VEILED

VEILED

A Novel

KARINA HALLE

First edition published by
Metal Blonde Books July 2016
Publisher's Note: This is a work of fiction. Names, characters, places, and
incidents either are the product of the author's imagination or are used
fictitiously. Any resemblance to actual events, locales, or persons, living or dead,
is entirely coincidental.
Copyright © 2016 by Karina Halle

Cover design by Hang Le Designs
Edited by Laura Helseth
Metal Blonde Books
P.O. Box 845
Point Roberts, WA
98281 USA
Manufactured in the USA
For more information about the series and author visit:
http://authorkarinahalle.com/

ISBN-10: 153483463X
ISBN-13: 9781534834637

Also by Karina Halle

Contemporary Romance Novels
Love, in English
Love, in Spanish
Where Sea Meets Sky (from Atria Books)
Racing the Sun (from Atria Books)
The Pact
The Offer
The Play
Winter Wishes
The Lie
Smut
The Debt

Romantic Suspense Novels
Sins and Needles (The Artists Trilogy #1)
On Every Street (An Artists Trilogy Novella #0.5)
Shooting Scars (The Artists Trilogy #2)
Bold Tricks (The Artists Trilogy #3)
Dirty Angels
Dirty Deeds
Dirty Promises

Paranormal/Horror Romance Novels
Veiled
The Devil's Metal (Devils #1)
The Devil's Reprise (Devils #2)
Donners of the Dead
Darkhouse (Experiment in Terror #1)
Red Fox (EIT #2)
The Benson (EIT #2.5)

DEDICATION

For everyone who asked (except for Sandra).
But *mainly* for myself.

"If life is but a dream, wake me up."
–*Keep Your Eyes Peeled*, Queens of the Stone Age

"What if you could look right through the cracks?
Would you find yourself afraid to see?"
–*Right Where it Belongs*, Nine Inch Nails

Note: Veiled is a new adult paranormal romance/urban fantasy novel. It is a spinoff of the Experiment in Terror series but is a standalone – meaning people do not need to read EIT to understand or enjoy this book. In fact the book is perfect for those who haven't read or even heard of EIT. If that's you, thank you for picking up Veiled and keep on reading! I hope you enjoy the ride!

However, *if* you are a reader of EIT and you have NOT finished the last two books, Ashes to Ashes and Dust to Dust (particularly Dust to Dust), reading Veiled will completely spoil Dust to Dust for you. Seriously. It will *ruin* the last EIT book for you. Dex and Perry's journey deserves better than that. *You* deserve better than that!

So if that's *you* put this book down and go read Dust to Dust. When you're done, come back here. The book will be waiting.

CHAPTER ONE

I wake up with a gasp that freezes in my lungs.

My body is strained, nearly paralyzed, a stark contrast to my heart which races erratically inside my chest, as if looking for a way out.

It was the noise that woke me.

That same noise, night after night.

One knock.

Two knocks.

Three knocks.

Like someone's at my door, even though they never are.

I wait, trying to suck the air deep into my lungs, realizing I couldn't move even if I tried. There's nothing else to do but wait and hope my heart calms down and I don't die from a fucking heart attack.

It's in your head, I tell myself. *You know this. You looked it up.*

But after growing up with a sister like Perry Palomino, it's hard to know what's in your head and what's real. I much prefer it when my mind plays tricks on me.

Even so, I lie there in the dark, listening to every sound in my room. Outside a cricket chirps once, twice. A light breeze rustles the trees and I feel the air as it comes through

1

the open window and washes over my body, my limbs that are outside the sheets. It's been stinking hot in Portland this summer and this breeze is nearly cold. It would be refreshing if I wasn't so rattled.

Strength slowly returns to my body. I'm able to suck in a breath and let it out carefully, even though it's far too loud for my liking. I'm still trying to listen, still trying to figure out if the knocks are part of my dream or part of something real.

I've had this condition for about as long as I can remember, though it was only recently that I looked it up and discovered it was quite common. It also has a disturbing as hell name: Exploding Head Syndrome. Yup. Ada Palomino's head might explode on occasion. Hope you're wearing a poncho.

Apparently though, it's not that big of a deal and it doesn't mean your head is just going to spontaneously combust, like that dude in *Scanners*. Now, I've never seen *Scanners* because it looks like a terrible 80's movie, but anytime someone's head explodes, that's the movie they refer to.

Instead it just means it's an auditory hallucination, one powerful enough to wake you up. Some people hear cymbals crashing, others hear a bang or gunshot. I hear three loud knocks. I used to think it was someone at my door, so I would get up and answer it, thinking it was Perry. No one was ever there. Sometimes I'd have to go downstairs and check the front door, usually with a steak knife or blunt object in hand, but it was always the same deal.

No one there.

Then this spring, when I slept over at my ex-boyfriend's cabin in Astoria, I woke up convinced someone was trying to get in the place. My ex, Dillon, was already awake, having gone to the washroom and told me he hadn't heard a thing.

Finally, I had to look up on the internet what the hell was going on. I discovered it had a name (albeit a pretty shitty one) and that many people suffered from it, usually women and usually when they were overly tired.

I've had it a few times since, but sometimes it's just so real that it's hard to imagine your brain could come up with something like that. Not to mention that often my body goes rigid, paralyzed, for a few moments after.

Then there was that one time I was pretty sure I felt someone sitting on the end of the bed, only I was on my side and couldn't look.

The weight lifted, as if someone stood up, and when I was finally able to move, no one was there. I'm going to assume that's part of the hallucinations as well.

I sigh, relieved that my heart is no longer racing, even though I'm still faced with that overall sense of unease and *what the fuck*. My throat and mouth feel desert dry, so I slowly get out of bed, grabbing the empty glass on my bedside table, and head to the washroom. The air from outside now feels warm, like it has been all summer.

In the bathroom I flick on the lights and wince, but make a point not to look at myself in the mirror. On nights like this, when I wake up in the middle of the night, either because of my apparent condition or for no reason at all, other than this feeling of dread, I feel the mirror holds the truth. I'm terrified that if I look at my reflection, it might not be me. And if it is me, I might be different.

But who can blame me for thinking the impossible? Because, after all I've been through, I know nothing is impossible. And even though on the surface I have a pretty average life for an eighteen-year-old, beneath the surface I'm anything but average.

Luckily, very few people scratch beneath the surface. If they did, they'd either run screaming or have me committed.

Sometimes I think the latter might be preferable.

After I fill a glass with water from the tap, I flick off the lights, my reflection still unseen, and creep past the nightlight in the hall back to my room. My father sleeps at the end of the hall, but ever since mom died he's been a light sleeper. In fact, I see him popping his sleeping pills every night. When he doesn't, I can hear him downstairs in his study during all hours.

I inherited my sister's room since she moved to Seattle. It's a lot bigger, brighter, and better than my old one, which is now a (much-needed) extension of my closet. The only problem is, it's hard to forget all the shit that went down in this room. For all of my fifteenth year, Perry's bedroom was a miniature house of horrors with some very big, very real, scares.

I down some of the water and crawl into bed, the breeze still wafting in. The streetlights provide comfort and a faint orange glow that not only keeps the room from being pitch dark, but reminds me that I live in the suburbs. There are neighbors on either side of the house and neighbors across the street. Our yards are big enough that everyone isn't up in everyone else's business (though tell that to Mrs. Hedley down the street), but close enough that I don't feel all alone.

With my mom dying and Perry moving out, it's been really fucking hard not to feel alone. The last two years have been a special kind of hell.

I let my head sink back into the cool of the pillow and close my eyes, finding that current of peace and contentment that will hopefully pull me under, when I hear a faint scratching sound.

Oh god, I think, just wanting to drift away, just wanting the world to go black so I can wake up with the sun and have the world light again.

But it goes on. Not louder, just more…deliberate.

I slowly sit up and hold my breath, listening. The scratches sound like nails against a door. The closet door, to be more specific.

I swallow hard and my heart begins to thud. It's not my imagination. I'm not asleep.

The sound continues, the strokes longer, the sound succinct, almost echoing throughout the bedroom.

It could be a mouse. A really large mouse. Okay, it could be a rat. A really large rat. God, I hope it's a rat. If it's a rat it can just stay in there until I get my dad to deal with it in the morning. Anything other than some type of animal is completely unacceptable.

I ease out of bed carefully, not making a sound, and stare at the closet, feeling frozen in place. There's no way in hell I'm opening that door, but there's no way in hell I'm going to spend the night in here either. I wonder if I should wake up my dad, but the man needs his sleep more than ever and knowing my luck, the scratching would stop when he gets here and there'd be nothing in the closet after all.

I'll sleep in the other room.

I can't help but pause by the closet on the way to the bedroom door.

The sound changes. A flurry of wings now, flapping against the closet door, the scratching louder.

My breath is caught in my throat. It sounds more like I have a chicken in the closet than a mutant rat, but even though I know there's something funny about that scenario, this doesn't seem funny at all.

Because a giant rat is plausible and a chicken is not.

And the wings don't exactly sound like feathers either.

The flapping is thick, like someone throwing slabs of raw meat against a wall.

I am zero seconds away from either vomiting from fear or literally losing my shit, but if I keep standing where I am I feel like I'll be stuck in the room forever.

And then I hear it.

A rough yet somehow familiar voice comes from the closet.

"Let me out," it croaks and the sound is a fist in my lungs.

The closet door rattles as someone on the other side knocks.

Three times.

I wake up.

. . .

6

"New purse?" Amy asks me as I get in the passenger seat of Smartie, her Ford Focus she bought second-hand a few months ago after saving for every pretty penny.

I look down at the micro YSL bubble-gum pink purse that's slung over my shoulder, which I chose to save up for instead of a car.

"Kind of," I tell her. I bought the purse on an online sale a couple of months ago, I just hadn't found the opportunity to wear it until now. I buy new things all the time—I mean, I'm a fashion blogger, it's kind of my job—but more often than not I get stuck in the habit of using the same bag over and over again.

Today though, today I needed some cheesy bubble-gum brightness in my life. I'd been having the worst sleep for the last few nights, ever since that dream upon a dream and the knocking and the chicken thing in the closet. Thankfully I hadn't experienced that again, even though I was giving my closet a wide berth now. The irony, that I'd be afraid of it when I'm about to start art school for fashion design next month and would probably be spending more time in my closet than ever before, wasn't lost on me.

But I had been dreaming about a guy I met once, and in some ways those dreams were worse. I'd wake up in this happy, warm state, like my heart was glowing and I was just floating through life. The opposite of waking up from a nightmare. Because even though I couldn't remember the specifics of the dreams, I knew I was with this guy and I was safe and I loved him. I couldn't even tell if he loved me back, it was just this feeling of being on top of the world, something I'd never really experienced.

And that's what made it worse. When you wake up from a nightmare, the reality comforts you. When you wake up from the best dream ever, reality is a burden, a slap-in-the-face reminder that you could feel this, you could have this, but you don't and you won't.

What's really weird is that I can't really recall the guy. Like in most dreams, he starts off as one person and then morphs. I lose focus. But I just have this image, this feeling, that he was this guy I met at Perry and her husband Dex's wedding two years ago (still weird to think of Dex as her husband—my brother-in-law—and not some douch-ecanoe that hangs around).

His name was Jay and I really wish I hadn't swigged so much champagne at the wedding because, just like the dream, the real-life details of him are kind of blurry. I know he was tall, maybe in his mid-to-late-twenties, which to my then sixteen-year-old-self seemed all sorts of ancient. He had reddish brown hair and manly scruff on his strong jaw. I'm not really sure why I think I know the feel of his rough stubble—I think if we kissed I would have at least remembered that.

Regardless, there was something about him that was vaguely magnetic and, considering my aversion to gingers, that said something. And what it said was that the last time I felt real butterflies around a guy was ages ago, I was drunk, and I never saw him again. How sad is that?

"Are you okay?" Amy asks as we head across the Fremont Bridge, the Willamette River sparkling below us.

I slide my eyes over to her and give her a tepid smile. "I'm heading to Sephora. Of course I'm okay."

Amy Lombardo is pretty much my closest friend. She's been there for me through everything from losing my virginity with Dillon (okay, she wasn't actually there for *that*, but she helped me deal with the aftermath), to breakups, to cramming for final exams. She, along with her boyfriend Tom and our friend Jessie, make up our little posse that has managed to last throughout the crazy high school years and now into this scary big world of the beyond. Jessie has already gone off to school in California, so our pack has dwindled to me being the third wheel most of the time.

Amy takes her eyes off the road and slides her sunglasses down on her nose, inspecting me with her chocolate brown eyes. "You sure?"

Her voice is soft and I know she's worried about me. The first year after my mother died, I was practically inconsolable. I'm surprised I even finished high school to be honest. Life was just a blur and when it wasn't a blur, when I was feeling things too deeply, too much, I made it a blur. I never thought I'd follow in my sister's footsteps, but I turned to drugs and alcohol in order to get through the days.

But the nights were always worst. The drugs never helped me with the nights. The dreams would come for me, no matter how doped up or drunk I was.

Somehow I got out of it. The days seemed brighter, steadier. When I hurt, which was all the time, which still is all the time, I was able to absorb it, deal with it. I was able to think, to actually see myself, my life, and distance myself from the substances. I leaned on Perry, my father, even Dex.

Amy, Tom, and Jessie were there too. My ex bailed when I was too much of a mess, but he was just extra baggage anyway. The heartbreak over losing him was nothing compared to losing my mom.

I know Amy worries about me still. I know I'm not the same person I was before it happened. It doesn't help that Amy doesn't know the truth about how my mother died. The truth about me. The truth about my family.

I need to keep it that way. I've seen what our ghostly afflictions can do to someone. I know that my grandmother, Pippa, saw dead people and could enter a realm called the Thin Veil, and that in time she was committed and eventually died alone because no one believed her. I know that Perry has been haunted since she was fifteen, that she was put on a cocktail of medications that did no good, that the world wanted to lock her up because it didn't understand her. I know that my mother saw the truth—far too late.

And the truth killed her.

Even my brother-in-law comes from a lineage of fucked-upness. Dex was also plagued by ghosts from a young age, did a stint in a mental institution, and relied on medication to keep it all away. When he went off the meds—and had his infamous ghost-hunting show with Perry—things only got worse until he discovered his own brother was taken over by a demon and literally tried to take us all to Hell while we were in New York. Worst vacation ever.

Then there's me. I've seen so much, been through so much, that even if I did admit to my best friend that my sister's now defunct ghost-hunting show was totally true, that I've seen the world behind the curtain, I've seen exorcisms and monsters and the devil himself, I wouldn't know where to begin nor how to make it all sound remotely believable.

So I let Amy think that I'm tired and on edge because I'm still grieving and not because my dreams keep getting worse and worse and I feel like each day is leading me down a dark path I might not be able to come back from.

"I'm fine," I tell Amy, loudly, struck by the sudden need to convince myself of this as well. I quickly reach over and shut off the annoying poppy shit on the radio and flip to my favorite alternative station.

When Nine Inch Nails comes on, Amy makes a sound of disgust. "So now you think One Direction sucks?" She rolls her eyes, clearly not amused as we take the exit to downtown. "You really are turning into your sister, you know?"

In more ways than one, I think to myself. But even though Amy chides my sudden change in music tastes and I'm becoming a bona fide 90's grunge and metal lover even though I was born at the end of that decade, I'm not ashamed of it. I look up to Perry, more than she'll probably ever know. Besides, seeing ghosts and demons just lends itself to listening to White Zombie and Slayer and Fantomas on repeat. One Direction and Selena Gomez are for the girls who don't see dead people every fucking day.

Not that I was seeing dead people every day. I mean, maybe I do, but half the time you don't really realize it unless they're covered in blood, or maybe standing in a white dress in the middle of a road, like every cliché you can think of. Most of the time, the dead just kind of... blend in. They're innocuous and usually harmless. Sure

11

they can scare the pants off you but that's usually the extent of their damage.

I gaze out the window as we roll through the Pearl District, watching the throngs of people on the sidewalks, everyone in shorts and tank-tops and billowy dresses, trying to beat the heat.

Then, for just a second, I see a flash of a familiar face as he gets off a bus. I straighten up and blink, trying to see better but he's gone.

It couldn't have been the guy from the wedding, the guy from my dreams, could it? God, I really am getting delusional.

When we finally find parking and I'm swallowed by my mecca that is Sephora, I'm feeling better. There's nothing like sipping on syrupy Coca-Cola from the mall's food court while perusing the white, backlit-beauty of a million makeup products. It's like being in heaven, really, if angels wore all black and enough foundation to paint a house.

Amy and I literally spend an hour here, trying on everything and filling our baskets until our lips are rubbed raw from the makeup remover and our hands and wrists are rainbows of different swatches.

Then it happens.

I see him again.

Standing just beyond the doors to the store.

Staring right at me.

And for once, for once, I can see him clearly.

He's tall, well over six feet. Broad shouldered and barrel-chested under a black leather jacket and black shirt, black jeans and black boots. He's pale in a way that brings to mind a classical sculpture, or maybe it's his face, which is exactly as my mind has tried to piece together.

His jaw is chiseled, his chin square and sharp enough to cut glass, covered by light scruff and complete with a chin dimple. His forehead is wide, expressive even, as he stares at me with piercing blue eyes under arched brows. His hair is chin length, slicked off his head, dark cinnamon. A ginger, just as I had remembered, though he's probably the sexiest, most enthralling male specimen I've ever seen.

"Can I help you with anything?" a Sephora saleswoman with stripes for cheekbones steps in front of me, blocking my view.

I shoot her a dirty look, because I *never* need help in Sephora, and dart around her.

But he's gone.

I hand the bewildered assistant my bucket and walk quickly through the store until I'm outside the doors, my head whipping around. People are going to and fro but the tall guy from my dreams, *from my fucking dreams*, is nowhere to be found.

Maybe he was never here at all.

Suddenly I'm hit with a queasy, stomach-churning feeling, my skin immediately clammy.

"Ada!" Amy calls from behind me but her words barely reach.

I can only just stand here, shoppers walking past me, bumping into me, wondering if I'm slowly going insane. Am I actually seeing this guy? Is it one of those cases where you dream about someone and then see them the next day?

Is he really the guy from the wedding or was there even a Jay at all? Did I imagine everything?

I'm having trouble standing upright and tilt back just as I feel Amy's hand on my shoulder, holding me up.

"Hey, are you all right?"

I nod, licking my parched lips as I slowly turn around to face her. Everything seems so swimmy, woozy, like I'm underwater.

"Got dizzy," I manage to say. "It's the Coke crash."

She frowns at me. "Why are you out here?"

I blink a few times, trying to get my thoughts together. "Nothing. Thought I saw someone but it was nothing." I take in a deep breath and give her a broad smile. "Okay, I think I've got some makeup waiting for me."

We head back into the store.

CHAPTER TWO

My head is still swimming when Amy drops me off at home and I blame it on getting my period rather than the mysterious dream man I saw in town. I give her a wave with my Sephora bags and watch her drive off, standing next to the For Sale sign on our front lawn.

I hate that our house is for sale. It adds another level of uncertainty to my life, not knowing if I'm going to spend half my school year here, or in an apartment with a roommate I don't know. I know the market is slow right now and my dad is asking for a bit much, maybe because deep down he doesn't want to move either, but our neighbors sold their house in just a month, so who knows what will happen.

Speaking of neighbors, one of my new ones has spotted me as she exits her house, the driveway full of boxes. They only moved in yesterday, a retired couple, who had a group of brawny movers helping them and providing mucho eye candy as I watched through my bedroom window.

Normally I would march right into my house and feign ignorance, but with my mom gone someone has to step up as woman of the house.

"Hello," the woman says to me, coming over to the fence and holding a pan of what looks like brownies. She's gorgeous even though she has to be in her mid-sixties. Her hair is curly and pulled back, a stunning shade of grey, and her face is pale and freckled giving her a youthful appearance.

I walk over to her and smile, always feeling a bit awkward in these types of situations. You know, the ones that require being polite and normal.

"Hi," I tell her. "You must be our new neighbors."

Well. Duh. Good one, Ada.

"We are," she says, smiling with perfect teeth. "I'm Dawn." She offers her hand and I reach over the low fence to give it a light shake.

"Ada," I tell her.

She nods over at the For Sale sign. "Though perhaps we won't be your neighbors for long."

I sigh. "Yeah, believe me I'd rather not move."

"Lived here long?"

"My whole life," I tell her, feeling my heart pinch. I swallow and attempt a shrug. "Though I am starting college next month so I guess it's time for me to hit the road anyway. My older sister moved out and it's just my dad and me." I don't know why I'm blabbing on to this woman but there's something about her that makes me think she'd understand. I pause. "My mom died a few years ago and I think the house just holds too many memories."

Her face softens. "I'm so sorry. That must be so tough. I lost my mother when I was younger...you never quite get over it."

Great. But hell. At least she's telling me the truth. Everyone else makes it sound like death is something you forget with time.

"Here," she says, passing the brownies over the fence. "I'm not the best cook even after all these years, but you can bet I can bake the shit out of brownies."

I can't help but smile. I like her already. I take the pan, the Sephora bags sliding down my arms. "Thanks. These aren't special brownies, are they?"

She laughs. "No, I'm sorry. But those are my specialty too. My husband and I moved from Washington so we're used to being knee-deep in pot brownies on the regular." She tilts her head as she looks at me and I feel like she's really taking me in, seeing everything. "You should come over sometime. I mean, I know it's probably the last thing a girl like you wants to do, hang out with a bunch of old geezers. But I promise you we're fun. Do you like music?"

I frown. "Who doesn't like music?"

She shrugs. "Weirdos."

The perfect answer.

I'm about to tell her that would be great, though I'm not sure if I'd actually follow through with it or not, when an old beige Mercedes pulls up to their curb and Dawn turns her attention to it.

A tall man wearing sunglasses and a baseball cap comes out of the car and strolls toward us, holding a bouquet of flowers. I wonder if this is her husband.

"You're early," Dawn says to him.

"Your new house is easier to find than I thought," the man says, speaking in a thick Cockney accent. "Lovely though. I was getting a bit tired of that dustbowl you were living in before."

Okay, definitely not her husband. The man stops in front of me and I can almost feel his gaze beneath his sunglasses. He's probably in his fifties, a craggy yet charismatic face, crooked smile, with red hair peeking out beneath the baseball cap. His nose is broad, looking like it's been broken a few times, while freckles and pockmarks scar up his cheeks.

"Getting to know the neighbors already," he comments to her. He takes his sunglasses off, sliding them in the front pocket of his mustard yellow shirt, and gives me a steady look. His eyes are hazel, nearly amber, the kind of eyes that you know have seen a lot, been through a lot.

"Of course," Dawn says. She nods at me. "This is Ada. She lives here with her father." She lowers her voice. "She lost her mother a few years ago."

"What a shame," the man says frowning. "Death doesn't always discriminate, does it?" He offers his hand. "I'm Jacob. Family friend."

"Nice to meet you," I tell him, his hand nearly crushing mine.

The way he keeps his eyes on me is unnerving until he winks, breaking into a crooked smile. "It will be good for the Knightlys to have someone young next door, keep them breathing and all that." He takes his hand back and looks to Dawn. "Where is the husband anyway, napping? You know you should be careful, he's almost seventy. Wouldn't want him to break his hip taking a shit or something."

She rolls her eyes. "You are terrible."

"That's why even Hell didn't want me," he jokes smoothly.

"Well he's already taken over the basement and turning it into a jam room. If he's breaking anything it's his back from hanging guitars all over the walls." Dawn gives me an apologetic look. "I best be showing Jacob the grand tour. This man doesn't know what patience is. Let me know how you like the brownies."

"Will do," I tell her, raising up the pan in a show of thanks.

"Come on Rusty," Jacob says, putting his arm around Dawn's shoulder and leading her to the house. "It's been a long drive. Take me to the gin."

I watch them disappear into the house before glancing down at the brownies. That whole exchange was kind of strange and there was definitely something odd about that redheaded fellow with the Michael Caine accent. I think I'll give the brownies to Dex, just in case. He can handle poison better than anyone.

I head inside the house, my dad puttering around in the kitchen trying to make dinner. I feel a pang of guilt knowing I should have been at home helping him instead of out buying makeup I don't need with money I don't have.

He doesn't even glance at the bags as I plop them on the counter. He stopped harassing me about spending money a long time ago. I think he figures I'm trying to shop my way out of grief just as he's taken up gardening tenfold. Even though we're trying to move, he spends most of the day out in the back garden. It looks so lush and extravagant now that you can't even tell it was once the sight of a séance, a witch bottle filled with toenail clippings and hair and all the negative energy of the house buried there.

Then again, what backyard doesn't have that? It could almost be a selling point.

"I met the neighbors," I tell him, sliding the pan on the island. "Though I'm not sure if the brownies are poisoned or not, so proceed with caution."

He glances at them briefly as he stoops to take a tray out of the oven, the scent of roasted vegetables wafting out in a cloud. "Oh. I met them earlier this morning." He starts turning over the beets and carrots. "Interesting couple. Turns out the man used to be in a seventies rock group, though I can't say I've ever heard one of their songs. Your sister would probably know. Or that husband of hers," he mumbles under his breath.

"What band?"

"Hybrid? I can't remember. Something that would induce a lot of drug use, I'm sure." A silence falls between us, thick and uneasy. I know he's thinking about Perry when she was younger. I know he's thinking about me last year.

I clear my throat. "Well that's good that they're cool," I tell him. "Need any help? What time are they coming over anyway?"

There's a brief knock at the door before we hear it open. Dad sighs. "I suppose that's them."

"Hello?" Perry calls out from around the corner. She comes into the kitchen and drops a giant duffle bag on the floor that's nearly the size of her.

VEILED

"You're here for a night, Perry," my dad chides her, putting the vegetables back in the oven. "You've gotten just as bad as Ada at packing."

"She wishes," I mumble before going over to Perry and giving her a hug. I catch a whiff of cigarettes in her dark ponytail. "Ugh, have you taken up smoking?"

"No," she says exasperated as she pulls back. "Guess who thought he could smoke one cigarette and not get re-addicted?"

"My ears are burning!" comes Dex's voice from outside.

"No, that's your fucking cancer stick that's burning!" Perry yells right back. She looks back at me and shakes her head. "Asshole."

"Language, please," my father says, rolling his eyes before coming over and giving her a tight embrace. I'd just seen the two of them a few weeks ago when I went up to their place in a Seattle for a few nights, but my dad hasn't seen them in at least a month. And while he can do without seeing Dex, I know he misses Perry dearly.

She's looking good. Her weight fluctuates like most women's, though her giant boobs are always constant. I definitely wasn't blessed in that department. I may have inherited our mother's blonde hair and long limbs but Perry got all the sultry Italian curves from our dad's side. The only thing we really have in common are our sky blue eyes. Oh, and the whole seeing ghosts thing.

Which sucks.

"I've tried to get him onto E-cigarettes," Perry says to dad.

Dex's laugh comes loud and clear along with a waft of smoke, and I figure he's on the front steps finishing his cigarette.

"You want him to vape?" I ask Perry, raising my brow. "You might as well as staple the word 'shitdick' to his forehead."

"Ada," my dad admonishes me.

Dex laughs again and the front door closes. He appears in the kitchen entryway, looking at Perry with raised brows. "You see? Only shitdicks vape. Your sister knows what's up."

"I always know what's up," I tell him dryly.

He shrugs, conceding, and nods at my father, tipping his newsboy cap at him. "Daniel."

"Dex," is his reply before he turns around to busy himself with more food.

"Can I help with anything?" Perry asks but our dad shoos us away.

"Go put your stuff away and relax," he says, opening the fridge. "Dinner will be ready in a half hour."

Dex scoops up Perry's bag, his large bicep muscles flexing beneath the sleeve of his grey tee shirt. He grins at me, wagging his brows and I immediately make a noise of disgust, looking away.

Okay, here's the truth about Declan "Dex" Foray. He bugs the absolute shit out of me, always has since he first waltzed into our lives all those years ago with his wannabe Robert Downey Jr. mustache and goatee and video camera. I thought he was here to exploit my sister, roping her into their YouTube channel as they investigated ghosts and the paranormal. Instead, he saved her. Changed her life in more ways than one. And I couldn't be happier that he's my brother-in-law now.

He also happens to be hot. I cringe when I find myself admitting it from time to time and I would *never* tell him or Perry that, lest his ego get even bigger than it is, but it's true. He's not exactly my type. I'm pretty tall and Dex is around 5'9", but there's still something about him that sets your heart aflutter sometimes. Maybe it's because he's ripped as shit, maybe it's his expressive dark eyes, the way he carries himself with so much "I don't give a shit" confidence. Or maybe it's that in some ways he's almost superhuman.

Could be anything, really.

But most of the time, he lives to annoy me, just like any brother would.

"Put your muscles away," I scoff at him as he brushes past, moving toward the staircase.

"Don't act like you don't like it, little sister," he calls over his shoulder, heading up the stairs.

"I think I liked it better when you called me Little Fifteen!" I yell after him. "Though I guess Little Eighteen doesn't have quite the same ring to it."

I step out into the hallway, about to head to the living room, when Perry intercepts me, putting her hand on my shoulder and squinting at me.

"Are you okay?" she asks softly.

"You think I'm offended because your husband is flexing for me?"

She frowns. "I'm serious. I hate to sound like a bitch, but you look awful."

I shrug away from her hand and go into the living room, flopping onto the couch and pulling out my phone to busy myself with fashion bloggers on Instagram. "I haven't been sleeping right."

She sits down beside me and I can feel her stare deepening as she leans in closer. I give her a quick glance. "Don't tell me you're going to try and read my mind. We had a deal."

She sits back, looking mildly embarrassed. "It doesn't work like that," she says in a clipped voice. "And you're right, we did have a deal."

I eye her warily. She says she can't just read my mind, though I'm pretty sure that's how she found out I lost my virginity to Dillon. In the backseat of his 1995 Toyota Tercel. Something I wish could be erased from my memory. Sadly there hasn't been anyone since him.

"I'm worried about you," she says after a moment, her voice quiet.

"Why?" I ask, afraid that she'll have all the good reasons.

She shrugs with one shoulder and looks down at her hands in her lap. "Just a feeling I have."

Perry and her *feelings*. It's never good news. She's never like, "I have a feeling we're going to win the lottery and you'll be swept off your feet by a charming billionaire." It's always "I have a feeling you're in danger and everyone around us is going to die."

Unfortunately, she's usually right about her feelings. She's always been intuitive, even when she was all screwed up, and ever since all her incidents—some of which have become my incidents—her intuition has doubled. That, along with her ability to project her thoughts into other's heads. She says she can't read minds in the same way but I just don't believe her. Sometimes I think about investing in a Magneto helmet around her when she starts pulling this Professor Xavier shit.

I sigh, wishing my heart wasn't starting to kick up a few notches. "What feeling?"

"I don't know. I'm having dreams," she says. "You're in them."

I swallow hard and look back down at the phone. "Anyone else in them?"

"No." She puts her hand on my knee until I look at her. Her eyes are rounder than ever as she stares at me. "You're having them too."

I quickly tuck my hair behind my ears. "It's nothing."

"Tell me about them."

"Tell me about yours," I counter. "Perhaps you'd better start from the beginning," I say, mimicking the opening lines of White Zombie's "Electric Head Pt. 1."

She exhales slowly. "Okay. Well I've been having them for the last two weeks."

Me too, I think.

"It's pretty much all the same. We're in the Thin Veil. Remember when we there in New York?"

"You mean remember when I went to another dimension in the middle of Bryant Park to rescue you?" I repeat dryly. "Yeah. I remember, Perry."

"Right. Well it's like that, except it's on an island. It kind of reminds me of this island I was on once with Dex, you know where the lepers were."

"All your episodes kind of blur together," I tell her, motioning with my hand for her to speed it up.

"Anyway, you're standing on a cliff at the edge of the ocean. I'm down in a boat and I'm yelling up at you not to jump."

A shiver rocks through me.

She goes on. "And you stop just before you're about to go over. You listen to me. Then someone appears behind you. A shadow, a hand. And they push you."

"Great."

"You fall straight into the ocean and sink and I jump off the boat and swim for you." She pauses, biting her lip for a moment.

"And?" I coax her, knowing this ain't going to be good.

"You drown. No matter what, I can't get below the water to get you. I see you sink. And...well, you're not alone." My heart stills. "Mom is with you too."

I whistle slowly, breathing out. "Wow. I'm not sure what that means."

"Neither."

"Now I'm scared shitless."

"It's just a dream Ada, it doesn't *have* to mean anything. It's something my psyche is trying to work out."

I give her a levelling look. "We both know your psyche isn't normal. Especially if I'm having dreams too. Which, by the way, are nothing like yours. I just...well you know my exploding head syndrome?" She nods gravely and to her credit doesn't laugh at the name this time. "It's like that. I'm dreaming something is in my closet, then I hear the knocks and wake up. Or I'm with a guy but..."

"What guy?"

I shake my head. "I'm not really sure. Like, I have a feeling I know who he is but I don't really get a good look at him. It's almost like...Do you remember a guy at the wedding named Jay?"

I don't bother telling her that I thought I saw him today. One crazy thing at a time.

Her groomed brows pull together. "I remember you were drunk and walking around barefoot holding your heels in your hand and looking for a guy called Jay but that's it."

"So you don't remember inviting someone there by that name?"

She gives me a wry look. "Ada, I don't know who half the people there were. Ask dad, he's the one who went nuts with the guest list. Or Dex. A lot of people from his old work were invited. That whole day was such a blur."

"Ask me what?" Dex asks as he enters the room. He stops in front of us, folding his arms across his chest. "Am I interrupting girl time?"

"It's fine," Perry says. "Ada's been having strange dreams too."

Dex nods, sliding his fingers across the stubble on his jaw. "Well, I wouldn't worry about it. Ada is going off to school and our second wedding anniversary is coming up in October, which is enough to make any woman lose their shit. Two years as Mrs. Foray, it's a lot to handle."

"Tell me about it," Perry says under her breath, though there's a hint of a smile on her lips as she stares up at him.

Lord, the two of them make me so sick sometimes with their love for each other. Sick and, I must admit, jealous.

Perry continues, "Did you know a guy at our wedding called Jay?"

Dex shakes his head, giving her a lopsided grin. "The only thing I knew that day was you, kiddo."

"Oh, barf," I say, sinking back into the couch.

He flashes his smile to me as he sits on the edge of the coffee table. "Sorry I'm not of any help. I guess we could go through the wedding photos. What's this all about? You hook up with him?"

"No," I say quickly, glaring at him. *I don't think so.* "I just feel like he's appearing in my dreams." I straighten up. "Anyway, weird dreams aside, I'm fine. Just..."

"On edge," Perry supplies.

"Well I am now since you told me you've been having feelings about things."

"Perry is always having feelings," Dex says. "It's usually her period's fault."

"Dex," she hisses at him. "Stop blaming everything on PMS."

He cocks a brow. "Right. Like you don't turn into a murderous she-devil once a month who plows through an entire cake even when you swear you're all gluten-free." He looks at me. "She makes me buy gluten-free bread for us. Have you ever tried that shit? It's like chewing on dried-out dogshit."

I raise my palm. "Stop. How would you even know what that tastes like?"

"Someone want to set the table?" Dad hollers from the kitchen.

Both Perry and I look expectantly at Dex. He can use the brownie points.

He sighs and gets up, trudging into the kitchen to get the plates.

I look back at Perry. "He's probably right you know."

"About the dried-out dogshit?"

"Yes. And also it being a stressful time of year for us. Me anyway. Maybe I'm just stressing and you're picking up on it and it's manifesting itself into dreams."

"You're nervous about starting school," she says sympathetically.

"Actually I'm excited. I just...you know. I wish mom was here for it."

Perry sighs and leans back into the cushions, running her hand over her face. "Yeah. I get it. I think of her during the stupidest times. Like, I'll pick up a pomegranate at the supermarket and think, would mom know what to do with this? I know I can Google it, but it's not the same. I just wish I could ask her advice on things, anything. Even though we weren't close, not like you guys, I thought—I knew—that in time we would grow closer."

My chest is weighted, the heavy hands of grief starting to climb up from the inside. Sometimes I forget that she and Perry weren't as close as we were. My mother treated her like the bad seed, the black sheep, because she was too afraid to see Perry for what she really was. When they finally began to reconcile...it was too late.

"I'm sorry," I say quietly, trying to keep my voice strong, even though we've talked about it many times before.

Perry's head lolls to the side and she smiles softly at me. "Don't be."

"Also, I don't want to move," I add.

"Still?" she asks, looking around the room. "I couldn't wait to get out of here. Aside from the fact that it's way too big for you and dad, doesn't this place scare you?"

"No," I tell her. Totally lying. Because this house *does* scare me. But at the same time, I feel compelled to stay here. It's not just because it's everything I've known, that I'm hanging onto memories of my mother. It's because it *needs* me to stay.

"All right ladies," Dex says poking his head around the corner. "Let's eat before your feelings turn to *hangriness*."

Dad made roast chicken and vegetables with mashed potatoes that he calls "special potatoes" even though the only thing that makes them special is the fact that there's bacon bits and truffle salt sprinkled in it. Well, that and they are damn good.

We gather around the table, helping ourselves to the food and conversation that doesn't involve feelings and dreams and death.

"Hey I saw you have new neighbors now," Dex says between mouthfuls of chicken. "Poor people don't know who they've moved next door to." His brows raise at Perry. "Had they moved in a few years ago, they wouldn't have lasted long with all the shenanigans and whatnot."

Shenanigans. What a simple way to describe everything that went down here.

"Actually," I tell him, "I met the woman today. She's really nice. They're old though." My dad coughs on purpose and I shrug. "Sorry, *older*. Retired. And apparently the husband was in a '70s rock band."

Dex cocks his head. "What band?"

"Hybrid?" my father says before taking a sip of wine.

"Holy fuck!" Dex exclaims, pressing his hands down onto the table, his dark brown eyes looking half-crazed. "Are you shitting me?"

"Who is Hybrid?" I ask, looking between him and Perry.

"They were massive back in the day," Perry explains. "Totally influenced Kyuss, Melvins, and Queens of the Stone Age. Sounds a bit like Black Sabbath. Weird shit went down with that band."

"Who is the guy, do you know?" Dex asks eagerly.

My dad shrugs while I say, "I didn't get his name. But the woman's name is Dawn. Dawn Knightly."

Now he's even more impressed. "Holy shit."

"Dex," my dad warns him.

"Look, *dad*," Dex says. "I'm thirty-five years old and I can say holy fucking shit if I want to."

My dad glares at him.

I can tell Perry is trying to kick Dex under the table. "That might be true but don't forget my dad—*our* dad—is a theology professor."

"Who is Dawn Knightly?" I ask, attempting to breakup their showdown which happens every time we all get together. "Was she in the band?"

Dex tears his eyes away from my dad's death stare and looks at me in such a way that I know I'm about to

31

get an earful. "No. She was the music journalist who Sage Knightly, the guitarist, fell in love with. Documented the rise and fall of the band on their last tour before everything went to hell in a handbasket. You want to talk about infamous tours, that one is for the books. There's a whole mythology built around it, which now I wonder if it could have been real after all." He leans back in his chair, taking off his cap and running his hand through his thick black hair, eyes going to the door. "Damn. I wonder if I should go over and introduce myself."

"And say what?" I ask. "Ask him for his autograph?"

He gives me a withering glance. "Sage Knightly had a bunch of solo albums after Hybrid. I wonder if he could give me permission to use some of his music in my documentary. Fuck knows the Deftones will never respond to me."

"Will you ever tell us what the documentary is about?" my father asks gruffly. "You've been talking about it for ages now."

After Dex and Perry called it quits with their Experiment in Terror YouTube show (*they* were the original YouTubers), they were both at a loss of what to do with themselves. Luckily it didn't take them long to figure it out. I thought that they might go the paranormal investigator route much like the Warrens (you know, the real life couple *The Conjuring* was based on), but they seem to have put everything scary behind them. For now, anyway. Can't say I blame them.

Instead they opened up a company together, Haunted Media. Dex uses his prowess as an editor, cameraman, and musician to make music videos for some major artists. I never thought you could turn making music videos into a career, especially in the age where MTV plays nothing but the Kardashians, but Dex has a dark and creepy tone to his work that goes over well with so many bands and artists. Perry is the manager of the company, the brains and the beauty. She keeps Dex in line, which he needs badly, and is the key liaison between the business and the customers. The saying *behind every man is a great woman*, is totally true in this case.

But then there's this documentary that Dex keeps mentioning but never tells anyone what it's about. Even Perry shrugs when I ask. I know he has aspirations to be a legit filmmaker beyond the music video business, so a documentary makes the most sense as a stepping stone, but he's always been strangely cagey about it. Then again, Dex is a pretty cagey guy by nature, so I don't read too much into it.

"You'll find out once I know," Dex says and I know he won't give us anything more than that.

After dinner I head up to my room to work on my blog for a little bit, which means going through and editing a slew of photos I took with Amy and Tom last week. I admit, I've been slacking on my blogging duties which isn't good since that's really the whole reason I got into my design school. They liked my sketches of course, but it was the whole social media aspect of being a fashion blogger and the fact that I've had my blog since I was fifteen that helped seal the deal. They wanted to take on someone who already had a personal brand and a platform to move forward with.

Perry and Dex are downstairs watching a movie on Netflix and even though I'm working on my sketches, trying my hardest to get the right forms for a leather jacket—maybe a leather jacket partially inspired by the one I thought I saw today, the one belonging to the man who may or may not exist—but I just can't get it right.

I guess I doze off with my head on the sketchpad and a charcoal pencil in my hand.

Three hard knocks seem to ricochet through my brain.

CHAPTER THREE

My head snaps up from my desk and I let out a muffled cry, heart bouncing in my chest as I try and rescue my thoughts from sleep.

I pull off the paper that's stuck to my cheek and quickly look around. My bedroom is dark except for the light above my desk. I'm alone, though I could have sworn those three knocks came from someone pounding on the desk, beside my head. That's how much it rattled me.

I try and catch my breath, taking air in deep and slow. I reach for my phone to check the time, wondering how long I've been asleep, wondering if Perry and Dex are still downstairs watching TV, when there's a flutter at the window.

I gasp and whirl around, nearly falling out of my chair.

Something black flashes past outside the window, the light's reflection on the glass obscuring most of it.

Holy shit.

I'm on the second floor but that doesn't really matter because once upon a time, Perry saw a demon on the roof and then fell off said roof trying to run from it. I could never figure out why she even went out there but now I know.

Complete morbid curiosity.

I slowly get out of my chair and edge toward the window, heart in my throat, watching my reflection get closer as I approach it. I reach for the window edge to open it the rest of the way.

I'm just about to open it when an intense chill runs over my limbs, like someone's just dumped a bucket of ice water down my arms and back.

A slow, laborious *creak* comes from behind me.

From the closet.

I freeze.

Suddenly the window doesn't seem so interesting anymore.

Bony fingers of terror skitter down my spine and I'm turning around.

The closet door is open a few inches even though I know it was closed before.

Maybe it was the wind, I tell myself.

There is no wind. If anything, the room has become still, like all the air and smell and life has been sucked out of it and the only thing left is dust.

Maybe I'm dreaming.

I'm always dreaming.

With that in mind, my feet start moving across the room, the rug cold on my soles. I'm poised, every nerve in my body ready to spring, my heart beating so fast I swear it has wings.

I stop outside the closet door and stare dumbly at the crack. The space taunts me with the dark depths behind it. In this moment it feels like it's not a closet at all, instead it's something infinite. A doorway to something horrible.

My hand slowly reaches for the doorknob.

I pause, my hand shaking, losing all nerve to grab it. Then...

"Help me, Ada," a faint voice rasps from inside the closet.

The voice of my mother.

The light in the closet goes on.

I scream.

My whole body launches backward and I'm running for the door out of my room and into the hallway.

I run right into Dex.

"Ada," he says, grabbing my shoulders. "What is it, what happened?"

My mouth flaps open, soundless as I stare at him and then Perry as she appears behind him, coming out of my old bedroom.

"Something is in my closet," I manage to say, my whole body trembling now.

The door at the end of the hall opens and my dad stares at us, slipping on his robe and sliding his glasses down on his face.

"It's past midnight. What's going on?" he says gruffly, voice hoarse from sleep.

I look up at Dex, not sure what to say.

"She had a dream," Perry says to him quickly. "It's nothing. Go back to sleep, dad."

We stand there in the hallway, halfway to my room, watching my dad carefully. Thankfully he takes the bait, even though I know, I *know* I wasn't sleeping this time. He frowns at me with a mix of exasperation and concern on his face before stepping back inside his room.

"Stay behind me," Dex says, pushing me so Perry and I are behind him. Like hell I'd want to go back in first.

Dex walks to the middle of my room while Perry and I hang around the doorway.

"This closet?" Dex asks, pointing at it. It's still open a crack though the light is off now. "I only ask because it feels like Perry and I are sleeping in an extension of your closet too."

"Yes," I tell him, too afraid to be annoyed. "But the light was on. It turned on, *by itself,* just as I was about to open the door. I heard..." I trail off, not sure if I should say anything else.

Perry is watching me closely. "Heard what?"

I swallow hard and give her a pleading look. "I heard mom," I whisper.

"You know that's not her," she says to me but I can't quite agree.

Dex frowns at us, then looks around him. He quickly moves to the desk and grabs the pencil I was using to sketch and holds it like a knife.

"What the hell are you going to do with that?" Perry hisses. "Draw the ghosts?"

He tilts his head, giving her an incredulous look. "Have you ever been stabbed with a pencil in the eye? No, because if you had, you'd probably be dead. Anyway, no one said anything about ghosts."

"No one has to say anything about ghosts," I say. "But I don't think this is that. I know when I'm dealing with a ghost and when I'm dealing with...well, I don't know. If I'm not dreaming then I'm going fucking crazy."

Perry quickly pinches my arm, hard.

"Ow! The fuck?" I cry out, shying away from her.

"Not dreaming."

Dex takes in a deep breath and whips the closet door open.

My hands fly to my face. I don't know what I'm expecting.

But it's empty. Just full of my clothes, shirts hanging from the rattling hangers. Dex stoops, sticking his hands into the bottom of the closet, shuffling through sandals and heels and clothes that have fallen.

"There's nothing," he says, straightening up. "Except that you have an obscene amount of heels that belong on a stripper named Candy."

"Shut the fuck up," I tell him, glaring.

He raises his palms, walking over to us. "Hey, I've known some mighty fine strippers in my day. It's not an insult. Unless your name is Candy."

Perry rolls her eyes. "I thought you were fond of the ones called Marla."

"Ah, you remember," he says happily.

Perry ignores him and turns to me. "So what exactly happened?"

I point at the desk. "I was sketching and fell asleep. I woke up. I heard the knocks."

"Good ol' exploding head syndrome," Dex comments.

"Yes. That. But I swear it was right here, like someone was pounding on the desk. Of course I woke up and I was alone. Then there was something outside the window."

Dex walks over to the window and hauls it up, sticking his head out for a moment.

"There's a giant ass bird in the tree right there," he says. "Could it be that? Looks like a raven."

"Oh, well there just happens to be a fucking raven outside my window, can't mean a thing," I tell him, coming over.

I peer outside and sure enough, there's a raven sitting at the end of the tree, its silhouette lit up by the streetlights. It cocks its head at me, staring at me with beady, glassy eyes, then flies off, its wings beating heavily as it goes.

I shudder again. There aren't a lot of ravens around here, only crows. And I've certainly never seen any past midnight, nor hanging around the tree outside my window.

"Ignoring the bird for now," Dex says, though from the hard look in his eyes I know he's thinking something of it too, "then what happened?"

"I heard the closet door open. It wasn't open before. It was closed. I swear it. Then I went toward it."

"As you do when you think there's something horrible in your closet," Dex says.

"And then I heard my mom's voice. She said, help me, Ada." I look at Perry with wide-eyes. "It was her. I know it was her. She sounded so far away, so...strained. Then the light went on and I screamed and ran."

Perry and Dex exchange a look.

"What?" I ask.

"Nothing," Perry says, coming over to me. She puts her hand on my shoulder and gives it a squeeze. "Want to sleep with us tonight?"

I wrinkle my nose. "No thanks. You do believe me, don't you?"

"Of course we believe you," Perry says. "You could tell me my old stuffed animals are trying to kill you and I'd believe you."

"Wait, what?" I ask, my eyes flitting to the bed where I know her stuffed animals are stored in a box underneath.

"But I also think you're stressed and exhausted and liable to seeing things. I know sometimes when I was seeing shit it wasn't because there were actual ghosts, I was just so on edge that everything seemed out to get me." She looks at Dex. "Sorry baby, I'm sleeping with my sister tonight."

He shrugs. "Suit yourself. You girls need anything, you know where I am." He leaves the room, stretching his arms over his head. "Love you," he calls over his shoulder. "You too, Perry."

She raises her brow in mild amusement and looks back to me.

"You don't have to stay here," I tell her.

"You've done the same for me before," she says. She looks around her. "Though honestly this isn't my favorite place to be." She climbs into the bed, moving to the other side. For a moment I'm transported back two years when Perry still lived here, our mother was still alive and things, at least for me, were more or less normal.

But my brain won't let me pretend for long. Even though Perry is still just twenty-five and looks pretty much the same as she did, there's a world-weariness to her eyes, the kind that old souls have, the kind that says she's seen too much and can never go back to the way she was.

I quickly get changed into my matching camisole and boy-short set and get in bed beside her, feeling like a little girl again under the covers.

I turn over on the pillow to look at her. "You know what this reminds me of? When we used to go to the cabin when we were little."

She rolls over to face me, folding up the thin pillow underneath her head. "Was this when you said I had an imaginary friend and I'd go and talk to him through the window every night?"

"But he never was imaginary, was he?"

She shakes her head, frowning. "No. Nothing ever is." She closes her eyes. "Nothing ever is."

You'd think it would be impossible for both of us to sleep, but in seconds she's out like a light.

Then I follow.

. . .

I'm dreaming.

For once, I know it.

And I know exactly where I am.

I'm in the Thin Veil, a place I've only been to once and here I am again; here but not.

The world is both red and grey, a desaturated hue that seeps into everything, my hands, my clothes, the crunchy, dead grass beneath me.

I'm sitting on a cliff overlooking the ocean, much like the one Perry had mentioned earlier, the one in her dreams. Only she's nowhere to be found. There's only the empty sea with waves crashing below, faraway islands in the distance. There is a forest of fir and hemlock behind me, a dark, seemingly fathomless thicket.

Hi.

I whip my head around to see a man, *the* man, the leather jacket wearing ginger who may or may not be a man named Jay, standing over me.

I stare up at his hulking body, no jacket this time, just a plain t-shirt that shows off every taut muscle, and jeans. He gives me a half-smile.

Mind if I sit down?

He's speaking to me, right into my head, without opening his mouth.

I'm not a fan of this.

I open my mouth and am surprised when the words, "Can I talk?" come out.

"Of course," he says. "I understand it must be strange for you. It's still strange for me."

I frown at him. My dreams have been so lucid lately, but never the ones that have involved him. I've never been able to just exist like this, to interact with him and have it be so real.

I need to take advantage.

"Who are you?" I ask him. "I mean, I know I'm dreaming."

He stares down at me, his smile twisting slightly. My god, this dude is even more handsome up close. I'm starting to think there is no way in hell that I met him in real life because if he really was the guy from the wedding, I know I would have remembered every detail of his face, no matter how blackout drunk I got.

"*Are* you dreaming?" he asks, easing himself down to sit beside me. He props his elbows on his knees and gives me a sidelong glance. "Or are you awake?"

All the hairs on my arm stand up and I can't tell if it's because he's so close or the way his eyes seem to gaze right into the heart of me, or because I'm starting to think maybe I am awake after all.

"You never answered my question," I tell him, shifting away slightly, his proximity to me producing a strange push pull, like two magnets about to connect. "Why do I keep dreaming you? Have we met before? What's your name?"

"So many questions, Ada, so little time" he says. There's something so soothing about his voice, both low and silken, even in such a dead place like this where all sound is worn down, dull. "But you have met me before. At the wedding."

"I knew it," I whisper, feeling mildly triumphant.

"I guess it doesn't say much about me that you don't really remember," he says with a wince, a piece of wavy hair flopping on his forehead. "Or maybe it says a lot."

"I blame the champagne," I tell him. "So now I know I've met you before. Am I conjuring you up because I found you absurdly handsome and I'm hoping to pick up where we left off?"

Okay, normally I'm not this forward with guys but it's my dream, I can do what the hell I want.

The corner of his mouth quirks up. He has damn fine lips. "We didn't really leave off anywhere. You took off your shoes and went to get champagne. I never saw you again."

I'm wondering if that's true or if it's what my subconscious wants me to believe. After all, it's pretty much what Perry had told me earlier.

"You're here," he says slowly, his face falling slightly, "because I have something to show you."

He gets to his feet in one fluid motion and reaches down for my hand.

Without thinking, as if my hand has a mind of its own, it goes to his and I feel an immediate jolt of electricity running through me. Not just the electricity you read about in romance novels. I mean actual voltage. My lips are buzzing.

"Sorry," he says, hauling me to my feet, still holding onto my hand. "The connection in here can be a livewire."

A livewire? It's magnetic is what it is, it feels like my palm is stuck to his and our hands meld together like they were always meant to be this way.

Fuck. Though the respite from the horror is welcome, I'm not sure all this Twilight-like, magnetic, electric bullshit is any better, dream-wise.

Come on, he says in my head. *And use your inside voice.*

Okay, I say, hearing my words escape, despite not opening my mouth.

He leads the way, his large form in front of me as he takes me toward the forest.

The forest of darkness and death.

My chest feels heavy and he pauses, looking at me over his shoulder.

You'll be fine with me. I won't let anything happen to you.

What are you showing me? I ask him. *I don't even really know who you are.*

I'm the one who has your back, he says. *And I've been watching you for a very, very long time.*

I don't have the luxury to puzzle over his remark. We enter the forest and I immediately feel this sense of doom slide over me, as if evil has taken up residence here and it's just oozing from the trees. The light in here is nearly gone and I can barely make out the tree trunks from the shadows. Everything is the darkest, grainiest red, a world seeped in blood.

Without realizing it, I'm holding his hand for dear life. He's leading me further into my nightmare and I don't even know his name.

It's Jay, he says, glancing at me over his shoulder.

Oh great, Jay, the thought reader.

Sorry, he says. *It's impossible not to when we're in here.*

You keep saying in here, I say as I give wide berth to a flowering vine that's reaching halfway across the path. I swear there are eyeballs at the center of the flowers, watching me as I go. *You mean my dream.*

He doesn't say anything for a moment. *Things aren't always as they seem here.*

No shit, I mutter to myself.

Suddenly he stops and I run into his back. A nice, hard, firm back. I yearn to run my fingers over his muscles and reach up to do so, because again, it's my dream and it's been forever since I've had a sexy one, but he says, *listen*.

I take my hand away, my other still grasping his, unable to let go, and cock my head in concentration.

I hear a flurry of wings beating and look up to see the faint shape of what looks to be a bat the size of an eagle flying overhead, a black blot beyond the dark reaches of the tree limbs.

Not that, he says.

I close my eyes, straining to hear more.

At first I just hear my own heartbeat, a strange thing to pick up on in a dream, and for a moment I wonder if I'm still in bed with Perry, if my heart is racing in real life, if I'm tossing and turning.

Then I hear it.

Again.

"Help me, Ada."

My mother's voice.

I grasp Jay's hand tighter. *What is that? What's going on?*

It's not your mother, he says, glancing down at me, his brows low. *That's what I want to show you, what you need to know.*

I peer around him.

The path in front of us widens, but as the trees fan out, it doesn't become lighter. It becomes darker. Instead of a forest it's a black veil, like we're standing on the edge of a starless universe. And there, just feet away in the earth, is a large gaping pit with a sole hand sticking out of it.

I know without a doubt that it's my mother's hand. I know her hand. I feel her near, a connection that can't be broken.

I start for it but Jay pulls me back, his hand going to my elbow and taking a firm hold.

It's not your mother, he warns.

Help me, my mother cries out, her voice soft and ragged all at once, like she's barely holding onto life.

47

Even though she's dead.

Please, I tell him, trying to wrestle free from his grasp. *She needs me.*

My mother screams bloody murder, her hand gripping the side of the hole, fingers digging into dirt, barely holding on.

I know you're there, you can save me, she gasps. *You need to save my soul. They have me and won't let me go.*

"I'm trying!" I yell, wishing I could see her face, wanting to grab her hand and pull her up.

Shhh, Jay hushes me, eyes blazing into me as his grip tightens. *They might know.*

More giant bats start flying overhead, one landing a few feet from my mother's grasping hand.

Who might know? I cry out in frustration. *It's a fucking dream and I'm either saving my mom or I'm waking up.*

I won't let you, he says. *This isn't over.*

I stare at him incredulously. *Won't let me?*

He points at what I can only assume is the pit to hell. *That is not real. That isn't your mother. This is what I had to show you, why I had to show you myself.*

Of course it isn't real, I snap, my chest heavy, as if loaded with bricks. *It's a dream.*

Listen, Jay says, placing his large hands on my shoulders, an iron grip to keep me in place. He lowers his head, his eyes inches from mine and searching. *And listen carefully. No matter what happens, you mustn't believe your mother is in any danger. She's dead and she's safe.*

That's an oxymoron if I ever heard one, I mutter, trying to ignore my mother's cries, even though they stab deep, like hot knives.

Whatever it is, she's okay. Don't attempt to seek her out. Don't attempt to interfere.

How can I interfere?

Let it be and ignore it.

I think I'd really like to wake up now. I look around, staring at the darkness. "Wake up, wake up, WAKE UP!" I scream.

"Shhhh!" Jay hushes me. "I'm not supposed to be here with you."

A dozen more giant bats land on the earth around us with soft thumps.

Jay looks over his shoulder at them and then back at me.

He gives me a small shake of his head. "You need to go to sleep now."

Knock.

Knock.

Knock.

Three knocks reverberate through the air.

In a flash I'm sucked backward through darkness, Jay, the bats, the forest growing smaller and disappearing.

Suddenly I'm back at home.

Standing downstairs in the kitchen.

In the dark.

I gasp for air, as if I haven't been breathing this whole time, and lean against the island for support, my legs suddenly going weak. A wave of nausea rolls through me and I barely have time to make it to the sink before I vomit. I stay hunched over, trying to get through it, catching my breath, until I have enough strength to get a glass from the cupboard.

Grimacing, I rinse my vomit down the sink then splash water on my face before filling my glass from the tap and downing it. I am beyond thirsty even after that and have to fill it again.

When I'm done, I push the glass away and look around the kitchen warily. I'm in my camisole and short shorts, barefoot, and yet I feel like I've spent the last few hours trudging through a forest.

It was a dream, I tell myself. *A bad one.*

And now I'm apparently sleepwalking. That's a new one for me.

I take in a deep breath and absently walk over to the window that looks out onto the street.

The air leaves my lungs.

There's a man standing in the middle of the road.

His form dark and faceless against the streetlights.

I freeze, wide-eyed, watching him.

I feel him watching me.

Neither of us move.

Then he turns and walks away.

Goes right next door.

To our new neighbors, the Knightlys'.

CHAPTER FOUR

The next morning over bacon, eggs, and an obscene amount of coffee, Perry and Dex decide to stay an extra night. Perry says it's because she wants to check out the Saturday market downtown, though I know it's because they both don't feel right about leaving me. They have their friend Dean looking after their dog, Fat Rabbit, anyway, so they're squared.

Actually I do want to go to the market and peruse the handmade clothing and eat from the food trucks. I want to be in the sunshine and as far away from this house as possible. I even want to be around a crowd of sweaty strangers, just so I'm not alone.

I didn't go back to sleep last night. I was too scared. After the thing in the closet and the dream about my mother and Jay and waking up in the kitchen sleepwalking, plus seeing one of my neighbors outside on the street in the middle of the night staring at the house (or was that a dream too?), I went back upstairs, climbed in bed with Perry, but spent the rest of the night on my phone. I literally went through every single fashion blog and magazine there is and even bought a few things from shopping sites I'd banned myself from. Anything to keep from closing my eyes, to risk going through it all again.

Needless to say I'm exhausted, my brain is full of fog, and I've barely spoken two words all morning. But Perry knows, as she always does, that I'm even worse today than yesterday. So they're staying and I'm not protesting one bit. Even though Perry and Dex are known for attracting trouble, there's no one else I feel safer around. Dex has Perry's back and he has mine too.

But in my dream, so does someone else.

I'm the one who has your back. And I've been watching you for a very, very long time.

Jay.

It was so incredibly real, incredibly vivid and arguably the most fucked up dream I've ever had. It just felt...like I wasn't in control of it. Like it was being projected into my head. And the more I think about it, about my mother and the Thin Veil and Jay, the more my head spins.

I'm mulling that over as I grab my purse and head out the door with Dex and Perry, the stark sunshine feeling incredibly good on my skin while bird song erupts from the trees. I close my eyes briefly as Dex unlocks the doors to his black Highlander and try to let it the summer light wash away the darkness.

"Hmmph," Dex says and I open my eyes to see him staring over at the Knightlys', his brow furrowed as he sticks a cigarette in his mouth.

I look behind me, a chill coming over me. "What?"

The boxes are gone, there's no car in driveway nor the '70s Mercedes that the Jacob man drove. It looks quiet.

"Nothing," Dex says, lighting the cigarette and taking a drag. He blinks, seeming to relax before my eyes and blows smoke out of the corner of his mouth. "Anyway I was hoping maybe I'd see Sage Knightly."

"I'm sure you can harass the new neighbors tonight," Perry says as she walks around the hood. "And you're not smoking that in the car."

He gives her a salute. "Yes ma'am." He promptly puts out the cigarette on the back of his lighter and shoves it back in the pack before getting in the driver's seat, sighing despondently.

During the drive to downtown, Dex has Soundgarden blaring and Perry keeps eying me in the rear-view mirror.

I'm fine! I yell inside my head, using the "inside voice" Jay told me to. I'm not sure if she can hear me or not because her expression doesn't change. She's studying me as if not quite sure who I am.

"What?" I finally ask her out loud, my voice sharp.

She looks away and now Dex is peering at me in the mirror.

"You all right back there?" he asks. "Overdosing on teenage angst?"

I flip him the bird and look out the window.

Portland's Saturday market has always been one of the best parts of summer in the city, and I've only made it out once this year. It stretches from the McCall Waterfront Park into the downtown area, and has grown a lot over the years. Portland's famous food trucks are all over the place, there's live music, and vendors selling everything from hand-tooled leather bags to vintage furniture. There's a water park that you need on a humid day like today, and street performers everywhere.

After we find parking blocks away, we're sucked in by the crowd and for a moment it feels like my problems are disappearing. In fact, it makes me feel like I never had any problems at all. Maybe it's the epic collection of people, the weather, or the good vibes, but I feel a twinge of excitement run through me. In three weeks I'll be starting school, and even with all the changes going on in my life, that's one change that brings promise.

Maybe I can start again.

"So you know how to smile after all," Dex muses. He's got a phallic-looking corn dog in his hand and waves it at me. I didn't even realize I was smiling.

We're standing outside a vendor tent while Perry is trying on clothes inside. Ironically I'm of no help to her. I can't stand shopping with other people and am apt to tell them everything looks fine just to get it over with.

I pretend to knee him in the groin and he waves the corn dog like a fencing sword to fend me off until it goes flying onto the grass. His face falls dramatically.

"Son of a fuck," he says, tossing the empty stick in the nearby trash and taking out a cigarette. While he lights it he glances at me. "Anyway, smiling is a good thing. You seemed a little rough this morning."

"Well I had a rough night," I tell him, suddenly occupied with picking strands of my hair off my black linen dress.

He exhales, the smoke wafting away. Silence strums between us for a beat. "You know, Ada," he says in a careful voice, "I hope you know that what you're going through is perfectly normal."

My eyes snap to his. "What I'm going through?"

He nods, taking a drag, eyes all squinty. "Yeah. Puberty."

I let out a tired groan.

"Seriously though," he goes on, giving me a quick smile. "I mean about everything. Your mom. Everything that's happened since. Everything that happened before. Normal people don't go through all that."

"Then how can you say what I'm going through is perfectly normal?" I question.

"I mean in the sense that I've gone through it. So has Perry. We're still going through it. A lot happened." His eyes grow hard and he blinks, looking away. "We lost people. We lost...chances. We gained truths we didn't want. Fuck. We literally all went to hell and back and that changes a person. It's changed Perry. It's changed you. And it sure as hell has changed me."

I've never heard Dex admit anything like this to me before and I have to say I want him to keep talking. I usually want him to shut up.

"Yeah?" I ask quietly.

He nods, flicking his cigarette. "Yeah. If you think you're the only one who has weird dreams, you're wrong. I have nightmares all the time."

"What about?"

"Everything. Everyone. Every place. It doesn't really end." He sighs and rubs his hand along his chin, eyes darting over the passersby. "We know monsters are real. They exist in this world. They can be disguised in a crowd. They can be buried in your head. And they are definitely somewhere...there." He waves his hand in a circle, focused somewhere in the distance. "Beyond what we can see. We know they're there, fighting to come in. It's been two years and we've all recovered, distanced ourselves, and have tried to move on. Yet, deep down, I know we're not in the clear. This isn't over, little sister."

"Gee," I tell him softly, "you sure know how to wipe a smile from a girl's face."

He gives me a half-hearted grin. "One of my many talents. You're too young to know the rest." He puffs back on his cigarette, his dark eyes observing me just as Perry's were earlier. "Sometimes I know what your sister is thinking whether I want to or not. Extremely handy in the bedroom. Not always handy outside of it. She's worried about you. A lot."

I swallow uneasily and absently look down at my nails, not wanting to hear this. "I'm fine."

"You're not," he says simply. "And neither are we. And we'll probably never be fine. It's okay to admit that. And it's okay to tell us if something is going on, whether you think it's a silly dream or stuffed animals trying to kill you."

"Okay, why do you guys keep mentioning the stuffed animals? Because I swear I'm piling them all in your car and you're taking them back to Seattle for Fat Rabbit to chew on."

"Fair enough," he says with a shrug. "Better them than my boots. My point is...you have us. We're only three hours away. Use us."

"Did Perry put you up to this?" I say suspiciously.

He shakes his head, looking downright solemn. "She didn't. Believe it or not, I care about you."

I can't help but grimace, completely uncomfortable with any affection coming from this douchecanoe of a brother-in-law. But secretly, deep down, I'm touched.

"Don't worry," he says quickly as Perry comes out of the tent, a plastic bag of clothes in her hand. "I'll go back to annoying the fuck out of you in no time."

She holds up her bag triumphantly. "Dresses made from old concert t-shirts."

"Sweet," I tell her, mentally filing that idea away for my own designs.

"I don't know about you," Dex says, putting out his smoke. "But I could use a beer or twelve."

There is a little beer garden over by the stage, but I'm only eighteen so I obviously can't take part, and my last fake ID got seized by a bar Amy and I had tried to sneak into a few months ago.

"You guys have your beer," I tell them. "I'm going to look around."

"Are you sure?" Perry asks. "I'm sure Dex can keep his alcoholism in check until we get back home."

Dex's mouth drops open in false shock. "Woman, do you even know me at all?"

"I'll see you in a bit," I tell them, heading over toward the water fountain. I look back over my shoulder just in time to see Dex grab Perry's hand, holding on tight as they walk away, lifting it up to his lips and kissing it while Perry beams back at him.

I feel a squeeze on my heart, a warm fuzzy feeling combined with a flash of my dream.

The feel of my hand in Jay's, the way it felt like it was made just for me to hold.

You're a fuckwad, I tell myself. *It was just a dream.*

I repeat that to myself as I meander through the crowds. I start taking pictures of the local fashion, street style to post on my blog, and of course I seek out our own Jimi Hendrix and get a selfie with the market legend. It's tradition.

I'm standing outside a Korean taco stand, trying to figure out if I want a bibimbap wrap (honestly I just like saying "bibimbap"), when I feel a presence beside me.

I look over to see Jacob standing right there.

"Hello," he says in his thick accent. "Bloody brilliant weather we're having."

I blink at him for a moment, taking him in. He's not wearing a baseball cap this time and has a thick mop of red hair for someone his age, though his sunglasses are covering up his eyes. I remember their amber color quite well. Just like yesterday he's wearing an ugly shirt, this time a burnt orange short-sleeved shirt that matches his hair.

"Jacob," he supplies when I don't say anything. "We met yesterday. You're Dawn and Sage's neighbor. Ada, isn't it?"

I swallow, trying to find my voice. I'm not sure what it is about this man that makes me feel off-kilter. Not necessarily in a bad way, it's just...something.

"Yeah, Ada," I manage to say.

"Well, Ada," he says smoothly, looking around, "I have to tell you it feels good to see a familiar face in this crowd. I don't know Portland at all. First time here."

We shuffle forward in the line as it gets shorter. "Where are you from?"

"Aside from England?" He asks. "Oh, I've been all over the place. You name it, I've been there."

"But Dawn and Sage, they moved from Washington?"

He nods. "They're a nice couple. I think you'd like them."

I give him a wry smile. "To be fair, you don't know me so you can't know what I like."

He tilts his head back and I can feel his eyes on me despite the sunglasses reflecting back my own face. My dark circles stand out more than anything and my blonde hair is thwarted by fly-aways. I look like absolute shit.

"No I suppose I don't know you at all," he says finally, his attention back to the menu on the side of the stand. "Bibimbap," he repeats. "Fun word, isn't it?"

"So how do you know them?" I ask. "The Knightlys." I pause. "Is it true that Sage was in the band Hybrid, that Dawn was a journalist?"

"Who told you that, love?"

"My dad. He's not a fan or anything. He was just talking to them earlier."

"Well if they told him that, it must be true."

"And so..."

"I'm a family friend," he supplies. "Here to help them settle in. I've always been a helper of sorts for them. Anything they need, they know they can count on old Jacob." He adds sympathetically, "They're getting older, you know. Their minds still run like it's the '70s, but bodies don't keep up so easily. Such a shame, really. How unfair life is in that regard.

They say you're only as old as you feel but try telling that to a ninety-year-old on their deathbed, just wishing he could do all the bloody things he wants to do."

Jeez. Second Debbie Downer conversation in the last half hour.

"You have youth, love," Jacob says, nudging me to move forward when the man behind the counter beckons me forward. "A young body, a young heart, and endless courage. That last part is the most important. Don't let anyone tell you any differently. Why do you think we used to send so many kids your age off to war?"

I'm trying to absorb what he's saying while placing my order for the bibimbap wrap. When I'm done paying, I turn around to face Jacob.

But he's gone.

There's only a pair of teenage girls with obnoxious neon sunglasses, staring down at their phones.

I step away from the line and look around but Jacob is nowhere to be found.

Now I'm wondering if I'm going crazy. If he was really there at all.

The girls can't tell me since they've been on Facebook this whole time and when I get my food and ask the guy behind the counter if he remembers the man behind me, he says he's not paying attention to who's in line and goes back to handling a myriad of orders.

Despite being confused, I still manage to shovel the food in my face and head back to Dex and Perry. Thankfully they're just leaving as I'm coming over.

"I think I'm ready to go," I tell them quickly.

They exchange one of their glances. It either means *moody Ada* or *crazy Ada*.

I'm not sure which one I am these days.

As we're heading back to the car, I blurt out, "I think I'm seeing ghosts."

They stop walking.

"What?" Perry asks, pulling me to a stop.

"I mean, I know I normally do. We all do." I glance at Dex. "It's just that I feel like one is repeatedly seeking me out."

"The guy from your dream?" Perry asks.

"No," I say carefully, though now I'm wondering if he's a fucking ghost too, finding some way to invade my brain. "No, this guy I met yesterday and…" I trail off and scrunch my eyes shut, pressing the heel of my palm into my forehead. "Never mind. He can't be a ghost. Dawn Knightly introduced us. I mean, he drove a car and everything. You remember seeing that old Mercedes outside yesterday."

"Yeah," Dex says. "Sweet ride. But even ghosts need cool cars."

"No. No, he's not a ghost then. I just thought…I don't know, I ran into him here and he said some cryptic shit and then pretty much disappeared."

"Into thin air?" Perry asks.

"No, just when I was ordering my food. I guess he could have walked off. I don't know, there was just something so odd about him. A feeling, something familiar, but I can't put my finger on it."

"Do you know his name?" Dex asks.

"Yeah, Jacob. He's a family friend of the Knightlys."

KARINA HALLE

Dex's eyes nearly bug out. "His name is Jacob?"

I frown. "Yes."

"What did he look like? How old was he?"

I shrug. "I'm not good with ages. Maybe mid-fifties?"

"That's impossible then," Dex says, shaking his head and I have no idea what he's talking about.

"Well impossible or not he was about dad's age, maybe a tad older. Tall, red hair, really cool eyes, like amber glass, face looks like it's been beaten up a few times but still handsome in a weird way."

Dex is on his phone, frantically typing in something.

"What is it?" Perry asks, peering over his arm to look at the screen.

Dex holds up his finger, motioning for us to wait, then he shoves the phone in my face. "Was this the guy?"

I take the phone in my hand, staring at the picture. It's a black and white photo, grainy, but in it is Jacob, smiling with a cigarette in one hand and a drink in the other, wearing what looks like a horrible checkered suit.

"Yeah, that's him. Who is he?" I ask, handing it back.

"Are you sure he looks exactly like this?" Dex asks.

"Yes," I reply testily. "He looks like that. No different. Who is he?"

"He's Jacob 'The Cobb' Edwards. One of the world's most famous band managers."

I nod. "Cool."

"No," Dex says. "Well yes, cool, but also not cool because this photo was taken on the infamous Hybrid tour. In 1974."

I try and do math. It's not my strong suit.

"That was forty-two years ago and he was definitely fifty-something back then," Dex goes on, back to scrolling.

He pauses. "Oh. Right. So aside from the fact that he should technically be in his nineties, he's also dead."

"What?" Perry and I say in unison as we both look at his phone.

There on the Wikipedia page for Jacob Edwards is his picture, plus his birth date in 1919 and his death date in 1975. It says he died in Prague during Sage Knightly's European solo tour when a crypt collapsed on him.

"I'm remembering it now,'" Dex says slowly, looking off into the distance, "just the mythology of the band, how the curse that befell them, the deal with the Devil, didn't really end on the first tour. People say Jacob was doing some weird voodoo shit down in that crypt and we all know how weird voodoo shit turns out." He pauses and looks at me. "Except for you Ada, but you can imagine it ain't good."

"So he's a ghost after all."

"A ghost that our neighbors can see," Perry muses, "let alone hang out with."

"So he faked his own death then?" I guess.

"I think we need to talk to the neighbors," Dex says, starting to walk down the sidewalk.

Perry and I follow. "So you can harass Sage about music rights?" Perry questions with a quirk of her eyebrow.

"Kiddo, I always have an ulterior motive."

. . .

Though during the drive back to my house the conversations in the car turned to lighter topics, such as the music video Dex was creating for an up-and-coming band called Only Mostly Dead, the minute we pulled in behind my dad's Taurus in the driveway, silence fell between us.

As the three of us walked up the stone path to the front door, The Knightlys' house looked as empty as it had earlier—no cars in the driveway, no lights in the house, no noise.

I really wasn't sure what was going to happen. To be honest, the fact that Jacob either faked his death or was already dead, wasn't too much of a concern. If anything I just wanted to know what his comment had meant, the one about the young having courage. That wasn't a throwaway line. That meant something and it meant something for me.

Dex knocks at the door, three quick raps and I automatically tense, thinking I might wake up any second and this is yet again a dream.

But nothing happens. Perry reaches out and squeezes my hand, sensing what I'm feeling, reminding me that this is all very real in the here and now, even if it feels kind of silly. What exactly are we going to say if someone answers?

And it doesn't seem like anyone is going to answer anyway.

"The cars are gone," I point out, my voice hushed for some reason. "No one's home." I start pulling back on Perry's hand but then there's the sound of someone on the other side of the door and I'm pretty sure all three of us just sucked in a collective gasp.

The door opens and a tall, bulky man of Hispanic descent with thick white hair, green eyes, and golden skin appraises us, a dark brow raised in curiosity even though he doesn't look all that surprised.

"Can I help you?" he asks.

I expected Dex to talk but he's actually gone mute. Speechless, maybe.

"Hi," Perry says, elbowing Dex to the side. "We're your neighbors." She gestures to the house with a tilt of her head. "I'm Perry, this is Dex, that's my sister Ada. We just wanted to come over and introduce ourselves."

The man's eyes fix on mine. Though he's got to be pushing seventy, he's handsome and I'm a bit stunned by his gaze. "My wife talked to you the other day. I'm Sage."

"From Hybrid," Dex is finally able to say. He clears his throat, composing himself. "Big fan."

Sage gives a wane smile. "Have you listened to my solo stuff?"

Dex nods enthusiastically. "Sage Wisdom, Bloody Twat, Tricky Times, An Album for the Dead and Dying, The Devil in Shasta." He lists them all off without missing a beat.

And it seems to impress Sage. It's impressed me, the fact that the man standing before us has had quite the career. It kind of makes me wish I spent some time listening to his music, then again I wouldn't want to turn into a grinning fan-boy the way that Dex is all of a sudden. Dex has always had an aura of cool about him but right now he could be just about any dork drooling over his idol. What a twatwaffle.

"Wow," Sage says slowly, maybe even with a touch of embarrassment. "You really do know your stuff." He opens the door wider. "My wife isn't home right now, but she'd love it if you came in."

We enter the house. I'd only been in here a few times when the old neighbors were here, my mom having dragged us all over for dinner once or twice. Even though the Knightlys just moved in, the place already looks different. It feels different. I'm a strong believer in houses having vibes, and the vibe of this house has totally changed. In fact, every hair on my arm is standing up and I feel hyper-aware. It's not a bad vibe per se, just one of energy, like the walls are brimming with static.

I eye Perry and she gives me a little nod, feeling the same thing.

We follow Sage into the living room, past stacks of boxes. The furnishing is fairly sparse but somehow I can tell it's because of their personal style and not because they haven't unpacked. Maybe because Jacob had mentioned them being stuck in the '70s, mentally anyway, there is a bit of that feeling thanks to the orange and earthy tones, as well as shag carpeting, but it's done up in a modern way. Plus the walls are adorned with all sorts of art that range from tribal and primitive to downright creepy. One painting is the album cover for Led Zeppelin IV, except instead of a man, it's a horse in ragged clothing.

"Can I get you anything?" Sage asks, gesturing for us to take a seat on the couch. "Beer?"

"That would be great," Dex says, his eyes dancing, clearly thrilled to be offered beer by a hero of his.

Perry shakes her head no and then everyone looks at me. I'm underage but obviously that doesn't mean anything.

"Sure," I tell him with a big smile. Hey, they got to have their beer garden fun this afternoon while I was getting cryptic talk from Jacob, it's my turn.

Speaking of Jacob, while Sage strolls into the kitchen, I turn to Perry and whisper, "Are you going to do the talking or is Dex?"

She gives me the gesture to calm down and chill out. I sigh and sit back. She wasn't the one who had been talking to someone who is supposed to be dead.

For once, I guess.

Sage comes back with the beers and a glass of water for Perry and we immediately lapse into easy small talk.

Sage is one interesting old dude. Even though what we're talking about is completely mundane—the farm they lived on before, the new neighborhood, Oregon versus Washington—there's something enigmatic about him that makes you sit up and pay attention. It's the way he speaks, carries himself. It's his eyes that hint at a million things he's seen and experienced, far more than anyone else his age. He's, quite frankly, legendary.

But small talk is impossible for a legend and the conversation easily moves into his own fame and notoriety.

"So," Dex says cautiously, leaning forward on his elbows with his nearly empty beer in his hands, "Ada here tells me that she met your friend, Jacob."

Sage looks my way and I freeze, wishing Dex hadn't thrown me under the bus like that. But he merely gives me the subtlest of nods before focusing back on Dex.

"Jacob had mentioned that," he says. "He's staying with us at the moment. Old family friend of ours."

"Well, uh," Dex falters, running his hand over his jaw and shooting Sage a boyish look, "the thing is, I thought Jacob was dead. I mean, that was Jacob Edwards, wasn't it? Your manager who died in Prague in 1975."

Sage stares at Dex for a moment and I'm afraid he's going to ask us to leave, that Dex is being too nosy, too pushy, that we've stumbled upon something no one is supposed to know. Oh my god, what if there isn't a jam room in the basement at all but a dungeon and that's where the three of us will go in a few seconds, once Sage grabs the guitar in the corner and starts using it as a sword?

But then the corner of Sage's mouth lifts up and he leans back in his armchair, his large, weathered hands palming the wooden adornment on the ends of the arms. "I shouldn't be surprised you know this, considering you're a fan."

"Well it's kind of urban legend," Dex admits. "It only added to your mystique."

Sage's smile is tight. "Yeah. I know." He sighs and looks away, his fingers kneading along the end of the chair. "But how many urban legends actually end up being true?" He gives us all a steady look. "Jacob is a friend to me and Dawn. A very, very good one. Whether he's alive or not doesn't make much difference, does it?"

I can tell the answer is supposed to be "no it doesn't," but I mean *hello*. Of course it makes a difference! But I know I'm supposed to keep my mouth shut so I shove the beer in my mouth and swig back the rest of it.

"The fact is," Sage goes on, "Jacob is here, where he should be. He did a brave thing, sacrificing his own life to save Dawn's. I know that's not how they say he died, but that's the truth. There was no voodoo, nothing except bravery and selflessness. What they don't tell you is both Jacob and Dawn died the day that the crypt collapsed. And they both came back. But she never would have without him. As such, I owe Jacob my life. I owe him the world. Even to this day. You see," he says, looking at Perry now, "it's not easy having to deal with things you can't explain. Things that the world judges you for. The fact that you see the world differently. Or maybe the world shows itself differently to you. When you find that person who understands...you hold onto them with your life. And if there is anyone out there who can...give that person back to you, you're in debt to them forever."

I feel like this is totally a moment for Perry and Dex, considering they've been to Hell and back (again, literally) and seem to understand each other on this basic, soulmate kind of level. I guess it's kind of inspiring to see a couple such as Dawn and Sage still together, considering they seem to have gone through something similar. True love binds.

Of course that makes me have a tiny pity party for myself, complete with festive hat, confetti, and party horn that makes a pathetic little toot, since I also seem to be damned with these afflictions and yet I'm still alone. Finding someone who understands me seems pretty much impossible.

That said, Sage didn't really answer the Jacob question, whether I was talking to a ghost or not. It seems to be important only to me.

"So then what really happened during the Hybrid tour?" Dex asks point blank.

Sage grins at him. "What Dawn wrote for Cream magazine in 1974 is completely true. Everyone passed it off as clever metaphor. But it wasn't. It took us a long time to even think about it, let alone talk about it...people died.

And that still hurts. But time heals and we've had a good, easy, simple life since then."

"So that means if the myth is true," Perry surmises, "you made a deal with the Devil for fame and fortune and when you turned twenty-seven, he decided it was time to collect. That's why your tour went awry, why people started getting hurt and dying."

Sage gives her a quiet smile. "Sounds like a load of bullshit doesn't it?"

She shakes her head. "Not at all. I believe it completely. It's just something tells me you don't tell this story to just anyone."

He shrugs. "You're right. And if I get too drunk or high and do, I can usually pass it off as ramblings of a tired old man, still living in the past. But I knew you guys would understand." He fixes his green eyes on me now. "Even you."

Especially you.

I can almost feel that radiating off of him. I think my paranoia amp has been cranked up to eleven lately.

He looks to Dex. "You play an instrument, Dex?"

It's music to his fucking ears, no pun intended.

"I'll play anything you give me," Dex says, wide-eyed. "Just let me smell your guitar and I'll be happy."

"Dex don't be weird," Perry admonishes him under her breath.

I know Sage doesn't want to discuss the past anymore and I know that Dex is a gifted musician in his own right, able to play any instrument he wants, let alone sing like a motherfucker, so the question easily swings the conversation back into neutral territory.

We head downstairs into the basement, which is in fact a funky jam room crammed with guitars, instruments, and band memorabilia (AKA not a dungeon). While Perry and I stare at framed platinum records on the walls and photo albums full of Sage and Dawn with Jimmy Page and Roger Waters, Sage and Dex start jamming together. It's actually kind of an epic sight and I even record a few minutes of it on my phone just in case. Not that my blog followers would care, but you never know.

Finally Perry suggests it's time to leave. I know Dex wanted to keep rocking out with a legend and I wanted Dawn to come home, maybe even with Jacob in tow, to get more answers but we can feel when our time is up.

We leave and I tell Sage he and Dawn are welcome over any time for dinner (my dad will sure as hell be surprised) and he heartily accepts. But while it was nice to get to know Sage and see his house and get to know a bit about him, I know I've only scratched the surface when it comes to our new neighbors.

And I'm not really sure what I'll find next.

CHAPTER FIVE

"Ada."

A breath of a voice floats past, barely audible, like it's more of a memory than anything.

I groan, my eyes too heavy to open and try and take stock of where I am, how I got here. My memory jogs and then stutters and I come up with nothing except the here and now: my cheek pressed against cold, hard ground, with dampness seeping in my clothes, going straight into my bones.

"Ada, come find me."

The voice again. My mother's. Here but not here.

Somehow I open my eyes and am faced with a grey world. I'm face down on frosted grass, sprawled against unyielding earth. Slowly I raise my head.

And I see her.

She's standing a few yards away, her back to me. We're on the island again, this place that only seems to exist in my dreams, only now it's not an open space overlooking the sea, we're in frozen woods of birch and hemlock. On the other side of my mother is a large, dark pond, a layer of thin ice stretched across like a spider web. I have this unsettling feeling that the pond keeps going and going and going underneath and there is no bottom.

It's a door.

To someplace beneath Hell. A darker place where there's no air, no life, no escape.

The thoughts rattle me and I'm afraid. I'm suddenly afraid that the door is real, that this is real, and that my mother might actually be in front of me and she'll be lost to me forever.

"Come find me."

She starts to walk.

"Stop!" I cry out.

She does.

I try to move, to get up, but every part of my body is heavy, swollen, and by the time I get to my feet, I'm sweating, my face red hot with strain.

She's still standing there, dressed in jeans and a peasant top, the clothes she was wearing when she was last seen alive.

When she threw herself onto the train tracks of the New York Subway, before my very eyes.

She knew that if she killed herself, the demon that was possessing her, the demon that was intent on destroying us, destroying our world, would die along with her.

The memories hit me like a sledgehammer and I feel myself cracking into pieces.

My mother shouldn't have died, it should have been me. I should have realized what was going on, I should have been strong enough. The demon was inside me first, albeit briefly, and I should have been the one to kill myself and the demon inside, not her.

But I hadn't.

I wasn't strong enough to fight.

And honestly, I don't know if I would have been strong enough to throw myself in front of a moving train either. The fact was that if I had been in my mother's shoes, if I had the choice, I may have been too much of a coward to do the right thing. Jacob had said that the young have courage. But I was only sixteen. And I had none.

"Mom," I say softly, the ache in my heart growing and growing, adding to the weight, my body already so heavy, being pulled to the earth. "Please."

I don't know what else there is to say. What can I say?

Too much.

Not enough.

"I miss you," I whisper. "I love you. I wish you were still here. That I'd wake up and come downstairs and you'd be in the kitchen with Dad. I wish we were all happy again. I wish everything was normal."

My words float in this airless land and I feel she can't hear me. Maybe it doesn't matter anymore.

She starts to walk, straight into the pond. The ice melts instantly with a hiss and puffs of steam rise as her foot touches the water.

I can't go after her. I can't move an inch.

She gets in to her knees and slowly starts to turn her head. To look at me over her shoulder.

I suck in my breath, terrified that what I'm going to see won't be my mother, will be a horrible demon instead.

Instead, it's worse.

She's my mother.

As she's always been, as I've always remembered.

Just being able to look into her eyes again brings me to tears.

You're stronger than you think, she says in her inside voice. *Come find me.*

"Mom," I sob, nearly falling to my knees.

She turns her head forward, goes in further, one step at a time, until the dark water is at her throat.

You're stronger than you think, she says again. She pauses, her head cocked, almost as if she's listening. *You need to be. To fight him.*

My eyes widen. "Fight who?"

She glances at me quickly and in her eyes I see nothing but utter torment.

The one who died with me.

Her head goes under. She disappears beneath the water, only a faint ripple to tell that she was ever there.

The one who died with her?

"Mom!" I cry out and suddenly I can move. I stagger across the frozen ground, tripping over branches and low brush until I'm at the pond's edge, beside the crooked, bare limbs of a birch tree.

I frantically peer into the water, expecting to see my mother.

A scream strangles in my throat.

My mother isn't there.

Instead there is a girl with wisps of blonde hair cascading around her face like a veil.

It's me.

I'm floating in the water, just underneath the surface.

Dead.

Suddenly my eyes pop open in alarm, staring right at me through the water.

My mouth opens in an underwater scream, bubbles rising, breaking the surface.

Hands, dozens of hands, some with peeling skin, some just fiber and bone, reach up, grabbing my body. Skeletal, rotten fingers digging into my hips, thighs, shoulders, arms, dragging me down and down until I'm fading before my eyes.

All I can do is stand there and watch until I'm gone, drowned in the depths.

Prisoner of the dead.

The pond is still and dark once more.

I turn around slowly, unsure where to go, what to do, the forest suddenly seeming to close in on me, growing thicker, darker.

A hand grasps my ankle.

I can't even scream.

I'm yanked to the ground, my fingers clawing into the cold dirt, trying to hold on as I'm pulled back toward the pond.

"Come find her," a disembodied voice says, raspy and metallic, like a monster over a radio. "And you won't come back alone."

. . .

I wake up with a jolt, my heart beating so fast in my ribcage I'm certain I'm on the cusp of it failing all together.

I open my eyes to the blackness and for one horrible second I think I'm underwater, drowning, that I'm floating in the depths of a watery Hell.

But my eyes adjust quickly.

I'm in my bedroom, the covers thrown aside, my limbs sprawled across the mattress.

I want to sigh in relief, to shed the nightmare from my heart. Fucking hell, that was a doozy.

But I can't.

I can't move.

Sleep paralysis, I remind myself quickly, trying to quell my racing heart. *You know this happens with the syndrome. It happens all the time when you wake up. That's what the internet doctors say.*

Knowing doesn't change anything.

I *can't* move.

And I'm not alone.

Everything in me suddenly freezes, like my blood is paralyzed as well, and I'm acutely aware of everything around me, down to the molecule.

I'm aware that the room is quiet and absolutely still.

Unnaturally still.

I can hear my heart beating in frantic thuds.

I can hear the tick of dying bubbles inside the half-drunk can of soda by my bed.

I can hear a low, ragged *breath*.

A breath that isn't mine.

Someone is else is in the room with me.

My heart skips.

Heavy breathing comes from the foot of the bed. The same place where there is immense pressure on the edge, just to the side of my bare, exposed feet.

I can feel them, *it*, sitting there in the dark, breathing in raspy little gurgles.

But I can't move.

I can't see them.

My whole body feels awash with dread, colder than the ground in my dream, a frozen kind of panic that prickles at me, steals my breath and holds it.

There's someone in my room.

Someone.

Someone.

Another rough, guttural breath.

Something.

The terror has never felt so great, so overwhelming. I am nearly enslaved by it.

I close my eyes, trying to breathe, trying to find the strength to move. I will my limbs, my muscles, my bones, and nothing happens. I can't even open my mouth to scream.

It could be in your head, it could be in your head. I'm practically crying on the inside. *Perry, Perry, Perry!*

I don't know if she can hear me and it doesn't matter.

Because there is now another sound.

The closet door slowly creaking open.

I can see it out of my periphery, opening by itself until it's wide and there is nothing inside the closet but a black, gaping hole.

The pressure comes off the bed, weight lifted.

It brushes against my foot and I scream internally. The fear is so sharp.

I see a dark, tall shape glide toward the closet, my eyes fighting to adjust, to pick up the form from the darkness.

Something thick and about two feet long drags behind it, rustling on the carpet as it goes.

The being steps into the closet.

The door slams shut.

And suddenly all feeling returns. Like chains and shackles have fallen off me all at once and the breath flows into my lungs so fast I nearly choke on it.

I'm up, out of the bed, on my feet and panting, wheezing, slapping my hands up and down my arms, my neck, my face, trying to make sure I'm alive, I'm awake.

It went into the closet.

That motherfucking closet.

I stand there beside my bed, unsure of what to do, where to go.

There was someone here.

Something.

It was real.

It wasn't a dream.

And it's in my closet right now.

I have to go to Perry.

I start walking across the room quickly, afraid to look at the closet again.

Then I hear it.

Her.

"Ada, please."

I freeze.

My mother's voice again, crying out from the closet.

"Please, he's here with me. He won't stop. He won't stop."

I try to swallow and can't.

"You have to be brave sweetie, you have to be brave."

"Mom?" I manage to whisper. Because this isn't a dream now, this is real, this is *happening*.

I move toward the closet, each step I take becoming lighter, like the closet itself is pulling me in. I have a vision that if I closed my eyes and let myself go, I would fly through the air, into the darkness, into my mother's arms.

I open my eyes and suddenly I'm right there. My hand is inches from grasping the knob. It wants to. My palm burns and my hand twists involuntarily, desperate for contact.

"Don't."

The voice comes loud and clear across the room.

I gasp and spin around.

There is someone standing by my bed. Tall, broad-shouldered, faceless in the night.

Sweet fucking bejesus.

My mouth opens, words on my tongue, a scream building in my lungs.

But nothing happens. I stand there, staring, unable to move again.

"Don't touch that door. Don't go inside."

His voice is hard and commanding, yet instantly familiar.

But it can't be.

"You're not dreaming," he says, softer now. "Not this time."

I lick my lips, my throat parched. "It was you," I manage to say. "You were sitting on my bed."

The man shakes his head and I wish I could see more than just his form against the windows. "No. That wasn't me."

"Who was that?" I whisper, my voice trembling, every single cell inside me trembling. I'm legitimately concerned I might pee right here and now.

"Something you don't want to meet," the man says smoothly, his voice still taking on an edge.

But for whatever reason, the man in my room now is much less terrifying than the thing that went in the closet.

"Who are you?"

Warmth floods into my limbs and I take a step toward him, able to move.

He doesn't answer.

I keep walking, slowly across the room. I'm about a foot away and his features are coming together. Even the smell of him is familiar.

He stiffens.

"Who are you?" I repeat, making out his sharp jawline, thick neck. The swoop of long hair. "Jay?" I whisper.

He sucks in his breath and the pause between us deepens. "I'm your—"

"Ada?" Perry's voice shatters the room.

The door opens and once again I'm jumping from fright and whirling around to see her shadow at the door, the hall light on behind her. "Ada are you okay? Who are you talking to?"

There is panic in her voice and she fumbles for the lights.

They come on, too bright and I wince, covering my eyes, before looking back to Jay.

He's gone.

I'm standing by the bed, facing the wall, and no one is there.

"Ada?" Perry comes in voice higher now, quietly shutting the door behind her. "What happened?"

"I..." I stammer, blinking at the place Jay was. He was here, I know he was, just as I'm sure that some being went into the closet.

Even now, the closet seems to pulse and hum with its own kind of malevolent energy.

I look over at her with wide-eyes, my heart sinking because I know what she's going to say. "Didn't you see him?"

"See who?" she asks, frowning.

"I was talking to a man," I say quietly, pressing my lips together.

"You were sleepwalking," Perry says.

"I wasn't," I tell her sharply. "You weren't sleepwalking when this happened to you."

"Ada," she says. "It's the middle of the night and you're suffering from a sleep disorder."

I march over to her, the blood in my face hot with anger. "You of all people should know that these things can't be played off that easily! You should know nothing is so easily explained with us. I wasn't sleepwalking Perry. There was a man here and before that, there was something on my bed."

Her eyes dart to the bed and back to me.

I go on. "I had a terrible dream about mom. I woke up, paralyzed. You know, like the syndrome sometimes does to you. But there was someone else in this room with me. Something. I could hear it breathing. I could feel the weight on the end of the bed."

A flash of fear comes across her eyes but she quickly buries it, raising her chin. "You know that the sensation of having someone at the foot of your bed is part of the syndrome, it's common."

"And then it *got up*. The thing, the person, whatever it was got up and I felt it. It touched my foot! And then I saw it. I saw that it was *real*. The closet door opened wide all by itself and the, the being walked inside. Perry, it had a fucking *tail*."

She swallows, her jaw tense and she looks over at the closet, staring at it in a strange way, like it's compelling her.

"I got up," I tell her. "I went over to the closet and it was almost like it wanted me to open it. I heard mom's voice again, Perry. Just like in my dream. Telling me to find her, help her, that she wasn't alone. In my dream she told me that the Michael demon died with her. It's with her now."

"It was a dream," Perry whispers, voice shaking. Her eyes are still focused on the shut closet door. "You said so yourself."

"So I almost opened the closet door. Then a man told me not to. I turned around and there he was." I gesture to beside the nightstand. "He told me I wasn't dreaming, that I shouldn't go inside."

Perry nods absently and starts walking toward the closet.

"Perry," I warn her.

She shakes her head, gingerly raising her hand to shush me. She stops just outside the door and closes her eyes.

I come over to her, keeping a safe distance, watching curiously.

"Perry?" I whisper, wondering if she's asleep on her feet.

Her eyes snap open and she leaps backward, her hand at the Kyuss logo on her faded band t-shirt. "No," she cries out softly.

The skin on the back of my neck prickles, my fingertips numb.

"No what?" I ask her, afraid. Because when she's afraid I have more of a reason to be.

"I don't know," she says, voice shaking. She looks at me, her brow creased. "I don't know, but this is bad. There is something very bad about all of this."

"No shit!" I yell, unable to keep it to a whisper. "There was a creature who went into my closet and then a strange man appeared in my room right afterward!"

The door to my room opens and both of us yelp in unison, jumping in place.

"What the fuck is going on in here?" Dex asks as he pokes his head in, brow furrowed as he takes us in.

Perry brushes past me to him and points at the closet. "There's something in that closet. I don't know if it's there now but it was there. And that isn't a closet. It may have been when you looked last but it's not anymore. I don't know what it is but I can feel it all the way in my bones that this is very, very bad." She looks over at me. "Ada, I think you should come back with Dex and I tomorrow to Seattle."

"What?" Dex and I say at the same time exchanging a glance.

"I'm serious," she goes on, rubbing her lips together, her eyes darting back to the closet. "I don't think you should sleep in this room anymore Ada, let alone this house. All those feelings I had before I was possessed. I'm having them here again."

"Are you sure?" Dex asks, grabbing her hand.

"I think so," she says, looking to me. "I believe you Ada. Whatever is here isn't good. Whatever went in that closet might come back."

"Wait, what?" Dex says, raising his hands. "Can you ladies catch me up to speed here?"

"Ada woke up with something in the room with her. It got off her bed and went into the closet. It had a tail..."

Dex eyes me, raising his brows. "Well holy shit then."

"I also saw someone else in the room. I was talking to him. And he was real."

I think.

Perry eyes him and I can't read what she's thinking. "When I walked in here she was talking to someone. I never heard another voice."

I frown. "That doesn't mean there wasn't someone here with me. I'm telling you there was."

"Regardless, that closet is a fucking slice of horrors, and that I can feel," she says. "Whoever you were or weren't talking to I can't say but I can comment on *that*." She points at the closet with a shaking hand.

"What did the guy look like?" Dex asks me and I'm forever grateful that at least someone is interested in the strange man in my room.

"Well actually," I say. "The guy from my dreams. The guy from your wedding."

Perry purses her lips in surprise. "That Jay guy?"

I swallow. "It was him. I've seen him before you know. In real life."

"What? When?" I catch a twinge of hurt in her voice for not filling her in on it earlier.

"When I was at Sephora," I tell her.

"So he's a metrosexual ghost as well?" Dex asks.

I glare at him. "No. He was outside of the store. But I saw him. We looked right at each other. Then I lost sight of him and he was gone." I pause. "I wasn't dreaming then."

Dex scratches at his sideburns. "Well I suppose that's better than being haunted by a guy that shops at Sephora. You know you're more than welcome to come stay with us till your school starts."

"More than welcome?" Perry repeats, coming over to me. She grabs me by the elbow and looks me deep in the eyes. She's nothing but determined and when she's determined, I feel safe. "You *are* coming with us. And tonight, you're sleeping with me in your old bedroom. Dex you can sleep in here."

"Delightful," he comments dryly. "Okay, in Seattle can I at least sleep with my wife?"

Perry leads me out of the room and I eye my father's door down the hall.

"What about dad?"

"What about him?" she asks as we get into my old bedroom, the bed in the middle of the room, the window beside it illuminating all my extra dressers and rolling racks full of clothing.

"We can't leave him here all alone," I tell her.

"Dad will be fine," she says. "He's not like us. He'll always be fine. You know that."

But I didn't.

"I'll make sure to talk to the Knightlys before we go, let them know he's alone. I'll talk to Debbie down the street too, I'm sure she'd be more than willing to keep an eye on him."

"Do you trust the Knightlys?" I ask.

She bites her lip, thinking as she goes around to her side of the bed. "I'm not sure. Sage was nice, even if he was keeping a lot of things close to his chest. But I think we have to trust them for now."

I wasn't sure either but deep down I felt they were just older versions of ourselves. If we went on to have a badass rock star career, of course.

I get into the bed, the room strangely cold despite the persistent heat wave. I know it's kind of silly to be sleeping with my sister for the second night in a row, like a frightened child, but I'm grateful for it all the same.

"Is Dex going to be okay in there?" I ask her softly after a few moments, the night settling back around us. "I mean, if it was Michael in the closet..."

Two years ago, Dex, Perry, and I were sitting here, in this house. They'd just come back from filming their last episode of their Experiment in Terror show. Dex was upstairs editing. I was doing a workout video in the living room. Perry went for a walk. My parents were out somewhere. Then a man showed up at the door, claiming to be Michael, Dex's estranged brother, and all hell broke loose.

I mean Hell *literally* broke loose.

Michael made me black out and when I woke up, he was gone and so was Dex. Only Perry and I remained. We immediately hopped on a plane to New York to get Dex back, who we figured had been manhandled by Michael. And my parents, once they learned where we'd gone, did the same. That brought everyone to Manhattan like one big happy family. Except we weren't happy—we were being used and manipulated by a demon that had possessed Michael a long time ago. Me, my mother, Perry, Dex, and his friend Maximus all ended up in the house that Michael and Dex grew up in, a place that wasn't a house at all but a portal to Hell, existing in its own horrific reality.

My mother wasn't the only one lost thanks to Michael's demon. Maximus died as well. And we were all forever changed.

Look, I never said my backstory was easy.

Or normal.

"If that is Michael, or whatever demon it was who possessed him," Perry whispers, "Dex has nothing to fear. He has defeated him once, he could do it again."

"Perry, Dex died," I point out, even though I'm sure she never needs reminding of that horrible moment when she found him lifeless on the floor in the house of Hell. "He made the same sacrifice that mom made, only you were able to go in and get him out, bring him back to life."

She falls silent and I feel I've hit a nerve. "Not that you would have been able to do that with mom," I quickly add.

She just nods, swallowing thickly. "Dex will be fine. But you, you won't be."

Normally I would protest over something like that, get defensive or find it belittling, but in this case Perry is right and I'm not about to argue.

I'm not fine at all.

And I don't fall asleep, no matter that Dex is in my room, no matter if I'm safe here or not. I just can't.

My mind keeps playing it all over and over again. The dream, the pond, my mother's words. The thing in my room. The closet.

Jay.

He could be a ghost, I could be going insane.

But there was no doubt he was in my room.

A dream brought to life.

CHAPTER SIX

I don't know how long I lie there in the bed beside Perry, praying for that first show of dim morning light, the sign that you've made it, that you're going to be okay.

It doesn't seem to come, though. I can hear Perry's soft snoring, and if anything the room grows darker as the night wears on.

Finally I get up, wanting a glass of water.

I slowly ease of bed, careful not to wake Perry. I stand there, trying to figure out whether I should go to bathroom or kitchen, both equally creepy on nights like this, when a light illuminates my face.

I glance at the window that looks straight into the upstairs window of one of the Knightlys' rooms.

A man is staring right at me, backlit by sickly fluorescent lights.

Jay.

We stand there, gazes locked, before he breaks the spell, turning around quickly and disappearing into the depths of the house.

Oh no he fucking doesn't.

I don't even think twice. As quietly and quickly as I can, I head for the door and down the stairs until I'm bursting out onto the front lawn. I'm about to head straight over to the Knightlys when I see a man walking down the street away from the houses. He's wearing a dark jacket, hands shoved in the pockets, taking long strides, his head down.

I'm barefoot in just a skimpy white t-shirt and my boy-short underwear (with sugar skulls on them, naturally) and yet I couldn't care less because I hustle over to the street and then start running down it after the man.

"Hey!" I call out, my bare feet echoing on the pavement.

He stops, the glow of the streetlight illuminating him in dim orange. He doesn't turn around.

"Look at me," I tell him, stopping a few feet away. "Tell me what's going on. Who are you? Why were you in the Knightlys' house?"

"I'm a family friend," he says, his voice low.

"That's what they all say," I tell him, taking a step closer. Whatever fear I had is gone. I want answers above all else and I want them now.

"Turn around," I tell him.

He doesn't. A hot breeze whistles past, ruffling his hair, making it glint blood red in the streetlight.

I put my hand on his arm, somewhat surprised to find him solid, and pull back, turning him around.

He stares down at me and I'm suddenly very aware of how real he is, how tall and well-built, like he's about to pull up a tree by the roots. The sharp bones of his face create shadows in this light, his eyes looking deeper, darker, the hollows beneath his cheekbones carved out.

He's eyeing me warily, not quite afraid just...unsure.

I'm not sure how I look to him, standing here in my underwear. Probably a little of the same.

"Are you a ghost?" I ask him.

Though his face remains stern I see a spark of humor in his eyes. "Your first question is if I'm a ghost? Usually most people leave that conclusion to last."

"You appeared and disappeared from my bedroom," I tell him, surprised at how easy it is to talk to him in real life. "You appear in my dreams. And you should know by now I am not *most people*."

He raises his chin, not breaking his gaze. "Definitely not."

"So," I go on, "are you a ghost? Because believe me, I wouldn't be surprised. It would be the only thing lately that makes any sense."

His mouth quirks up in a wane smile. "No. I'm not a ghost."

"Did I really meet you at the wedding?"

He nods. "Yes."

"Was I the only one who could see you?"

Oh god, was I walking around talking to myself the whole time?

He gives a slight shake of his head. "No. People could see me. See us. I'm not invisible."

"Except when you want to be," I point out.

Just then I hear a door close and Dex's voice. "Ada?"

I turn around to see him jogging across the lawn to the road. Though he's distractingly shirtless, at least he had the sense to pull on some pajama pants.

"What are you doing?" he asks, his voice in a hush down the quiet street.

Oh shit, this whole thing in the bedroom is going to happen again. Jay is going to disappear and I'm going to look like I'm talking to no one.

But when I turn around, Jay is still standing there, albeit a bit stiffer now, on alert.

"Are you okay?" Dex asks as he comes closer, brows lowered as he takes us in, like a prowling dog. Which is a good thing because for once I know he sees him too. And from the edge to his voice I know he's about to go nuts on Jay if I don't say something. "Who is this?"

"I'm fine," I say quickly. "This is Jay."

Dex stops, peers at Jay with a brow raised. "The metro-sexual ghost?"

"Not a ghost," Jay corrects him quickly.

"Just a guy that shops at Sephora, then? That's okay, I get it."

I would tell Dex to shut up but the fact is we're both up to speed. He knows about as much as me now.

"No," Jay says, clearly unamused.

"So," Dex says, folding his arms and looking between the two of us, "what is this? I mean, why are you standing in your underwear and talking to a stranger in the middle of the road, in the middle of the night?"

"None of your concern," Jay says, his jaw firmly set.

Dex flashes him a caustic smile. "Oh really? None of my concern? Right." He looks at me. "Just say the word, Ada."

I roll my eyes. "You can't just go around beating up every boy who talks to me."

Dex scoffs, gesturing to Jay with his chin. "This ain't a boy, sister, this is a man. And a ginger one at that." A strange look of clarity comes over Dex's eyes as he says the words.

"What?" I ask him.

Jay is watching Dex carefully and I feel like something is transpiring between them, I just don't know what.

"Maybe you should run along," Jay says.

Dex stiffens, his eyes taking on this round, half-crazed look that I've seen way too many times before. "I'm sorry, what did you say?"

Jay takes a step closer, his height dwarfing Dex, his eyes boring into him. "I said, this is none of your concern. So turn around and head back into the house and go back to bed."

A vein pulses on Dex's forehead beneath a messy swoop of hair. I eye his fists as they clench and unclench, the muscles popping on his arms, his chest.

This isn't good. Dex fights like hell. Dirty and mean.

But Jay. Well, aside from his height and bulk, he also can disappear into thin air, so that's something.

I'm about to step between them like some girl in a fifties greaser movie, trying to keep the two rivals apart, when I hear, "What the bloody hell is going on here?"

We all turn toward the English accent. Jacob, wearing slippers and a pair of pajamas that look like Hugh Hefner crossed with an old polyester couch from the '70s, comes marching toward us.

Jay mutters something under his breath, taking a step back from Dex.

Dex stares at the infamous Jacob "The Cobb" Edwards as he stops in front of us all, glaring at us with an air of authority, like we're a bunch of petulant schoolchildren and he broke up a playground fight.

Jacob brings his eyes, even more orange and vivid in the streetlight, over to Jay and shakes his head mildly. "I really thought you were going to handle this in a more, well, subtle way."

Next he looks to me, eying me over. "And you, love, you've got a thing or two coming, running after a man you don't know in your underwear. I said courage belonged to the young but I guess so does stupidity."

My mouth falls open and he turns to Dex, extending his hand out. "And this is the infamous Dex Foray," Jacob says smoothly. "Pleasure to meet you."

Now Dex's mouth is open for a moment until he gains his composure and shakes Jacob's hand. "Infamous?" Dex repeats, looking pleased as punch. "That's a new one."

"Well don't let it go to your head, boy," Jacob says, withdrawing his hand. "Another inflation of your ego and your head might just float away."

I frown at Jacob. "How do you know of Dex? Because I know him well and honestly he's not that special."

"Hey," Dex chides me, looking hurt. "Easy there, BJ."

I curl my lip. "BJ?" I repeat in disgust, ready to throw down at him despite what's going on.

"*Bleach* job," he explains slowly, eying my hair. He tilts his head back at Jacob. "But if anyone should be infamous, it's you. I mean, forget being one of the world's best band managers back in the day. You're...*dead.*"

"Obviously you can see I'm not," Jacob says in a tepid voice.

"Right," Dex says. "Because you're either a ghost or you faked your own death. Good job on that, by the way. Dying in a crypt, buried by a pile of bones in Prague? Legendary death for a legend like yourself. You know we talked to Sage about you but couldn't quite seem to get a straight answer."

Jacob exchanges a glance with Jay and for a moment I'm struck by how similar they look. In fact, seeing them together makes me think they might even be related.

Before I can say that though, Jacob gives Dex a levelling look and displays his palms. "I'm not a ghost but I did die. One hundred per cent. Went straight to bloody Hell."

"And how did you come back from that?" I ask, suddenly fearful, hopeful that this is something that could actually be done. Never mind the fact that Jacob went to Hell, which is a concern of its own since that place isn't usually reserved for good people.

"A friend got me out," Jacob says, looking Dex squarely in the eye.

Dex frowns at him.

"A friend got you *out*?" I say, not happy with the vague response.

"I believe you knew him," Jacob says then beams at both of us. "But I'm getting far head of myself here. I'm not of importance right now. What is of importance is Jay and Ada. Or *Jayda*, if you like cute nicknames. I don't."

Dex and I both look at Jay, who is staring off into the distance, determination still set in his jaw.

"Dex," Jacob says, "why don't you go inside, back to your wife. Jay and Ada have plenty to talk about."

"Right now?" Dex asks. He gestures to me. "I'm not leaving her."

"Dex, you of all people should know that we mean no harm."

Dex squints. "Who exactly are you?"

Jacob sighs, tilting his head back and looking up to the stars. "Once upon a time I was just a man. Before that I never knew who I was. Now, I'm not too sure either. But I always have your best interests at heart, even before you do."

Dex stares at him for a moment, blinking, before he says, "Well that's the weirdest shit I've heard all week. I'm not sure what's going on in Keith Richards' house over there," he jerks his thumb at the Knightlys, "but you should really lay off the ludes and the pot brownies. Also, I'm not leaving her." He crosses his arms, legs wide in an assertive stance. "Not only do I happen to care about Ada's wellbeing, but you can bet I don't want the eternal earful from Perry after she finds out I let her sister walk off with a bunch of gingers, both of whom she doesn't even know and one who admits he went to hell. Though it totally proves my theory that the lot of you are soulless."

I'm torn. I don't feel fear with Jay or Jacob. I want to know what's going on. I feel like I'm on the cusp of something great, something life changing, something that will give me purpose in this life.

On the other hand, I know Dex would never leave me alone. I'll always be fifteen to him, too young to make sound decisions, even if my instincts and gut are guiding the way. I should be flattered, and I normally am, but right now I wish he'd go away.

"Dex," I say softly, trying to find a chance. "Go back to Perry. I'll be okay."

"Even if you would be," he says, "have you not seen your sister's wrath? I know you haven't been around her a lot lately, but I'm telling you she has gotten *fierce* with marriage. I always thought it would mellow her."

"Well she's married to you, what did you expect?" I sigh, rubbing my hand over face. "I just want someone right now to tell me what's going on."

"Fine," Jay says and before I know it he's at my side, grabbing my hand and pulling me backward.

There's a great popping sensation, like all my bones are hollow and clicking in and out of place and the scene in front of me, Jacob's face furrowed in disapproval, Dex's one of shock, starts to shimmer and warp like I'm passing through liquid.

Suddenly everything is grey, Jacob and Dex are gone, and my ears are filled with immense pressure, like I dove too deep, too fast.

It's enough for me to grab my head and fall to my knees, groaning at the pain, begging for it to stop.

I feel a warm hand at my back.

"It will pass," comes Jay's voice, softer now, like he actually cares. "Just breathe."

But there is no air to breathe. There is nothing at all. Everything inside me feels absolutely devoid of life, and if it wasn't for his hand on my shoulder blades, I would think I'd actually died.

My lungs keep working though and air or not, I keep breathing. Eventually I look up.

I'm still on the street, in a grey deserted world, my house in the distance. Not another soul to be seen.

"Welcome to the Thin Veil," Jay says, standing in front of me. "I'll be your guide."

CHAPTER SEVEN

I blink, trying to take it all in, the world of the Thin Veil. It's not hard. There's nothing here. I should be grateful we're alone, that spiders the size of cats aren't skittering toward us, wanting to slice and dice.

"I know you've been here before," Jay says as I get to my feet and take a few tentative steps toward my house. "But there are layers to the Veil. We are only in the first step of immersion, barely below the surface. It's the safest for you."

"Safe?" I repeat, looking around, my hands rubbing along my arms even though I'm not cold. "I'm not sure how safe I'm supposed to feel considering you kidnapped me in front of my brother-in-law and took me to another dimension."

When he doesn't say anything I turn around. His eyes flit off into the distance but I caught that. He was staring at my ass! I guess I am still in my underwear but the fact that his gaze was lingering on my sugar skulls tells me that whatever he is, he's still a full-blown male.

My stomach warms at that thought and I have to remind myself that this no time to indulge my ego.

I clear my throat. "Why am I here?"

"Because I needed to talk to you alone," he says.

"You could have just invited me out for coffee like any normal person."

He raises a brow, those intense eyes of his locking on me. "What were you just saying about being normal? No. I couldn't have. You ran after me, in case you forgot, and I knew it couldn't wait until morning."

I cross my arms, staring at him impatiently. "Well, talk."

He chews on his lip for a moment, his eyes staring at the ground, deep in thought. It irks me how much I enjoy staring at him.

He sighs and rubs his fingers along his jaw. He's got nice, long fingers. Strong hands. More things I shouldn't be focusing on but I guess my brain is just trying to find the normalcy in all of this.

"I'm not sure how much of this you're going to believe," he says.

"Try me." I gesture to the fact we're in another world. "I'm pretty open-minded."

He studies me for a moment and then nods sharply. "How familiar are you with the Jacobs? And no, not Jacob himself, I mean the term for…"

"Supernatural redheads who can't mind their own business?" I ask. Then it hits me. It's been so damn obvious this whole time. "Oh my god. You're a Jacob. You're *my* Jacob."

"Tell me what you know about them," he says, ignoring that.

I'm still spinning over my epiphany so it takes me a few moments to remember what I know of them. It's been awhile.

"Perry had one," I tell him slowly. "Dex had one. Even Pippa had one. They're supposed to—*you're* supposed to—help guide or instruct certain people when dealing with the afterlife. Ghosts and demons and all that bunch of nasty stuff. Right? So I'm guessing you're my guardian of the non-angelic kind."

I mean, shit, if this is true, that means he's *mine*. This gorgeous man. I'm not sure if that's lucky or extremely unfair. "Even though," I quickly add, "I also know not all Jacobs are good."

"We aren't good or bad," he says simply, as if he's rehearsed it before.

"So you say. But Perry's was bad. He made her burn down a house." At the time I was so young and naturally thought Perry was losing her mind when she torched a house at fifteen. I wouldn't have believed the truth back then, that she was under the influence of a supernatural "guardian."

"I can't speak for that Jacob but I know the details," Jay says. "He never made her burn anything."

"No, you can only manipulate the young and put suggestions in their head." I pause, studying him. "Is that what you're trying to do to me right now?"

Jay starts walking around me, hands clasped behind his back making his massive shoulders pop. "The Jacobs are the liaison between the afterlife, the underworld, the Veil and the land of the living. I don't like to call it the 'real world' because all the worlds are quite real. But we don't always have the same roles. Essentially we are beings who are immortal, can live forever, though every time we are assigned to someone, we begin again. That is, we don't remember who we were before and we never remember the human that we once were. Sometimes bits and pieces come through, enough to color us like any past life would."

"And how long have you been around the block?"

His eyes drift off, a darkness coming over them. "Honestly, this is my first time."

"What?" I exclaim. "Your first time?"

How fucking fitting that the first time I need guidance with the afterlife that I get assigned a goddamned rookie.

He glares at me. "We all start somewhere. I was alive, someone else, and then I wasn't. I don't know how the process works and I don't care to know but the next thing I knew I was talking to Jacob and I understanding some very deep and real part of me. Whatever makes one of us, well, one of us, it happens at an innate level. We don't go to school. We just begin. On pure instinct."

I have hard time taking all of this in. "And Jacob, was he one too? I mean, is that why he didn't die like people say he did?"

"Actually, Jacob went rogue. Just as your friend Maximus did. It means they gave up their immortality and role to live a normal life. To die a normal death."

"Like having a crypt of bones collapse on you is a normal death," I mutter, kicking away a pebble with my bare toe. It hops across the road but doesn't make a sound.

"But your friend Maximus also went back in and saved him. Pulled Jacob right out of Hell. Jacob died sacrificing his life to save Dawn. When a Jacob does that, after they've gone rogue, it doesn't mean the end for them. They can come back. But there are consequences."

"What kind of consequences?"

"It's not relevant to you," he says, putting his hands in his pockets and taking a step close, his icy eyes spearing mine. "Ada, I'm here because I have to teach you the ways of the Thin Veil. To protect yourself and others from the dangers. Dex had Maximus to show him, Perry had her Jacob, Pippa, your grandmother, had another. Jacob himself had a different role, he managed a contract between the Devil and Sage Knightly. We all have different ways of handling those who we are assigned to. But I can promise you I have your best interests at heart. I always have."

"Always have?" I pause, licking my lips. "I had dreams about you. In them you told me you'd been watching me for a long time."

He nods, not breaking his hypnotic stare. "I have been."

I wonder how much he knows, how much he's seen. If he knows me at all or if he's basing everything on assumptions. "And my dreams, were those real or not?"

"They were dreams," he says. "Real dreams. In the dream state, I can take you places, to far deeper levels than this, to where the real threats are. I can take you there unseen. It's an invisible entry. Only your spirit, your mind, travels through while your body stays behind. Just like in a dream, you can't change anything or do anything."

"I did in my dreams," I tell him.

"And we all know there are people who are lucid dreamers too. It doesn't mean things are actually happening. You may talk to and interact with people in the dream at your will but it doesn't mean you are. You could kill someone in your dream but in reality they will go on like nothing happened."

"This is so *Inception*," I say under my breath. "And it's leaving me equally as confused. Too bad you're not Tom Hardy."

Jay looks puzzled briefly and I wonder if he has any clue about the movie or about pop culture and real life in general.

He goes on. "Then there are the portals. Your whole body passes through and if I accompany you through a permanent portal, no one will know you're there. It's the safest way. The only way."

"You say no one...like other people?"

"Like demons. You know the threats and consequences of visiting the deeper levels of the Veil. When you go in, you weaken the walls. If you can come in, demons and the undead can come out. You're created a door for them. And when you're in there, they can see you. They can hunt you. Kill you, and that's where your soul will forever stay. And, more than that, they can hitch a ride back. You can be possessed by them, or they can piggy-back onto anyone else you love." He pauses, scrutinizing me. "That's if you go in on your own, of course, or create a portal where there shouldn't be one."

It's so much to take, even though so much of it sounds familiar. "What about my mother?" I ask quietly. "In the dream you said—"

"And I meant it," he says quickly. "This is why I'm here. We don't always have to show ourselves, we can watch from afar if we choose. But you're tempting the Devil himself here and we can't have that."

"I'm not doing anything," I tell him haughtily. Sometimes I have no idea where my nerve comes from. I had just pointed out earlier that he could be very bad indeed.

"That's not your mother," he reminds me. "The demons are manipulating you. They want you to come in of your own will, to find her, to seek her out. She's somewhere safe. She's not in Hell. But that's where they will trick you to go. To keep you there. Or, even worse, to come back out with you. I'm sure that's how the demon that took over Michael, Dex's brother, came to be."

I exhale noisily, running my hand through my hair, trying to think what all of this means. "So you're saying that you're watching over me, interjecting yourself into my dreams, because you think I'm just going to create a portal to the Veil – or *Hell* – and waltz on in, looking for my mom."

"Pretty much."

"And if I promise not to do that? I mean, I might be a little stubborn at times, perhaps impetuous, but after all I've seen I know the last thing I want is to be fooled, let alone bring the Devil back into this world."

A small smile graces his lips. "I'm afraid I can't quite take your word for it."

"So what next?" I ask with a shrug. "I'm not sure if you've noticed you're late on this whole guardian thing, but I'm eighteen. I've been dealing with Dex and Perry and my grandmother and seeing ghosts for years now. Are you supposed to enlighten me too? Or just ensure I don't trespass?"

"I should have known what I was getting into with you."

"Oh, please," I tell him. "I am a motherfucking delight."

Another hint of a smile. It breaks the graveness of his face, making him look younger. I can't help but wonder who he was before all of this. Why did the Jacobs pick him to be one of them? Did they pick the hottest ginger that ever lived on purpose? Isn't he curious about his life before?

"So," I say. "Are we just going to stand here in Bizarro World and talk? I mean, what else haven't you told me? I'm going to assume there's a lot."

"There is a lot," he says. "But we have time. Now that you know."

"Now that I've been warned."

"She's not your mother," he says again, his voice low. "I can't watch you twenty-four seven. There has to be trust here."

"You're an immortal guide," I remind him. "You have all the time in the world to watch me if you want."

"It doesn't work like that. I'm human, despite everything."

"You're dead."

"No, I was dead. Past tense. I breathe, eat, live, shit, even sleep the same as you."

I scrunch up my nose, surprised at his humor. "TMI, BTW."

"I do anything except speak in abbreviations. I use proper words, like everyone else."

I roll my eyes. "Fucking supernatural grammar police. You're going to make my life a living hell, aren't you?"

His eyes pause briefly at my lips, before locking in my gaze. "I'm here to prevent exactly that." He then abruptly turns and looks back to the house. "I suppose I should take you back. I think your brother-in-law might be getting unruly and even someone like Jacob might have his hands full."

"And then what happens? You're going to sequester me into the Twilight Zone whenever you feel like it? Inter-dimensional kidnapping at random?"

"I'll be next door, living at the Knightlys," he says.

"Doing what? Is that the new halfway house for gingers?"

He glances at me over his shoulder. "As I've said, keeping an eye on you. For as long as I have to."

"Oh great. Are we going to talk about demons over the fence, all 'Hi ho there, good neighbor'?"

He obviously doesn't get my *Home Improvement* reference. I'm starting to think most people wouldn't. "We can talk some more about all of this," he says. "In a different place, under different circumstances. Coffee?"

I can't help but smile, my hands going on my hips. "You're asking me out for coffee?"

His brow remains expressionless. "Or we can meet here again."

"No thank you," I tell him. "Coffee is just fine."

"Good," he says, holding his hand out expectantly. I eye it and he sighs softly. "If you hold my hand, it makes it a more gentle transition."

There's a '*That's what she said*' joke on the corner of my lips but I suck it up and take his hand.

Just like before, in my dream, there's a faint buzz of electricity as our palms touch and his fingers curl over mine. It sends a wave of warmth straight to my core, down between my legs.

I swallow hard, hoping he can't sense it off of me. His gaze tells me nothing.

Then the grey dead air in front of us begins to warp and shimmer and before I know it, it feels like my head is being filled with steam and gravity has gone haywire. I'm pulled forward through a vice and...

Suddenly I'm back on the street in the dark, light purple-grey tinging the corners of the east. The air is warm and smells like dry grass.

And we aren't alone. Jacob, Dex and now Perry are standing on the lawn. The moment that Perry sees me she runs forward, enveloping me in a frantic hug.

"Oh my god!" she cries out, practically flailing. "I thought I'd never see you again!"

"It's okay," I tell her, pulling back and trying to get her to see that I am indeed A-OK. "I'm fine. We just had a talk."

"You took her to the fucking Thin Veil," Perry spits out, turning to Jay. "What the fuck is wrong with you?"

He exchanges a glance with Jacob who raises his arms up in a shrug.

"Sorry," Jay says to Perry. "I assume Jacob filled you in?"

"He did," she says sharply, her eyes boring into him. Jeez. She's acting just as protective as Dex had been. "That doesn't mean I trust him and I definitely don't trust you. If you'd have been me at fifteen, you would understand why."

"And yet your friend Maximus, the one who sacrificed his life to save you," Jacob pipes up smoothly, "that doesn't matter at all. Listen, love, I know your Jacob scarred you for life but one sour apple doesn't spoil the bunch."

"Maximus had gone rogue by then," Perry says quietly. I know his death still wears on her conscious a lot. "He...he was a friend. Not a stranger. And it took a *long* time to trust him. In fact," she looks over at Dex who is standing there with his arms crossed, "I'm pretty sure Maximus became a better person when he wasn't a Jacob. When he was one, he led Dex through hell. What does that tell me? That for all your righteousness and entitlement, you're just about as crooked as cops are, except you get to live forever."

"Perry," I tell her, grabbing her arm and turning her away from them. I look her square in the eyes. "I believe them. For now, anyway. Jay is just warning me, that's all. And he took me into the thinnest part of the Veil, there's no real transference or side effects."

Okay, I'm making that part up but as I look to Jay he just nods.

"Now, let's go to bed and tomorrow is another day," Jacob reminds us in his band manager voice, like he's trying to corral a bunch of wayward rock stars.

"Tomorrow you're coming back with us," Perry reminds me, pulling me toward the house.

I pull right back. "Wait. No, I'm not."

"Ada!" she exclaims. "I've sensed what's in that closet. That's a portal in itself, straight to Hell, isn't that right?" She looks over at Jay and Jacob.

Jacob slowly nods. "That's what we think," he concedes. "But as long as Jay is here, Ada will be in no danger."

"Right. Like she's in zero danger having the doorway to Hell in her bedroom." She looks back at me, her eyes blazing in determination. "You're coming with us where you will be safe."

"There is no safe place anymore," Jacobs says mildly, examining his fingernails like he's utterly bored of our middle of the street, middle of the night, pajama-clad drama. "If she goes with you, you invite this into your house. And as skilled as you two seem to be when dealing with ghosts, neither of you know how to handle this. Jay does."

Dex raises his hand in mock politeness. "Um, I'm pretty sure we sent a demon back to Hell."

Jacob doesn't even look up. "No. You didn't. That was Mrs. Palomino who did that. Their mother."

Both Perry and I flinch, his words burning despite the truth.

"And are you willing to do the same should the situation arise?" Jacob goes on, finally looking over at us, the lines deepening in his forehead. "Or perhaps it would be best not to test it and put anyone in any danger. Ada should stay here. Jay will take care of her as it's his duty and I'm here as well."

"Micromanaging?" I question.

"Overseeing," he says with a quick smile. "Of course, Ada, the choice is yours. You're capable of making your own decisions regardless what we say or your family says."

"I'll sleep on it," I say dryly, though with the sun rising slowly in the distance, I know there won't be any more sleep for me. Not that I could have possibly fallen asleep anyway after all that. I also know deep down I'm not going to Seattle with Perry and Dex.

Jacob and Jay head back inside the Knightlys' house, while the rest of us go to ours. I can tell Perry is stewing, wanting to yell at me for who knows what. I know she's scared shitless that I'm going to get hurt and to be honest, I'm scared too.

But at the same time, as much as I feel safe with Dex and Perry, as much as I trust them, something tells me that I'm going to need Jay a lot more than I think. I know I've just "officially" met him, but there's a lot to be said for an immortal being that not only invades your dreams but can whisk you off to another dimension.

And I definitely don't want to expose Dex and Perry to any danger. They've got their own life going on in Seattle, they've put all of this shit behind them. What kind of sister would I be if I made it start all over again? I've already lost my mother.

I'm not losing them too.

CHAPTER EIGHT

It turns out I got some sleep after all. After we headed back into the house, unnerved by our middle of the night rendezvous, Dex and Perry went about making a nervous, silent kind of breakfast while I got dressed and lay down on the couch, trying to recoup my thoughts.

Next thing I know, it's eleven a.m. and Dex and Perry have packed up their stuff and are loitering in the hallway, talking to Dad.

"Hey sleepy head," Dex says as I stagger out of the living room, sleep in my eyes. "We didn't want to wake you, you seemed like you needed it."

Dex is giving me an easy grin though I can tell from his eyes that it's kind of forced for Perry's sake. It's nice to know he doesn't harbor any hard feelings about my decision, but my sister is another story.

In fact, she's not even looking me in the eye.

Dad glances between the two of us, not sure what's going on. "Well, I'm sorry to see you off, pumpkin," he says to her. He only glances briefly at Dex and gives him a head nod. Dex responds in kind. Such guys.

Perry softens slightly at her pet name and hugs dad, closing her eyes tight. It's only when she pulls away and promises to call when she gets home, that she finally looks me in the eye.

"Take care of yourself," she says to me stiffly before picking up her giant duffel bag and heading out the door.

Dex shoots me an apologetic look. "Let me fix this," he says then trots after her, pulling her to a stop in the middle of the yard.

"You two fighting?" my dad asks me uneasily as we watch them walk across the lawn. We used to fight all the time but haven't since mom's death. I'm not sure if he's seeing this as a good thing or a bad thing.

"Something like that," I tell him and go out after them, my dad wisely staying in the house.

"Don't be stubborn," Dex is whispering to Perry, taking her bag for her and sauntering over to the Highlander with it.

I hold out my hands in surrender as I approach Perry. "Look, I'm sorry I'm staying but it's the right thing to do."

Perry's mouth is held in a thin white line. She shakes her head. "You're supposed to trust me, Ada, not them. We don't even know them. I'm your sister. We've been through so much...I don't know what I'd do if I let something happen to you."

Now she's near tears. I rarely see her cry so it already brings my defenses down a couple of notches.

I come over to her and pull her into a hug. "Hey," I tell her while she sniffs on my shoulder. "Nothing is going to happen to me. I'm not choosing strangers over you Perry. It's just that I trust Jay. And Jacob too. I know it sounds crazy, I can't explain it." I pull back and press my hand into my sternum. "I feel it in here."

She wipes her nose on her sleeve, narrowing her eyes at the Knightlys' house. "They're already fooling you."

"Well what do you expect me to do? I start school soon. I couldn't live with you and Dex forever. You wouldn't want me to anyway."

"We would manage." She sighs, flipping her ponytail back over her shoulder. "You're right. The whole school thing. I just figured that maybe whatever it was would blow over by then."

"I don't think things are that easy," I tell her. "I think I have to deal with them as they come up. We both know we can't sweep shit like this under the rug."

"Yeah," she reluctantly concedes. "I tried for years. Didn't work."

"And I was there to watch you try." I put on my bravest smile, which of course comes across as totally cheesy. "Hey, there's nothing stopping you from staying here anyway," I point out, flipping the tables on her. I actually wouldn't mind if she stayed at all.

"I'm going to try," she says. "Dex has so much work to do but I might be able to get a day or two off. He can be a tyrant, you know." She says this as if she's not the tyrant at work, keeping Dex in line. "The minute anything gets worse, the second you think you're in trouble or you don't trust Jay, you let me know. Yell, phone, text. Anything. I'll be here as quick as I can."

I take in a deep breath, hoping it doesn't have to come to that. Hoping that I am doing the right thing after all is said and done.

"I promise," I tell her.

But as the Highlander goes down the street, disappearing around the corner, I feel loss in my chest, a solid, heavy thing. It's not just that I care about Perry more than anything, that I miss her when she's gone.

It's that the fear is creeping back in.

Inch by inch.

The hairs at the back of my neck rise, a cold rush flowing through me. I slowly turn around, afraid to look where I want to look, my bedroom window. Afraid that I'll see something there.

Watching me.

But there isn't anything. Just the reflection of the tree on the glass.

I exhale loudly and head back inside, grateful to hear my dad puttering around in the kitchen. He's busying himself, which is what he usually does after Perry leaves and right now it's bringing me comfort to know he's home, that I'm not alone, even if in many ways I am.

I'm not sure what to do about my room though. Dex seemed to sleep in there without any incident, otherwise I'm sure we would have heard about it, but now that it's just me, and after I learned all that shit with Jay and Jacob, I'm not sure if I want to step foot in there ever again.

"Dad," I say to him as I pass by the kitchen.

"Mmm?" he asks, cleaning out the fridge that probably doesn't need to be cleaned out.

"I think I'm going to move back into my old bedroom," I tell him.

He pauses and peers at me. I have his attention now. "Why?"

I shrug, not sure he'd buy my "I think it's a portal to Hell" story. "It doesn't seem right. You know, Perry comes by quite often and it doesn't feel right having her sleep in my old room. And, I don't know. It's just never felt like mine."

He studies me. I know he doesn't believe me but I also know he wouldn't dare ask for the truth. "You know the house could sell any day," he points out. "Do you want to bother moving twice? I mean, you can do what you want, Ada. But I won't be helping you. There's enough to do around here as it is."

I nod, not sure if I'm even brave enough to start moving shit alone. I may have to sequester the help of someone next door.

I make my way upstairs, needing a shower something fierce, even though all my good clothes are in the bedroom.

For a few moments I stare at the door handle, wondering what I'll find when I open the door. What if I run in there and the door shuts on me and I'm trapped? Would I call for Jay? Would he just appear in my room? What if he was occupied—he did say he couldn't watch me all the time. Does that mean he can't respond all the time? Was he even aware of what I was doing right now?

Good lord, could he somehow watch me in the shower? Has he been?

Odd thoughts to have and normally I wouldn't even entertain that notion since Jacobs are immortal guardians, something above and beyond human, but I had caught Jay staring at my ass last night. And I could have sworn there was some sort of heat behind his eyes, as if he liked what he was seeing.

Well if you can hear or see this, I think to myself, *mind your own business.*

I decide to skip my bedroom completely and get something to wear from the other room. Then I get in the bathroom and take a one hell of a long shower, trying to wash the last few days from my skin. Naturally even taking a shower is fucking terrifying and I refuse to draw the curtain across the tub out of pure paranoia. Thanks, Hitchcock.

When I'm finally clean, my hair dried and straightened, I've got a hefty dose of makeup on, and a black shitkicker boots and olive green sundress combo going, I start to work up the nerve of approaching Jay. I don't have his cell phone or anything like that so there's nothing to do but go next door.

But just as I'm heading down the stairs, there's a knock at the front door.

I freeze midway as my dad goes to answer.

"Hello?" I hear my dad ask, puzzlement in his voice.

"Hi. I was wondering if Ada was home."

I practically run down the rest of the stairs to see Jay on the front steps. My dad eyes me over his shoulder.

"Ada, you know this man?" He's already got fatherly disapproval all over his face, not that he's particularly liked anyone I've dated. Obviously I'm not dating Jay but I know what this must look like. Plus there's the fact that Jay is a hulking beast of a man dressed all in black, from his well-fitted t-shirt to his jeans to his boots. His broad jaw is dusted with dark stubble, his cinnamon hair pushed off his forehead, curling at the nape.

"He's our new neighbor," I tell him quickly, flashing my dad an innocent smile. "I met him yesterday."

"Are you the Knightlys' son? I didn't know they had one," my dad says.

Jay offers a tight smile. "I'm a family friend. Just renting a room in the house for the time being."

"I was going to show him around Portland," I fill in, remembering our arrangement for coffee.

My dad raises his brow, studying me again. I'm completely ready to deal the "I'm eighteen and a legal adult" card, which I have been known to do from time to time. I can't blame my dad for being protective, but still.

"Fine," he says reluctantly. "I'm making cannelloni tonight though, so be back for dinner."

"I will." I brush past him and join Jay outside. He gives my dad a polite wave before we both turn and walk down the path.

The moment we hear the door close behind us, Jay says, "Is your father always so suspicious?"

"He's not a fan of strange men showing up at the door and taking me for coffee," I tell him, falling in step beside him. A heady feeling grows in my chest, a strange mix of feeling giddy to be beside Jay and yet completely at peace simultaneously. I'm nervous but not afraid, just as I was last night when he pulled me into the Veil.

"I'm sure he'll get used to seeing me soon enough," he says.

"Well unless you start taking shortcuts into my room," I tell him. "Which, by the way, I've decided to move out of. I can't sleep in there again, especially with Dex and Perry gone and especially as neither you nor Jacob refuted the idea that my closet is a portal to Hell."

"That's probably smart," Jay says but gives me nothing more.

"I'll need your help moving all my stuff over," I tell him cautiously as we head down the street. "I'm not doing it alone."

He squints at me. "I just helped the Knightlys. In fact, I'm *still* unpacking."

"So then you have experience. Which is great since you're a rookie at life and all."

He stops walking. "Just because this is my first time as a Jacob, doesn't mean I don't know how to function in society." He nods at the beige Mercedes beside us, the one Jacob was driving. "I can even drive us downtown."

"Jacob doesn't mind?" I ask him, eying the Knightlys' and half-expecting Jacob to come charging out and shaking his fist, a gaudy gold watch rattling.

Jay shrugs. "He's fine."

I've got the feeling that Jay isn't really supposed to take Jacob's car but for some reason that makes Jay a lot more interesting than he already was. In fact, looking back at last night I'd venture to guess that Jay is a bit of a button-pusher. He not only stood up to Dex but Jacob as well. Maybe all Jacobs are this way when they're first starting out, but since I'm a rabble-rouser myself, maybe the match works.

Except it's not a match, I remind myself. *He's my guardian. The Giles to my Buffy.*

A smile curves his lips as he opens the car door.

"Can you hear what I'm thinking?" I ask him as I get in the passenger side. The leather seats squeak beneath my bare legs, already hot from the sun, and the air inside the car is sauna thick, smelling of mothballs and cigarettes and something else. Something nearly indiscernible, maybe spicy. I realize that's how Jay smelled in my dream, something hot, spicy, primal, almost like a pheromone.

"Thinking?" he asks. "No. I was just imagining Jacob's face when he finds out his car is gone."

At that he starts the car, the diesel engine rumbling, and we quickly peel out onto the street, doing a U-turn that makes my head thud back against the headrest until we've straightened out and are zooming away from the houses.

Looks like he can drive just fine after all.

In fact, as we navigate the highways taking us from northeast Portland into the city, it seems like Jay is more than just good at it. It's almost like the traffic and the lights are responding to him and not the other way around. Not to mention he drives like he knows the city like the back of his hand.

"How long have you been in the city?" I ask him. "Watching me," I add.

"Since your mother died," he says.

My eyes nearly bug out. "Two years?"

He nods.

"Two years," I repeat. "The Knightlys just moved."

"I've been around," he says vaguely. "In dreams you don't remember. Ever since the night at the wedding. I had to...be near you. In person. To really get a hold on you. To know you after that."

I blink at him, feeling all sorts of violated. "You don't know me," I sneer at him, on the defensive in a second.

He shrugs, not seeming to care. "In some ways yes, some ways no. You can learn a lot about a person through their dreams. It's your subconscious, split open and bare for all to see."

"You mean for *you* to see." I try not to shudder, wondering what he saw over the years. It's not fair that I couldn't remember him being there, not fair that I myself can't interpret my own dreams, discover my own subconscious. "Was it just my dreams you were poking around in?"

He rubs his lips together, hesitating. I don't like hesitation. "I can go in your dreams, from anywhere I am. It's like looking through a window, into your head. Sometimes I step through that window."

"You didn't answer my question."

"Yes, it's just dreams."

I don't believe it. "You haven't just...*portaled* into my life at some point or another?"

"I haven't needed to until the other night," he says, eyes sliding to me. I can read nothing in them. "I won't do it again, unless I have to."

"Right."

"You're my ward, Ada," he says gravely. "I've been connected to you since the wedding. I can't read your thoughts. I can't see into your conscious mind. But I can feel you, from anywhere. Sense your state of mind, what you're feeling.

"Can you sense what I'm feeling right now?"

He nods. "You don't like this. You feel violated. Like I'm an intruder. You feel vulnerable. You don't like me. And yet part of you still does."

I roll my eyes. "What part?"

Wait, don't answer that.

"I think you know," he says, his gaze on me again, scrutinizing. I quickly turn away, feeling like my body has betrayed me and then realizing he probably knows that too. "I don't mind. It's important that I be likable to you, Ada."

I let out a dry laugh. "It's important you be likeable? Do you realize how much of an android you sound like right now?"

"Sorry," he says quickly. It's probably wishful thinking that I see an ounce of shame in his expression. "I don't mean to sound callous. Impersonal. It's just…"

"The way you are?"

He nods, reaching down to turn the radio knob. The car looks like it only gets AM and crackly blues song comes on. "When you're immortal, you don't have a fear of death. If you don't have a fear of death…"

"Then you're not human."

"Fear gives people their humanity. Fear of loss. I fear nothing."

And for the first time in a while, I feel afraid being around him. It's unsettling, this slightly robotic version of himself. He's being honest, too honest, lacking the very human fear of judgement.

I look out the window, the properties becoming smaller as we approach the city. "You must fear failure. Otherwise you wouldn't care what happens to me."

"I don't fear failure but I also don't welcome it. In fact, it's not about fear at all. It's about duty. My job comes from deep within my bones. It is to protect you until you can protect yourself."

Somehow our conversation has gotten even more interesting. "What do you mean until I can protect myself?"

He doesn't say anything for a moment.

"Jay?" I coax him. "You can't say that and nothing else."

He breathes in deeply and I wonder what it's like to breathe yet have no use for it. "Each Jacob's job is different for each person. As you know. My job is to guide you through the now and protect you until you are strong enough, smart enough, to protect yourself. Then I move on. Start again as someone else, for someone else."

"But what am I protecting myself from? I mean, other than demons in the closet."

"Well that's precisely it. Because that's one tiny piece of what's happening around you." He chews on his lip, brow furrowed as he thinks. I can tell he wants to tell me something, maybe something he shouldn't.

"And what's happening around me?" I ask quietly.

"I haven't just been in your dreams," he admits. "I've been watching you. In real life. From a distance. Sometimes closer. You've never noticed me. Until the other day."

At Sephora. "Why were you there?"

"To watch over you. To make sure you weren't harmed."

My eyes widen as I sit up ramrod straight. "Harmed? What the hell would harm me? The people in the kiosks in the mall, throwing hand cream and cell phones?"

"Ada, you've been seeing ghosts for some time now. But those aren't the only things that can harm you. It's the demons you aren't seeing yet. They sure as hell see you."

A soul-deep chill runs through me. I shiver. "Demons? I haven't seen anything..."

"As I said, you aren't seeing them yet. And until you do, you're vulnerable. There are many slips and portals in this world, places for them to sift in and out. They know your smell, they have for years now. The more powerful you get, the older you get, the more...adult, womanly, you become, the more they'll want to seek you out and take you."

Demons have been fucking hunting me all this time and I never knew it? I hold up my hand, unable to comprehend any of this. "Wait, wait, wait. Perry was twenty-three when she really started to lose her...see ghosts. My grandmother, she—"

"You are not Perry," Jay says quickly, his gaze hard, piercing right into me. "You are not Pippa. You are Ada Palomino and your story is completely different. You are completely different. You have a fight ahead of you, one that goes far beyond what you've seen in your dreams."

Well, fucking *shit*. "Please tell me some good news," I whisper to him, my nails digging into my palm. "Your bedside manner sucks."

"*I'm* your good news."

I glance at him. Of course he's completely serious.

"Right," I mutter. "Bound by supernatural duty."

"And I am bound," he says. "To watch and protect. To make you open your eyes. To teach you to fight back."

I shake my head. I'm pushing everything he's saying away. It's much easier this way. "I'm starting school soon. I'm still struggling with what happened to my mother. I'm going to pretend I didn't hear any of this. I'll keep out of the closet. I'll ignore my mother in my dreams. And I'll keep being used to seeing the occasional ghost. But that's it."

I may not have loved my life at the moment but at least I knew what to expect from it. I knew to move on, I knew what to accept and get used to. No one asks to see ghosts but I was still managing it quite well in my day to day life. Everything Jay just said to me has no place in the life I'm supposed to have.

"Life isn't fair, Ada," he says, a rare hint of softness to his voice. "You know this. Sometimes we're dealt a hand we never see coming. Sometimes there are only two choices. To live. Or die. And sometimes there is a third choice." I glance at him. "To suffer in Hell for all eternity."

"I'm not sure I want coffee anymore," I mumble.

But within minutes we're downtown, finding the perfect parking spot right in front of one of my favorite coffee shops. The same one my sister used to work at, Stumptown.

I peer at the shop as I get out of the car, happy to see it crowded and full of people. I need a caramel mocha with extra whip cream and syrup, stat, and I need it delivered by a barista who pronounces my name wrong (saying "Ad-a" instead of "Ay-da"), and I need to be surrounded by yuppies and hipsters and life as usual. I don't even bother asking Jay how he knows I love it here.

We get in the shop and he offers to grab my coffee. I'm not sure what money he's paying with, how and if Jacobs get paid at all, but I'm not arguing. My blogging revenue is low these days with my lack of posting and I'm more than happy to snag a seat.

As it happens, my favorite spot, a small booth by the window, is free. I'm wondering if all this good fortune is serendipitous or if it's somehow connected to Jay. Because if he can arrange for no traffic and a great parking spot and my favorite seat, then surely he can arrange for me to not be stalked by demons. I would assume, anyway.

I watch him as he gets the coffee. He's not one for small talk, even with the gorgeous and overly chatty barista that is giving him the eye and leaning over just enough so her cleavage is popping out over her apron. She obviously finds him as ridiculously handsome and stupidly manly as I do. He doesn't look down though, doesn't indulge her seduction attempts. Only smiles politely.

I suppose, being an emotionless immortal, he probably doesn't care about those kind of human appetites. Then again, I had caught him staring at my ass. And I sometimes feel this heat behind his gaze, something instinctual rolling off of him. Granted that mainly happened in the dream and in my dreams my subconscious is as horny as anything.

And what had he said? That he knows how I like him? He knows I'm attracted to him and doesn't care?

Typical fucking guy.

He comes back with the drinks in hand. The barista had called out my name wrong as I thought.

"You must get that a lot," he says, sliding me the cup. "Ada is a pretty name though. Do you know what it means?"

"Nobility," I tell him, removing the lid and taking a good hard whiff of all the sugar and caffeine. "My mother was sure to remind me of that often."

"It suits you," he comments.

I take a sip, eyeing him. "Thanks." I'm not sure how to take his compliment. I have a feeling he doesn't dole them out often. I clear my throat, letting the sugar flow through my system, calming me. "So. Did you pick the name Jay or did you just wake up with it?"

He palms his cup of coffee, staring at me over it. He waits a beat. "I woke up with it."

"And you don't remember the name of who you were before?"

He shakes his head.

"Do you know at least where you came from? The century? How old you were when..."

"Jacob says I am, I was, in my late twenties."

"Too old for me then," I comment dryly.

He just stares at me.

I manage a smile. "And that's all you know?"

He nods slowly before taking a tepid sip of his coffee. He sits back against the chair, eyes going to the window.

"There is a wall in my head," he tells me, voice low. "There is a door. It's black. Heavy. It's locked. And I don't want to know what's on the other side." He pauses. "It doesn't make a difference what's there. I am Jay, now. Who I was before doesn't matter."

I feel like he's trying to convince himself of this.

"But aren't you curious?" I tell him. "What if who you were could influence the way you are? What if the way you act isn't just instinct from being a human being, it's from being a *specific* human being?"

His Adam's apple bobs in his throat as he swallows and he gazes at me with cold eyes.

"It doesn't matter," he says again. "The past is the past."

"The past makes us who we are," I tell him.

"As a human, yes," he says, looking around to see if anyone is listening. Thankfully the coffee shop is pretty loud. "In case you need a reminder, I am not like you. I may look like I am but I assure you I'm not. And even if that were the case, the past doesn't define us. It's what we do here and now, today, that does. This world was built on second chances."

His eyes go to the street, a strange flash of clarity coming over them. If I wasn't watching him so closely, I wouldn't have noticed. His brows come together, his hands tightening on his cup. Then it's gone and his gaze is back to being cool and opaque, indifferent to the world. I wonder, if just for a second, he was tempted to try and unlock that black door inside his head.

I swallow thickly. "You're a strange date."

He nearly smiles at that. "I suppose you're right." He looks back out to the street again and stiffens noticeably.

I follow his gaze. For a moment I think I see a person, a long, shadowy black figure with no face, just an ever-widening hole, standing by the entrance to a laundromat. But when I blink I realize it's just my eyes playing tricks on me. It's only a shadow of the building and a black crow hopping about, pecking garbage up from the ground.

"Do you see that?" Jay asks quietly.

"The crow?" I ask.

"Did you see anything else?"

"I...I thought I saw a man. Or a creature. Like a living shadow. But it was just a trick of the light." But even my voice sounds weak, like I can't be convinced of it myself.

"That's how they're starting to appear to you. How you start to see them. It's not a trick of the light. What you saw was real."

Another sickening chill runs down my spine. In this heat of summer, I'm starting to think I need a sweater on me at all times. "Where is it now?" I whisper.

Jay nods at the crow. "Animals are perfect conduits."

I think back to the raven I saw the other night outside my window.

"So what am I supposed to do?" I keep my voice low, not because I'm afraid someone will overhear me and think I'm crazy, but because I can't muster the strength. "What would have happened if you weren't here?"

"Probably nothing," he says.

"Nothing?" I repeat. "You said they are *hunting* me."

"They are," he says, staring down into his coffee like he's facing the abyss. "And like many hunters, they study their prey first. Find their weaknesses. They come after you because they sense what you have. But they don't know how you'll use it. They fear you and want you at the same time."

I look back to the crow but it's gone now, as is the shadow. "How long has this been going on?" I ask quietly. "How long have I not been seeing it?"

"As I said before, years."

"So why now am I in danger?"

A couple walking past the table give us a weird look. I hunch over and lean in close to Jay as he speaks.

"As I said before," he repeats slowly, a flicker of impatience in his blue eyes, "you're coming into your own. You're an adult. A woman."

Is he hinting at my own sexual awakening or some new-agey bullshit?

"For the record," I tell him. "I'm not a virgin. And I've been a woman for a while."

He cocks his head at me, frowning. "Oh, I know." He pauses, studying my expression, which must be one of horror because I don't know want to know how he knows that. "The impetuousness of youth. You may be eighteen but you have a lot of growing up to do. And you're about to grow up really, really fast."

"Ada?" Amy's shrill voice comes from across the shop.

"Shit," I swear, wishing I could hide. I tell Amy everything and she's not going to like the fact that I'm having coffee with a strange man.

"Your friend is here," Jay says quietly.

Amy comes to the table, her boyfriend Tom in tow behind her. Both of them stare down at me like I'm someone they don't even recognize.

"Hey," I tell her.

"Hey yourself," she says testily. "You might want to answer your texts, I've been harassing the hell out of you. What, you can't bother to reply?"

I honestly haven't even checked my phone in the last day. I nod at Tom, who despite his indignation for Amy's sake, is usually mellow as fuck. "Hey Tom."

He nods back. "Sup, Ada."

"Sorry," I say to Amy, offering my sweetest smile. "I've been busy."

"I can see that," she says, her attention now on Jay, inspecting him with a look of utter disapproval. "And who are you?"

"Jay," he says, holding out his large hand.

She eyes it before shaking. "Jay who?" She winces a little under his grip.

"Jay," he says, taking his hand back, and for a moment I wonder if he even has a last name. "Jay Abrams."

"J.J. Abrams?" she repeats suspiciously, like she can tell he totally made up that name on the spot.

He nods. "Yes."

Ugh. He doesn't get it.

"Jay just moved in next store," I tell her quickly. "He's renting a room. I'm showing him around Portland."

Amy seems to relax a little. "Oh. Well, welcome to the neighborhood. Where did you live before?"

I expect him to be vague but he says, "Ramona, California."

"Cool." She looks back to me, her brow arching high. "Well, maybe text me later if it doesn't kill you, okay?"

She and Tom wave goodbye and they're gone. I can't help but let out a long sigh of relief.

"She doesn't know about you," Jay notes. "About your family. Your truth."

"No," I tell him. "Believe me it's a lot better that way."

"Is it?"

I give him a questioning look. "Of course it is. She'll think I'm nuts."

"How do you know? Isn't she your friend?"

"How do I know? Because I would think she was nuts if the situation was reversed."

"But you would still stay her friend."

"Of course I would. I love crazy people."

He exhales sharply out of his nose as he stares at me. "Can I give you a bit of advice, Ada?"

"You can give me all the advice," I tell him. "Please. Especially the advice that's about how to not get eaten by demons."

"You should tell her. Get it over with. Right now, things are easy for you."

"Easy?" I repeat.

"They're about to get harder. You need to know whether you can rely on your friends or not. You need to find that out now, while you can still stand on your own two feet. Because if you put your trust into someone and the going gets rough and they bail? The fall might kill you."

I don't want to think about it. I don't want to talk to Amy about any of this. She's my friend. She's my escape to a normal life. I can't risk losing her, losing that.

A few moments of silence pass between us, Jay looking back out the window, his eyes searching the passersby. Meanwhile my heart is in knots because I know I should follow his advice, and my stomach is churning, possibly because of the sugar and coffee, possibly because I can't come to terms with anything that I've been told today. Even the monster thing I just saw is something I have to push aside for now. If Jay can have a locked door in his head, so can I.

"Is your last name really Abrams?" I ask him.

He smiles quickly. "No. I don't have one. I suppose I should. I just thought of the guy who directed the new Star Wars."

So the immortal knows some pop culture after all.

CHAPTER NINE

We didn't stay out for coffee too much longer. Jay took me back home and even though our conversation wasn't as deep as before, I did pick up some interesting tidbits.

Such as:

- In time, not only would I be able to spot demons but I would be able to put them back where they belong, forever, through various methods he would one day explain to me.
- Life was going to get harder before it got easier.
- The Thin Veil was off-limits to me and visions of my mother weren't real.

You know. The usual shit.

Can't say I arrived home for dinner brimming with confidence. I was sullen and quiet over the meal, as was my father though I assumed for different reasons. Perry had texted and called a million times over the course of the day, checking up on me and assuming the worst when I didn't answer right away. I didn't tell her much though. If I didn't understand it, neither would she and she'd be worrying even more over something she can't control.

After dinner I cleaned up and thought briefly about enlisting Jay to help me move shit into the other room, but to be honest, I wanted some time to be alone to come to terms with things.

Not that I was coming to terms with *anything*. Because every time I started to think about what he told me, I laughed. It's funny how your mind can be open, expansive, to almost anything but when there's a hard limit, something your brain can't make that extra leap for, it all shuts down. I believed in ghosts. I saw ghosts. I believed in demons. I've seen them a few times too. I believed in a lot of things, including the fact that I would never have your average, normal life, no matter how hard I tried.

But the fact that I wasn't even like my sister, or my grandmother, the fact that my trials were different, that *I* was different from even them, was a hard thing to try and accept.

It made me feel fucking alone.

Not to mention scared.

Not to mention ridiculous.

Me, a demon fighter? Why? I mean, why was that even a *thing*? And why did they seek me? I'm tall and thin, but it's not like I'm loaded with muscle. I'm coordinated, but for things like Dance Dance Revolution, maybe tennis. I'm smart but I'm not that smart, and my idea of a good time is smoking some pot and perusing fashion blogs until I feel inspired enough to put together an outfit. Why did I somehow possess the power to fight back against demons of all things and what the fuck was the goddamn power to begin with? What was in me that enabled me to do such a thing?

Who was I?

And more importantly, who was I becoming?

I had no answers. Jay had them all but I couldn't think about them, face them, with him around me. He watches me in more ways than one. It's not just that he's looking out for me, it's that he's trying to know how I think, how I act. I can sense that behind his eyes.

And more than that, I can sense something else about him. I think he's more human than he'd care to admit, even to himself. I think he's had a peek behind that door once or twice. I think there's a reason he keeps it locked.

So while my dad was in the garden, watering the hostas while there was still light in the sky, I filled a highball glass with his whisky and went upstairs to my old bedroom. I sipped the drink while pretending everything was still as it ever was. In fact, I went beyond that. I pretended my mom was downstairs and Perry was in her room and everything was normal. I wrote blog post after blog post, making up for lost time, all whilst getting drunk. Until I couldn't type about fucking rompers and bucket bags anymore.

But now, now everything is different.

I'm back on the island.

In the red.

The Veil of my dreams.

The moon is full and disturbingly close. If I stare at it long enough, I can see faces trapped in the surface, mouths open and distorted in silent screams, blood seeping from terrified eyes.

I turn around, my heart already racing away from me.

Instead of being by the ocean this time, I'm on a rocky knoll above a steep slope of trees, a single, narrow path twisting down through salall bushes and shrubs.

Jay is nowhere to be found. I would have assumed that if I fell asleep again, he would be there in my dreams, to protect, to watch.

Jay? I cry out in my head.

There is nothing, no one. Just myself and the dark crimson trees and the horrible moon.

This world is empty, barren, and very, very cold.

Despair.

Grief.

Shame.

The feelings seem to grow up from the ground like weeds, wrapping around my legs, sinking deep inside until I'm on my knees. I want to weep, to cry out, to scream, to beg for it all to stop. Too many feelings, too many emotions cutting too deep with sickening precision.

I grab my head, my fingers pressing on my scalp, praying for it all to stop.

I am sadness.

I am torture.

I am death.

And beyond death.

The words jab into my brain like an icepick and I have an even worse feeling that there's someone inside my brain with me.

Not Jay.

Not anyone good.

Then suddenly it stops, so fast that I'm knocked flat on my back, sprawled on frozen ground and the moon seems to float away, to the other side of the sky.

I gasp, taking a moment to catch my breath before getting to my feet.

There's someone here.

Down the path, heading away from me.

I can't see them, I can only sense them.

And there is singing too.

Light as air, melodic and dainty. It's halfway between human voice and chiming crystals.

And yet it's familiar in a way that breaks my heart.

On the darkest of the nights
With a blood red moon so bright
Your mother will call you, dear
To put away your fear
Follow her quick down the hill
As they will not hesitate to kill
Her and all she could be
Then you, for all you see
So hurry now and listen
Run to the pond that does so glisten
Step in before she dies
And now you know it's he who lies.

It's my mother's voice, changed into something inhuman, but still astoundingly beautiful. It's a siren song that compels me.

I am unable to resist.

Jay! I yell out but my legs are moving and I'm running down the path, following her enchanting voice as it sings again and again its morbid tune.

Brushes scratch at me as I run, sometimes tugging at my skin and clothes like tiny clawed hands, my feet are bare and quick as I stumble across moss and rocks, occasionally sinking into something warm and sticky.

I try not to think about any of it, only thinking of my mother. I know I'm not supposed to believe it's her, I'm not supposed to do anything. But Jay isn't here and the more I run, that blood red moon filled with screaming faces swinging past me in the sky like a crimson pendulum, the more I don't care.

I feel like I've snuck into someplace other than my dreams, where I can go unwatched, where nothing else matters. Jay can't help me but I can't help my mother.

Not real.

Not real.

Not real.

Not her.

His words still find their way into my brain, light as smoke. I shake it off, keep running through the thicket until the ground levels out and the trees close in.

The forest here is dense, tall firs soaring hundreds of feet high. The canopy blocks all but a tiny sliver of the moon and above me I hear the thick slap of leathery wings.

I don't dare look up.

"Your mother will call you, dear,

To put away your fear."

She sings, nearly weeping over the melody.

I keep walking. My fear is locked up. I have just one thought. To save her.

Finally I stop, a cold breeze blowing down the path toward me, as alive and strong as an oncoming train. It freezes me to the bone, coats me with a thin layer of ice.

I stare at my skin, sparkling now, but as the ice melts, I bleed.

I lift up my arm, watching the dark rivulets run down, mildly fascinated.

ADA!

My mother's voice slams into my head and I'm nearly knocked backward.

HELP ME.

I start running.

The dark woods seem to stretch on forever, moving up and out into a dark infinity. I can feel hot breath on my neck, the cold wind at my front, and yet I know I can't fear, can't think, can't stop.

It's wrong, it's wrong.

But I must keep going.

I run, run, run.

QUICK!

THEY HAVE ME!

The woods suddenly stop, opening up to a pond, bare, skeletal trees rising up from the banks like bones. I've been here before in my dreams, the same but different, always changing.

This is a land of change, I think to myself, my first coherent thought in a while. *A land of lies.*

ADA!

Lies, lies, lies, I chant to myself.

"You're not real!" I yell, suddenly emboldened, remembering all that Jay had told me. "You're at peace, this isn't you!"

"But it is, sweetie, it is."

I whirl around.

My mother is standing ten feet behind me.

I try to scream but no sound comes out.

I am trapped in horror.

Not because she scared me.

But because she's not alone.

On one side of her is a tall, thin figure, black as sin. He hurts to look at, he seems fathomless, no shape, no details, just a black hole that will eventually suck in your sanity and soul. I can feel the very essence of myself being stripped away and I know the more I stare at him, the more I'll cease to exist. He reeks of a million siphoned souls inside and grabs onto one of my mother's arms, her veins turning black where he holds her.

On the other side is Michael. Or at least the body he incorporated back when he was a demon in our world. Tall in a pinstriped suit, he could almost be called dashing, except for the fact that he's smiling so cunningly, his eyes putrid black holes, that he's horror personified. Any resemblance I once thought he had to Dex is gone.

"We can stop," Michael says, his voice so inhuman and terrifying, it makes me grind my teeth together. Liquid spurts from my eyes and I can't tell if it's blood or tears as it runs down my cheeks. "We can stop it all right here. We will spare your mother if you just come with us."

I stare at them. I stare at her.

Her eyes are pleading.

Her eyes are...real.

She's staring at me and she's crying. She's in pain. She's trying to hide it all but she can't. Her brave face isn't brave enough.

This is real.

This is her.

And I have no idea what to do because I know what coming with them entails.

As if my mom senses that she slowly shakes her head.

"Don't do it," she whispers. "Wake up, Ada. Run away!"

I don't know what to think. First she's telling me to save her, singing a song about following her, now she's telling me to wake up and run away.

Which is it?

I look at Michael. "What do you want?"

His grin never falters. "You know exactly what we want. It's you."

Even though his voice makes my eyes bleed, I push on.

"You're not real. This is a dream. Nothing is really happening." I look at my mom. "She's an illusion you've made. Maybe even one I've made, to play on my guilt." I nearly choke on those last words. My tongue tastes the blood from my eyes.

"They lie to you so well," he says. "I suppose they want to protect their latest guinea pig. You're nothing but a tool to them, you know that, don't you? You can feel it. How they only give you so much information, just the right amount, to make you complacent and afraid." The Michael demon's hand tightens around my mom's arm until her eyes close in silent, debilitating pain. "He's not who you think he is. He's not even who *he* thinks he is."

I don't want to ask who he's talking about, even though I know it's Jay. It doesn't matter. It's not real. It's my own subconscious, my own doubt.

"Do your worst then," I tell him, finding strength somewhere in the depths of me.

Michael's head jerks back like he's not hearing me correctly and in that one sickening instance, I'm afraid. Truly fucking afraid. Because that reaction was a little too real.

The black, nebulous creature reaches over to place its hand over my mom's chest.

"Last words?" Michael asks my mother. "Until I do it all over again?"

My mother eyes me with so much sorrow my heart breaks.

"Don't come find me," she whispers frantically. "No matter what happens, Ada. No matter what I say. No matter what—"

The black being pushes its hand into her chest until it's a gaping black drain. I see galaxies among arteries, planets around her beating heart.

"No!" I scream despite myself.

My mother's mouth falls open, choking, no words, no breath. Blood trickles from her mouth.

With sickening quickness, the black thing brings its hand downward, severing my mother's body in half from her collarbone down like a hacksaw on a carcass. I turn my head, blood splattering hot against my skin, coating me from head to toe.

"You can stop this," Michael says and he's at my ear, breath that ices. *No*, he's inside, in the middle of my chest, burrowing deep. I can feel evil in my blood, sinking into my cells and beyond. There is no escape. "You can stop this Ada. Or she'll be tortured for eternity."

I'm crying. I'm screaming. I'm tortured and yet if I turn my head and open my eyes I'll see who is really suffering.

So hurry now and listen, Michael's agonizing voice whispers from within me, permeating my brain. *Run to the pond that does so glisten.*

I try and push him out of my head. I put up a black wall, tall and eternity-bound.

Step in before she dies.

Another wall. I concentrate as much as I can, seeing that dark wall block me from him.

"Ada!" I hear another voice whisper.

And now you know it's he who lies.

"Ada!"

Hands on my shoulders.

I gasp for air like I've been underwater. Panic floods my bones, my body ready to run. All feeling is back, clarity like nothing else.

I'm in my room. My old room. Sheets tangled at my legs.

It's dark but there's air and I'm alive and this is real.

This is life.

And my father is in front of me, face white, his eyes darker than ever in the black. For a moment I'm afraid he's possessed, that this isn't him.

"Ada," he says again and steps toward the window, to the light. I watch him, breathless, my heart racing, so afraid of what just happened in my dream that I can't even speak. I'm not even sure if any of *this* is real.

Is this what it's like to go insane?

"I'm sorry to wake you," he says, running his hand down his face. It seems like my father, that I'm awake, but I can't be sure. Will I ever be sure? "I just...I couldn't ignore it."

Somehow I find my voice. "What?" I sit up straighter, trying to get my bearings. The dream ended so horribly, so suddenly, that I'm afraid I'll easily slip back into that gruesome scene.

My dad paces back in forth in front of me, hands behind his back, and I know now that this is real. But the thing is, my father has never woken me up in the middle of the night before. It's always been the other way around.

Suddenly I'm so acutely aware of how it is now. How it's just me and him in this big old house. That's all we have here.

He stops, looking down on me with such fear that I'm not even sure I knew fear until this moment. I have never seen my dad afraid. Wrought with grief, yes. Inconsolable, yes. Angry, ignorant, deceitful, smug, arrogant, condescending, stubborn, all a million times *yes*.

But afraid? My father is a highly-regarded professor of theology. He is never afraid. He has God on his side after all.

"I might be going crazy, Ada," he says softly. He looks away, like he can't even bear to see my reaction.

"Okay," I whisper, clearing my throat. "What happened?"

He sits on the edge of the bed, looking absolutely despondent as he stares forward at the wall. "I don't know," he says, almost inaudible. "I don't know. Your mother."

I sit up straighter. I can see the black thing slicing her in half, the look in her eyes, the plea for me to run.

KARINA HALLE

"Your mother," he goes on, pain creasing his brow. How I wish for my strong, unfeeling father at this moment. "She was in bed with me. She was right there. Right there." He sobs and puts his head in his hands. "It was her. It was her, Ada. I wasn't asleep. It wasn't a dream."

And yet, despite how disturbing this is, how heartbreaking it is to see my dad crumble, it gives me hope. Because she was fine. She was with him and okay, nothing at all like my dreams led me to believe.

"She was there with me."

I reach over and put my hand on my dad's back. "It's okay. She's trying to tell you she's good. She's happy," I say softly.

"No," he says abruptly. "She was dying. All over again."

I can't breathe. I stare at him, unsure how to approach this, how to make sure we're on the same page.

"Dad, mom's already dead."

"I know. I know she is. But she wasn't just now. She was dying. She was gasping for breath and I heard her voice in my head. She said...she said..."

Oh god. I close my eyes, praying that it's not the same.

"She said, don't come find me. No matter what happens."

"No matter what I say," I finish quietly.

He gives me a sharp look and the fear has transformed. He's no longer just afraid of what he saw.

He's afraid of *me*.

"I had a dream," I explain. "She said the same thing to me. Just now. Before you woke me."

He's staring at me in disbelief, blinking hard.

"Dad. What happened after she said that?"

He still seems out of it, like he's having a hard time with the two realities. "She...I...." He closes his eyes, taking in a deep breath. "I pulled back the covers and she wasn't even there from the neck down. It was just blood. Just blood. So much blood."

I don't know how to fix this. I know my father is looking for the most reasonable explanation but I'm so terrified that after everything that has happened so far in our lives, I'll be another daughter to blame. He saw what happened in that subway in Manhattan. He saw what happened to me then, he saw what happened to Perry months before and yet he never believed. His faith never let him believe.

"Do you believe in ghosts?" I ask him. My voice is trembling now and there's nothing I can do to stop it.

He stares at me and it's almost like I can see two parts of him grasping for control. I already know which one will win out. It's the only thing he knows, that he can rely on. His faith.

"No," he says gravely. After all that he's seen, to admit to seeing ghosts would shake his very foundations.

"Then this is a dream, dad," I tell him gently. "Go back to bed. She won't be there. You'll wake up in the morning."

I'm not sure how much of that he can believe but still he gets up, tells me he loves me, and leaves the room.

I wait with my breath held, wondering if I'll hear him talking to her. If he'll cry or scream. But there is no sound. I have no doubt she was there but she's gone now.

I lie back down and close my eyes. I want to think about what it all means but I'm exhausted and, more than that, I'm horribly sad. My chest feels like it's being crushed from the inside out.

I shed bloodless tears and sleep.

CHAPTER TEN

By the time I'm up the next morning, the sun is slanting in through the window, which means I've been in bed for way too long.

But to be honest, I don't care. I could sleep all day. I didn't have any dreams (after the main one, of course) and with that in mind, I want to just cocoon myself in the covers and pretend that nothing is wrong. I want to sink into deep oblivion, mindless and dark, and stay there for a long time. Nothing is bad. Nothing can hurt me.

I don't want to think about last night. Not one bit.

A knock at my door nearly makes me scream. Apparently my subconscious has no chill.

"Come in," I say, assuming it's my dad.

The door opens.

I suck in my breath.

Definitely not my dad.

Jay stands, large and in charge in the doorway, my mug that says *Coffee First, World Domination Later* is in his hand.

"What...what?" I ask and then realize I'm sitting in bed in just my bare camisole (holy nipple city). I grab the covers, hauling them up to my shoulders. "The fuck?"

"Nothing I haven't already seen," he comments mildly as he eyes the blanket, stepping inside the room. "Brought you some coffee."

"How did you get in here?" I cry out, still so fucking confused. "Did you teleport in?"

He shakes his head, placing the coffee on the bedside table. "Knocked on the door. No one was home. Your dad left a note saying he'd be back later. Coffee pot was still warm."

Now that he's closer to me, I can smell that distinctive scent of his, the spiciness that gives me a jolt of warmth. He's dressed in all black again—boots, jeans, a thermal shirt that clings to every inch of muscle. I'm both vaguely thrilled, nearly turned-on, from him being in my room beside me like this, and totally annoyed he's here at all.

I eye the coffee, even though it looks amazing and promises to fix what ails me. "So is this a Jacob thing, to just waltz into people's homes uninvited?"

He crosses his arms over his broad chest and casts an inquisitive eye over all the clothes piled in the room. "It's a Jay thing. So this is where you used to sleep. Did it always look like an outlet store?"

"An *outlet* store?" I practically hiss at him. I'm not sure if he's trying to be insulting or not but I'm not taking any chances.

The fact that he's hard to read doesn't help.

He stands over me expectantly and eyes the coffee.

"Have a drink," he tells me. "Clear your thoughts. And let's discuss last night."

"Last night?" I repeat.

He nods at the coffee.

I sigh and pick up the mug. It's like he knows I'm mostly incoherent unless I have caffeine in my blood.

Somehow the coffee is perfectly hot, tasting a million times better than what my dad usually makes. Though he's Italian, his taste in coffee sucks.

"What happened in your dream?" he asks me once I've had a few sips.

"You tell me," I say. "Dream interpretation is your specialty."

"I couldn't see you," he says, frowning. "I tried but you put up a wall. To keep me out."

I raise my brow and take another sip, hoping things will make more sense when I get to the bottom of the mug. "I didn't put up anything. I was dreaming. You weren't there. It would have been nice if you were." I trail off, the gruesome image of my mother being sliced in half flashing through my mind.

"What happened in it?"

I swallow thickly, staring down into the coffee for a moment, gathering up my wits before I tell him what happened. It's impossible not to hear that disturbing song ringing through my ears, the feel of Michael speaking to me from the inside, the nebulous matter of the dark.

When I'm done, he's staring at me just as he was before, a bit of indifference, a lot of nothing.

"So what do you believe?" he asks calmly.

"Well I believed it was a dream," I tell him. "Until my father comes into my room moments after, telling me my mother has visited him in his bed. And I know my father…

it took guts to admit that. This was the first time." When Jay doesn't say anything, I continue. "He saw her. Then he saw her dead. Just like in my dream. Repeating just what was said in my dream."

Jay briefly holds his lower lip between his teeth, his eyes still focused hard on mine. I'm aware once again that this giant, mysterious beast is standing in my bedroom and I'm scantily clad in bed. It's actually a lot better if I ignore that and concentrate on the horror at hand instead.

"Do you believe them?" he finally asks.

"Believe who?"

"The demons. What they said in your dream, not to trust me."

I look down and anxiously run my hand along the blanket, looking for a loose thread to pick at. "If actual demons are invading my dreams and telling me this, then no. If my subconscious is telling me this...that's a different story." I pause. "And wouldn't you say that's all this is. My subconscious?"

I glance up and meet his eyes. I swear I see them shift from ice to slate and back again. Considering who, or what, he is, I wouldn't be surprised to learn they do that, only I have no idea what it means.

"I suppose your subconscious has a lot of...letting go to do."

My eyes narrow. "As if you know what it's like to lose someone and let go. As if it's that easy."

His lips twist into a placating smile. "I can't pretend that I do. And I was talking about letting go of your distrust of me."

I nearly roll my eyes. "Right. Like that's easy too. When it comes to dealing with human beings, trust is something that is earned, not given."

If I hadn't been watching him so closely, I think I would have missed the flash of sorrow on his face, as if I had insulted some deep part of him. But the look is so quick, I wonder if I saw it at all.

He nods and walks over to the window that looks over at the Knightlys'. "Regardless, it would be helpful if you didn't put up your walls."

"I don't have walls," I hiss at him. "You weren't there. Anyway, how did you know I had a dream?"

"It's a given at this point," he says. "But when I tried to step in I couldn't. I had no idea if you were alive or not. So I came over."

I realize I'm staring at him horrified, a chill running over me. "You had no idea if I was alive or not? Why the hell wouldn't I be?"

He slowly turns around to eye me and gives me a mild shrug. "Life is never a given, princess."

This guy is unbelievable. I shake my head.

"So is that all?" I repeat tersely. "You just came in to check if I was alive or not."

"Pretty much," he says, eyeing my mug. "And to bring you your coffee. Though don't expect this to be a day to day thing."

"Thank god," I mutter under my breath. Not that it would be so horrible to have him in my room every morning, bringing me coffee or otherwise. I clear my throat. "So what do you expect me to do next time this happens?

When the walls go up, or whatever? I was calling for you in the dream, you know."

"I could hear you," he says grimly. "I just couldn't see you. Don't worry. I'll find a way next time."

"Right." I finish the coffee and put it back on the bedside table. "And so what does it mean then, the fact that my father saw the very mother that I dreamed. Is my subconscious powerful enough to project itself? I know Perry's is."

He shakes his head and takes a step closer to the bed. "It means demons are real. And they're starting to reach the unbelievers."

To his credit, he doesn't say it lightly.

I find it hard to swallow. "Will they come after him?" I ask, unable to mask the tremor in my voice.

"No. They're just appearing as a way to get to you. Your father is safe."

I study him, searching his face for the truth. I think I can glean it from his eyes, the determined set of his jaw. He's asked me to trust him and sometimes I wonder if I have a choice.

My cell beside the bed suddenly beeps, making me jump. I pick it up and see a text from Amy, wondering if I'm still going with her to the music festival today. I'd totally forgotten all about it.

The Northwest Music Fest runs for three days in downtown Portland at the waterfront and other venues, showcasing a bunch of bands. This year Amy and I decided to get tickets to see Duran Duran on one of the nights and it totally slipped my mind that tonight was that night.

"What is it?" Jay asks, mildly curious.

"Nothing. I just forgot I had plans with Amy tonight." Honestly, even though I know going out to a music festival is probably the best thing for me, I'm tempted to cancel on her. But I know she loves the band as much as I do and I really haven't seen her since all this crazy shit happened.

Still, it's hard to pull up my fucking big girl panties and put all this Jay and dreams and demon shit behind me and pretend to be a normal girl. In fact, the last few days I've started to realize that the normal I've always wanted to be will now never be reached. It was always in my grasp... but it's just smoke in my hand.

Silence falls between Jay and I as I get dragged into the depths of my head. He's watching me, waiting for me to say something else, or maybe he's not waiting at all. Maybe he's trying to figure me out, to piece together the "me" he knows in my dreams with the me he sees before him. Maybe he's just observing with tepid interest, like the way we watch animals in a zoo. We watch them because of how alike us – and unlike us – they are.

"Are you going?" he finally asks.

I sigh and slide the phone onto the table. "Yeah. I should. Get out of the house. Pretend the big bad wolf isn't at my door." My eyes flit to his and he stares back at me openly. "I'd invite you but..."

He shakes his head quickly, raising his palm to stop me from going on. "Don't worry about me. I'm sure the Knightlys have some chore they want me to do. Or Jacob does."

"So how does it work there? I mean, why are the Knightly's letting you and Jacob stay there? Did they just move there for me?"

VEILED

"It's complicated," Jay says, slowly walking over to my door. "As most things are." He opens the door and gives me one last steady look, a gaze that seems to tip the room over, leaving me untethered, ready to fall. "Take care of yourself, Ada. I'll see you later."

Then he's out of my room, closing the door behind him, and the room returns to a dusty chill, like he was never here at all.

. . .

"Hello stranger," Amy says to me as I climb into the passenger side of Smartie. I breathe in her lavender air freshener that hangs from the rear-view mirror and immediately relax at the sense of normalcy it brings me. All lies, but I buy into it.

I give her an apologetic grimace. "Sorry I kind of dropped the ball on all of this."

She gives a little shrug and clucks her tongue as she does a U-turn in the middle of the street, eying the Knightlys' house as we go past. "You're excused." Then she gives me a sassy smile. "I mean, if I had a giant hunk of man meat living next door to me, I think I'd be a little distracted too. Don't tell Tom I said that."

I sigh. "It's not like that," I tell her and it's the truth. "He's just a friend." Mmmm. Okay, maybe that part is a stretch.

"Sure, sure," she says, tapping her fingers along the wheel to the beat of an obnoxious pop song. For once, though, I let it play, hoping the auto-tuned songstress can trick my mind into thinking everything is okay and life is as fun as it is in her song.

155

And it kind of works. As we drive into the city, Amy launches into the latest fight that she and Tom had, then starts going on about a show she started watching and before I know it I've completely forgotten about this morning, last night, the last few days. To escape, even for a car ride, is amazing.

It isn't until we find parking and start the long walk to the concert, following hordes of music-lovers drinking beers out of paper bags, wearing large sunglasses and laughing loudly, that Amy turns the subject back to Jay.

"So how come you never mentioned him to me before?" she asks as we turn the corner past where the 24 Hour Church of Elvis used to be. In the distance, across the river, dark clouds are building up ominously. Even though the air is hot and muggy, I get a slight chill at the mention of his name. Or maybe it's a thrill. It's hard to tell these days.

"I honestly only just met him," I tell her. "We went out for coffee, that's all."

"How old is he, twenty-five? Thirty? Like, a lot older than us, I know at least that much."

I give her a wry look. "Then it's a good thing he's just a neighbor, isn't it?"

She grins at me, the sparkles in her lip gloss catching the afternoon light. "You know, Ada, it wouldn't be the end of the world if you hooked up with someone. Even someone older. You're eighteen, totally legal and shit. Why not hit that? Seriously, why not have a fling with someone, anyone?"

I roll my eyes, even though her remarks make me uncomfortable, just reminding me of things I don't have. "No one interests me." It's something I've said again and again.

"This guy did. I could tell. And I've seen you around hot dudes before. This one though, you're *into* him, this J.J. Abrams."

"Fine," I concede with a sigh. We both stop at an intersection, waiting for the light to change. I can hear the dull bass of the concert coming from the river, whatever band is playing at the moment. "I'm into him. I mean, in a way. He's...stupidly good-looking. But that doesn't mean he's into me." And what I really want to say is, there is no way he could even be into me because he's not even human and he's actually my protector and I'm sure that's forbidden anyway since it distracts from the demon-slaying and all that.

"There you go again," she mutters. "Forgetting that no guy would ever turn you down. Sometimes I think you don't even own a mirror. You should take a look sometime, you weirdo. You're hot."

I ignore the compliments and want to remind her that I'm not quite ready for anything, not after my mom. I don't want to go through again what I did with Dylan, even though it's a tired excuse at this point. But before my brain even has a chance to decide on it, I'm struck with this cold, sharp sensation of hands traveling up my stomach, to my chest, where they close around my heart.

I gasp and Amy's eyes are on me but my eyes are across the street.

There on the other side of the road stands a long, thin man, the one from my dreams. Black, nebulous, never-ending. A void that's void of everything around it. It's the eater of dreams, of life, of souls. It's hungry. It vibrates with evil. My mouth tastes like pennies.

It extends a hand toward me and before I know it, my feet are being dragged against pavement as I'm pulled forward across the busy intersection, like he's pulling a rope attached to my gut.

Only it isn't so busy now. The traffic has stopped. The world has stopped.

"Ada," I can hear Amy in my ear, shaking me and somehow this makes me come to a halt. I find my footing in the middle of the road, while the thin black man is still reaching for me, even though the vibrations, that churning hunger inside him, the magnetic pull of my body towards his like a star into a black hole, has stopped.

I turn around and I see myself back on the other side of the road. Frozen, mouth open, eyes wide in fear. Amy's hand is on my arm, she's staring at me in concern.

"Are you okay?" she asks.

And then the world explodes into blue stars and smoke and it's spinning and suddenly I'm back where I was. No longer two people, just one and Amy's grip on my arm is tight, her eyes filled with worry, while I teeter off-balance. The need to puke is strong.

"Are you okay? Talk to me?" she asks louder and I'm aware that other pedestrians are crossing the road, some bumping into me, some others glancing at me curiously. The lights are green.

I swallow and try to speak, looking back to see the man. He is gone.

"I'm fine," I manage to say, taking in a deep breath as if I've been under water for minutes.

Amy slowly removes her hand and then sighs in frustration as the light turns red again. We missed our chance to cross.

I can't share her frustration. I want to know what the fuck just happened. Jay said there were demons around me, things that were showing themselves to me, things I wasn't seeing. But how did he make time pause like that, take me out of my body like he was shucking a peanut? If Amy hadn't brought me out of it, what would have happened?

I look at her, my closest friend, and realize that what Jay said was right. I have to tell her, tell her now before it gets worse. I have to come clean, no matter how badly the truth might cost me.

"Amy," I say slowly. My heart beats wildly though I'm not sure if it's from the fright I just had or the fear that I might lose her, the only normal thing in my life. In the distance thunder rumbles and, even though the sun is still shining, I swear it's dimmed, like a restaurant at the romantic hour. "I have to tell you something."

She bites her lip, shooting me a quick, wary glance. "I thought you never would."

My brows come together. "What do you mean?"

She exhales loudly, her attention going to everything but me. "I don't know. It's been pretty obvious that something is wrong with you. I mean, more than just your mother dying. It's been two years Ada. We can't tell if you're holding onto sadness because you want to feel sad or there's just something majorly wrong with you."

Amy can be really blunt, so I try not to let her choice of words get to me, nor the fact that she said "we" which means it's something she and Tom have discussed, possibly even Jessie.

"It's…complicated," I tell her. "And you're not going to believe a word of it. I understand. I wouldn't believe it and I still fucking don't. But it's the truth and it's my truth."

My truth. It sounded so fatalistic.

"Okay," she says warily as the lights go green again and we cross.

As we walk, I wonder if our relationship is going to change from beyond this moment to the time we get to the festival. I wonder if I'll ever hear "Hungry like the Wolf" the same way again.

I can feel the sweat building in my palms as I take in a deep breath. I have to do this like pulling off a Band-Aid.

"The truth is," I say, keeping my eyes focused on the street ahead, not daring to look at her, "well, you know the movie *The Sixth Sense*? That's my life. Minus Bruce Willis. But yeah, that's pretty much my problem. I see dead people."

I pause but still don't look at her. To my surprise she hasn't faltered in her strides beside me. Far-off thunder rumbles again, as if on cue.

I go on, quickly, the words bubbling up in my throat like champagne in a bottle. "It's always been this way. At least it started with Perry. Three years ago she told me she started seeing ghosts. That the show she did with Dex was real. He saw them too. I thought they were nuts but at the same time, I believed her. She was like that at fifteen too, but I was too young to get it. I do now. Because I'm just like her. It took a while for it to happen to me though.

And when I was fifteen, I started seeing things. My dead grandmother mainly. But demons too. It's...been a learning experience since then. I'm not crazy though. I mean, I think I am sometimes but I'm not. It just is what it is."

We stop at another intersection and I hear Amy suck in her breath. I dare to look at her and something inside me breaks. She's staring at me like I have some sort of disease. It's the look she used to give me when I was grieving, wild on drugs, doing anything to escape my head. But instead of the worry and pity, there's an extra emotion there.

She thinks I'm lying.

I swallow hard, my throat raw and dry. "It gets worse, too." I mean, fuck, I've gone this far. Let's rip the lid off the can of worms. "When my mother died, she was possessed by a demon called Michael, even though that really wasn't his name. He'd taken possession of Dex's brother who knows when. That's why we really all went to New York to begin with. His demon brother had taken Dex and we went to get him back, and all the while we were walking into a trap. In the end, the demon even possessed me until my mom overtook him." I pause, not because I'm aware that I'm raving like a loon and attracting the looks of people walking past, but because the memories burn. I know how ridiculous it sounds the moment the words leave my lips but it doesn't stop it from being an open wound. "My mother jumped in front of the train to save us all."

Heavy silence falls between us, so much so that even the distant thunder and the bass of the concert, just two blocks away, is muffled, like someone has put a sheet over the city. The air grows hotter, thicker, while my skin seems to chill from the inside out.

161

I glance at Amy as we walk, my heart in my throat. She's looking straight ahead, blinking slowly, not looking at me, not saying a word.

"I know it's a lot to take in," I coax her, wanting her to at least say something.

She nods, eyes darting around her like she's already trying to distance herself from me.

I think we go an entire block in silence, every step I take I regret opening my mouth, wishing I hadn't told the truth.

Finally we stop on the grass of the waterfront park, the crowd around us becoming thicker, the security lines forming by the gates. In the background a pop rock group is between songs, making remarks about the storm in the distance. I don't have to look over my shoulder to know the clouds are darkening and coming right for us.

Amy sighs, a long and harsh exhale, and gives me a look I can't read. Usually I can read everything on her expressive face, but not now. Not when I need to the most.

"Ada," she says softly, almost like a whine. "I'm not sure what you want me to say."

"That you *believe* me," I implore. My voice is shaking and I'm surprised that so much is riding on her simple—or not so simple—belief in me.

She runs her hand over her face, as if lifting away a veil. "But I don't," she says bluntly. "I can't. You're... you're either a terrible friend Ada or you need help. From a professional."

Her words hurt more than I thought they would. Puncture wounds all around my heart. "But I'm telling the truth."

"Then your truth is fucked up. Ghosts are real? Your mother died because she was possessed by a demon? Jesus Christ, at least try and have some respect for your mother's death instead of making up a story."

"It's not a story!" I cry out. "It happened. I had to tell you everything, I had to be honest. It's been killing me for years having the burden of all of this, to keep it all inside."

"And what did you think I'd say when you told me?"

My mouth shuts, for a moment, lips clamped hard together until I can feel like blood run out of them. "I thought you'd believe me. Because you're my best friend. You know I'd never lie to you, Amy."

Her eyes narrow for a moment. "Never lie? Apparently you have been. You just said so yourself. All this time you've been thinking you're seeing ghosts, that your whole damn family is haunted. You've kept this to yourself, away from us. Why tell me now?"

"Because I have to," I manage to say, looking down at the concert tickets in my hand that I've absently taken out of my purse on the walk over. "What's happened before, it's only going to get worse. It is getting worse. And I'm going to need your support. I'm not asking you to do anything except just stay my friend and believe me."

I search her eyes, begging for her to see my sincerity, to see the sanity I can only hope is there.

"Ada," she says flatly and it's then that I know it's all over, and just like you know when your boyfriend is about to give you the "talk," I know that our relationship has crashed and burned around me. "I am your friend. I always will be. But you're asking too much of me. I don't believe in ghosts. I don't believe in the supernatural or demons. And I know that even though that's what you think is going on, that it's not. I'll help you get the help you need but you have to help yourself first."

I can't even speak. She doesn't understand. Not even close.

She thinks I'm fucking insane.

God, I wish I were.

I wish this whole thing was something that could be fixed with high doses of anti-psychotics and a short-term stay at the hospital. If only.

"So that's it," I say weakly. "You don't believe me. You think I'm sick in the head."

"Grief does funny things to a person," she says.

"Oh what the fuck do you know about grief," I snap. It's like I've been bound by an elastic band, unbeknownst to me, and with one sharp, painful snap my worry and fear has been replaced with anger. Vicious, rolling anger. "You get to sit there with your boyfriend and look down on me, 'Oh poor fucking Ada, going through so much shit, will she ever be better?' I see your pity, I know you wish I could just get over it, become the person I was before. Well guess what? The person I was before was no better. I still saw the unexplainable. And you still would have called me insane."

She's staring at me with wide eyes and I realize I've never yelled at her before. In fact, we've never even had a fight. I always thought it was because we got along so well, that it was a testament to our relationship. Now I realize it's because she never really knew me and I never really knew her.

I definitely didn't expect this to go this way.

"Look," she says when she finds her voice and it comes out hard. Any sympathy gone. "You don't make things easy on anyone. You're difficult even when you're pretending to be normal. You live in some bubble where it's just you and no one else. Maybe your clothes, maybe your blog, sometimes your family. But it's just you and it's always been you. You've been shutting all of us out for years."

"Yeah because I was afraid to tell you the truth!" I'm yelling now, raising my arms. Thunder trumpets again. "And I had a right to be afraid! You think I belong in a mental institution!"

"Anyone would think that!" she yells back. A few people heading for the security lines give us a look, a guy sniggers at the impending catfight. "Ask anyone here!" She gestures to the crowd, to the stage where the band has started up playing again. "They'd all agree with me. Ada," she grabs my arm, "you're not well. And the sooner you come to terms with that, stop hiding from it, stop blaming it away, the sooner that everything will go back to normal."

But there is no normal. And I think she knows this. Though she believes I'm fucking nuts, she also knows this is it. She cares about me but not enough to go the extra mile. Not enough to just let me be the way I am. She won't be there if I let this go any further.

I have a choice but it's really like no choice. Get help, or pretend to get help and admit that it's all in my head, and keep my friend. Or stay true to course. Live out my truth, no apologies.

And lose her.

KARINA HALLE

"I'm not going to the doctors, Amy, because there's
nothing wrong with me. Nothing they can cure. It is what
it is and I am what I am and yes, I'm majorly fucked and
totally fucked up. But I'm not crazy. It's not in my head.
It's all very real, too real, and it happens to be something
I'm going to have to deal with for the rest of my life. I wish
it wasn't this way. But we don't get to choose who we are."

She watches me for a few moments, the hostility on
her brow melting away, becoming something close to sorrow, before she closes her eyes. When she opens them, her
expression is blank. Closed off. I know that expression too
well. It's how I should be feeling, trying to protect myself
from the hurt.

But it's too late. I'm hurting.

"That's where you're wrong," she says after what feels
like eternity. "You always get a choice as to who you are."
She looks behind her at the concert. "Look, I'm not sure
I quite feel up to this anymore. I'd offer you a ride home
but...I need time to think."

Ouch. I try not to grimace. It's not exactly easy to get
home from here using public transit, which means I'll have
to call my dad, but I wouldn't have ridden back with her
anyway.

And at that, she turns and goes, not even bothering to
find someone else to take her concert ticket.

I'm dumbfounded, standing there and watching her as
she weaves through the crowd, until she's across the street
and around the block, until she disappears and I'm not sure
how long I've been frozen in a sea of people.

It's only when some drunk dude bumps into my shoulder, spinning me around and offering a harsh "Sorry" as he tries to catch up with his friends, that I'm spurred into moving.

I glance at my ticket and briefly think about going into the concert, being swallowed up by the music and the crowd, maybe grabbing a joint off of someone.

I don't have it in me.

I turn away and stagger off toward the riverfront walk and start walking aimlessly along it, heading south, not really sure what to do next.

I'm numb. Angry. Terrified.

Sad.

So fucking sad.

I guess I always knew deep down that Amy wouldn't believe me. That she would reach for the most logical explanation, even though she knew that to not believe was to hurt me. I knew and that's why I had kept it to myself.

It's Jay's fault, I think bitterly as the dull thuds of the concert and chatter of the crowd slips behind me. I have no choice but to blame it on him. The whole thing was the fucking ginger's idea. He probably saw this coming himself, I mean how could he not, he's most likely psychic. Most likely sees that I'm going fight demons through sardonic wit and end up friendless and alone. Future Ada will have blood on her hands after a hard day of fighting the dead and eat Lean Cuisine meals with her cat.

I smile bitterly at the thought, doing what I can to keep the sorrow at bay, that cutting sensation around my gut that tells me things will never be the same after this.

CHAPTER ELEVEN

The storm is now billowing through east Portland.

In a few minutes it will pass over the river and hit me, and the music festival, head on. It's like I'm conjuring it up myself, the elements matching my mood, instead of being a typical late summer thunderstorm.

I didn't bring a jacket or an umbrella and I have no idea where I'm going. I'm wandering, aimless, just trying to understand what's happened, wanting to come to terms with my friendship with Amy but still feeling things too clearly. If I let myself dwell on it too much, I'll fall into another downward spiral and this time I'm not sure if I have the strength to crawl out all on my own.

I've turned down a street past a row of food trucks, near the university where my father teaches when the sky goes dark, slowly, like someone pulling a dimmer switch. The air grows heavier. I can feel the weight on my skin, producing a sheen of sweat, the hairs on my arms standing with electricity. Yet a shiver slowly makes its way down my spine, icy fingers feeling along each bump of my vertebrae.

A drop of rain falls on the bridge of my nose and I look around for shelter, knowing it's going to come down hard any minute. There's a coffee shop up the next block but I've only made it a few feet before the deluge happens. The sky opens up and dumps rain on me like an overturned bucket.

I shriek and start running, as does everyone else on the street, laughing as they go. I know I won't make it to the coffee shop without drowning so I quickly duck into the shelter of a parking garage.

It's fairly empty which is odd, considering how hard it was for us to find parking for the concert (the thought of Amy sends another worrying jab into my heart) but at least it's dry. I look down at my clothes, assessing the damage. I'm partially soaked, mainly my hair and shoulders. I should be glad I didn't wear the white sundress like I was going to earlier since it would have gone totally see through, and opted for a black tank and shorts instead, but I can't seem to muster the emotion of being glad about anything.

I stand by the entrance, just under the concrete roof, occasionally glancing up at the sky to see if there's a break coming, but if anything the clouds seem to grow larger, lower, pressing down on me. Rain streams down from the upper levels of the parkade, splashing noisily into an ever-widening puddle a few feet away.

I think I'm alone. I checked when I ran in here, a quick survey over the empty stalls and the few cars parked here and there. It's one of those garages that don't have an attendant, you pay via a ticket from the machine.

But the skin on the back of my neck begins to tighten, like the electricity from the storm but not quite, and the most subtle but unnerving sensation begins to build from the inside out. It's like I have hundreds of ants crawling all over me but they're not crawling over my skin—they're crawling *underneath* my skin.

I shudder, trying to get the sensation to leave, shaking out my arms and legs when I hear a harsh, wet breath from behind me.

I gasp and whirl around, expecting to see a monster. In fact, I think I do, just for a second, red eyes and black matted fur, a creature waiting in the dark depths.

But it steps forward out of the shadows and I realize it's a nun, which should put my galloping heart to rest but doesn't.

"Keeping dry?" she asks me in a quiet voice as she stops beside me, her grey habit perfectly ironed. Her eyes study me, not the rain, but there's no harm in them, just what looks like kind-hearted curiosity. Only I have a strange feeling that it's *supposed* to look like that, that her true face is buried underneath.

I have to blink a few times to get the feeling to go away and even the ants under my skin seem to hush.

"I didn't bring an umbrella," I say meekly, looking away from her inquisitive gaze.

"The forecast called for sunshine," she says brightly. "Even I didn't see this one coming. But sometimes God likes to mix things up."

I nod, feeling that heaviness in my heart again over Amy. "He sure does."

"Do you believe in God?" she asks me.

Oh here we go. The problem with so many of the Christians who come knocking at your door is that even when you tell them you do believe in God (if you do), they don't think it's good enough. It's not enough to just believe, they want you to believe the same way that they believe.

Still, I muster up a smile because one must never be rude to a nun and say, "I do."

She smiles broadly though it doesn't quite reach her eyes, like she knows the reaction she's supposed to give yet doesn't feel it.

The ants crawling under my skin start to prickle again.

"Good," she says, looking back to the street. "It's impossible to not believe in God when you see all the good in the world." She almost seems to laugh over those last words. "He must have blessed you more than others. You're very pretty."

I frown slightly, pretty sure that prettiness and vanity aren't exactly things to be congratulated on in a religious sense. I don't say anything to that, just give her a polite smile. Conversations with strangers have never been my strong point, let alone nuns.

"Does something ail you?" she asks me just as I'm looking across the road, my eyes attracted by a tall shape lurking behind a dumpster, a shape that moves with a familiarity that makes me even more uneasy. Is it just a homeless person sifting through the trash, or is it something else? The sky seems to darken by the second, the rain becoming thicker so that looking across the street is like staring through darkened gauze. The drumming sound of the rain turns hypnotic.

The nun's cold fingers rest on my arm. I jump, a yelp mercifully muffled in my throat.

"Are you well?" she asks again, seeming genuinely concerned.

I glance across the street to where the dark form is, only now it's standing in front of the dumpster. It could be a man dressed in black, it could be a demon. With the rain it's impossible to tell. I can't even tell if it's facing me or not, even though I swear I can feel its gaze.

"I'm well," I say softly, afraid to take my eyes off of it. "I'm good. I'm just..."

"I understand," the nun says, removing her fingers. It's only then I realize that my arm was going numb from cold while she was touching me, the heat and feeling coming back with a fury. As soon as this weather clears, I'm heading straight home, making a pot of tea and getting into bed. This is what I get for trying to go outside and be social. I lose my best friend, get caught in a thunderstorm, and have to deal with a nosy nun, not to mention the weirdness across the street.

"Sometimes it's easy to turn inward. Toward the darkness," she muses, her voice chipper. "Sometimes the darkness is our friend."

I keep my eyes on the figure—still not moving—even though I want to look at the nun and see just where she's going with this.

"Do you believe in the Devil?" she asks sharply.

Somehow I'm not surprised she asked that.

I might be staring at him right now, I think to myself. I clear my throat. "I do."

"Have you felt him?" her words take on a hiss, reminding me of a snake or something crawling out from a swamp.

I finally look at her, expecting the worst. But she's grinning at me. Her teeth are all missing, just black and blue gums, something I hadn't noticed before. In fact she

VEILED

looks like she's aged even more, her skin yellow and papery thin, the lines on her face like greying canyons.

"Felt who?"

She looks away to the road and if she sees the dark figure standing there, she doesn't let on. "The rain will stop soon. You will be on your merry way. Tell me how the darkness sings to you. Do you have God's grace to ignore the siren song? Or are you like so many others, wanting more, demanding fairness in their tiny little lives?"

Okay, now I'm really getting uneasy, wondering if heading out into the downpour, near the shadowy figure, is a better bet than my present company. I sigh and start scratching at my arms, the creepy crawling in my skin feeling intensifying.

"I'm not...sure what you're talking about," I say, stumbling over my words, my tongue feeling foreign.

"Never you mind," she says, bright again, like all is well with the world. "I know how weak humanity is, how they crawl on their knees, begging for salvation, for escape and hope. But God never responds to them. So they turn to the one who does. Why else do you think the world is turning into vile shit?"

Now I'm shocked. I stare at her with wide eyes, trying to come up with something in response, maybe along the lines of "I wasn't aware you were allowed to swear," but my tongue still doesn't want to obey.

She eyes my arm where I'm scratching. "You have them don't you? The sensation of ants crawling under your skin."

I still. Attempt to swallow and can't. *How do you know that?* I try to ask but the words don't come.

"Because," she says, taking a step closer to me. A whiff of something musty and sour, like the earth and rotten fruit, comes flowing over me. "That's what it feels like when he is near."

It gets worse, suddenly, sharply. I shake out my arms again, my nails now drawing blood, wishing I could rip off my skin and shed them all out.

"When who is near?" Somehow the words come out of my mouth, my tongue finally working again. Every part of me trembles. "God?"

Her eyes widen. She now has cataracts, milky, yet I know she sees me more clearly than ever. "No, not God," she hisses. "Never God." She crooks a bony finger toward the hazy figure on the other side of the road. "*Him*."

My blood runs cold. My eyes dart between her and the shadow, still standing across the street.

"There is no escape, only surrender," the woman says, her voice unnaturally low, like it's coming from another place. Then she drops her arm and starts scratching at her neck. "I have the feeling too." Scratch, scratch. I watch, horrified, mesmerized. "Beautifully unbearable."

The figure across the street begins to move through the rain, and even though the deluge isn't letting up, the closer he comes, the less clear he is. And that's when I know he can't be human.

It is who—what—the nun was talking about.

It is *him*.

I back up, slowly at first as the figure approaches, just twenty feet away, my feet stumbling over themselves though I don't fall down.

The nun stands there staring at me through white eyes, scratching hard at her windpipe, drawing blood that flecks down onto her white collar.

"I-I think someone is following me," I stammer to her as I keep backing up, thinking that because she's a nun, she'll be able to protect me if it's a demon. If it's not a demon and just a man, then having her with me might make him think twice. Because whatever the thing is coming across the rain-screened street, I know he means me harm. More than that, he's smiling. I can't see it, can't see him clearly even now, but I can feel the smile all the same.

One that says killing me will be fun.

"I think that person is after me," I tell her, eyes darting to the approaching shadow, "Please. Help."

The nun doesn't even look to the figure (who is just ten feet away now, almost to the garage entrance!) just keeps her eyes on me, shiny white orbs. She keeps scratching. "Like ants underneath the skin," she murmurs, her lips appearing to move too fast for what she's saying. Her tongue comes out briefly and waggles in the air, like a snake trying to smell. Her lips smack together wetly, spit flying.

And then the first ant appears.

It crawls out from under her nose, heading over to her cheek.

Yet another follows.

Then one from her lips, heading down over her chin.

I can't even comprehend what I'm seeing and the air is filling with a sickening hum, like a frequency that no human should ever be subjected to, and the bad thing is coming. I just watch, my eyes glued to her face as yet another ant slowly emerges.

Then her check splits open, a long, jagged-edged gash the color of rusty blood, and hundreds of ants come pouring out of her at once, covering her face like a black moving mask.

I scream. I scream at her, I scream at the shadowy figure who is now in the garage with us. I scream for help. I scream for Jay.

Then I turn and run, though the last thing I see as I do so, such a quick flash, is a long, slick tail protruding out the back of the nun's dress.

I run faster.

I head straight down the middle of the lane, into the darker depths of the garage, knowing how stupid I'm being but I don't have much of a choice. I can't run toward them, there's no attendant in this lot, the only thing I can hope for is to run for the roof and hope I see someone, whether it be a shopper going back to their car or a security officer.

I don't even know if it's following me, if *they're* following me, I can only feel the ragged breaths in my chest, my boots slapping on the concrete, echoing coldly.

I turn the corner and start running up to the second level, my feet slipping and I crash to the cement, my hands and knees taking the brunt of it. Everything stings. My skin wet with blood. But I keep going.

There are more cars on this level but no one to be seen. And underneath me, from the first level, I hear fast, heavy footfalls turning into something else. Quicker. More than two legs. Claws scratching on concrete.

An animal scurrying on all fours.

Hunting.

I contemplate continuing to run, but I'm halfway down this level and I know that it will turn the corner and see me before I can get to the next level. Not that I'm trying to pretend I'm not here. It knows I'm here. It's just I can't think, I can't do anything but go where my feet guide me.

I hope my instinct won't get me killed.

BLAM!

Without warning all the car alarms on the cars go off at the same time, each car turning on, their headlights shining like they've all come to life at once and are rioting.

My heart leaps into my throat and for a split second I'm frozen in the middle of the lane, enveloped by the cacophony, before I remember that I don't have a split second anymore. I duck behind a black Chevy Escalade, moving my body back so that my legs are hidden by the back wheel, my butt to the wall as I'm hunched over.

I've literally painted myself into a corner here. I'm not sure what the hell I'm thinking. That I can hide behind a car and the *thing* will simply go away?

But my saving grace comes with an EXIT sign, five spaces down from me, only a little hatchback between me and the staircase leading to freedom. And possibly a demon nun. But mainly freedom.

Suddenly all the car alarms cease, the horns stop honking, the engines still and the space is brought back into a silence so thick it seems to bounce off the walls.

Except there is one sound.

The *tic tic tic* of sharp claws slowly coming my way.

Then the raspy, wheezing breath, not of something having troubles breathing but of something that shouldn't have lungs to begin with. Something that's trying out our air for the very first time.

My mouth is sandpaper dry as I hold my breath, trying not to make a sound. I eye the staircase again, calculating how much time I think I have, how close I think it is. I can't think about the alternative. I can't think about what happens if I fail.

This is no dream.

This is life or death.

I decide to go for it. It's now or never.

I burst forth from the Escalade without even a glance behind me and start booking it as fast as my legs will carry me.

It starts running too, what sounds like a fast yet lumbering gallop, like a grizzly picking up speed. It's coming closer and closer and the exit sign bobs in front of me as I'm one stall down, two, three.

Four.

Almost there!

My hands are in front of me, reaching already for the handle and the thought of it being locked flashes through my mind and there's hot breath at my back and a gurgling, growling and I can feel the immense heat and dread and utter despair that seems to be thrown over me like a net.

I'm not going to make it.

I cry out in utter sorrow, the last grasp of life slipping in front of my eyes, knowing in the next second the beast will be upon me and it will be too fucking late. I'll be caught with one hand on the door.

Death is horrible for those left behind. It's even sadder for the ones who have to die. I never realized how much I loved *life* until I knew it was being taken away.

Then there's a SNAP and everything warps and bends and the space in front of me becomes a wall I crash into, solid, cold, and then spin off of until my back is flat against the door and I'm facing the other way.

It's Jay, literally appearing out of thin air, all six-foot two hulking beast of him, ready to take on another beast. He was the wall I bounced into.

He doesn't even glance back at me, his shoulders are hunched up, muscles and veins in his arms popping as they get ready to what I can only assume is fight the monster.

I see *that* beast now in all its glory. Something so horrible it's almost indescribable, like my brain can't make sense of it, as though its protecting itself against future nightmares.

What gets through my eyes to my brain is black matted fur in some places, gaping lesions in other places, filled with eyes and mouths, like the creature has swallowed souls—people—and they're fighting for a way out through the bloodied skin. There are six-inch claws that attach to legs that belong to a spider, a tail that belongs to a crocodile or serpent and then a face that's more disturbing than everything else put together. It's nearly human, like a child but not a child. Innocent and full-cheeked and dead wrong. A bald, elongated head, holes for ears, tiny eyes set so far back in its sockets that they're nearly in the brain.

Red eyes that burn into mine. Eyes that hold me in place, making my heart and gut and soul double-over from the pain that happens when you stare at pure evil.

We finally meet, it hisses at me. An inhumane voice, no gender, no emotion. It's a voice that only brings suffering.

But not for me. Not now.

Because Jay is going for it. He's not here just to protect me. He's here to kill this thing.

And I have no idea how.

The beast turns its red child-eyes to him and for a moment it stares at Jay like it recognizes him. A sort of shock that quickly turns to disappointment, if it could ever feel such a thing.

Jay notices this long enough to make him pause.

Then Jay and the beast lunge at each other.

I have no idea what to do. Do I run to safety? Jay isn't telling me to run. It's like he wants me to watch.

The fight doesn't last long though. The beast snaps at Jay with a beak filled with serrated teeth that comes out of its widening child mouth, like a scene from *Aliens*, while its claws go for Jay's arms.

It gets him too, a gruesome gash across the forearm, then the upper thigh, the stomach. Jay grimaces in pain, blood pouring from his wounds, but it doesn't stop him from wrapping his large hands around the beast's neck.

Somewhere, one of the faces from the beast's wounds screams.

And then...

Jay *rips* the fucking beast's head *off* with his bare hands.

Like a kid twisting off the head of his teddy bear. One motion clockwise, then one hand pulls the head one way while the other hand pulls the body the other and the garage fills with the sickening sound of flesh and bone and sinew being torn in half.

The head goes flying to the floor with a dog-like whimper, blood spraying across the both of us as it lands with a wet thump.

The body tries vainly to stand, then collapses, twitching once, twice.

It is dead.

Jay killed the beast.

I suck in my breath, trying to breathe, as that moment of stillness comes around me, the type that precedes me fainting.

I crumble to my knees, gasping for air, at the horror that I've just seen, at how close that just was, at how unfair this all is, at everything, everything, *everything*.

Jay is crouched beside me, his hands, his decapitating hands, grabbing me by the elbows to keep me from rolling back onto the concrete.

"Did they hurt you?" he asks gently, though there's a tone of panic in his voice. "Are you okay?"

"I'm fine," I tell him. Then I look up at his face and know that I'm not.

I burst into tears.

"Hey," he says softly, sitting down beside me. He wraps his arms around my shoulders and tries to pull me into him.

I resist. Stubborn, even as I'm a hysterical, crying mess.

But then the strength drains out of me and I let him hold me, my face buried into his chest. The tears keep coming, my body wracked by my sobs, so much that they rattle him. But he just holds me and I feel his heart beating. It calms me like nothing else.

CHAPTER TWELVE

The next hour or so is a blur. I'm not even sure if time passes the way I think it has.

One moment I'm crying into Jay and he's holding me (oh fuck, did it ever feel good to be held) and we are sitting on the second floor of that parking garage for what feels like forever. It could have even been forever—I seem to have a never-ending supply of tears—but the sound of a car entering below brought us to our feet.

The demon wouldn't be visible to the average person, so it was okay to leave the dismembered body where it was. Shortly it would turn to flames and burn off anyway.

But there was the still the real fact that we were a long way from downtown Portland to my house and Jay obviously hadn't driven to get me.

Jay took my hand, opened up a portal to the thinnest part of the Veil again (which I've now nicknamed the "Thinny"—yes, after *The Dark Tower* series) and while I don't remember much of what happened next, whether due to the Veil or everything else that happened, I do know that the world became desaturated, like someone playing in Photoshop. My ears popped. Jay took me down the stairs and into the empty streets of Portland and then I was sitting cross-legged in my bedroom.

I still am, leaning back against the headboard and staring at Jay who sits on the edge of the bed, watching me.

"It's a lot to handle," he says and I stare at him blankly, trying to piece together the journey over here but coming up blank. He goes on. "I sifted you. It takes a lot of energy from me to do so. Usually I prefer to walk, drive, or run when I'm in the Veil. But there was no other way to get you here in a hurry."

Now that he mentions it, he looks tired. Dark half-moons under his eyes, though this doesn't diminish how beautiful he is. It almost enhances him, making him look more rugged and manly than before. Someone with experience, who has experienced more than anyone should. It makes him look more human.

I clear my throat. "At the risk of sounding terribly ungrateful, next time I'm about to encounter a demon or two, you might want to show up earlier."

He frowns, looking momentarily pained. "I would have. I couldn't...Ada, you put up walls, all the time, I'm sure without meaning to. But they're there and it makes you nearly impossible to track. It's only when you're most frightened that they come down. I'm lucky it wasn't too late."

"Lucky," I repeat. A bit of an understatement. A second later and I would have been dead and for all my faith, I don't think I would have gone *up*. I would have been dragged down.

"Who was that demon?" I ask, as if it has a name. Still, I remember the way it looked at Jay when they fought, as if it were Caesar, before Brutus stabbed him in the back. *Et tu, Brute?* "And who was the nun?"

"They were both the same demon. In other forms, it can occupy many vessels, appear as many different forms. But in its real form, it can only be one. We call them a Splitter Demon. I didn't know that one's name. But it wasn't Legion."

"Legion?"

He nods, looking down at his hands. "Legion is notorious. Has been since the dawn of time. You remember the Bible?" I give him a look that says, *are you kidding me?* He ignores it. "Jesus came across a possessed man and was set to exorcise him. He can only do this when he knows the demon's name—names have true power. And the demon said 'My name is Legion. And we are many.'"

I can't help but shudder. "And did he exorcise them? Sorry, my Bible studies are a bit weak—there's a lot to remember in that book." My dad would legit cry if he could hear me right now.

"He drove the demons out into a herd of pigs nearby that ran into the lake and drowned. But that was never the end of Legion. The demons come back. They always do. It might take centuries. But they always come back. And Legion, being composed of an army of them, is one of the worst."

I swallow uneasily. "How can there be worse than what I saw today?"

He flashes me a sour smile. "There is always worse. Today, I did what I can do. But if that were Legion, it wouldn't be so easy. An army of evil, an army of many, has far more strength than I do."

"So let me get this straight," I tell him. "You the other day said that I had to fight these demons. Do you mean, fight them like you? Because, I'm sorry, but there's no way I'm doing hand-to-hand combat with them. I don't even know how to throw a proper punch without hurting myself and I hate breaking my nails."

"There are different ways to fight against them," he says. "And freezing them, dispelling them, banishing them, is one. No one expects you to wrestle. Though I can't promise you won't break a nail, princess."

His lips twist into a small smile at that. Oh my god, is he actually making fun of me?

I give him a dry look. "Sorry if I'm not laughing. I nearly fucking died..." I trail off, suddenly overwhelmed by throat-pinching panic. I suck in a breath, trying to get it in my lungs, the room starting to spin.

Jay is suddenly beside me on the bed, his large mass squeezed between me and the edge, taking my hands in his. "Ada, Ada. Deep breaths." His voice is so calming, so commanding, I have no choice but to obey. It's like my body wants to respond to him without my permission.

We sit shoulder-to-shoulder and the warmth from his thermal shirt floods through to mine. It should be awkward, maybe even a bit uncomfortable, being in such close proximity to him. But honestly, it's anything but. Even though he's just holding my hand, it feels like it's something he should do. Like it's right.

I try not to turn my head even an inch to look at him, far too conscious of how close his face is to mine. I know he's studying me, as he does, trying to figure me out. He may be my Jacob, but he's still a rookie, still doesn't know me no matter how long he's been watching. I get this feeling that he wants to know, that I'm some puzzle for him to solve, as well as a student to teach and a girl to protect.

The thing is, I want him to solve me. Give me answers to who I am and why I'm this way. Anything other than the fact that it just is what it is.

"Feel better?" he murmurs, giving my hand a firm squeeze.

And I do. My breathing has returned to normal. The room has stopped tilting on its axis. But it doesn't bury the fear, nor the pain. I'm not sure how far I'd have to shove that shit down to never feel it.

He lets go of my hand and mine feels cold without his skin.

"You're going to be all right," he says, his voice low and rough and reaching deep within.

"How?" I manage to ask. "After everything, how?" I swallow, licking my lips and finally have the nerve to turn my head toward his.

His eyes peer into mine, searching, his full lips terribly close. He doesn't move back—I'm pretty sure he has no notion of personal space.

"You told your friend, didn't you?" he asks softly.

My eyes drop to his lips. I quickly whisk them upwards. "Amy?"

He waits for me to go on.

I bite my lip and look away, the pain too fresh. "Yeah. How could you tell?"

"Because you're not just scared. You're sad."

Then he puts his fingers on my cheek, pressing slightly. His contact both makes me freeze and supress a shiver. "I can feel that," he says. "Your emotions."

Oh great. Yet another partial psychic. An empath.

"Do you even know what feelings mean?" I ask him, rather spitefully.

He doesn't flinch but he does pause before he says, "I do. I know that hurt. Maybe not as much as it should hurt someone, but it was an insult and I'll take it as one."

I dare to meet his eyes. He certainly doesn't *look* hurt. His expression hasn't changed at all. "Sorry," I mumble.

"Don't be," he says. "I'm sure that because I'm immortal, you think I'm not quite human. But here's a secret, Ada," he leans in until his lips are at my ear, "the longer I'm around you, the more that I'll *feel*." He pauses, his breath tickling my ear. I close my eyes to it, to the warmth that floods down my neck. "That's something that Jacob never told me. I'm not even sure if it's supposed to happen. But the more time I spend with you…the more like you I become."

He pulls back and I'm left with that heavy, yet strangely flattering, confession. I'm not sure what I should say.

So I awkwardly mumble, "Well, be prepared to become totally awesome."

He gives me a small smile. "So I take it your time with Amy didn't go well, then."

I shake my head, my heart thumping to a sad little beat. "No. It didn't. It went pretty much as I thought it would."

"But you still had hope, deep down. Otherwise you wouldn't be this hurt."

I sigh and stare down at the blanket. "Yeah. I had hope. Hope that she would be a friend. That she would at least *try* to believe me. I didn't think her first thought would be that I was lying. I didn't think her second thought would be that I was nuts. If it were the other way around..."

"She's not you, Ada. She's someone else entirely. Maybe someone you didn't really know. She couldn't have known all that much about you, if you were able to keep all of this a secret."

I shrug, even though I thought it earlier. "She knew that I was fun to be around and I had a successful fashion blog and I wanted to be a designer and I liked tall guys with goatees..."

He scratches at the light scruff along his jaw and chin. "Goatees, huh? Perhaps I should give this wee beard a shave."

At first I'm struck by the fact that he's almost flirting with me. Then I'm struck by the fact that for that last sentence, his accent came out totally Irish.

I nearly laugh. "What did you say?"

He gives me a puzzled look, which on his stony face means a very subtle frown. "When?"

"Just then. You sounded Irish."

He purses his lips and gives a half-shrug. "Not sure what to tell you. But listen. Trust me when I say it's best that you told Amy now. Any later and it could have been trouble. For both of you."

I exhale loudly through my nose and look up at the ceiling. There are still faint green star stickers from when I was a little kid. Back then I had no idea what course my life would take.

Or did I? I remember very clearly the way that Perry dealt with seeing things. I didn't think she was crazy. I didn't think she was lying either. I was jealous. Because she was part of a world I wasn't. I must have had some feeling though, deep down, that I would be like her. That I would follow in her footsteps. Maybe that's why I rebelled so hard against her. I wanted to be like her and that scared me.

"I guess," I tell him. "I know I'm glad she wasn't with me when that fucking nun came around. Would she have seen it, if they had showed up?"

He nods. "Yes. The closer a demon gets, the more chances that someone like Amy would see them. And then there's the fact that you'd be reacting. Your reaction and interaction brings apparitions to life. To the demons, they wouldn't care if she saw them or not because they'd finish her off the same way they would have finished you."

I try not to shudder. "And if you hadn't showed up and ripped its head clean off," I begin, finding the strength to ask, "what would have happened to me?"

"They would have dragged you to Hell," he says simply. "That's where they want you. That's why they're pretending to be your mother in your dreams. They want you however they can have you."

"Why?" I whisper.

"Because you're you," he says, his eyes turning warm. "You're a threat to them. They know what you're capable of, even if you don't yet. And you're special. Anyone with power and abilities is even more enticing to them. If they had possession of you...they could do a lot of damage to the world."

"So that's why Perry and Dex have always been targets," I muse softly.

He clears his throat. "Well, yes. But it didn't help that your sister and brother-in-law purposely sought out situations that put them at direct risk. We're doing the opposite with you, until you know how to handle yourself. That will take time."

"How much time?"

The corner of his mouth quirks up and he slowly gets off the bed. "I don't know. A few years."

My mouth drops open. "A few years. Of this? Just trying to sleep through the night and not get killed in the day?"

"It will get better," he says as he stands at the foot of the bed, arms crossed. "What happened to you today was rare. Most of the demons you will see aren't as strong and won't have the nerve."

"And my dreams?" In some ways, the dreams scared me most of all.

"Keep ignoring them. Eventually they'll give up."

"Sounds so easy," I mutter.

"You're doing good, princess," he says as he moves to the door and this really irks me. Like he's treating me like a little kid, even though minutes ago he was whispering in my ear about how I make him feel.

"Wait," I say, despite myself. "Is my dad downstairs?"

"He saw me bring you home."

This is a surprise to me. "You didn't just, what's the word, sift me into my bedroom unseen?"

He shrugs. "If I did that, your father would hear us talking up here anyway. Doesn't make much sense. No, I sifted you into the Knightlys' living room, then I took you over here. You told your father you weren't feeling well and I said I was bringing you to your room."

"And he just let you do that?"

He almost looks proud of himself. "Invited me over for dinner too," he says. "But I had to turn him down. You're eighteen, Ada. Pretty sure you're allowed to have a man around you. Back in the day, you would have been my bride at sixteen."

"Back in the day?" I repeat. "You're a rookie. You're brand new."

"Back in anyone's day," he says quickly as he pulls the door toward him.

"Jay," I call out after him, wishing my voice didn't sound so needy.

He pauses and eyes me curiously.

"Um," I say, scratching absently at my arm, the horrors of earlier all too close. "This might sound weird. And it's definitely not something my dad would be okay with, no matter how 'back in the day' you make your argument. But...do you mind spending the night with me? In here. I don't want to sleep alone. I'm too afraid of what might happen. In my dream or otherwise."

His brow softens. "Of course."

But then he's out the door.

. . .

Dinner is kind of awkward with my dad.

First of all, he's made a meal I just can't eat. Rare steak. The sight of the blood running out with each slice makes me want to gag, brings back images of Jay fighting with the demon.

So there's that.

Then there's the fact that my dad isn't talking much. This isn't new, but you'd think he'd at least be more interested in my day other than "you feeling any better?" You'd think that he'd want to discuss Jay in some way.

So I sit there and push the steak around and am about to make up some excuse to leave the table when he says, "Jay seems like a nice...man."

I raise my brow at him while I take a sip of water. "He is nice."

"How old is he?"

Ah, I knew he'd be worried about that.

"I don't know," I say honestly. "Maybe twenty-five." I'm shooting for the lower end even though he's ageless. "But it's cool, dad. I'm not with him like that. He's just a friend."

He nods thoughtfully. "I'm not worried. I can tell by looking at him that he's not interested in you that way. He's also older than twenty-five."

Ouch. Well gee thanks, dad. I'm going to pretend that wasn't a blow to my ego. I'll also pretend I don't feel a twang of disappointment.

"But," he goes on, shoving the last of his steak in his mouth and taking his time chewing, "he's still older and you're just eighteen. I just want you to be smart. I don't want to be overprotective, pumpkin, but you're all I've got."

Oh geez. Please don't let me dad get any more emotional because today I can't handle it.

"I'll be fine," I tell him. "It's nice to have a friend... someone close by."

He stares absently out the window, the sky darkening in the distance. A couple of kids from down the street walk past, flashlights and Frisbees in their hands, probably heading to the Blue Lake disc golf course. They're laughing and teasing each other and enjoying the balmy summer night now that the storm has passed, the freedom before school begins.

School. I haven't even given it any thought. It seems so…useless now, to go to design school when I have to worry about demons and dreams.

But I have to. No matter what happens, I have to hang onto what I can. I won't be normal, but for the sake of my father, I'll try.

"Speaking of the neighbors," my father says. "I was thinking we should invite the Knightlys' over for dinner next week. Get to know them."

"Are Perry and Dex coming? Because he will flip if he can't probe the musical mind of Sage."

He grunts, wiping his chin with his napkin and throwing it on the empty plate. "No. They don't live here, we do. It's up to us to forge relationships with these people."

"Even though we're selling the house and might be moving soon."

He watches me for a moment, debating something, before sitting back in his chair and letting out an empty sigh. He takes off his glasses and starts polishing them with the edge of his sleeve.

"I'm not even sure if I want to sell the house anymore. I don't think the timing is right."

Now, a few weeks ago this would have been music to my fucking ears. But despite having the convenience of cool neighbors who won't think I'm crazy, plus having my god damn guardian angel, devil, whatever he is, within reaching distance, I've been leaning toward the idea of getting out of here. Somewhere else, where there aren't memories to hold me down, let alone a monster in the closet, has started to seem like a pretty good idea.

But though my dad has no idea about the closet portal (or maybe he does, but if he does, he'll never bring it up), I can see why the memories held here are both a reason to go and a reason to stay.

"Okay," I tell him as I get up, not wanting to do anything other than what he wants to do. This is how it will always be I think, this tip-toeing around, not wanting to upset each other because we're all we have in this house.

"You're not going to eat that?" he nods at the steak and before I can tell him no, he's spearing it with his fork and bringing it on to his plate. I briefly have a vision of the demon swiping its claws at Jay's arm, the way they cut through to the bone and yet, at some point between there and now, his wounds have miraculously healed.

I move to put the plate in the dishwasher when he says, softly, barely audible, "You know, grief takes shape in many different forms. It follows you. The loss. The pain. It's a ghost in its own right. Don't forget that, Ada."

I murmur something in agreement and head up the stairs, wishing it was just that easy.

It's almost midnight when I decide to go to sleep. I've spent the evening on my phone, scrolling through Facebook (Amy hadn't deleted me so that said something) and my IG feed, perusing the usual online stores for some pre-fall bargains that I really can't afford, and finally drawing up a sketch of an evening gown made from flames. Orange and red silk, layers of tulle, and a jeweled, low-cut neckline—perfect if you were going to the Oscars as Satan's date.

But really, I'm just wasting time. I'm waiting for Jay to appear and when my eyes start closing on themselves, that's when the air in the room changes.

If there was a barometer in here, it would go haywire. My skin prickles and I expect a flash of lightning but instead the air warps and shimmers, tiny splashes of light, and then Jay steps out of nowhere.

He just appears, like earlier today, and he brings with him a rush of cold air.

I stare at him for a moment.

He stares right back at me.

He's wearing black sweatpants and a white wife-beater, which would look thuggish on anyone else but him. In fact, his pants are of a rather thin variety, like a silk-cotton blend that shows *every* little detail.

I only notice this because of my fashion background.

Like, I know my fabrics.

I swear.

I immediately avert my eyes and if he's caught me staring at his dick print, he doesn't show it. In fact, I don't think he's even capable of feeling anything close to embarrassment or shame.

Then again, he did say that being around me made him *feel*.

Feel what, I don't know.

Maybe that's the real reason I wanted him to stay over.

I realize I finally have to say something because this whole staring into each other's souls thing is only pulling my head into a tailspin (not to mention my hormones).

"Took you long enough," I say with just enough edge to my voice.

"Sorry," he says, not sounding sorry at all. "I was caught up with something."

My heart skitters. "Hopefully not another demon."

He shakes his head. "No, just Jacob." He looks around. "So, uh…"

Right. How did we want to do this? More like, how did I want to do this?

Oh my god. It's awkward already.

"Look," I tell him, "I was just scared earlier. You don't have to stay the night. I'm fine, really."

He cocks his head, a wisp of a smile. "I'm staying. You asked. I'm here."

I should protest some more. But honestly, as weird as this all is, I'm glad he's insisting on it.

"Get some rest," he says. "Nothing is going to hurt you. I won't let it. You know this now, don't you?"

Did I fucking ever. And I try not to thrill over his protective words.

Nothing is going to hurt you. I won't let it.

I'm going to start swooning any moment if I'm not too careful.

But I don't pull the covers over me. "Are you just going to stand there?"

His eyes go to the easy-chair in the corner that I nicknamed Pinkie. It used to be downstairs, back when I was kid, and I convinced my parents to bring the ugly pink recliner with the stuffing coming out of one corner to my room. Now Pinkie is a million colors and textures, having to be subjected to years of sewing experiments.

Yet as much as it was a good chair, it isn't right for him to sleep on it. I don't even think his bulky frame would fit.

"I'm here to watch you, not sleep," he says, as if knowing what I'm thinking.

"You have no idea how creepy that sounds, do you?" I ask, watching as he walks past the foot of the bed toward the chair. He moves with such ease, like each movement is silk, calculated to use minimal exertion. Despite his dark cinnamon hair, his limbs are tanned, the muscle distracting. This is the first time I'm really seeing him without a long-sleeved shirt or leather jacket and I can't take my eyes away.

Which, naturally, is only adding to the tension in the room. I'm completely aware that the tension is only in my head, totally unfelt by him, but it's enough.

He eases down in Pinkie. I was right. He barely fits. But he doesn't look uncomfortable. I wonder if it's some supernatural ability to just adjust to every single situation, every single chair that life gives you.

"Get some rest," he says.

I can't help but laugh. "Is this so if my father walks in here, you won't get your ass kicked?"

He raises his brow, a wry twinkle to his pale eyes. "Is your father known for that?"

"He's punched Dex in the face before."

"That doesn't surprise me."

I chew on my lip, thinking, stalling even. The moment I turn off the bedside lamp, the moment this ends. I like having Jay in my room, his company, talking to him like he's just some normal guy.

"What are you going to do?" I pause. "Do you sleep?"

"We already went over this," he says. "I sleep. I do whatever else humans do, because I am, more or less, human."

Yet the fact that he says that only brings out the fact that he's not. Humans should never have to clarify what they are.

"Not everything," I say under my breath.

"What was that?"

I try and think of a less nosy, less awkward way of saying this. "You obviously don't have sex."

The words seem to explode over the room. I regret opening my mouth and yet I'm watching him closely for his response.

He frowns at me, adjusting himself in the chair, the muscles in his biceps popping. "What makes you so sure I don't have sex?"

Actually nothing. I just want to know. Because he's here in my room and for better or for worse, I should know just what kind of a man he is. For safety reasons. I swear.

"Don't you take an oath?"

He lets out a soft laugh. "An oath? There is no ceremony. We aren't sworn in. We just...are."

"So there are no rules then?"

"There are rules," he says carefully. "Mainly common sense."

"So have you had sex or not?"

"Have you?" he counters.

Tables have turned. "That's none of your business," I say stiffly.

"Then my sex life—or lack thereof—is certainly none of yours. It's irrelevant to our relationship."

"Doesn't sound like a fun relationship." Okay, I know I'm being overly bold now but there's something about our dynamic that has me wanting to keep pushing. Find out where our boundaries are. I have a good idea.

"But...do you feel it? Do you have those desires?"

He swallows at that and looks away and I think he's a bit uncomfortable for once. Good. I like seeing him more human, not this immortal, perfect being.

"We have instincts," he says, his eyes swinging back to mine, blazing with something dark. "Some more *animalistic* than others."

Now it's my turn to swallow. Jesus. I'm not sure if he meant that to come across the way it did but suddenly I'm glad he's way over on the chair. Not that I'm scared of him. I'm scared of me. That look, those words...I'm throbbing everywhere, like he's driven a beam of heat between my legs.

I'm not myself lately. And I can't be trusted.

"Good night, Jay," I tell him, reaching over for the lamp.

"Good night, princess," he says his voice rich and throaty.

The room goes dark.

CHAPTER THIRTEEN

I've never seen my dad fret over a dinner so much.

It's been exactly one week since he had the idea to invite the Knightlys over. Of course they accepted when the both of us went over to ask, my father and I appearing on their doorstep like door-to-door salesmen.

As would luck would have it though, Jacob answered first and by the time Dawn and Sage came to the door, looking very happy to see us, Jacob and Jay had both gotten invites as well.

Then came a week of trying out recipes, getting new kitchen supplies, going through the old china and silverware and place settings. Either my father has been hard-up for new friendships since mom passed, or he subconsciously gets how important it is to have people like the Knightlys next door, people who understand this crazy fucked world.

My week was blissfully uneventful. After Jay spent the night (and somehow I slept the whole night through, no dreams, no midnight bathroom breaks) we ended up being rather inseparable. I don't know if it's because I was putting out signals that I wanted him around (*need* is such a strong word) or that he felt the need to protect me but either way it meant where I went, he went.

Of course I didn't mind. In fact, I'd grown accustomed to spending every minute with him. It's not just the constant eye candy or the way he makes me laugh at the most absurd things. It's something else, something deeper, that I can't quite put my finger on without sounding like a total asshole.

He may not have spent the night again after that first time, but we did go and play disc golf once (he kicked my ass). He drove me to the school so I could pick up a package from registration and we had a look around where my future career might be born. We even moved the rest of my stuff out of the old bedroom and into the new one, turning Perry's bedroom to the giant walk-in closet.

Speaking of closet, the whole area felt completely benign. Whereas before I could almost feel evil lurking behind it, now it seems like a closet. But I was still not moving back and I refused to even be in that bedroom by myself.

Somehow, Jay made everything safe. But I didn't want to test just how safe he made me.

"Ada, they'll be here any minute!" my dad yells from downstairs.

I'd spent the last few hours helping him in the kitchen (he decided on rack of lamb after the Knightlys assured him that no one was a vegetarian) and have only had a few minutes to try and make myself presentable before the "guests" come.

"I'll be right there!" I yell from the bathroom, staring at my reflection with a sigh. I've been sleeping a lot better lately—no bad dreams—so my dark circles are pretty much gone with a hefty dose of concealer. But still...there's something almost foreign about my face. It's like I've aged in the last few weeks. Not in a bad way—I still think I've got it going on (even if Jay doesn't seem to think so), but it's at least noticeable to me.

I add some hot pink matte lipstick, realizing it's the first time in a while I've made a real effort with makeup (a fact that the old me would be having a hissy fit over), then go into my room and quickly rifle through my clothes, looking for something sexy yet suitable. It's not that I'm trying to impress Jay tonight but...okay. Well. Maybe there's a small part of me that wants to show myself off in a different light. You know, not the student (although the giant ginger hasn't taught me anything) and not the damsel in distress. And not just an ordinary eighteen-year old girl.

I want him to see me as a woman.

And *I know*. I know that's completely ridiculous, not to mention probably taboo. I mean, he never came right out and said that...you know what? No. Not going to even indulge myself with these thoughts. The man can have animalistic sexual instincts all he wants but that doesn't mean he'll ever use them on me.

A damn shame.

I end up picking a black dress (I can't stop looking like Morticia Adams lately). It's low-cut and even though my boobs are on the small-side, I think collarbones are sexy and the thin lacey straps hint at lingerie without being totally out of place for a family dinner. I add a gold Grecian belt around my waist and then slip on a pair of leather snakeskin flats in a similar gold-tone and admire myself in the mirror. I put my hair up, something rare for me, but eschew any jewelry.

I look pretty good.

Eat your heart out, J.J. Abrams.

I take in a deep breath and head out the room and into the hallway and...

Creak.

Panic rushes up my spine.

The door to my old room, Perry's room, slowly creaks open as I pass it.

I go still, my skin erupting in goosebumps, my eyes stuck to the door.

Creeeeak.

It opens a little bit more.

I want to blame it on the wind. A breeze coming in through the window. But today is humid and heavy, the air as still as my body is right now.

Move, I tell myself. *Stop staring at it. Keep walking.*

Yet I still stand there.

The door creaks open just a little bit more, the sliver of room growing. I see the edge of the bed. One of the windows.

A tall shadow in the corner.

Then the door starts to shut, blocking the shadow out before I can get a better look at it.

"Ada," my mother whispers from inside the room.

"Ada!" my father yells from downstairs.

Before I can think, I'm running down the stairs at a rapid rate and practically spilling into the kitchen, breathless, my heart running away on me.

What just happened?

VEILED

"A little help?" my dad chides me, turning around with the rack of lamb between his hands. He frowns at me. "What's with you?"

I shake my head, trying to compose myself, trying to ignore the knot of cold clay in my stomach. "Fine. I'm fine."

"Well, help me set the table then," he says, before giving me the eye. "Is that what you're wearing?"

I roll my eyes and grab the homemade mint jelly from the counter, yet I'm secretly relieved that his ribbing is putting things back to normal.

Five minutes later, the neighbors are ringing the doorbell.

"Answer it!' my dad howls from the kitchen, having a last minute problem with the wild rice side dish.

"I was going to anyway!" I yell back, feeling myself slip into fifteen-year old mode at the worst time. I close my eyes, breathing in deeply through my nose, then open the door.

Dawn and Knightly are on the stoop, Jay and Jacob lingering on the path behind them.

Dawn holds up a tin-foil covered tray and smiles with perfect white teeth. "Dulce le leche cheesecake. Sage says it's the best you'll ever try."

I offer them a smile that I hope isn't shaky. "And what do you say it is?"

"Pretty good," she says with a laugh. "Sage is the expert in all things sweet."

"Especially you," he says warmly, kissing her forehead. She giggles like a child in response.

Aw. How disgusting.

I welcome them in, relieved to see they've somewhat dressed up. Dawn is wearing grey slacks and a silk green sleeveless top, her arms pale, slender and covered with freckles. She kind of reminds me of an older Julianne Moore, same kind of smile and calm energy. Sage is wearing khakis and a black and grey Hawaiian shirt. And flip-flops.

I try not to dwell on his footwear and glance at Jacob and Jay who are still on the path, as if they only planned to escort the Knightlys over and are about to head back.

"Well are you coming in or what?" I ask them, hand on my hip.

They exchange a glance I can't read. Typical.

Normally my eyes would be fixed to Jay but Jacob looks more cagey than normal. It doesn't help that his suit is pale green, his dress shirt underneath bright orange. The man really needs a new wardrobe, I don't care if he's been to Hell and back.

"Well?" I repeat. I can feel Sage and Down hovering behind me in the foyer.

Jay shoots me an apologetic smile. It nearly makes me weak at the knees. "Sorry. We don't want to intrude."

I tick off my fingers. "A, you were invited. And B, if you don't come in, all that extra lamb is going to go to waste and you don't want to see my dad when he's angry."

Jacob gives Jay an ever-so subtle nod and then smiles charmingly at me. "Of course, love."

They come inside, Jay brushing up so close against me as he passes that my stupid girly brain is trying to figure out if it's intentional or not. Also, he smells fucking amazing and I have to pretend that I'm not breathing in a huge whiff of his deliciousness.

Christ, this is worse than high school.

My dad comes out of the kitchen before I can make a fool of myself. Even though everyone knows each other, polite introductions are made again (with Jacob thanking him profusely for inviting the "renters") and everyone takes a seat at the dining room table. My dad and I are at the heads of the table, which reminds me, in a creepy way, that I'm posed like my mother.

The usual pleasantries are exchanged as my dad displays the food ("Oh, that looks delicious, I haven't had rack of lamb in so long" from Dawn and "You shouldn't have gone through all this trouble for us" from Sage) and everyone settles in nicely.

I watch my father closely as he folds his hands and bows his head. He looks up, shooting me a sheepish look that also says *is this inappropriate?* Saying grace is very important to him.

"Dad," I announce, clearing my throat. "Would you like to say Grace?"

A flash of relief flits across his brow. "Yes, sure," he looks at the others. "Do you mind?"

Every mumbles no, of course not, even Jay and Jacob who, for all their godliness and demon dealings, don't strike me as the type. Then again, I'm pretty sure Jacob owes the man upstairs something big for getting him out of Hell and all.

My father leads the Lord's Prayer, short and simple, with a low voice brimming with reverence. Everyone has their head bowed and I sneak a peek at Jay who is sitting to the left of me, his knee brushing against mine every so often.

He's watching me, eyes transfixed.

I blink at him, trying to smile but there's something terribly off-putting at the way he's gazing at me. It's like he doesn't really see me. More than that, it's like it's not really him. I have the distinct and unnerving feeling that I'm staring at a stranger.

And he's not a good man.

Then Jay suddenly shakes his head, like he was lost in a daydream, gives me a startled smile and goes back to praying, or at least paying lip service.

"Amen," everyone says and I repeat it absently. I can't quite get that unsettled feeling out of my chest.

Dad starts passing out the plates, lamb headed down one way via Sage, rice headed down the other via Jacob. But now it's Jacob's face I'm paying attention to as everyone else starts talking about the food and murmuring thanks.

He's agitated. While he's smiling here and there as he listens to the conversations, he keeps fidgeting in his seat, twirling his tacky gold watch around his wrist, eyes darting around as if listening to conversations coming from outside the room.

I think my father picks up on this because he watches him for a moment before he asks. "So are you and Jay related? Father and son?"

This makes Jacob laugh, putting him at ease for a second. Even Jay smiles.

"No. But he often feels like a son to me," Jacob explains. "Won't bloody do what I tell him!"

They both burst out laughing like it's the funniest thing on earth and pretty soon everyone else is joining in. But beneath the laughter, I can see the strain in everyone's eyes, like this is just for show. It makes me wonder what has everyone on edge, or if we're all just feeding off of each other.

"And Dawn, Sage," my father says, pointing his fork at them. "How did you two meet?"

The couple exchanges a look with raised brows. I know what they're trying to figure out—which story to tell.

"It's a funny story," Sage says, giving him a jovial smile and I already know which version my dad is getting. "Dawn was a music journalist sent to cover our tour. She rode on the bus with us and everything, all freckles and long limbs and unruly hair, asking all the wrong questions, digging for soundbites. I truly hated her."

Dawn nudges Sage in the side, her smile lines deepening. My eyes go to Jacob, who I now know was there on that tour, but he's not paying attention at all. It's as if he's still listening to something none of us can hear and he doesn't look too happy about it.

"So it wasn't love at first sight?" my dad asks. Despite what's going on, my heart melts for him. I know it was that way for him and mom.

"Oh, it was," Sage concedes. "I just didn't know it yet."

"And I was in love with him before I even met him," Dawn adds. "Every girl worth their salt, or with at least great taste in music, had a poster of Hybrid on their wall."

My dad then goes on to talk about actor Gregory Peck and how his wife was a journalist sent to interview him. Then Dawn brings the conversation around to me and my fashion blogging, my design aspirations.

When we're almost done with the lamb and some of us are practically licking the plates, Sage excuses himself to use the bathroom down the hall.

"And Jay," my father says. "What kind of job are you in the market for?"

I stare at Jay, not sure what he's going to say, then give my father a look, thinking he's being too nosy.

But Jay is cool and collected as always. "I'm looking for freelance work. I'm a graphic designer."

Graphic designer? That's the first I've heard of this. Then again, he could be flat-out lying and I wouldn't know. In fact, I wager he is lying.

Dad pretends to be impressed. "Interesting. I guess you would work from home then."

"That's the plan," he says with ease, "Got a few jobs lined up already."

I nudge him under the table to say *that's true?* but he ignores me. I'm tempted to reach down and give his leg a squeeze when Sage comes back over, his brow furrowed in thought.

"Are Dex and Perry here?" Sage asks casually as he sits back down.

I roll my eyes. God. Always Dex and Perry. All anyone ever wants to talk about are Dex and Perry.

"No, they're back in Seattle," Dad says before taking a sip of wine. "Should pop by next month."

"So there's no one else in the house?" he asks, a thread of worry in his voice.

My heart stammers. "What? No. Why?"

"Nothing," he says as he looks to my dad. "Thought I heard talking coming from upstairs. I'm sure it's the TV or something."

"I'm sure," my father says even though I was the last one upstairs and I know there was no TV on.

I think the others know this too, judging by the deepening scowl on Jacob's face, the way Jay's attention has turned to me now, asking with his eyes if this is something we should be worried about.

Then...

DOO-DO-DO-DO-DO!

Horn instruments erupt from the kitchen, the swing big band music of what can only be Glen Miller comes blaring, making us all jump in our seats.

"Goodness," my dad says, hand at his heart. He shakes his head as he gets up, shoots everyone an apologetic smile. "I thought I turned the radio off! Sorry about this."

My heart is bouncing around like it's in a squash court now. My dad listens to AM when he's cooking but I know for sure he turned the radio off earlier on when he was concentrating on the mint sauce.

He heads to the kitchen and the moment he's out of earshot—which isn't a problem considering how loud those trumpets are—Jacob leans in and says, "I don't like this. I didn't like it before and I don't like it now. We're pushing our luck."

"Why, what is it?" Dawn asks, worry lines appearing on her forehead.

Suddenly the music turns off and my dad comes back in the room before Jacob can continue. "Strangest thing," he mutters to himself as he comes. "The radio was already off. I had to turn it on and then back off again to make it stop."

"That sounds like it defies the laws of physics, dad," I tell him, wishing for once that he wouldn't find a rational explanation for every damn thing.

"It's an old radio," he warns, eyes cutting into mine over the tops of his glasses. I know the last thing he wants is for me to bring up ghosts and the supernatural. Oh, if only he knew who he was dining with.

He's just about to sit back down when Dawn slowly gets out of her chair. "Maybe this is a good time to bring out the—"

She's cut off.

Because the lights flicker and then die, the entire house is plunged into darkness.

Dawn lets out a gasp.

I yelp.

"What on earth now?" My dad cries out in the blackness.

"Power failure," Jacob says in a flat-voice that I find even creepier considering I can't see a god damn thing.

"Why would the power go out?' I ask, my voice getting shrill with fear. "Is it just our house?"

It's past eight pm and the sun has set, though there should be enough twilight coming through the dining room window. Yet the room is so dark, it's like someone has put blackout drapes on.

Finally, a light comes on, a blinding stream from Sage's iPhone. He quickly flashes it around the table and checks to make sure everyone is here, the whites of his eyes shining with a fear I know is familiar to him.

"Where's your breaker?" he asks my dad.

"In the basement," my dad says. "I'll go take a look. Maybe I did something screwy when I was fiddling with the radio."

"No," I say quickly and the flashlight blinds me. I shield my eyes until Sage lowers it. "It's dangerous to go down there in the dark. Maybe the whole block is out?"

"I'll go with you," Sage tells him, getting out of his chair. "Supply the light."

I still don't want my dad to go anywhere, let alone the basement. It's a place I avoid like the plague, always afraid I'll get to the bottom and the door will close on me.

The two of them walk off, the light flashing off the walls. For a moment I think I see a shadow standing in the corner, its back to us, motionless. Then the light is gone and everything is black again.

I left my phone upstairs but Jacob pulls his out and shines it around the table. Just four of us now. I can hear my dad stumble over something down the hall, Sage asking if he's all right, then the sound of the basement door opening.

"Why is the power out?" I ask Jacob, leaning forward in my seat until my breasts are practically on the table. There's this dark cavern of emptiness at my back that feels dense and immeasurable, like a million shadows are lurking, staring at my exposed spine.

"I don't know," he says, voice still flat, eyes beady in the darkness. "I'm sure we'll find out soon though."

"Day-O," Jay sings softly under his breath. "Me say *daaaay*-O."

"That's not funny!" I hiss at him, not even bothering to ask when he managed to watch *Beetlejuice*. I half expect the lamb carcass to reassemble itself and start doing a jig to the Banana Boat song.

"What were you saying earlier?" Dawn asks Jacob. She can't hide the fear in her voice either and probably isn't too happy that Sage volunteered to take my dad to the basement.

"I was saying," Jacob begins. Then he pauses, head cocked. Listening again.

"What is it?" I ask. When Jacob raises his finger to shush me, I turn to Jay. "Jay. What's going on, what's happening?"

He's watching Jacob closely too, gives me a slight shake of his head.

"The power is only off in this house," Jacob finally says. He looks me dead in the eye, a sly grin twisting his mouth. "This was a bad idea."

SLAM!

A door slams shut from somewhere in the house, causing us to flinch, even Jacob.

The noise is followed by echoing footsteps.

Shouts.

"Hey!" Sage yells, muffled from the basement stairway.

We all get out of our seats, Jacob with the light which leaves me banging my hip into the edge of the table.

"Motherfucking shitfuck," I swear, grabbing my side.

Then Jay's taking my hand and holding on tight.

"Stay with me," he murmurs in my ear. "There's something not right here. I can smell it."

"You mean literally?" I ask as he leads me out of the dining room and down the hall where Jacob is shining a light on the basement door.

He grunts his answer.

"The door won't open," Sage says from the other side and the doorknob turns back and forth in vain. He pounds on the door again.

"We're here," Jacob says, passing the phone to Dawn and seeing if he can open it. "Are you both all right?"

"Yes," my father says, his voice sounding weak.

"Why don't you go back down and try the breaker, I'll try and fix the door," Jacob says.

A muffled agreement comes through and the sound of their footsteps as they walk back down into the basement.

Jacob lets go of the knob and looks at us, his face ghostly white in the light Dawn's holding. I wonder if this is how so many of Perry and Dex's shows started out. Only they didn't have two Jacobs with them, which should make me feel safer but it doesn't at all.

Well actually that's not true. Jay is still holding my hand and I'm pressed up right against him, afraid to stray from his body heat for even a second.

"It's trying to separate us," Jacob says grimly.

"It?" Dawn and I cry out in unison.

Jay squeezes my hand harder, his body stiffening against mine.

Then...

Laughter.

From upstairs.

Cold, sinister, utterly inhuman laughter.

Familiar but not familiar.

Primitive.

Every cell in my body revolts, terror striking my marrow.

"Oh god," Dawn says softly. "What is that?" She looks back to the door, the phone shaking in her hand. "I have to get to Sage."

"He'll be safer in there than out here," Jacob says. "You know to trust me on this, don't you, Rusty?" He looks to me. "Ada, stay with Jay."

I wouldn't dream of protesting.

Especially when a light from upstairs goes on. The hall light outside my bathroom. It shines down the stairs, illuminating the bottom.

A shadow passes through the beam, someone walking along the upper hallway.

I can't. Even. Breathe.

Then it goes dark again.

Light to black.

It was just enough to let us know that it's there, whatever it is.

And it's *waiting.*

Jacob starts walking away, down the hall toward the stairs, in slow, controlled movements.

"Don't you need your phone?" Dawn hisses softly, holding it out to him with a shaking hand.

He only raises his arm in dismissal before he disappears out of reach of the light. I'm pretty sure Jacob can see in the dark. I'm pretty sure Jay can too.

I'm pretty sure there are some things in the dark that we're not meant to see.

The three of us wait outside the basement door like we are in some kind of limbo. My dad and Sage are stuck in the basement. Jacob is walking up the stairs to tussle with some monster.

"Now what?" I whisper. "What's he going to do?"

I hear Jay swallow thickly. "Something like I did last week. I'm not really sure. Jacob warned me about tonight, saying that there would be too much energy in one place. It would bring the demons out of the portal and whatever else has been lying dormant on the other side of these walls and the walls you can't see."

"Oh my god," I cry out. "Why did you come over then?"

"We were debating," he says. "But we couldn't know for sure."

"I'm so sorry," Dawn says. "I had no idea."

"Don't be sorry," Jay says quickly. "It's better this way."

The laughter erupts again, seeming to come from all corners of the house, our heads swiveling around trying to find the source.

"How is it better this way?" I ask incredulously, so close to peeing my pants. The laughter feels like its permeating my very soul, turning it sour and black. "I can't stand this!"

"Easy now," he whispers to me. "I've got you." He glances at Dawn and then holds his hand out for her. "Come here. Nothing is going to happen to you either."

She takes it and if I wasn't scared shitless, I'd be swooning a little over Jay, taking an older woman's hand and making her feel safe.

And so there we are, two girls in the dark, hanging onto his hands for dear life.

"Is Jacob going to be okay?" I ask. "I don't hear anything."

Even the laughing has stopped. Upstairs sounds like radio silence.

"Jacob will always be okay," Jay tells me soberly.

"You can say that again," Dawn says, trying to sound light about it but failing.

"Because he's immortal like you," I point out to Jay.

"More or less."

"But what if his head gets chopped off?"

Jay gives me a strange look. "If his head gets chopped off? I don't know."

"What if *your* head gets chopped off?" Not the most appropriate question considering the circumstances, but hey it's preventing me from thinking about what's really going on. AKA, it's preventing me from really losing my shit. Besides, I've always wondered.

"You are such a morbid girl," he comments, almost sounding amused.

"You rip the heads off demons and travel to a dead world," I tell him. "You shouldn't talk. Also, you're not answering my question."

"Well," he says, licking his lips. "I assume I would die. I would at least hope I'd die. I don't want to operate with my head doing one thing and my body doing another."

"Why not, most guys are like that." I pause. "So if you can die, then you're not really immortal are you?"

He sighs. "Semantics."

"But vampires—"

"Can we not talk about this right now?" Dawn pleads.

Suddenly there are knocks at the door beside us.

A scream dies in my throat.

"Breaker isn't doing anything," comes Sage's voice. This time there's a tremor in it. "And, um, I think we're not alone down here."

Oh. My. God. My dad.

"Dad are you okay?" I cry out.

"Yes sweetie," I hear him say, though his tone is equally as strained. "I think there's a raccoon down here. A rabid one. Must have gotten in somehow and..."

I glance at Jay. We both know that's not a fucking raccoon.

Jay promptly takes my hand and gives it to Dawn. "Don't let go of each other." He turns to face the door squarely. "Stand back from the door," he commands.

"But that means going down to the racoon," my dad says shakily. There is something so terrible in knowing two grown men are scared.

"Come on," Sage says and I hear them walking down. He's trying to sound brave. "Mid-way, it's enough." He pauses. "Okay Jay. *Hurry*."

Jay comes at the door foot forward, easily stomping the door open with one quick blow. The door swings hard against the wall and comes off the top hinges, the front of the door caved in where Jay's boot met it.

There are a few seconds where I'm sure something has happened to them, where they don't appear and it's only dust motes floating among the iPhone beam.

Then comes my dad, face pale and shiny with sweat, and Sage, who towers over him but looks equally as rattled. Sage nods back at the door.

"We might want to find a way to keep that closed for now," he says edgily.

Jay nods, reaching past him and pulling the door shut. I'm not sure what exactly we're supposed to do now with something in the basement *and* something upstairs, when suddenly all the lights go on with an electrical CRACK!

The house hums back to life. The fridge in the kitchen, the fan in the living room.

The five of us stare at each other in that relieved kind of way, like all fears are erased in the light.

But I know that's not true. There's still something to be done about the basement and the upstairs and I'm about to ask if we should check on Jacob when he comes back down the stairs, wiping his hands.

"Power is back on," he says, charming smile on his face. "Wish I still felt like having desert."

"No, no," my dad says, his shoulders slumping as he walks down the hall. "That's perfectly all right. After all that, I've lost my appetite. Plus I have a raccoon in the basement to deal with now. I better call pest control."

He goes into the kitchen and I hear him talking to someone when Jacob grabs my arm and leans down toward me, the smile wiped off his face. "I was able to fix this temporarily but you need to get out of here now."

"What, why?" I ask, eying his grip on my arm.

He looks over my head at Jay. "You need to take her away for a few days. Three. Maybe five. This house needs to be cleared of all the energy in here. There's been too much with all of us, it's like a bloody feast for them and they will continue to feed off you Ada, long after we all leave."

"Where am I supposed to go? I start school in two weeks, I have to start preparing for that."

"You'll figure it out," he says, more to Jay than to me. "But listen. If you leave, I can close it permanently. Your dad will be safe, don't worry. I'll keep an eye on him. But he won't be if you stay. And neither will you."

I try to breathe. Everything is happening so fast. "I. I guess I can go to Dex and Perry's."

"No," he says sharply. "Not right away, not yet. They're looking for you closer now. They *know* you. Being around Perry and Dex is too dangerous, the three of you have two much power between you." He jerks his thumb at Sage and Dawn who are standing nearby, watching this unfold. "Just like them. All of us together like this is a recipe for disaster and it's my fault for letting it happen."

"Well then why the hell did you guys move next door!?" I exclaim.

Jacob gives me a dry look. "For your protection on all levels. But we can't predict everything."

"Oh really? Finally something you can't do." I sigh and rub my hand down my face, stopping before I smear my lipstick. "Okay. I'll go. Do I have time to pack? I don't even want to go back up there. What do I tell my dad?"

"Jay will pack for you," Jacob says, nodding at him. Jay obeys and goes running up the stairs, taking them two at a time with ease.

"Oh my god, he doesn't know what I want to wear!" I cry out. Not to mention he's going to have to rifle through my underwear drawer. Fuck. I hope all the dirty laundry is in the hamper.

Bigger things going on here, Ada, focus.

"Your dad," Jacob continues, ignoring me, "tell him that you're going out to the movies. Then call him later and tell him you're spending the night at a friend's house. Then lie some more. You're his daughter, love, I'm pretty sure you know how to get away with murder."

"And the raccoon?" Sage asks, gesturing to the door.

Jacob gives him a crooked smile. "That wasn't a raccoon but I think you know that, old boy. No matter. It's not there anymore. The pest people will come but they won't find a trace."

"Like it's all so easy," I mutter.

"Oh no, love," Jacob says grimly. "Going forward, nothing will be easy."

CHAPTER FOURTEEN

"What if your arm gets chopped off? Can you grow a new one?"

I don't have to see Jay's eyes in the darkness to know he's probably rolling them. "Again, I don't know," he says. "And I'm not about to find out."

It's been like this the entire drive to...actually I'm still not sure where we are going. The moment Jacob told us to get out of the house, we did. My dad didn't seem to have a problem with me leaving to spend time with "Amy," especially when Jacob volunteered to help him clean up. Jay packed for me, the duffel bag is in the backseat of Jacob's Mercedes which we were told to borrow.

Jay's been driving for about two hours and all I know is we're heading toward the coast. Cannon Beach, maybe. But the road along highway 26 is dark and winding and even though I'm sure Jay could drive all night, I'm nodding off here and there. Hence all my questions.

I guess it happens again because my chin hits my chest and I'm jolted awake as gravel crunches under the tires.

We've pulled into a parking lot of a roadside motel. In the dark it looks epically creepy and I have half a mind to tell Jay I'll sleep in the car because I've had just enough creepy for one day.

"It's nearly midnight," Jay says, turning off the engine and twisting in his seat to look at me. "We need some rest."

"Yeah but..." I say, staring at the motel.

It's not like the Bates Motel, thank god, but it was definitely built in the 50's or 60's. A long sloping roof slicked with wet moss, water dripping from the eaves even though it hasn't rained in a few days. There are ten rooms all facing out to the cars and an office at the end with a blinking neon sign.

"Looks like there's room," Jay says, there only being three cars in the lot.

"Yeah and probably with good reason," I tell him.

Still we both get out of the car and I grab the duffel from the backseat, along with his backpack. He eyes me over the roof of the Mercedes, his face looking sharp and white in the wane light of the single streetlight at the side of the empty highway. "Are you afraid of ghosts? Or just staying in a place that's not the Four Seasons?"

"Oh please," I scoff. "When the hell would I have stayed at a Four Seasons? And by the way, there are some hotels that combine luxury and the undead. Ever heard of The Benson in downtown Portland?"

He just nods at the office. "Come on, princess."

The office manager is a creep. Not in the "Welcome to my haunted hotel" kind of way and not in the wide-eyed, "I'm a good boy with secrets" Norman Bates kind of way. But in the way that he's staring at my chest the whole time Jay is signing forms and paying for the room, to the point where he licks his dried lips.

"Eyes up here, buddy," Jay says sharply, pointing his pen at the manager and then at his own face. I'd never seen Jay look remotely murderous before, not even when demon fighting, but murderous seems a good way to describe his eyes now.

"Huh?" the manager looks up at him with a dull stare, oblivious to all except my non-existent chest. He snorts in something awful and swallows it down before handing the keys to Jay. "Room seven."

Gross. Gross. *Gross.*

I abruptly turn and step out into the night air, trying to keep my dinner down, Jay coming right after me, the blinds rattling on the glass door as it slams shut.

"What a fucking creep," I swear as we head down toward the room.

"Fuck if I'll let anyone look at you like that," he says, his voice taking on the lilting Irish accent again. It would be extremely flattering—his protectiveness—if this accent business didn't throw me off.

"Uh, Irish accent alert," I tell him as we stop outside the door.

He frowns and gives me a quick glance while he fiddles with the keys. "What are you on about?"

"You sounded Irish again. You know. *Top of the morning to you, I'm a leprechaun,*" I say, myself sounding like a fucking Lucky Charms commercial.

"That's racist," he comments as the door opens. A whiff of musty air comes forward. He flicks on the lights showcasing a hotel room with a Super 8 meets mountain lodge appeal. Which is to say, no appeal at all. Thick yellowing curtains, a green carpet with a myriad of stains, a double bed with itchy looking bedspread. Shitty paintings of trees and pheasants adorn the walls.

Wait. Back up.

Double bed.

"Should we go get a room with two beds?" I squeak.

He steps in the room. "If I go back in there, I'll ending up punching that guy in the face."

Now that he didn't sound Irish, I take a moment to revel in his possessiveness. I like my alpha males and I'm not ashamed to admit it.

He locks the door behind us, slides the chain across, and then flicks on the noisy air conditioner underneath the window. The curtains dance. Then he throws his backpack on the bed and gives me a discerning look. "If you want me to sleep on the floor, I have absolutely no problems doing so."

"Don't be silly," I tell him, though the back of my brain is hemming over the fact that sleeping on the floor wasn't his first assumption. He automatically thought he'd be getting into bed with me. Which meant...

Well, probably nothing.

Unless...

Shut it, Ada.

I put my bag on my side of the bed and start rummaging through it, curious to see what he packed.

"Jay," I say slowly, flipping through my clothes faster and faster. "Did you pack me any actual clothes?"

I look up at him. He shrugs, bringing out those dangerously thin pajama pants of his from his backpack. "I just emptied a drawer."

"But this is all just bras and underwear," I tell him, holding them up in the air. Yes, I do have Victoria's Secret Angel Card. "Miraculously there's a pair of denim shorts in here but that's it."

He stares at me blankly. Although when Jay does blank, it's like he's still staring into your soul. "Guess you'll need to buy some clothes." He goes back to bringing things out of his bag and then pauses. "Sorry."

He says this like he's not used to apologizing. That might be true.

I sigh, loudly and like a little girl who hasn't gotten her way. It's the small things that comfort you when you're under epic stress and scared for your life, though I should be grateful for clean underwear because I have a feeling I'll need that most of all.

"Here," he says, reaching across the bed and handing me a t-shirt. "You can use that as a nightshirt."

I hold it up. It's a giant Led Zeppelin concert tee shirt. "Where did you get this?"

"Salvation Army," is his answer.

I hold it up to my nose and smell it. It smells like him, causing my heart to flutter.

"Do you listen to Led Zeppelin? Do you even know who they are?"

That stare again. "I'm not an alien, Ada. I know who they are, just as I know who most bands are. I have every album on my iPhone, from their self-titled all the way to Coda."

Well I feel stupid. "Good," I tell him. "That means you're not as weird as I thought."

Then before I say anything else, and before he keeps staring at me like that, I take the shirt and the duffel bag and head to the bathroom.

In here the tap is dripping and there are rust stains in the tub. The light is ghoulishly fluorescent and it takes forever for me to try and open up one of the little bars of soap.

I turn the water on until it's basically scalding and wash my face again and again and again. Jay luckily had the smarts to grab my tooth brush, toothpaste, deodorant and moisturizer, as well as my phone and my purse, which has my wallet, hairbrush and just enough makeup to make me look presentable tomorrow.

I sigh, trying to get air in my lungs, fighting against the feeling of the room spinning around on me. I'm too easily overwhelmed these days, but fuck if I don't have a good reason.

Putting down the toilet lid, I take a seat, my head in my hands and try to breathe. It's the first time I've been alone since dinner and my mind is chugging along, trying to catch up with all that's happened.

I texted my father during the drive, telling him I was going with Amy and her family to their cabin outside of Mount Hood. I've been there many times and he likes her parents, so even though it was an outright lie, he didn't question it too much. He did sound rattled though and I know that the dinner was weighing on him. It didn't quite go as he planned, plus there was the whole being trapped in the basement with Sage and a "raccoon." I know that had scared the pants off him.

Jay assured me that he would be all right, that Jacob would keep a close eye on him, as would Sage and Dawn, and that he was one hundred percent safer without me in the house for now. I believed that.

I wanted to tell Perry about it, maybe get her to come down and spend some time with him while I'm gone, but I'm not sure that would make anything better. She'd been texting and calling me every day for the past week, making sure I was okay and every single time I had to lie, resorting to snark and sarcasm to get her off my back. The truth is, I don't want her to worry and there's nothing she, nor Dex, can do, no matter how special they think they are.

A few times she did ask about Jay, though. Wondering if he was getting me to burn down houses like her Jacob had. I played it off like it was no big deal, that I rarely saw him but even with that, she would end that part of the conversation with "I don't trust him."

And in turn that always made me wonder if I should.

Just outside this bathroom door is a man who is supposed to protect—who *has* protected me—and yet I don't know a single thing about him. I guess he doesn't even know a single thing about himself.

Although that isn't true. He loves Led Zeppelin.

I sigh and take off the black dress that drew so much leering from the creepy manager (and yet zero leering from Jay, which is why I wore it to begin with) and slip on the Zeppelin tee shirt. Somehow it feels right, looks right, and is long enough to cover my butt. Not that he's a stranger to seeing me in my underwear.

I do my business—flicking on the fan and being extremely glad at how loud and rickety it is because the last thing I need right now is him hearing me—and then head back into the room.

Jay is lying in bed, the covers pulled over him, reading a book.

Shirtless.

My mouth drops open and I immediately clamp it shut.

He looks over the book to me, gives me a quick smile. "Are you doing okay?"

"Yup," I tell him, trying so hard not to stare at his chest. But I do, oh I do! "Just screwing my head on straight."

He nods and goes back to the pages.

I should walk over to the bed and get in on my side but I'm stuck here. My eyes are drawn to his chest.

It's massive. I knew it would be. Firm wide pecs, rippled abs you could grate cheese on, rounded shoulders, and everything just as it should be on a beast such as him (though with only a dusting of chest hair —he's not *that* much like a beast). And again, he's more tanned than I thought he would be, the summer sun being kind to him. He nearly glows golden in the light from the bedside lamp.

I feel his gaze on me and quickly bring my eyes to his. He raises his brow in question.

"Just trying to see what you're reading," I tell him, hurrying to my side of the bed.

"Milton," he says. "The graphic novel of Paradise Lost."

"You're kidding me," I say, throwing back the covers and peering at the book, glad for something to distract me from getting into bed with Jay.

He shows it to me. "It's graphic novel of Stephen King's The Gunslinger."

I can't help but give him a puzzled smile as I bring the stiff sheets over me. "I didn't know you liked those books. You're full of surprises tonight."

"You kept on calling the Thin Veil the "Thinny" so I decided I needed to know what you're were talking about." He pauses, cocking his head. "Not quite the same."

"That's good to know." I pull the rest of the blankets up, not really sure how I should sleep. My back to him seems like the best, least awkward way (especially as he then can't wake up to the sight of me drooling in my sleep), but it also seems a bit like a brush-off.

He decides it for me, shutting the book suddenly with a *thwap* and putting it on the table. He leans over to reach for the light switch on the lamp and I steal a glance of his torso as he twists in place, his muscles straining, the hint of boxer briefs under the sheets.

My god, he's mesmerizing.

The lights go off and I promptly roll to my side, eyes open and adjusting to the dim room. The air conditioner kicks off and then on again, loud, but I can still hear him breathing beside me.

I wonder if I should say something.

Good night?

Thank you?

I've never slept with a ginger before?

But all my words stay inside my head, my mouth dry, my body too tense to relax. Having him beside me like this is confusing. I feel like I'm going around and around, unsure how to deal with this, even though this is nothing more than two friends (partners?) sleeping beside each other.

Nothing more.

Then, out of nowhere:

"You looked beautiful tonight, by the way."

Oh jeez. Be still my fucking heart.

I try and swallow, his words, the sincerity in his voice rocking my world off-balance. "Which part? When the power went out or when Jacob went upstairs to fight a demon?" I joke. But I joke because I'm feeling this a little too much.

"All of it. You know why I call you princess?" he asks, his tone graver than before, like he's letting me in on a very deep secret.

"Because I'm a spoiled brat?"

"Because you're beautiful."

Well that shut me up. The sentence hangs in the air, larger than life.

He clears his throat and goes on and I have to fight against the urge to roll over and face him. "You have this way about you. You don't see it. But I do. Like you're born royalty. The way you hold yourself. Your walk. The face of an angel."

Butterflies take flight in my gut, spreading through my veins until my whole body feels like its floating. "Why are you being so nice to me? Am I going to die?"

He laughs softly. "I don't know why I'm saying these things. Just seemed like the things to say. You're destined for something great, Ada, I know this. And it's an honor to help see you through it."

His words cascade down on me like ashes from a fire. Where they land, I'm ignited.

Jay thinks I'm beautiful.

And more than that, he *believes* in me.

Silence settles over us, stealing time. I hear him breathing in the dark, steady as a heartbeat. He might even be sleeping.

But I can't even begin to shut down. My entire body, from the top of my scalp, down to my toes, is buzzing with heat and electricity. It's like everything I felt for him before, everything I try to ignore, is coming out in full force, responding to his words, to his body so close to mine. I can feel the warmth at my back, sinking into my spine, just from his presence alone.

I'm starting to have feelings for him. Not just in a he's a giant hulking beast who's here to protect me from the underworld way. But real feelings, slowly creeping into my heart, day by day.

The thought is terrifying in the same way that demons are terrifying.

They both might take possession of me.

They both might ruin me.

And I'm not sure how much of me I'll have left.

Stop being ridiculous, I chide myself.

I listen for a moment then say softly into the darkness, "Jay?"

He grunts in response.

"What happens after I reach my potential? When you're no longer my guardian?"

I don't know why I'm asking this. I think I want some kind of blow to the tender parts of myself, I want the truth to hurt, to warn me that my sudden stupid feelings are worthless and can only end in heartache or humiliation.

"I go on to help someone else." His voice is as soft as a cloud.

"Like, right away? Do I get a chance to say bye? Do I get to see you again after? You know, as a friend?"

He goes silent. I almost ask again, thinking he may have fallen asleep but with a heavy sigh he says, "No. As far as I'm aware, my memory is stripped. I start anew. I won't remember who you are."

I know he's said something like that before but for some reason I figured maybe I was an exception.

"Can you not? I mean, can you ask to have your memory for longer. I mean, why would it hurt you? If you go and help someone else, say some kid somewhere, how would staying friends with me interfere with that?"

"I guess because it's my job to commit to that person 100%. I don't think we're allowed outside attachments, other than other Jacobs."

Like Jacob himself. Forever the only constant in Jay's life. Would he have to start over getting to know him every single time too?

"I'd come find you, you know," I tell him.

"You say that now," he says. "But by the time this is all over, I'm sure you'll be more than happy to be rid of me."

I've been dreaming about Jay for a long time and I've been with him for a few weeks. In dreams, in the waking world, I feel like he's become as accepted as an extra limb. Awkward at first, ungainly, but later becoming a part of me that's indispensable. I can't imagine Jay not being beside me in some shape or form.

And that's fucked up, the naggy part of my brain goes. *To feel that attached to him already. That's not normal.*

"None of this is normal," I say out loud.

"You mean sleeping in a decrepit roadside motel with me as a way to escape the portal to Hell in your closet? No, I wouldn't say it's normal at all—for anyone else. You're going to have to adjust your reality. This is the new normal. I'm your new normal."

I don't know how long I ponder that. I think I see the moon pass through the curtains. Outside the highway is silent, no cars finding their way in the middle of the night.

"Jay?" I ask again.

"What?" he murmurs.

"Do you think maybe you were Irish in another life? Like your original life? And that's why you have an Irish accent sometimes?"

"I have no idea," he says tiredly. "Is that all?"

"Jay? Remember when you said I was beautiful?"

"Go to sleep, *princess.*"

And so I do.

CHAPTER FIFTEEN

Jay kissed me in my dream last night.

The details are fuzzy now, the dream draining from my head as soon as I woke up this morning, but the feeling is still there.

What I'm trying to figure out is if it was an ordinary dream where my subconscious conjured Jay up or if it was a dream where Jay inserted himself. I'm guessing that because I can't quite remember it, it's a normal one. All the other dreams are lucid to the point of being real.

Not that Jay is acting any different toward me this morning. When I finally woke up (and I'm pretty sure with a smile on my lips) it was because it was 10 a.m. and Jay was standing above me, telling me I needed to get a move on. He'd already showered and packed and was waiting for my sorry ass.

I showered as quickly as possible, shoving my wet hair in a bun since the room's hair-dryer didn't work, and decided to do my makeup in the car. I slipped on the same dress as last night—it was either that or wear a bra, and I'm not Carrie Bradshaw enough for that—but knotted it around my hips and added the denim shorts.

Actually it wasn't a bad look and, as we left the room heading toward the Mercedes, I tried to take a selfie or ten. Lame, maybe, but I hadn't posted to IG in a few days now and since I actually make money from my account for posting things like my outfits, then it's something I can't really neglect, demons or not.

"What are you doing?" Jay asks, leaning across the roof of the car and watching me curiously.

I chuck the duffel bag a few feet from me to get it out of the shot and try another angle, holding the iPhone far above my head. A lone scraggly-haired man in his pajamas exits his room, heading to the vending machine. He looks at me like I have a screw loose. Whatever. He probably takes dick pics so he should know all about getting the right angle.

"I'm trying to get a post to Instagram," I explain to Jay, refusing to feel self-conscious. "I have a brand to uphold, you know."

"Do you want me to take the picture?"

I pause, lowering the phone. "Would you mind?"

Normally I don't like anyone else take the photo because they have no idea what flattering angles are. I'd given the phone to Dex once and he took a photo of my boobs. Perry tends to shoot from angles that give me double-chins and fat arms, something I always suspected was sisterly sabotage.

"I'll give it a shot," he says, "no pun intended."

He comes around the hood of the car and takes the phone from my hands before motioning for me to turn around. "Stand in front of the doors. Look off to the left."

Huh? Direction. I like this.

I do as he says while he lines up the shot. Now the man by the vending machine is cracking open a Pepsi and watching the parking lot photo shoot. I give him a wink and go back to posing.

"Think I got it," Jay says when he's done, handing the phone back to me. "I'll take more if you want."

I quickly flip through the photos. I don't know how the fuck he managed to make this god forsaken place look like an editorial shoot for Vogue, but he has. The dull color of the Mercedes makes the dark green forest on the other side of the highway pop, the filtered sunlight making all the details crisp.

And I look fucking amazing, wet hair, no makeup and all.

I stare up at him in awe. "How did you do this? Are you a part-time photographer along with being a huge Led Zeppelin fan?"

"I said so at dinner last night. I'm a graphic artist. I know what looks good."

I frown. "But I thought..."

"We should get going," he says and I catch a smirk on his face before he heads to the driver's seat.

Hmmm. Like I said before. Full of surprises.

Luckily the drive to the coast is only an hour, a peaceful winding journey through thick forests with the occasional clear-cutting and deep streams that race the road. Only it's not so peaceful because my head wants to focus on the dream, as fragmented as it is, and revel in the afterglow. It reminds me when I was dreaming about Jay before, how I would always wake up happy, with a full heart.

I stare at him, wondering. His large hands wrap around the steering wheel, wayfarers covering his eyes. Not that I would be able to read much from him anyway.

"You were in my dream last night," I blurt out.

"Was I?"

"*Were you?*"

He glances at me briefly. "Not sure what you're getting at."

"You have a history of showing up in my dreams. I'm wondering if this is something you did, rather than something my subconscious did."

"What was the dream about?" he asks.

I clear my throat. "You tell me."

He sighs. "Ada, what was it?"

I don't want to. I want to see if he knows.

"Or are you embarrassed?" he goes on.

"I'm not embarrassed," I say quickly. "You're the one who kissed me."

He grins cockily, eyes on the road. "Oh did I?"

"Yeah. *You.*"

"I bet you kissed me back."

I clamp my mouth shut for a moment. "The details are fuzzy."

"Convenient."

I decide not to push it further. He has this uncanny way of twisting things around and I don't want to go there, especially after last night when every nerve in my body was begging me to go exactly there.

Please let us have two separate beds tonight, I think.

When we reach the coast, the highway forking left and right, we turn to the right.

"I thought we were going to Cannon Beach," I say.

"Checked the hotels this morning," he says. "All booked up. Peak season, you know. Managed to snag a room in Seaside instead. Right on the beach, with a balcony." He glances at me. "And yes, double beds."

"Good," I tell him, rather spitefully.

I have the feeling he's rolling his eyes underneath those sunglasses.

It's still early, just before noon, when we roll down the kitschy cool streets of Seaside. We used to come here a lot when I was really young, my uncle having a house just down the coast, and I always had the fondest memories of the arcades and candy shops. Nothing much seems to have changed, except that maybe it's more crowded.

We pull into a large hotel at the very end where the promenade begins. It's nothing fancy but it is right on the beach. The minute I exit the car I feel relief. The ocean breeze rolling off the Pacific is full in my face, a sharp, mineral wash that coats me from head to toe. It blasts away the humidity that had descended on Portland this month, banishes the cobwebs, even the fear.

I close my eyes, even though I'm standing in a parking lot, and just feel it. I breathe in as deep as my lungs will let me, then exhale.

When I open my eyes, nearly teetering off-balance, I catch Jay staring at me. Actually, I felt his gaze even before I looked, that way he can reach right into me like no one's been able to before. Or maybe it's around him that I'm finally making myself transparent.

I hold his eyes for a moment, wordless conversations passing through us, conversations I don't understand but I feel. Then I shoot him a sheepish smile as he holds the door to the hotel lobby open for me.

Being early, the room isn't ready yet so we park the car in the garage (far less scary than the last time I was in one) and head out to get some lunch.

Though Seaside is small, the main "downtown" area just one or two streets, we're immediately swept up into the crowd of vacationers. There are families pushing strollers dragging along kids with sticky hands and melting ice cream cones, young couples holding hands and gazing more at each other than where they are walking (which is into me on more than one occasion), groups of Germans holding maps (of what, the one street?).

And then there's Jay and I, whatever we are.

Jay has a hankering for some clam chowder, and judging by all the shops selling "The Best Clam Chowder in Seaside!" it isn't hard to find some. We settle on one that has a diner feel with red plastic booths and seagull figurines dangling from the ceiling.

Jay of course gets the chowder while I decide to be extremely boring and get toast. Normally I'd be polishing off the greasiest thing on the menu, but my appetite seems to be diminishing by the minute.

"Toast?" he repeats after the waitress takes our order, a girl no older than me that stopped snapping her gum for just long enough to give Jay googly eyes. I wanted to employ the same "Eyes right here, buddy" technique that Jay used on the hotel manager last night but the last thing I want is a catfight where hot bowls of chowder are scattered everywhere like landmines.

"Not hungry," I tell him and he frowns at that.

"You should eat more. You're skin and bones," he teases.

I give him my most withering look. "You need to work on your compliments, mister."

"Thought I gave you a pretty good one last night," he says sincerely.

Right. I was wondering if that moment would ever be brought up again or if he would pretend it never happened.

"And," he goes on, briefly reaching across the table to place his large warm hand on mine. Fire transfers through me. "I'm just worried about you, that's all."

"You sound just like my dad," I say, trying to sound light but there's no mistaking the tremor in my voice.

He removes his hand and the fire stops.

"Fair enough," he says. "You know I'll always look out for you."

"It's your job," I concede.

"And I'm rather fond of you."

I stare at him with startled eyes.

The waitress chooses this moment to plunk our coffees down and I immediately mainline mine, grateful for the distraction. She soon follows up with the toast and chowder.

When I've finished half the cup of Joe, black as sin, I wipe my lips on the napkin and say, "Speaking of my father. Do you think he's doing all right?" I'd texted this morning and he said all was well but I need reassurance from Jay.

"I'm sure he's forgotten all about last night."

I doubted that. He would brush the scares under the rug as he always does (ask him about the time a pig carcass was found in the kitchen and his office was splattered with blood. Oh wait, you can't, because he pretends it never happened). But he's all about impressions ever since mom died. Like he's picked up the reins. And he probably thinks he failed at his first dinner party. I make a mental note to cheer him up big time when I return. Whenever that is.

"So how does Jacob close a portal? And why doesn't he just close all of them?"

He picks up the bottle of tabasco and shakes a dangerous amount of it in his chowder, staining it orange. "I don't know how exactly. He just can. But the moment he closes one, another pops up. It's an endless cycle. Which is why we need more legs on the ground."

"Meaning me."

He stirs the chowder and points the spoon at me. "Meaning you."

"So why don't you just create more Jacobs instead of pulling in recruits like me, who don't know a thing about closing portals and killing demons and would much rather spend their Saturdays at the mall."

I know I'm testing his patience with all the questions but hell, it's not like he's been forthcoming about any of this since I first met him.

"I don't have all the answers you know."

I give him a steady look. I'm not sure if I believe him. "Because you don't even know who you *are*."

His eyes narrow, a gaze that pins me to my seat. I mean, I physically can't move and my lungs feel stuffed with cotton. What the fuck is this trickery?

"I don't need to know who I was to know who I am," he says. His voice is rough, hard, and for a moment I'm terrified I've angered him beyond repair.

"I didn't mean to be insulting," I manage to tell him with a broken voice, displaying my palms in a peace offering, even though moving is difficult while he's staring at me like that. I feel like he's using some part of him, some type of ability, on me that he hasn't done before.

He keeps this intimidating gaze on me until he abruptly breaks it and looks down at his chowder. Suddenly I can breathe again. "I don't have all the answers because that's the nature of the game. It's something I live with. Something you'll have to live with too, no matter how curious you are or," he pauses, "demanding you get. But I do know that all Jacobs come from somewhere. We weren't ordinary people to begin with."

"You're not? What are you?"

He glances up at me. "People like you. People with abilities. Power. Sometimes power that lies latent inside them their whole entire life."

"So the person you were before, the person that you have no clue about," (*or so you say*, I add in my head), "was someone just like me. But obviously not a woman. Why so sexist?"

"Maybe because women are unpredictable," he says simply.

"Excuse me?" I practically snarl, my hands pressed down on the table. "We are *not* unpredictable. When did you become such a caveman?"

He has a spoonful of chowder, then gives me the slightest of grins. "How do you know I wasn't a caveman to start out with?"

"Well I wouldn't be surprised."

"What I meant to say is that women are more emotional. That's what I get from it anyway. They attach to

more things. For example, their children. That's a difficult
bond to break, even when you die."

I swallow down the pang of sadness, feeling it saturate
me. My mother. No wonder I dream about her still, no
wonder my subconscious wants to see her, no wonder the
demons use her to trick me. They know about that bond
just as anyone does. How, even in death, I sometimes feel
my mother is as attached to me as always, an invisible
thread that links us and will never break.

"Anyway," Jay goes on, eyes flicking to mine, softer now,
and I know he can feel the sorrow coming off of me, "that
must be one of the reasons. I don't know for sure but I bet
that's part of it. It's harder for some people to let go of love."

"That still sounds a bit sexist," I mutter before I shove
the toast in my mouth.

He shrugs, not bothered.

"So, since you don't really have answers but seem to
have opinions, when do you think I'll be able to, um, begin
my training?"

He flags down the waitress and gestures for more coffee
for the both of us. He turns back to me. "You've already
started."

"What I mean is, when do you stop being some guy
hanging around me and start turning into Mr. Miyagi?"

He cocks a perfect brow. "Some guy?" he repeats. "I am
not *some guy*."

Testy, testy. The more time I spend with Jay, the more
I get under his skin. I kind of like it.

"You know what I mean," I tell him. "When will it
all…begin?" I quickly add, "And don't tell me it's already
started."

"I'm not going to tell you anything because I don't know anything. To be honest, I'm not even sure how I'll know. Maybe I'll just wake up one day and it will be clear. Maybe Jacob has to pull me aside. I have no idea. But I know you shouldn't worry about it. Things like this don't happen overnight."

"So we're just supposed to just sit around and wait?"

"No. You go live your life. Go to school. Design. Study. Take selfies. I'll be the giant weirdo lurking in the background and occasionally taking your picture."

And you're my giant weirdo, I think to myself.

"And then one day," he goes on. "I'll tap you on the shoulder and tell you it's time. Throw you right into a pit of demons with nothing but a bible and the sword of destiny and you'll have to fight them all until you're the only one standing. If you live, then you've passed. If you die and go to hell, then you've failed."

The coffee is spilling out of my cup I'm shaking so hard.

"Oh my god," I squeak softly. "Oh my god."

Then he grins at me. It lights up his whole face, turning him into a rugged handsome man into something boyish.

And *dickish*.

"What the fuck?" I cry out. "Are you joking?"

Now he's sitting back in his seat and laughing. A full-on belly laugh that's both beautiful and aggravating.

"You asshole!" I seethe at him. "You are such a fucking jerk. I'm going to get you back for this so bad, I swear to God."

Jay tries to say something but his laughter won't subside. There are even faint tears at the corner of his eyes.

"Your face," he eventually says between laughs. "Oh, you should have seen your face."

"Is joking and laughing at my expense now a consequence of hanging around me too much?" I snipe. "Because I think I liked it better when you were a humorless robot."

He wipes underneath his eyes and lets out an amused sigh, still grinning.

"You're lucky you're hot," I tell him, sliding out of the booth. "I'm going to the washroom. Don't try anything funny."

"You think I'm hot?" he asks as I walk away but I don't give him the satisfaction of looking back.

Once in the bathroom, just as tacky as the rest of the place with plastic clamshells adorned around the mirror, I take a good look at myself. I'm scowly, that's for sure, but there's a glow to my cheeks that wasn't there before. I'm not sure if that's the glow of being embarrassed or the glow of something more pleasant than that.

I turn around, making sure the three bathroom stalls are empty before turning back to the mirror and saying to my reflection, "Suck it up, princess."

Then I take the middle stall and do my business, grateful for the privacy.

I'm just about to get up and flush when suddenly the toilet in the stall next to me flushes.

What the fuck?

I glance back at the flush handle on my toilet. Manual. But maybe the stall next door has an automatic flush that malfunctioned because I know there wasn't anyone in that stall—it was wide open—and I know no one else came in.

Suddenly the terrible sensation of ants crawling inside my skin swarms through me.

No. Not a good sign.

I hold my breath and listen, needing assurance that I'm all alone, that it's me being paranoid.

There's no one there, Ada, I tell myself.

But there is.

I can hear something...

Breathing.

Very faint. But raspy, gurgling, b*reathing.*

The blood-beat in my ears gets louder. I need to get out of here. I need to just get out the door and go. Just rip open that stall and run.

The crawling sensation intensifies and I absently itch my arm.

The whole bathroom seems to pause, as if holding its breath.

A sniffing sound.

Like something testing the air.

Oh god.

The image of the Splitter demon flashes through my mind.

Not again. Not on my fucking watch. I'm not going to have Jay rush into the bathroom to rescue me, even if I should be so lucky.

I take a deep breath, my body moving so slowly, like I'm in a dream but I know I'm not because now I can smell something too.

Something rotten, earthy, putrid. It stings my nostrils, like blood and malt vinegar, something that's been unearthed when it should remain buried.

I open the stall door, limbs sluggish and step out into the bathroom. The mirror is in front of me, reflecting my own image, my pale face and the stalls, their doors half-open. Nothing more. Nothing less.

I take peek around at the neighboring stall anyway, tepidly pushing the door open.

I hold my breath as it gently swings against the siding, hitting it with a soft *clunk*.

Empty.

I exhale in relief, feeling the blood in my veins run warm again, and turn back to the face the mirror.

There's someone right behind me.

A tall figure made of shadows.

No face.

Just red eyes.

And now, a slowly spreading smile showing off rows of shiny sharp teeth.

"Ada," it whispers, a voice that makes me want to drop to my knees and beg for mercy.

Instead I run.

I burst out of the bathroom and run into the restaurant, coming to a walk when I realize people are looking at me strange.

I round the corner and see Jay in our booth at the end, his back to me, and I'm so ready to grab his arm and make him leave with me.

Then I realize he's not alone.

I stop where I am, the waitress nearly slamming into me with a muttering of annoyance.

I don't care.

My *mother* is sitting where I was sitting in the booth.

She's leaning forward, panic in her eyes, saying something to Jay.

He nods but if he's saying something back, I can't tell.

After what happened in the bathroom, I know this can't be a coincidence. It has to be a demon's trick. But why is Jay indulging it?

And why do I know in my heart, the core of all I am, that this isn't a trick at all?

This is the first time seeing my mother outside of a dream.

She's made her way into my world this time.

I'm torn between wanting to run over to her and stay where I am, give her time to say whatever she's saying to Jay. God I wish I could just talk to her about him, about everything. *Hey mom, a lot's happened since you've passed on...*

Then she looks up and sees me. Her face falls.

She quickly gets out of the booth with preternatural grace and exits the restaurant faster than I could have predicted.

"What?" I say to myself and then start running down the restaurant after her.

I pass by Jay but don't even look in his direction, I just keep going until I'm swinging open the door and running out into the sunshine, nearly run over by an old man in a scooter as he putters down the sidewalk.

"Watch it," he grumbles but I pay no attention.

My mother is nowhere to be found.

I whirl around, out of breath, but all I see are tourists and storefronts, a car rolling past.

"Mom?" I cry out, disoriented as I keep spinning around in vain.

"Ada!"

Jay is bursting through the doors, grabbing my arm.

"Ada," he says again, his grip tightening as he pulls me to him.

"My mother," I whisper, eyes searching the street. "I saw her inside, talking to you. She just left. Why would she leave?"

"What are you talking about?" he asks.

I can only shake my head. How could she run from me?

"Ada, please, I don't know what you're talking about," Jay continues and I finally meet his eyes. They are icebergs laced with disbelief.

"It was my mother's ghost!"

"There was no one there," he says calmly, putting his hands on my shoulders. "I was alone the whole time you were in the washroom."

I shrug him off, refusing to be coddled. "Then it was a demon."

"Ada, I would have seen her if it was either one. It's in your head, okay. You said in the car you used to come here with your family when you were young—"

"No!" I cry out, squinting in the sunshine. "It was her. I saw her. You talked to her."

"Then what was I saying?"

I shrug helplessly. "I don't know. I couldn't see."

"Then how do know I was talking to her?"

"You nodded," I say feebly. "She was talking to you, she was scared, and you nodded like you understood."

"I could have just been moving my head to take a sip off coffee," he says. "Please. Ada. This is only doing you harm."

Tears are starting to well in my eyes. Fuck. Fuck. Fuck. I don't want to be the girl who can't get over her grief, the one who breaks down all the time.

"Hey," he says gently, brushing his thumb underneath my eyes, as if to clear the tears before they start. "Look at me, princess."

The way he says princess is disarming. Not sarcastic, not belittling. It's more than a term of endearment. In this moment, he's whispering it with tenderness that makes my heart feel soft and pliable. Warm. Full.

"Let me go pay," he says, keeping his eyes glued to mine. "We'll go back to the hotel. I'm sure the room is ready. We'll get some wine. Order some room service. Have a party."

I can't help but let out a weak laugh. "It's, like, two p.m."

"It's always five o'clock somewhere," he says. "Didn't a President say that?"

"I think that was Jimmy Buffet."

"The Margaritaville guy? I guess that makes sense." He gives me a kind smile. "Come on."

For a moment I'm terrified that he's going to leave me on the sidewalk, that he'll disappear into the restaurant and never come back out and I'll be forever lost. Not a rational thought but a terrifying one all the same.

But he grabs my hand, holding it in a vice-like grip, then leads me inside. He pays the bill, throwing down one more twenty than he should, and then we go back out into the ocean air.

We're only around the block when I mention to him what I saw—or think I saw—in the bathroom.

He sucks in his breath, giving my hand another squeeze. "Screw room service," he says and pulls me into a store selling liquor. He grabs a bottle of white wine from the fridge and a couple of packets of salt water taffy, pays at the register, and then leads me toward the sand.

We find a place among the small dunes, a stiffer mound of sand in between reedy grass, and hunker down. He hands me a salt water taffy and deftly unscrews the bottle, handing it to me.

"Drink up, buttercup," he says. "You need it."

I take it from him, our fingers brushing against each other, sending more shockwaves through my system. Even though the breeze is fresh, the pounding surf sounds like a lullaby, and the sound of squealing children nearby should be comforting, I need this wine more than anything. If not for what I'm seeing, for what I'm feeling.

Everything Jay.

I tip the bottle back.

And drink.

. . .

I am drunk.

Day drunk.

That's *way* more drunk than normal drunk.

I drank a whole bottle of pinot gris.

It's sitting right beside me in the sand, propped up like it's in an ice bucket and I'm some classy bitch.

Jay is right beside me, his large frame taking over my vision. Even though there's an endless beach in front of me and infinite ocean, Jay is all I see.

He's looking for a pen and paper. I told him I want to write a message and stick it in the wine bottle and throw it out to sea.

He's indulging me. He knows I'm drunk. He had maybe two sips of wine and that's it. I asked him if it's possible for him to get drunk, cuz I dunno, maybe his super fast metabolism keeps it from affecting him. I'm pretty sure vampires can't get drunk. Except on blood.

But Jay said it's possible and that's why he needs to refrain.

Then I called him a pussy.

He burst out laughing.

I love his laugh.

It's really only the second time I've heard it, this rich genuine sound of joy, coming from the soul of him, but I love it with every part of me.

Then he said, "You say that like it's a bad thing."

And I swear the Irish accent came out again. I decided not to bring it up. I just watched him and went on like nothing happened.

I have my theories though. That he was Irish in a past life. And if the accent is starting to come out, then maybe other parts of who he was are too.

The thought struck me as dangerous.

I ignored it.

Now Jay is handing me a receipt and I fish my eyeliner out of my purse and start writing the note.

"What are you going to write?" he asks me, utterly amused.

Good. I like it when I amuse him.

"Not sure yet," I tell him.

I put the receipt on my knee and have the eyeliner poised to write. I have to make the writing big so it won't be too smudgy. I glance at Jay out of the corner of my eyes and see his attention is on the crashing waves.

Without thinking, I write:

Help me.

Help me.

Help me.

Help me.

Before Jay can see, I quickly roll up the receipt and stick it in the bottle. Then I start using the bottle to scoop sand, like filling an hourglass.

"What are you doing?" Jay asks, peering over my shoulder. "It's going to sink that way, not float."

"I want it to sink," I tell him.

I'm pretty sure that direction is the only way it will get read.

"Maybe we should get you back in the room," he says. "We haven't even seen it yet."

I nod dumbly, not sure of the time. It's way past dinner, I know because my stomach is growling and the smell of fried fish and barbeque is in the air.

It's so beautiful out that I almost freeze to the spot. I'm hit with a pang of sadness that always comes with realizing summer is almost over.

Jay offers me his hand to help me up but instead I grab the wine bottle and scoot down the dune like a crab until I'm upright and running across the beach as fast as I can.

I smile into the wind, into the sun that burns bright on the horizon, and I run, run, run, the occasional giggle escaping my lips, my feet flying.

I know Jay is behind me. He's my shadow. A shadow I like.

A shadow I need.

A shadow I want.

Behind me.

In front of me.

Everywhere.

I stop at the ocean's edge, breathless, on the verge of hiccups, and wind my arm up.

The bottle goes sailing in an arc through the air, landing in the swell behind the breaks. It's probably not deep enough, but it will eventually get dragged out to sea, where it belongs. Maybe a mermaid will intercept it before it reaches the bottom.

Jay stops a few feet behind me. I can feel him. He's not breathing hard like I am (*he's not human, is he?*) but I sense him all the same, the way you know your shadow is there, even if it's overcast.

I watch the horizon for a moment, that big endless line, jagged with waves. I watch until it starts to scare me, like looking into the abyss and having the abyss stare right back.

That's the last thing I need.

I turn around and look at Jay.

He's so fucking beautiful.

And I'm drunk, I'm so drunk.

But he's so beautiful. And I want to tell him more than anything. I want him to understand that it's *okay*.

There he stands. Over six feet of muscle and mystery. The messy cinnamon hair waving in the wind. That chiseled

jaw. The sharp cheekbones. A look of being haunted and of
doing the haunting. His eyes that undo you, for good or
bad.

And right now, he's undoing me.

For good.

My world goes swimmy.

I'm not sure what happens next.

Suddenly we're in the room and I'm leaning against the
door with my back to it.

He's opening a bottle of water from beside the coffee
machine.

I want to tell him it's probably twenty dollars.

But my mouth doesn't work and my mind is probably
days behind.

He unscrews the cap and has a sip of the water before
striding over and holding it out for me.

"You need to drink the whole thing."

My lids are heavy.

I shift to the left and he's there, holding me up in his
arms.

Smells like the sea.

"Easy, princess," he says in that endearing way of his,
his lips at the top of my head. "I guess I wasn't exactly the
best guardian today, was I?"

I wrap my hands around his neck and hold on, holding
myself up so that my face is pressed into his chest.

Then I lift up my chin to stare up at him.

"Have you ever kissed a girl before?" I ask him lazily.

His eyes widen briefly before they become all squinty
and warm. "Me? No."

"Have you kissed a boy before?"

He gives a slight shake of his head, a lock of fiery hair falling across his forehead. "No. Do both of those answers disappoint you?"

"No." I lick my lips and say goodbye to reason, shame and good ideas. "Don't you wonder what it's like?"

I expect him to say no.

But his gaze becomes heady, almost lustful, and it drops to my lips. I can feel his eyes on my mouth, burning sweet, almost like he's already kissing me.

"I do," he says huskily, his tone dropping a register.

His answer, his look, it emboldens and sobers me all at once.

"You can kiss me you know," I whisper, staring at his full lips now, willing them. "I won't tell anyone."

He leans in closer, his nose brushing against the tip of mine. He closes his eyes. Murmurs, "I could. I very well could."

Oh god, please do.

He's breathing harder. Trying to compose himself. I can feel his pulse in his neck, beating against the heel of my palm. It's wild.

I want to undo him as he undoes me.

I want to show him what it's like to be mortal, to be human. To live, really live.

He said I made him feel. I want him to feel more.

Feel *me*.

"But you're drunk," he says softly, sadly.

"I'm sober enough."

"But it wouldn't matter." He moves his head back a few inches, his Adam's apple bobbing as he swallows.

"You…" he rubs his lips together. "If I were to kiss you, I wouldn't…I couldn't stay who I am. I couldn't go back."

I'm not sure I understand but it doesn't matter.

He's rejecting me.

"Do you really think I'm beautiful?" I whisper, closing my eyes and feeling that shame that moments ago I pretended didn't exist.

"Yes," he says emphatically, his breath catching. "You're more beautiful than this earth can handle. You belong in the stars, not here. You're walking stardust and I'm amazed I can hold you in my arms"

My brain wants to make a joke about him being a poet and not even knowing it. But there's nothing funny about this. I've never yearned for someone so much in my life. I've never had my body become so sexually aware before, like it's waking up for the first time.

Nothing less than Jay will do.

"Ada," he says, putting his fingers under my chin and raising it until my eyes open and meet his. "If you only knew how hard it is to say no to you. To say no to this. But I know what would happen."

"What would happen?" I say this softly, afraid I might break this spell. Our faces are still inches apart and he's moving closer without even knowing it.

"You would be mine. And I would be yours."

From just a kiss? I think, but I *know* it wouldn't just be a kiss.

"Is that so bad?"

He nods softly. "Yes. Because that's not how this works. I'm supposed to be with you and then I'm supposed to leave…"

"You can still leave," I tell him, knowing full well that it would destroy me.

"I couldn't." He pauses, taking in a deep breath through his nose, trying to steady himself. "Because my willpower is weak when it comes to you."

"It seems pretty strong right now."

"Please don't tempt me, Ada. I can barely handle it as it is. I won't be able to hold back and I'm not sure who would come out."

I want to tempt him. I want him to let go. I want us both to discover the hot-blooded man inside, the one with animal instincts. I'm playing with fire and I don't care if I get burned. I want the flames to lick every inch of me.

"I want to make you feel," I whisper into his ear.

He shudders, unable to supress a groan that I feel all the way down to my toes.

"You already do make me feel," he says thickly. "Too much. Too soon. And it's changing me, for better or for worse. But I can't afford to be anyone but Jay to you. I'm in charge of your life, your future. And I can't protect you otherwise."

He grabs my wrists and pries my arms from around his neck. "And most of all, you've had an entire bottle of wine," he says, his tone becoming jovial, pushing the distance from intimate back to casual. "And even more than that, I'm a gentleman. I'm not taking advantage of you. You would hate me for it tomorrow and I would hate myself."

I squint my eyes at him, the room seeming bright, my shame brighter. "You've got it wrong, Jay. *I'm* trying to take advantage of *you*."

He sighs and grabs my elbow, leading me over to the bed, placing the bottle of water on the bedside table.

I sit down and immediately fall back into the covers. He lifts up my legs and brings them around before slipping off my flats.

"How about we forget everything that just happened," he says lightly, tossing my shoes on the floor. "Chalk it up to too much wine and sun. Get some rest. Have a nap. We can always eat later, I'm sure they have twenty-four-hour room service here."

But I'm not really listening to him.

I'm feeling.

Reeling.

My heart is being dragged out with the tide.

And then I'm under.

CHAPTER SIXTEEN

"Ada, dear."

I expect to wake up with a raging hangover and a thousand regrets.

Instead I wake up in a cold, dark room. A single bed in the corner. A toilet half-hidden behind a curtain. A small shelf full of tattered books.

There's one window, up high, with bars on it.

I'm in prison.

I gasp, as if I haven't been breathing, and the air doesn't feel right. It doesn't feel like air; it feels like a vacuum.

I try and get something into my lungs but there is nothing.

"It's okay," a tired yet familiar voice says from behind me.

I spin around to see a person standing in the shadows by a thick steel door. There's a door with a sliding window open to the hall outside, the only source of light in this coffin of a room.

Everything is grey, even the person as she steps forward into the beam, revealing herself.

If I couldn't breathe before, I definitely can't breathe now.

It's my grandmother, Pippa. A person I never remembered from life, who I only met after she died.

She's staring at me with kindness in her eyes, looking to be about eighty or so, dressed in a long flowing gown straight from a classic film. Her hair is done up in victory rolls.

"Grandma?" I ask breathlessly.

"You'll find it's easier to not think about it," she says. "That there is no air. It doesn't matter. You're fine."

I swallow the lump in my throat and gesture to the room. "Why am I here? Where am I?"

"You're in the Thin Veil," she says quietly. "Not to where you've been going with that...Jacob. Deeper still."

My eyes widen. "It's not safe."

"It's safe," she says. "This place is a place I constructed from my memories. It's a place full of such pain and sorrow and torment that it has more power than anywhere else. The mental hospital where I was put away, the place where I died. It's where I can be and no one, nothing, can find me. You put up walls without knowing it. These are my walls." She pauses. "No one knows you're here, not even Jay."

I recognize it as the truth. I feel it in my bones. But even still, I'm on edge. The brief thought that this might not be Pippa crosses my mind. It would be an easy trap for a demon to set and make sure I could never come out.

But as I see her words as truth, I also know this is her. No tricks.

"Why did you bring me here?"

I try to think back to where I was before I woke up, though, and I come up with nothing.

"Because you're the only one who can help," she says. She shuffles over to the bed and sits down, pats the place beside her. "Come. Sit with your grandmother. I never did have a lot of time with you, even after my passing. It was always Perry who had to put up with hauntings. Poor child."

I know Pippa used to scare the bejesus out of Perry but here she looks gentle. Just an old tired soul with my mother's eyes.

I sit down next to her, afraid of what she's going to ask me to do. No ghost drags you into the underworld to ask for a *small* favor.

Especially if they're family.

I stare at her expectantly, absently realizing I haven't taken a breath in a good minute. So far, so good.

"I didn't want to interfere," she says, putting her weathered hand on mine. "I've done that too many times before. But I have to. She's my daughter."

"Mom?" I whisper.

"She's in a place she shouldn't be," she says. "I don't even know when it started. When your mother died, she was in limbo for a long time. Lost in the Veil. I pulled her to one side. The demon pulled her to the other. The one who died inside her. A noble sacrifice she made for all of you but a near damning one all the same." She pauses and lets out a heavy breath of non-existent air. "Eventually I won. I pulled her over. My own Jakob, the one I had my whole life, he helped too. She was in the light. She was home with me."

"But then..." I supply fearfully, because I know there has to be a "but."

She nods. "But then something happened. She found a way back to the Thin Veil. I told her it wasn't safe. I know all too well. But this is a game I've played for years. She was new. She went to the Veil because it was the closest glimpse she could have of you and Perry and Daniel. She missed you so much." She wipes away a tear that makes my heart break. "Missing someone is a dangerous emotion. It's hunger that can't be fed. It makes you vulnerable and weak and she wouldn't have seen the demon until it was too late. Lured, perhaps, by images and promises of you. The demons lie, they always do."

Her eyes trail over the room as if lost in thought. Then she pats my hand and continues. "She was sucked down to the other side. To Hell. And that's where they're holding her. To get to you. Only you Ada. Not Perry. Not me. You."

"So it's all real?" I ask incredulously, both horrified and vindicated. "That's really her in my dreams?"

"Yes. And those aren't always dreams, Ada. Sometimes they can find their way in and pull you under. That's why you put up the walls. It's your defense mechanism and it's a powerful one. It's one that your Jacob doesn't quite understand. There's a lot about you that no one understands, including myself."

"Tell me about it," I say softly. I shake my head. "I can't believe this."

"But you do. You always have known it was your mother. She's asking for help because she's suffering and will continue to be tortured for eternity. But at the same time she doesn't want you to sacrifice yourself to save her." Pippa looks me dead in the eye. "Please understand that

I have tried all that I can. Me and my Jakob. But there is nothing. I can't get to her. You can."

"Why not Perry? She can create portals out of thin air. She could pop in and get her. She did that with Dex."

Pippa laughs without mirth. "Are you not tired of living under someone else's shadow?"

I shake my head violently. "Not when there are shadows behind shadows."

"Perry has her own powers and her own path. She and Dex...they've covered a lot of ground. But you're just starting. And you're different, Ada."

"You sound just like Jay," I mutter.

"Oh, I'm nothing like him," she says bitterly.

I frown. "Do you know him?"

She shakes her head. "No. Not personally. I just...feel. You feel a lot of things here. That's why I know what's happening to your mother. I feel more than see."

"What do you feel about him?"

She gives me a steady look. "He's not who he says he is. He's not who he thinks he is."

"Can you blame him?"

"I don't mean the man has ill-will," she says. "Not as a Jacob. But he has been lying to you."

My heart stills. Blood rushes in my head. "What?"

"He knows your mother is in trouble. They all do. He knows she's in Hell, that the demons have her, that she needs you to save her."

"What?" I exclaim, getting to my feet. "How? Why? Why would he lie?" I pause, memories coming back to me. "Oh my god. I saw her today in the diner. She was talking to Jay. He denied it, denied seeing her. Was it her?"

She nods, slowly getting to her feet. She stretches, cracking her back. "It was her. She can appear sometimes when she's not being watched. She's almost always watched."

I'm so angry I could scream. "Why did she appear to him instead of me?"

"Because she's probably trying to convince him to let you come to her."

"And he lied to my face! That shouldn't be allowed. Jacobs are...are...they're on our side."

She snorts. "They are not on sides, they just are. They aren't good and they aren't bad. They skirt the grey and they're just as vulnerable as the humans they once were. My Jakob is a little devil sometimes. Forever this young boy, always playing games. He never means me harm but he's adept at manipulation. I've been around him for so long now that I know how to handle him. But you're new to this."

"And so is Jay," I say. "He's a rookie."

She raises her brow skeptically, as if to say, *is that what he told you too?*

"Regardless," she goes on, "you need to go to her. And you need to convince him to let you go because that man will follow you until the ends of the earth before he lets you go. And then, when you're there, you will put up the walls so that no demon, no damned soul, will ever see you."

"And how will I find her? How will she find me?"

"There is a bond that can't be broken," she says. "From me to her. From her to you."

She shuffles back across the room and brings me into a big hug, one I'm too shocked to return.

"Don't trust him," she whispers in my ear. "Don't trust yourself. Trust your heart. Your true heart. The inner compass. That will never steer you wrong."

Then she pulls back and pushes a piece of hair behind my ears. "Now, go back to your world. And do some good."

Suddenly the world shudders and my bones pop like bubbles are bursting inside and the grey air shimmers, stretched, until I see the haze of a hotel room.

And I fall flat on my face on the carpeted floor.

"Ada!" Jay's voice coming from so far away.

His hands on my back, feeling my neck for a pulse.

They travel down my arms until he gets a hold and then hauls me up to my feet.

I can barely stand but I'm no longer drunk. I'm just so disoriented I don't know what world I'm in anymore.

But this world has color. It has morning sunshine and smells of coffee.

It has Jay staring at me with a reddened face, brows drawn sharply together, looking both worried and furious.

"Where the fuck did you go?" he asks.

His language shocks me further awake. I blink and try and walk away from him. I get as far as the desk in the room before he grabs me again and whirls me around to face him. I'm vaguely aware I'm in his Led Zeppelin t-shirt, which means I was also wearing that in the Veil. Which means he must have undressed me when I slept. My mind can't even latch on to that idea right now.

"Where did you go?" he repeats, more frantic now.

"To a secret place," I mumble. I take a seat in the chair and blink back the sight. My brain feels like it's been siphoned. Perhaps I left it all behind in Pippa's cell.

Then it all comes back to me at once.

The rush of anger.

I glare at Jay with all the fury that's dying to be released.

"You bastard," I say through gritted teeth.

Now he's shocked. "What?"

I'm so angry I can barely breathe. "You lying son of a bitch."

He swallows and I see the first flicker of fear in his eyes that I've ever seen. He knows why I'm mad. Oh, he knows.

"I couldn't find you," he says, tripping over his words. "This morning you were gone. I searched everywhere. I tried to get in your head but...you put up those walls again. You have to stop putting up those walls, Ada. Stop blocking me out. Stop pushing me out. I'm only here to help you."

"Bullshit!" I scream at him, getting to my feet and jabbing my finger into his chest. "You aren't here to help me. You're here to lie to me!"

His eyes bore into mine but I don't care. I refuse to let him have that much power.

My refusal silences him.

"You told me it was a trick!" I yell. "You told me the demons were fucking with my head, that it wasn't real, that she wasn't in Hell, that she wasn't hurt. But she is! They have her and you've been lying to me!" With that I push against his chest which surprisingly moves him back, rocks him on his feet.

I brush past him, feeling the fury cascade through me. It's like a domino effect, but instead of dominos it's sticks of dynamite and they're going off one by one.

I whirl around, fixing him with the meanest glare, directing all that fire at him.

He looks scared. Honest to god, scared.

Of me.

Well, hell hath no motherfucking fury like a woman scorned.

"Don't you have anything to say for yourself!" I throw my hands up. "Maybe tell me the truth! Why you've been lying! I mean, god damn it Jay! You were talking to her today in the diner. One demon was distracted by me and my mother took the chance to talk to you and you just pretended it didn't happen. You made me think I was nuts!"

But Jay doesn't move. He doesn't even blink.

I'm not sure he's even breathing.

Uneasiness creeps up my spine.

I take a step toward him, feeling the hate and fire inside me dissolve momentarily.

Then Jay moves, stumbling forward a few feet, gasping for air.

I stop. "What happened?" I ask firmly, not liking how this is taking away from my fury. "What's wrong with you?"

He blinks at me. "You weren't doing that on purpose?"

"Doing what?" I ask with a sigh. "If you think you can change the subject..."

"I'm not, okay," he says testily. He comes over to me and my body stiffens in response. "I'm not changing any subject. I just need to know if you knew what you were doing just then."

"I wasn't doing anything. I was yelling at you because you're a big ginger-colored piece of shit!"

"Be that as it may," he says, reaching out and grabbing my wrist before I wallop him in the chest again. "You froze me with your stare."

My nose scrunches up. "I did what?"

"You did the same thing to me that I did to you at the diner."

My mind goes back a few reels. In the diner I'd pissed Jay off, insinuating he didn't know who he was. His glare caused a physical reaction in me. A bad one.

"I did that to you?" I ask. "Just now." Then I glower at him. "Wait a minute, you *are* trying to switch the subject."

"No, I'm not," he says. He sounds sincere. Then again he sounded sincere when he was lying about my mom. "Remember when you asked me when you would be ready? This is the first step. I don't quite know what you can do, Ada. But you can transfix me with your gaze in more ways than one. Which means you can do the same to a demon. A crucial skill to have, I would say."

"And I can put up walls," I tell him proudly, even though I have no idea how I do that either.

"About that," he starts.

"No!" I yell at him, ripping my wrist from his hand. "Explain why you've been lying to me! I'm supposed to *trust* you Jay. And I did. It took my own grandmother to rip me into some secret location in the Veil to finally tell me the truth!"

"I had to lie," he tells me, not seeming surprised about Pippa. "It's the only way to keep you safe."

"Safe!" I cry out, aware that I'm yelling at him full-blast and his face is a foot away. "Who gives a fuck about safe? What about my heart? My mother, Jay. You never had a fucking mother so you wouldn't understand, but my mother was everything to me. And she's being tortured for all eternity! How could you let that happen?"

271

He'd flinched at my comment but is back to being stone-faced and impassive. "It's not up to me. There are rules to follow and I follow them."

"Because you're programmed to follow them, is that it? Like a mindless drone."

He swallows. "You're not being fair."

"No, I'm being honest. You're not being fair. You could have gone and rescued her at least if you didn't want to tell me."

"I can't," he says gravely, shaking his head. "I would if I could."

"But you're not allowed," I say in a mocking voice. "You'll get in *trouble*."

"Ada, listen to me, please. You don't know how this all works. I do, all right? My job is to protect you at all costs. To protect and teach. I am bound to it, bound to you."

"For a limited time only," I mutter.

"And I will do that at all costs. For you to go after your mother is too risky. I can't afford to take that risk. I'm sorry, I would do it if I could, but I can't. I can cross freely into the Veil, to all the layers, but Hell is another story all together. First of all, going in there would mean leaving you alone and vulnerable. Then there's the fact that I don't have a bond to your mother the way you do. She wouldn't come with me. Then there's the fact that there aren't many portals from here going in."

"There had been one in my closet…if I'd only fucking known."

"I know, you would have stepped right in by your-self, if you weren't already dragged there by the demons. Obviously we couldn't have that. Jacob had to close it.

And it wouldn't have helped if you had gone in. The portals that the demons create are teeming with them on the other side, all dying for ways to break into our world. Sometimes they get caught in the middle, in the Veil, other times they pop right onto our streets. Find a vulnerable mind, an angry soul, and take over. The world is going to shit right now, shootings and bombings and so much fucking hate because the very anger and sorrow we feel makes us vulnerable to them. There are devils residing in everyone, all around us. And the worse the world gets, the more they spread. It's a vicious cycle and one that you can help stop. I hate to throw in the argument of saving thousands of souls instead of saving one, but I have to."

"Thousands of souls?" I counter. "Look, I'm sorry the world is destroying itself, but that's not my concern. My mother is my concern. I'm sure I sound despicable to you, but I would rather save her than all those people I don't know. People who are probably inherently evil to begin with."

He sighs softly, looking down. "You don't sound despicable, Ada. You could never because that's not who you are. You're a loving soul and a very loyal daughter. But you have to understand that if I told you the truth, you'd be in Hell right now with no way of ever coming out."

"But you didn't know that," I tell him. "You have no right to decide how I might react. Leave that up to me! You lied to me Jay and now I think you're lying about everything else! I bet you know who you are. Who you were. And you're afraid to tell me!"

"Because it doesn't matter, okay?" he yells right back, with force that shocks me. "It doesn't matter who I was, it has no bearing on what we are to each other!"

"And what are we to each other??"

He exhales noisily, eyes blazing, and runs a hand through his hair. "I wanted to tell you. I did. I went to Jacob and he said I couldn't. It was too risky."

"And you listen to everything he says," I say snidely. "He says you have to lie to me, you lie to me. He tells you to keep your hands off me, you keep your hands off me." I know I should stop talking but I'm like a freight train going off the rails, too much momentum to control. "He says I'm forbidden to you, and so I'm forbidden to you. Did you ever think you have free will? That you're a man of your own mind and heart and action."

"I have no heart!" he roars at me and I am transfixed to the sight, the fire in his eyes, the vein pulsing at his temple, the flush of red on his cheeks. "And I'm barely a man." He leans with his two hands against the wall, trapping me inside. He lowers his head, his hair flopping forward, and pinches his eyes shut. "Do you want the truth?"

I can barely speak. I'm sandwiched between his massive arms, watching him as if he's a lion let loose from his cage. "Yes," I whisper.

"I know who I was," he says, so low and gravely I can barely hear him. "Before I died. Before I became what I am. And I wasn't a good man. I wasn't a good man at all, Ada."

For some reason I yearn to touch him, to soothe him. My hand reaches forward to touch his hair as he's bowed over. He flinches at my fingers as I run them gently through his strands of soft hair. It feels like silk, brings me a strange sense of pleasure.

"Who were you?" I ask.

"My name was Silas Black," he says. "I was Irish. Born in Dublin in the 16th century."

I can only stare at him. My hand pauses. "What?"

He raises his head to look at me, my hand falling away. "It was a long time ago. Which is why what I was, who I was, has nothing to do with who I am right now, with you."

"But you're a rookie," I remind him carefully. Pippa's disbelieving expression when I told her the same floats through my head. "How could you begin again now, so far in the future?"

He cocks his head in form of a shrug. "I don't know. I try not to ask too many questions. Jacob warns about that. Says it can mess with your head. I believe him." He straightens up and I tilt my head back to keep his gaze. His arms stay on either side of my shoulders. "But my duty aside, I am not his prisoner. I do have free will. And with this free will I choose to protect you. In the very sense that some Jacobs will give up their immortality to go rogue, to be free and live and die a normal life. I have choices and I make choices every single moment of every single day. And no one, *no one*, has tested them quite like you."

"How am I testing you?" I say, nearly breathless.

He swallows thickly, his eyes dropping down to my mouth in a heavy-lidded gaze. He doesn't have to say anything. I already know. "I may be immortal but I am still a man with blood pumping in my veins." He moves an inch closer. My skin heats up. Every nerve is burning. "You are off-limits. You are forbidden to me. And all it does is make me want you more."

I shouldn't speak. Just keep my mouth shut and watch him as his expression turns more lustful. Predatory. I already feel like I'm one big coil ready to spring. In anger, in frustration, in shameless abandon.

But I part my lips, because I know what I want and that I'd die to get it, and ask him, softly, "In what way do you want me?"

"Every way. To feel you," he murmurs, his voice shaking like he's trying to hold himself together with all his strength. He slides one of his hands into my hair and I automatically close my eyes. "To taste you. Every inch of you."

My breath hitches.

I'm standing with my toes over the edge, ready to free fall.

I just need the push.

And so does he.

I put my hand on his arm, the one still planted against the wall, and lower it. I guide his hand to the small of my waist, hiking up his Led Zeppelin shirt just enough until the full heat of his palm is flush against my skin.

He closes his eyes, breathing deeply through his nose.

"You undressed me last night," I whisper as the touch of his skin on mine sends heat straight into my core, my legs automatically squeezing together in order to quell it. "You put this shirt on me." I pause, lick my lips. "Did you like what you saw?"

His eyes find mine, startlingly clear. Raw. I'm not scared by their intimacy. He's always stared at me too deeply, like he sees me for all that I am and encourages it.

"Did you touch me?" I go on, tone softer than air.

His gaze never breaks. The slight shake of his head. I believe him.

"You can touch me now," I tell him. I reach down and bring his hand further up, his fingers trailing over my ribs. His thumb brushes against the curve of my breasts, my nipples immediately going hard from even the lightest contact.

His eyes are boring into mine, flashing in shock, in amazement, in desire. He's flickering through emotions while the truth, our argument, my anger, all disappears from my head. All I feel is deep-seated lust, a primal force that's surging through me in ways I've never felt before, enough to make me bold and brazen and greedy.

I'm not myself at this moment.

And I love it.

His hand cups my breast now, thumb skirting over my overly-sensitive nipple. I can't help but gasp, every inch of me now awake and starving for him.

Jay groans, a throaty sound from deep in his gut and he leans in, his lips grazing my cheekbone. "I won't be able to come back from this," he whispers into my ear, sending even more shivers down my spine. "A side of me might come out, one I can never put back. A side better left hidden." He pauses, his thumb pinching my nipple until I'm gasping again. "The more human I get, the more dangerous I become. The more dangerous it is for us. And I can't promise a happy ending."

"I don't need your promises," I tell him, putting my hand behind his neck and holding him there. "I just need you. Right now."

I move my head back slightly so that his forehead is resting against mine. "Besides. I'm starting to get the hang of this whole danger thing. I might even like it." I smile. "You know I—"

His mouth is on mine in a second.

Hot.

Wet.

Feverish.

Hungry.

I'm instantly devoured.

Firm fingers at my chin, holding me in place.

His lips move against mine in a flawless rhythm, a kiss that nearly knocks me off my feet, a kiss that reaches through my mouth and down into the heart of me, erasing every kiss I've ever had.

I'm his first kiss.

And in a moment he's rendered me his equal.

His tongue slips inside my mouth, teasing, testing, sending shockwaves along every sensitive nerve. Warm. Lush. It's decadent, like sweet syrup and I'm drowning.

Where did you learn to kiss like this? I think but don't say because words are stolen from me and I am swept under.

I grip his neck for dear life, as if he'll be lost to me if I don't. His thumb pinches my nipple, hard, and I'm gasping from shock and pleasure, all rolled up in one merciless feeling.

He brings his mouth to my neck, sucking a bruise into my skin, nipping me, a little taste here, a long lick there. His body shudders as he comes closer, his shoulders dwarfing my frame, until his hips are pressed against me.

I swallow at the feel of him, hard and thick and hot along my bare skin. Just from feel alone his size is intimidating but it doesn't stop me from reaching down with my hand, to cup his girth in my palm.

He moans at my touch, a throaty primal sound that shakes his whole body.

"Ada." His lips move along my collarbone, his breath hard and heavy. "I'm not sure you want me to let go. I don't think I can be gentle." He raises up my shirt, exposing my breast before dipping his head. My body arches back, my eyes close, welcoming his mouth on my nipple, hot and wet and exquisite. The pressure between my legs is building, a fire uncontained, begging to be put out.

I don't want gentle. I want his hands lower.

"Touch me," I whisper, pushing his hand away from my breast where his tongue is teasing in slow circles. I lead it down the front of my stomach, my abs tightening as his skin brushes against me.

He hesitates before the band of my underwear, maybe having second thoughts. He pulls his head up and stares at me, this wild, barely caged beast in his eyes. I stare right back, wanting him, willing him. I've never been so god damn needy before in my life, never thought it was even possible to feel this kind of hunger, to chase my release like an animal after prey.

He shuts his eyes, his mouth finds mine again, our lips and tongues fused together, a rock against flint until we're sparking into flames. His taste, oh his taste. I could drink him in all day.

Then his fingers slowly slide down into my underwear, long and intimidating in their own right. Hands that seem to know my skin already, that possess an ease with the intimacy.

He sucks in a sharp breath when he finds how wet I am. I don't even have breath to begin with. My body has become a surprise to me, like it's finally showing me what it can do, what it wants, needs, craves.

His fingertips are rough and I am silk and he slides one finger slowly, deliberately, over my most sensitive flesh. Now I'm groaning, whimpering, feeling too much, needing too much. I feel myself opening wider as the pressure gets tighter. I grab onto his neck, his shoulder, my legs starting to give way as the blood inside becomes weightless.

He responds by dipping his fingers lower until I feel him inside me, then slowly drags it back out, pressing hard.

I can't stop it. Can't hold back.

I explode into his hands and Ada doesn't exist anymore. I'm boneless, jelly, reduced to a single-celled organism floating in the stars. I know I'm crying out loudly, that Jay is grunting into my neck, finding pleasure in my pleasure, my nails digging into him so hard that I'm sure I'm drawing blood.

I'm still not myself, still not of sound mind, still shooting across galaxies when he grunts "Fuck" and then picks me up, throwing me onto the bed.

I lie there, dazed, sated and yet forever insatiable, as he puts his hands at my collar and rips the t-shirt right in half. Totally unnecessary but Jay is no longer here, just like Ada is no longer here. His eyes tell a different story, one of an untamed beast who gets to hunt and eat for the first time in his life.

My underwear is deftly shucked off and I'm lying here on my back, naked and exposed to him for the first time.

His eyes rake over my body, taking me in, his nostrils flaring like a bull about to charge.

Yet, somehow he holds back. It's an effort. His face is flushed, jaw set, his muscles straining as he stands there at the foot of the bed, letting his eyes taste me.

Then he strips.

Shirt gone.

Jeans gone.

Boxer briefs gone.

And then Jay is naked.

I knew he was a chiseled, masculine work of art but I had no idea just how magnificent he was until right now. Every inch of his body is flawless, lightly golden, and cut like a diamond.

And he's hung.

As in *well-well-well*-hung.

I'd only felt him minutes ago, but it still takes me by surprise. I don't think I've ever properly leered at a man like this before, let alone a naked one. Dillon had a good body but it was one of a boy and he didn't wear it with confidence. The glimpses I got of him were quick and hurried, usually blurred by alcohol or clothing.

But not Jay. I see him clearly with hawk eyes that take in every hard inch. Jay is all man and he stands before me not giving two shits that he's naked. If anything, he wants me to stare, wants a reaction. He's been so skilled thus far that I keep forgetting that the man is a virgin in the loosest terms and adoration over his body might be exactly what he needs.

I don't fake it. My mouth has been gaping this entire time and the release I found moments ago is back to building inside me, just as greedy and eager for him now as I was before.

"Come here," I say, my voice choked with yearning. My boldness still surprises me, the fact that I lack any shame or insecurity. Being with him has made me want to own every beat of this moment.

He clears his throat, his eyes blazing at the invitation. "Are you sure?"

He's afraid to let go still, afraid he'll hurt me.

I don't care.

"Whatever you do to me," I tell him, "is exactly what I need and want." I slide my hand down between my legs, parting them slightly, giving him a look. "I can handle it. I can handle you."

He lets out what can only be described as a growl. "We'll see about that," he hisses and then he's on me in a flash, the mass of his body looming over mine. Impatience fuels his hands as they slip between my legs, as they slide up my sides, as they settle back into my hair and make a fist.

Lips find mine, open and messy and wild, and then his mouth is everywhere, my collarbone, my breast, my stomach. For a moment his head goes between my legs, his tongue, flat and hot, licking the inside of my thighs before it laps up my clit, causing me to teeter to the edge again.

I grab his hair and haul his face up and for a moment worry lines his brow until I say, "I don't want to come so soon."

He wipes his glistening mouth with his forearm and now he looks confused, probably wondering why I don't want to come all day every day. But the truth is, I want him inside me as quickly as possible. The cravings are getting too powerful to ignore.

He moves up my body, placing a hand beside my head to prevent his muscled frame from crushing me as his knee jerks my legs further apart. With his other hand he grips his dick, positions himself between my legs. His entire body is shaking with an urgency that I can feel in the heart of me.

This, now.

I need this, this, this.

Please.

Now.

Please.

But somehow there is still reason inside my brain. It speaks up. "Do we need a condom?" I ask breathlessly. Because that's been a hard fast rule for me, having used one with Dillon every time.

He almost looks amused, his mouth inches from mine. "Trust me when I say we don't." And in the real world with some other guy, I wouldn't believe that line. But this isn't a line. And this bedroom feels miles away from the real world and Jay isn't some guy. He's barely human, mostly supernatural, and I'm guessing he'd be shooting blanks.

Satisfied with that, I reach around and slide my hands down the hard planes of his back, all the way to his ass, impossibly round and firm. I grip him there and shrug him forward, urging him inside me.

His gaze is on fire as he stares into my eyes, the connection between us burning like an electrical fire.

"Oh you gorgeous creature," he murmurs.

Then he pushes in, just enough, a raspy hiss coming from the back of his throat. He teases, coming out again, testing me, taunting me.

"Please," I whimper, unable to keep it together, this insatiable want.

He growls again, an animal noise, and pushes in fast and hard and I can't breathe. He's heavy, hard, and so thick that when his hips push against mine, I'm close to being in pain.

But then the pain melts away to something else, my body giving way to his as his hips perfectly curl toward me with each and every thrust, the sensation of ourselves fusing together in perfect harmony, and now it's like I can't get enough of him. He's air and I'm gulping him down, needing him to survive every second.

He's grunting loudly now, sweat dripping from his brow, and I can see the restraint in him, that despite all he's warned me about, he's still holding back. I dig my nails into him ass and moan, "Jay. Harder. Rougher." Just to spur him on. "All of you, give me all of you."

It works.

Something in him unhinges, the cage door swings open and the wild beast is unleashed.

He comes at me with fury, his hands gripping my hips like a vice to keep me in place, the headboard starting to slam against the wall. Somewhere in the room a painting falls off and shatters. The sheets on the bed pop off and bunch behind me.

There is sex and there is fucking. I've never known the latter until right now, until this moment when something snaps within me, a wild creature of my own. Because this is pure and unadulterated and as immortal as he is.

And I'm enslaved to it.

I am equally as savage, desperate and crazed.

I rake my nails down his back drawing blood, and he's biting my neck until the skin breaks and we're two sweaty, frenzied animals who buck and pull and slam against each other at a breakneck pace.

He's grabbing the headboard now, pulling us both up so we're not falling off the bed and I watch with wide eyes as he hovers over me, each straining muscle, glistening with sweat. His face is the picture of pure determination as he works me hard.

He might pull that headboard right off, is my last thought before my brain gets gummy and the world swells with warmth. My body is close to the edge and I hover in the split-second before the fall as all the switches in me flick to on.

Keep going.

Keep going.

Keep going.

I pull him even closer, rutting up into him, hunting my release.

Keep —

I go off, the spark at the end of the fuse, and just before I pinch my eyes shut, unable to control any part of my body, I glance at Jay. He's staring down at me in amazement, maybe even pride, like he's seeing something most people never see, like a meteor shower at sunset, or dawn from the top of Everest. He's looking at me like I'm the most beautiful sight he'll ever witness and that I'm his and always will be.

Then the orgasm becomes too much and I close my eyes and I'm molten, lava flowing through me, igniting my soul as my legs quiver and my body jerks and I'm just completely obliterated. I'm sure there are bits of me all over the place, like I've exploded into fiery confetti.

Jay lets out a hoarse cry and starts slamming into me harder. The air crackles between us and time seems to slow down. Maybe it really is slowing down. I can see and feel everything he's doing to me in perfect clarity while the room starts to buzz, a glow entering all corners of my vision.

My eyes are glued again to Jay as he comes, his rhythm frantic and punishing and making up for so much lost time. His gazes at me in surprise, like he's caught off guard, and then his head is arched back, his neck exposed. A thick, inhumane roar comes from his lips as they fall open, then softens into a groan.

The strangest thing is that I think I can feel him as he comes, like he's filling me with heat and starlight and it's seeping through every inch of me. The sensation is as supernatural as he is.

His pumping slows and finally stills, arms braced on the headboard, his head hanging, the sweat dripping onto my chest. Then he comes down, his breath still ragged, and props himself on his elbows on either side of my head.

We don't speak.

Not with our mouths.

We speak with our eyes, the way he looks over me with so much tenderness and awe it nearly brings me to tears.

We speak with our hands, as my fingers skirt down his damp spine, as his thumbs brush the hair off my face.

We speak with our lips as he places his against mine, soft and sweet and still needy underneath.

We speak with our bodies as he rests inside me, still pulsing, and I wrap my legs around his waist. He's almost getting hard all over again.

And that's all we need to say to each other.

Our breaths are caught, our sweat is cooled.

And we start all over again.

CHAPTER SEVENTEEN

I've always been the first one to roll my eyes at Cosmopolitan when the cover promises "Mind-blowing Orgasms Tonight!" or when girls wax about how awesome some guy was in bed. I figured the whole world was lying to me, because when I had sex with Dillon, my mind wasn't blown. If anything was blown, it was him, a thankless job.

Sex was never horrible—except for the first time, in the back of his car, where it not only hurt because the asshole didn't believe in foreplay and I was too unschooled to know what I wanted, but it was awkward too. We didn't know each other's bodies at all and Dillon didn't really care. So sex during our relationship had just been okay. I never came and I only figured out the magic of masturbation after we broke up, but I put up with it because this was it, the thing that's supposed to change your life.

But now I get it. Now I understand and I understand in such a way that I'm thinking back to those Cosmo covers and I know they have no idea. No idea what mind-blowing really is.

Because what Jay and I have, what we share, goes beyond sex. The sex goes beyond sex. I'm sure if the rest of the world just experienced what I experienced, humanity would end up dead in their bedrooms. This is the kind of sex that makes you crave more of it, that has you forgoing food and water and sunlight and proper speech, just to have one small taste of ecstasy.

Needless to say, Jay has ruined me. In his warnings, I know he said I would ruin him, change him. And this might be true. The more insatiable sex we have, the more wild, more human, he becomes. But I never thought I would be reduced to such a primitive beast myself, a craving, lustful, starving creature that can't get her fill.

We spend four days in that Seaside hotel room.

We don't venture outside once.

We order room service, but we barely touch our food.

All we touch is each other.

Four days of him being inside me, making me come over and over, taking me every way he can, everywhere he can. The floor, the desk, the shower, the sink, even the balcony late at night when I have to bite down on his shoulder to keep quiet.

And somewhere in the back of my lust-addled mind, I know this isn't normal. I know that sex isn't supposed to be *this* good. I know that the man fucking me is a man in all the right ways, but not quite a man all the same. An immortal beast that's finally unleashing his deepest, most primal desires.

But I don't care. The sex has rendered me stupid and ignorant but incomparably happy all the same.

Until the outside world has a way of reaching in.

Jay's phone rings just as we're coming, our bodies entwined on top of the covers. My orgasm is ripping me apart and I'm floating so high that reason doesn't enter my head until I start to come down.

Jay had put his ringer to off.

Then my phone rings.

My ringer is also set to off.

Then the hotel phone rings.

And finally Jay is pulling out of me. It translates to instant hollowness, like I'm being denied a vital part of me. He brushes the hair from my sweaty brow, his sated eyes turning to annoyance. "I have a feeling if we don't answer, we're going to get a very unwanted visit," he says, getting off the bed and striding over to the desk, the morning light from the balcony making him light up like an angel. My eyes are fixed to his large thighs, the taught, round swells of his ass that are blemished with a few bruises of my own doing. I can't help it. With an ass like that, you have to bite it.

Jay snatches up the phone, clearing his throat. "Hello?" he answers but it still sounds husky, like he's spent the last few hours moaning and groaning. Which he has.

I can't hear the conversation but I already know it's Jacob. There's not many people who can make a muted phone ring.

Jay doesn't say anything except "everything is fine" and "yes." Then he hangs up, keeps his back to me. I momentarily admire his shoulders, made for an Olympic swimmer, before I ask, "What did he say?"

"Said the coast is clear," he says as he turns around, folding his chiseled arms over his chest, the very chest I like to run my nails down. "We can go back to your home."

Home. It sounds like a foreign word. This is my home now more than anything.

He's my home.

My eyes drift down to his cock, still half-hard.

"Ada," he says imploringly. "We have to go."

I sigh and flop back dramatically on the bed, my fingers curling around the sheets like it's second nature. "I don't want to go home. I want to stay here with you. Our cocoon."

"I'm not taking you home," he says, coming over and slipping on a pair of boxer briefs.

This has my attention. "What are you talking about?"

"Your mother," he says to me and images of her crash into my mind. Her in Hell, tortured, begging for help. It's all it takes to bring me out of the sex-haze and into the very real and very painful reality.

Oh god, I've been so heartless. This whole time I've been having sex with Jay and not bothering to remember what Pippa said.

"It's okay," he says, reading me. "You were handed a painful pill to swallow. They say sex is always used to keep the truth at bay. I get that now. You were trying to protect yourself."

Protect myself by sleeping with him? "Jay, that's not why we've—"

"I know that too," he says, pulling on a grey t-shirt. "But it certainly makes things easier. But your mother is still in Hell, she still needs your help."

I frown at him, the guilt lingering. "What are you saying? You've been trying to keep me from this."

"I know," he says, reaching down and tossing me the black dress I arrived here with. I honestly haven't worn any clothes since. "But you're right. I should have never kept you from it. It wasn't fair. And now I want to help you get her back."

I can scarcely believe my ears. "What?"

He sits on the edge of the bed. "You can put up walls, Ada."

"But I don't know how to do it. It just happens."

"Exactly. Which is why you can't do this on your own. I mean, how exactly would you wander down to Hell anyway?"

My brain is still fuzzy from the last few days and struggling to be used again. "Get Perry to make a portal?"

"It would be a portal to the Thin Veil and a dangerous one at that. She would have no idea how to get there and it would only harm her while endangering others. You have to go through a portal with me. And I know where one is."

"And you've been in this portal to Hell before?"

He shakes his head, gives me a twisted smile. "I've never been to Hell before, as far as I know."

"Then how do you know what to expect?"

He stares at me in that way of his, the one that says *I just do*.

I blink, feeling a rush of something new in my veins, clearing out the dreamy lust.

It's hope.

"So you're saying you'll take me to this portal and come with me to Hell to get my mother back? Sorry, I just want to make sure we're on the same page here."

Jay nods gravely. "It's the only option we have." He pauses, gives me a steady look. "But it's up to you. This is your choice. Your call."

"Well then. I guess we're going to Hell together."

He doesn't smile at that. Instead he gnaws on his lower lip, thinking. "This isn't going to be easy, Ada. People say things are going to be Hell without even the slightest notion of what Hell is."

"You said you've never been there."

"Just because I've never been there doesn't mean I haven't seen it. It's worse than your imagination can possibly allow you to comprehend. It's like trying to think of infinite space. You can't. Your brain won't be able to wrap around what you'll see. Or hear. Or smell. Or feel. It's your worst nightmare, when you're running from something but you're slowing down and they're catching up and it's that moment before it's on you, the anticipation of being ripped to shreds, and then actually being ripped to shreds. Then it's fifty times that horror. Over and over and over again, burrowing inside every cell until you don't even know who you are anymore and you're certain you never had a soul. You'll forget your name, where you came from, and who you were meant to find. You'll forget everything until all that's left is a pinprick of who you used to be and eternal damnation instead."

My eyes have been held wide open this entire time. If he meant to scare me, he's terrified me. But even so, I raise my chin and look him dead in the eye. "I'm going to get my mother back."

A ghost of a smile graces his lips, something like admiration. "Okay. But first, I have a request."

"Don't speak to the Devil unless spoken to?"

"Yes, *that*," he says. "Just like the Veil, there are specific rules we need to follow or it's all over. But, we have to head up to Seattle. To see your sister."

"Perry? Why?"

"Because of everything I've just said. Because you need to remember where you came from and who you're there to find. Perry's special, just like you, and your bond is just as strong as the one between you and your mother. You need to see her before you go. Even normal people feel comfort in having a loved one nearby. But you two aren't normal. She'll imprint on you for a few days, it's part of your abilities and your bond, how close you are. Your mother will be able to feel her too through you. It will make things a lot easier, trust me."

As weird as that all sounds, I know he's right. After I spend some time with Perry, I often feel her with me for a few days after.

"Okay," I say, picking up my phone from the bedside table and glancing at it.

A million missed calls and texts. One from Jacob, I'm assuming. Some from Dad. Most from Perry, even Dex.

I know I'm going to get an earful but I dial anyway. No way is she going to understand I haven't been in touch because I've been having a load of hot sex.

She answers right away.

"Oh my god, are you okay!? Ada!?" Perry yells so loud I have to hold the phone at arm's length for a moment.

"I'm fine," I manage to say before she erupts again.

"You asshole! Where the hell have you been? I've been calling and texting and calling and texting and you never answered! I was so worried! Fuck, Ada! I called Dad and he said that you were off with Amy somewhere and so I called *Amy,*" Oh no, "and she said you guys weren't really friends anymore. So that was a fucking surprise! How come you didn't tell me that? And then I started really freaking the fuck out because oh my god, what if you've been kidnapped. Or worse? So then I called Dad." Oh no! "And guess who answered? Jacob. He explained what's really going on, that you had to leave and Jay has you. Is that true?"

"Uh, yes." I'm looking at Jay with wide eyes. "That's true. I'm with him now."

"Is he being okay to you?"

I laugh.

"It's not funny, Ada. You don't even know the guy."

I roll my eyes with a sigh. "Yes, he's being *okay* to me."

Jay frowns and gestures to the bed in disbelief as if to say *I think I've been more than okay.*

I dismiss him with my hand. "Anyway," I say quickly into the phone. "We were wondering if we could come over tonight."

"Tonight?" she asks. "Where are you? He said you were in Seaside. If I didn't hear from you soon I was going to start calling every single hotel."

"We're here but we're leaving. I don't want to go home quite yet," I tell her this white lie.

"You know you have school next week."

"I know. Don't worry. So can we come say hi or not?"

"We?" she repeats.

"Well obviously Jay is with me."

She exhales noisily. A pause. "Yes. Fine."

Sheesh. What's up her butt? "Okay, great. So we'll see you in like four hours or something."

"Text me when you're near so I can run down and let you in the parking garage."

"Will do."

Pause.

"Perry?" I ask.

"Yeah?"

"Be nice," I tell her. "Dex is rubbing off on you a bit too much."

Then I hang up.

Jay raises his brows at me. "I get the distinct feeling they don't like me."

I shrug with one shoulder. "Eh. She's had bad experiences with Jacobs and I'm pretty sure she's against any guy I spend too much time with."

"But she has no idea about..." he trails off and motions to the room.

"Oh hell no," I tell him. "And she's not going to know. She's protective over me as it is."

"So am I," he reasons.

"She wouldn't understand. I'll always be fifteen years old to her, just a kid."

"You're still just a kid," he says lightly, eyes dancing.

I glare at him. "Compared to someone who is ageless and immortal, yeah I guess I am." I exhale and get up on my knees, about to slip the dress on. "So, when we get there, this can't happen anymore."

"Are you sure you'll be able to control yourself?" he asks, cocking a brow.

"Hey," I chide him.

"Because you came on to me pretty hard." He gets on the bed on his knees and crawls toward me. "Temptress."

"And you came *on* me pretty hard," I counter. It was such an easy pun, I couldn't pass it up.

"Wouldn't mind doing it again before we hit the road," he says, his voice taking on that throaty, thick quality that makes me want to surrender every cell to him.

He prowls over me, mouth going to my neck where he gently sucks.

I wrap my hands around his t-shirt and pull it off, reveling in the feel of his hard back muscles like I've been deprived for centuries.

We fall back into bed together, sighing softly.

Reality is put on hold for another hour.

. . .

We get to Seattle around four, the sun glinting off the high rises and the flat mat of Puget Sound. Perry and Dex live pretty much downtown, by the monorail tracks that have me singing *The Simpsons* monorail song every time I see them.

In fact, as we head down Fifth Avenue and I see the track, I start singing along.

Poor Jay has no idea what I'm doing.

I think I'm losing my mind, is what it is.

The whole drive I've been training myself to go back to thinking of Jay as I did before. Well that didn't help because I was always being a pervy girl after him anyway. But going from having our hands all over each other, sharing secrets with our sex and souls, to now just a strictly Jacob and student scenario (as if that's some common situation) is rough.

I want to touch him. I ache for it. I want to feel his body against mine. His lips. His breath. I want to keep him close, closer than ever. This is all so new for me, this transition from one reality (you can't have him) to another (have all the sex) and back again is disorienting.

I'm like every girl in that head-over-heels infatuation stage where he's all you eat, sleep, breathe, but it's been cranked higher and higher—lust on meth—to the point where I feel like we're fated for each other.

And fuck, as nuts as it sounds, we might be. Because otherwise there's no way to explain it. I can just guess that having constant sex with someone immortal might warp your mind, body, and soul in ways you've never expected.

But if Jay is straining against this new rule (which, I remind myself, was my idea in order to ward off Perry's wrath), he doesn't show it. He's back to a tight jaw, a harsh squint, as if nothing's happened between us at all.

Or maybe it's because the more time he spends with me, and the more human, the more emotional he becomes, the more that Silas Black peeks through. And the more we're apart (aka, not inside me every moment), the more he reverts back to his old self.

Of course he could be thinking about what we're doing after this. The going to Hell thing. I've decided to push that concept out of my poor brain and deal with it later.

And by later, I mean tomorrow.

I text Perry just as we pull onto her street and then twist in my seat to face Jay.

"Didn't Jacob say it was a bad idea to have all four of us in the same place together?"

He nods, chewing on his lip again. "He did. But that was then and this is now. And he's not always right you know."

"You mean the all-powerful Oz can be wrong about something?" I ask in mock shock.

"He has been before," Jay says. "He told me if I ever touched you, I wouldn't like the human I'd become. I can't say I agree with that."

Ouch. "He said that?"

"Don't worry about it. Scare tactics. He just wants me to do my job and this makes me want to do it better than ever." He props his shades up on his head so I can see his eyes. So piercing and blue, I almost gasp. "I haven't lost anything. I've only gained."

Perry comes out of the doors, breaking up our moment. She waves at me excitedly, then gives a stiff smile to Jay before walking to the parking garage and gesturing for us to follow. She waves her key card in front of the reader and the gates open.

We drive in and park in one of the visitor's spots.

In parking garage terms, I've had one demon incident the last two times I've been in one. Let's see what the third one holds!

But it's just Perry pulling me into a bear hug before she says, "You smell funny."

"Gee thanks," I say as she holds me at arm's length and inspects my dress and denim shorts combo. "I saw you wearing this on Instagram, like, last week. A repeat outfit, Ada are you feeling all right?"

She pretends to feel my forehead—which does feel flushed at the moment—and I knock her hand away.

"I didn't pack properly, it was last minute," I tell her, even though Jay packed for me. "I may need to borrow your clothes."

She raises her brow. "Everything will be huge on you."

I don't comment. She looks over at Jay. "Thanks for getting her here safely," she says with effort.

He nods gravely, his eyes flicking to me and back. "Not a problem. Thanks for letting us stay over."

She gives him a tight smile before she starts leading me toward the stairs. "You have a lot of explaining to do," she whispers in my ear.

"It's a long story and I didn't want to worry you," I tell her. "Plus Jacob said—"

"Not that story," she says in a hush. "Though I want to hear that one too. The one with you and this guy." She jerks her head back at Jay who is following behind us, carrying our bags and obviously overhearing everything. "You're in big, big trouble. I can tell. I can smell it all over you."

I grimace and resist the urge to give myself a sniff.

"I have no idea what you're talking about."

Moments later we're taking the elevator up to their floor and heading down the hall to their apartment.

Dex is at the kitchen island, pouring a glass of red wine. Fat Rabbit, their white fat French bulldog, comes scampering off the couch and running over to us as he normally does, all stubby limbs and wiggling butt.

He jumps up on my legs and I lean over to pet him when Jay steps in the apartment. Fat Rabbit snarls at him, barking repeatedly until he turns around and runs all the way to their bedroom.

"Hey you little fartface," Dex admonishes him, putting down the glass of wine and shooting us an apologetic look. "Sorry, I don't know what's gotten into him." He goes down the hall after him and I can hear him berating the dog in their bedroom.

I look behind me at Jay who is closing the door.

"I must have one of those faces," Jay says, not seeming too bothered by the fact that the dog just acted like he was a spawn of Satan.

"Yeah," Perry says slowly, giving him a skeptical look. "Anyway, do you guys want a drink? Jay, want a beer? Wine?"

"A beer would be great," he says.

While she pulls a growler out of the fridge and two glasses from the cupboards, Dex comes back into the room.

"Little fuck," he swears. Then he strides over to Jay and for a moment I'm certain they're going to have a pissing competition considering the last time they saw each other was when we were in the streets in the wee hours of the morning and Jay just kidnapped me to the Thin Veil. That feels like a different life, a different Ada.

A different Jay.

But Dex just takes the backpack and duffle bag from Jay's hands. "Let me take those." He holds up the backpack and starts walking across the room. "This one yours, Jay?"

Before Jay can tell him yes, he tosses it on the couch. Then he goes to the spare bedroom turned den turned office and chucks my duffle bag in there. "Jay you get the couch. Ada you get the spare bedroom."

"Cool," I say, trying to sound cool too. "Thanks for letting us stay over, by the way. I know it's last minute and you guys are busy."

"Ada," Perry says, handing Jay his glass of beer and me the wine, "you're my sister. You could have just showed up unannounced and it would have been fine."

"Besides," Dex says, taking the other glass of beer, "you're a great excuse to get out of the damn apartment.

I've been working too hard all week and if I didn't have a reason to stop, Perry was going to divorce me."

"Oh stop," she says. "But I was going to tell you that we've made dinner reservations for tonight."

"Don't tell me Zeke's Pizza again."

"No," Dex says dryly, knowing full-well that every time I'm here we end up eating at the pizza place because it's right around the corner. "A little place up in Fremont. They have Italian waiters who kiss you on the cheek when you come in. I love it."

"You mean The Olive Garden?"

"Well aren't you picky, little fifteen."

I stick my tongue out at him.

"Cheers for needed escapes then," I say, raising my glass of wine. Everyone else does the same, Jay reaching over me as we all lean toward each other to clink our glasses.

It turns out that the dinner reservation was actually for six people. When we get to the restaurant, around the corner from the famous Fremont troll, which, despite its cartoonish appearance, is terrifying to me in a completely irrational way, two other people from our party are already there, waiting by the doors.

I've met them before and I call them the odd couple because I'm not quite sure what's up with them. Rebecca is gorgeous, a British rockabilly pin-up girl type that could be an even prettier version of Kat Von D. With her is Dean, cocoa-skinned and cool as a cucumber. The two of them have a baby together but as far as I know she's a lesbian and he's straight. But hey, I'm not one to judge.

After the quick formalities—Jay is introduced as a friend of mine—we take our seats and get drinking, the Chianti (I get a Coke) and breadsticks flowing.

The conversation comes easy. Rebecca is talkative, as is Dex, and the two of them dominate the entire table to the point where it's almost a competition of who can be louder and more engaging.

Occasionally a question is hurtled my way and it seems Rebecca has a checklist about my design school. Actually it's nice to be able to talk to someone about this who actually cares and has an interest in fashion. It comes to the point that Jay goes and switches seats with Rebecca so she can grill me some more. Even having him a few chairs down from me feels hollow and wrong but Rebecca does a good job of making me forget every strange and horrifying thing that lies in my future. I'm pretending, just for a bit, that the only things I have to worry about are what kind of designs I need for my portfolio and what outfit I'll wear the first day of school.

"I'll tell you what," Rebecca says, her English accent coming out stronger now as she leans lazily on her elbows, swigging her wine. "If you need a model for your projects, count me in. I know I've had a baby but I can wear a corset like no one's business."

"Where is your child, anyway?" Dex asks, pretending to look under the table. "Lucinda?"

"Seb has her," she says, which makes everyone at the table laugh, except for Jay and I. That's the problem with hanging out with this crowd, you end up feeling lost all the time and missing all the inside jokes.

My eyes glance down the table at Jay and I can't help but smile at the sight of him. They might all have their own stories and their own worlds, but Jay is my story, my world. Perry and Dex may not trust him but this is the man who's willing to go to Hell and back with me. You can't ask for much more than that.

As if sensing me, Jay looks up from nodding at Dean over something and holds my gaze. It bolts me to the chair, the chair to the floor. Roots me there. Grounds me.

He doesn't say anything, his expression doesn't change to the naked eye but I know he's telling me he's there.

Perry clears her throat.

I look to her with an innocent expression as her eyes dart between the two of us. Jay goes back to saying something to Dean. I quickly dig into my penne pasta.

I'm about to shove it in my mouth but I'm hit with a sense of pressure, like the air has solidified.

The room goes mute.

I look up from the dish and pause.

Everyone at the table is staring at me with a grim expression. Even Jay.

The waiters have stopped moving. They are staring at me too.

It feels as if icy fluid has been injected into my veins, chilling me from the inside out, sticky and black and relentless.

I immediately drop my fork. It rattles loudly against the plate, the sound a gunshot.

But no one flinches.

Every single person in the restaurant is still staring at me. Some glaring. Some seething with disappointment. All absolutely still and looking right into my eyes.

I try to speak. To get them to snap out of it.

I can't.

It's like *Inception* when you're caught in a dream, but I know I'm not dreaming. This is real.

I do the only thing I can do. I very slowly get out of my chair.

The eyes follow me.

All of them, glued to my face.

All but Jay.

His are still frozen to where I was.

And they're wavering, like something is about to break out of him.

He knows. In this instant I know he knows something is wrong and he's trying to get to me.

But what exactly is this?

Oh my girl.

I stop where I am, in between tables, as this monstrous, disembodied voice descends on me from all directions.

You think you're so clever, it hisses, seeping into my bones like cancer. *I know exactly what you're going to do.*

I make eye contact with the waiter nearest me, espresso on his tray, still as a frozen lake. His eyes are murderous.

But I don't say a thing to the voice. I have nothing to say.

I see you, it says. It feels like something you might find at the bottom of the sea, something that lives in immense blackness, otherworldly, not meant for ours. *I see the both of you. Keep at it girl. Keep at it.*

Then it laughs, a laugh that makes me gasp for breath, my lungs grinding like they're stuffed with steel wool.

See you tomorrow.

A shadow slides into my field of vision and I watch as it glides toward the kitchen before it opens the swinging door and disappears inside.

Blood trickles out from underneath the door, as steady as a stream as it builds and builds, flowing into the restaurant and splashing along the legs of the tables like waves against a pier.

It's not real, I tell myself. *This isn't real.*

Even though the eyes are still on me, each soul unmoved, I go back to my seat.

Sit back down.

Pick up my fork and close my eyes, counting down from *ten.*

Nine.

Eight.

Seven.

The pressure ends with a sonic boom.

My eyes blast open, ears popping.

The blood is gone and the restaurant is back at full volume, everyone chatting with each other, drinking, eating, paying attention to everything else except me. Absolutely unaware of what just happened.

Everyone but Jay, who is staring at me in horror, a look that chills me.

"Excuse me, I need some fresh air," I say to Rebecca, immediately getting back up and heading out the door. I can hear Jay's chair being pushed back, feel Perry's concerned gaze but I don't turn around until I'm on the street.

It's busy out here with traffic and pedestrians and the night air is hot as fuck, but still I'm shivering like I've just come out of the deep freeze.

I turn around at the sound of the door opening, relief flooding me when I see Jay.

I immediately collapse into his arms, not caring if anyone inside the restaurant can see me. He holds me tight, kissing the top of my head.

"You're freezing," he tells me, then pulls away and takes me by the hand around the corner where the garish glow of the streetlights can't reach us. To be honest, I need everything bright and garish right now because I can't banish the darkness inside me.

"Something happened," I whisper when he doesn't say anything.

"I know." He's holding onto my hand, looking down the street, his jaw stiff. "I saw. I couldn't do anything." He nearly grinds out those last words. "I felt them."

Them. The term makes my heart drop. "Them who?"

"Legion," he says. "He is many. And he was there."

Legion. The demon of many demons. The one that even Jay can't defeat. Inside the restaurant with me.

"Why didn't he take me?" I question, voice trembling.

"I don't know," he says. He looks at me sharply. "He could have. And he shouldn't have been able to. I should have been able to move, to protect you." He throws his head back, stares up at the night sky which is filled with light pollution from the city across Lake Union. "I don't know what's happening."

My stomach churns, acidic. I don't want to see Jay like this. Remorseful. Confused.

"He said, he'll see me tomorrow," I say quietly.

Jay closes his eyes. "This is going to be harder than I thought."

"You thought going to Hell would be a piece of cake? You were the one scaring the pants off me earlier telling me what to expect."

He tips his head down to look at me. "My god, it's been impossible not to touch you tonight." He steps forward and runs his fingers down my cheekbone.

I immediately surrender to his touch. Powerless. Completely aware that I'm nothing but clay his hands, surrendering to his whim, and being completely okay with it. Old Ada would kill me.

His fingers slip down my cheek. Gently trace my jaw. Back and forth. So soft. His hands trail down my neck. He grips me there, gently, like he's ready to strangle me, his thumb against my windpipe, his fingers holding the back of my neck. He does this sometimes before he kisses me and my eyes start fluttering in anticipation.

"Sometimes I look at you and I wonder," he says, his voice taking on a strange quality, like it's being filtered, muffled, "what power your blood could bring."

It's not what he says at the end there that makes my blood run cold.

And it's not the Irish accent that he says it in.

It's that when I look at his eyes, I don't see Jay anymore. I see someone else entirely.

Stare into the abyss and the abyss stares right back.

Silas Black.

"Ada!"

Perry's shrill voice slices through the mounting horror.

I immediately pull back from Jay, as if we've been caught doing something, but the fact is I'm afraid, my gut feeling like it's coated in black tar. I refuse to look at him, too afraid to still see Silas there, and run over to her.

"What happened? You sick?" she asks, looking between me and Jay.

But the last thing I want is for her to suspect him even more.

"Yeah," I tell her and I'm amazed I'm able to fake a bored voice. "I don't know what was in that pasta but it did not agree with me. Thought I was going to puke everywhere."

Perry stares over my shoulder at Jay. "Are you all right?" she asks and at that I turn around to look.

Jay is staring into space, blinking, his chest heaving like he's been running for miles. Finally he realizes we're staring at him, his head swiveling in our direction.

"Jay?" I say loudly.

His eyes snap to mine, widen. Then he swallows, bites his lip. Runs his hand through his hair. Beyond agitated. "I'm fine," he croaks.

I know Perry's looking at this situation like we were just having a lover's spat but she couldn't be further from the truth.

"Jay," she says, waving him over. "Why don't you go back inside? I'd like a word with my sister."

Jay nods and strides past us, doesn't even look in my direction once. When he's gone around the corner I feel the connection between us sever, for better or for worse.

Perry turns to me. "Okay, spill. Tell me everything. Now."

"What?"

"Don't play dumb. Do you want me in your head or not?"

"You said it didn't work that way!"

She smirks. "We evolve."

I push at her forehead. "I'll let you in if you just stay out."

"Then tell me what the hell is happening! Are you sleeping with him?"

Point blank. Wouldn't have expected any less from her. And there's no point lying.

"Yes."

"Ada!" she shrieks, smacking my arm hard. "What the fuck is wrong with you?"

I rub at my arm, frowning at her. "Don't judge me or I'll judge you."

"Judge me for what?"

"I dunno, sleeping with Dex when he had a girlfriend?"

Ah, the look of death. I used to shrink from it. Not anymore. "That was different."

"How was that okay and this isn't?"

"*Ada*," she practically yells. I know she's trying not to smack me upside the head. "Oh my god. Are you hearing yourself? How is it okay? Um, gee, for one thing he's not even a fucking human."

"He was a human," I eke out, remembering his words, his look, when he became someone else. "His body is human."

"Do you hear your justification right now? I mean, seriously. Do you? Look, you can't sleep with your Jacob. How in the hell could that ever turn out okay? He's fucking immortal!"

I'm starting to feel small. Very small. Very young. Very over my head.

And I can't explain it except in the lamest ways possible.

I feel fated for him.

We're meant for each other.

I was blind and now I see.

But I don't know what I see now.

"You don't understand," is all I can muster.

She sighs, turning her back to me, as if drawing strength from the street. When she turns back, her face has softened. "I know you're going through a tough time right now. I know that. And I know he's there to help you. But you have to understand that this can never end well. You know that, don't you? And if you don't...you need to talk to Rose."

I frown. Rose sounds familiar.

She goes on, fiddling with the anchor bracelet around her wrist. "Rose was, is, just like me, like you. She needed a Jacob to fight the demons. That was her *plight.* Her destiny. She had one. His name was Maximus."

I suck in my breath, knowing exactly where this is going.

"Maximus trained Rose," she says. "They worked together as a team, banishing the demons or whatever back to where they came. But over time, or maybe it was in the blink of an eye, I don't know, Rose and Maximus fell in love. He went rogue for her. Gave up his immortality, his abilities, so he could live the normal life with her. All for her." She pauses, leveling me with her gaze. "Then she broke up with him. Broke his heart. And he eventually died. The end."

"Jesus Perry," I swear. "The other version of this story was a lot better."

"This is the cold hard truth version reserved for my sister. Do you want that to happen to you and Jay? Do you want him to give up everything for you, so he can die too? No, you don't. And then what happens? How do you have a normal relationship with someone who can't die? How do you explain to dad when you're sixty and he still looks thirty that he just has good genes? He'd be a damn test subject in a matter of seconds, absconded by the government."

I look away, knowing everything she's saying is true but I hadn't let myself think that far ahead. "He makes me feel good," I admit quietly. "Better than good. You have no idea. It's like..."

"A missing puzzle piece," she supplies swiftly. "Or a magnet. Your heart to his. Yeah. I get that. But in a case like yours, you have to think long term. Because living in the here and now with our lives doesn't work. You may be attracted to Jay because he's good-looking. And maybe he has some bond with you that I never had with my Jacob. But the fact is that you don't know him, he doesn't know himself, and you're just latching onto him because he's there. He understands you like no one else can."

But isn't that worth holding onto?

"You need to talk to Rose," she goes on. "I can put you in touch with her."

"That's Maximus and Rose," I tell her. "That's not Ada and Jay. And it's not Dex and Perry. Every single one of our situations is different, every single soul is different."

"Except for those who don't have one."

I still, my heart rejecting her words. "Jay *has* a soul."

"Whose soul does he have then?"

"I can't deal with this right now," I tell her, pushing past and storming back to the restaurant. I have enough on my plate as it is, I don't want to doubt Jay any more than I have to.

Back inside I avoid Jay's eyes and make excuses over the pasta. I pass on the espresso being served after dinner and manage to stealthily drink Rebecca's shot of Sambuca she had second thoughts on.

But from the restaurant and all the way back to their apartment, all I can think about is Jay. And he sits right beside me, like a ghost, locked in his own head and haunting himself.

Fat Rabbit greets us like he did before—excited wiggles for me, barking at Jay. This time Jay seems to take it to heart. I'd never seen his face crumble, like the dog was hurling violent insults his way.

We retire to bed. Dex and Perry scoop up the pooch and take him into their bedroom. Jay takes the couch. I go into the guest bedroom.

I'm lying here now, knowing that Jay's eyes followed me as I came in here. I could almost feel him flinch when I shut the door. I can feel him even now, this living breathing extension of myself. He calls to me whether he means to or not, the promise of our bodies fusing together, erasing our cares. I want to be back in that hotel room, where his pleasure was the only thing I had to care about.

That's the effect of sleeping with him, my brain pipes up. *That's the consequence. Losing yourself in him as he loses himself in you.*

Good lord, it's like I have a catholic school lecture going on inside my head.

I shake it loose and bring out my phone from beside the single bed, unable to sleep anyway.

The room is small, crammed full of computers and Dex's equipment, plus a bookshelf and music memorabilia. Despite the cramped quarters, the space glows ominously in the electronic light and I have the creepy feeling the shadows just outside of the glow are moving.

Crawling.

Creeping.

Closer and closer.

I have to keep pausing whatever fashion account I'm stalking and shine the light around, paranoid that there's something really there. I can almost hear it breathing when I'm not paying attention, but the moment I listen, it stops.

In time, though, I get more tired. My lids feel heavy. I almost put the phone down and try and make a go of sleep again when I have an idea.

Silas Black.

I enter it into Google along with the word Dublin.

A Wikipedia page is the first to pop up.

I click.

The page loads and my eyes eagerly scan it.

According to the Wikipedia gods, Silas Black was born in 1537, during the political strife of Ireland when the English administration destroyed the Fitzgeralds. His mother died in childbirth, it was believed anyway, and his father died trying to take over Dublin castle. After that the baby Silas was brought out to the Irish countryside by unknown people, some suspected relatives, others suspected it was a more sinister event such as kidnapping for rituals.

However, he later surfaced in his late teens in Meath, where he lived on a secluded farm near the Loughcrew cairns by himself.

Not much is known about Silas Black between that time and when he was twenty-seven, where he was known to predict a disease that would later take out a nearby village.

At twenty-eight he was seen holding a big bonfire on his property, the biggest ever seen in the area, and according to witnesses walked right into the fire and disappeared.

At twenty-nine he was found guilty of five counts of murder, children taken from their homes and then offered up as sacrifice that people at the time blamed on the Druids, even though their religion would never condone such a thing.

At thirty he had miraculously escaped a Dublin prison, vanishing right before the guard's eyes, leaving behind a cell covered in ash from floor to ceiling, the outline of his body burned against the walls in black soot, despite the guards insisting there was no fire.

He was never seen again but there are many legends surrounding Silas Black, particularly with his involvement with the Devil and black magic.

There's a lot more legend than fact about the man.

But it's all I need to know.

Jay wasn't exaggerating when he said that he had been a bad, bad man.

Silas Black had probably been in league with the Devil.

And that's his *human* side.

Which means the longer he's with me, the more that Silas gets pulled out.

The more that evil could potentially compromise Jay without him even knowing it.

Like that Irish accent coming out at the most intimate or humanistic times.

Like that look that came into his eyes while we were outside the restaurant.

The look that belonged to Silas Black.

Jay literally has the Devil's subject lying dormant inside him, waiting to come loose at my touch.

Our relationship just got a lot more complicated.

CHAPTER EIGHTEEN

I barely sleep.

All night long I have the sensation that there are things in the dark crawling toward me, wanting to curl up inside my ears and nose and spread a horrible evil inside my brain. Turn me into something I'm not.

Then there are the dreams. Fragmented and fleeting but upon waking—bathed in sweat—I have the feeling that it's the same dream over and over again.

A large bonfire.

Crackling. Embers into a night sky.

A moon severed in half.

People in robes, chanting with goat faces.

Jay stepping out of the flames, dressed in old fashioned clothing.

Eyes glowing red.

Grabbing me with clawed hands.

Pulling me into Hell.

Thankfully it's morning and daylight is streaming through the window, illuminating the dust, and the room has already taken on a hot, muggy feel. Maybe that caused the dreams, why I'm sweating. It's hot as Hell in reality.

But I know that's not why.

I glance at my phone and am surprised to see it say ten thirty. I slept way in.

I quickly shove on a dress, the concert tee one that Perry picked up at the Portland market weeks ago, noting that the whole apartment is strangely silent. Usually there's some sort of hustle and bustle in this place, either the scamper of Fat Rabbit's paws or the whine of the shower running or bacon sizzling on the stove. But the whole apartment buzzes like empty space.

Once I open the door and don't see anyone, I'm more assured it's empty. Everyone has gone and left me, even Fat Rabbit.

But as I step into the living room I see Jay out on the balcony, his back to me and showing in filtered waves as the white curtains dance from an unfelt breeze.

He turns around, an emptiness in his eyes as he takes me in. At least he's not Silas.

He has to know.

"Where is everyone?" I ask him.

He steps into the room, his frame seeming too big for the place, like the apartment is struggling to contain him. "They took the dog for a walk. Left a few minutes ago."

I rub at my eyes and move over to the Keurig to make myself a cup. "I slept in so long…"

"You had some bad dreams."

I freeze as I open the top of the machine, feeling his eyes at my back, like rays of sunshine. Warm yet probing, leaving me vulnerable. I pop the K-cup in. "You could tell?"

"More walls," he says.

I press on and as the machine noisily does its thing, I turn around to face him, leaning back against the counter.

"Jay…I had dreams about you. As Silas Black."

He nods, like he was expecting this. "I could read the fear off of you. I'm more closely connected to you than ever before."

"Which is a pretty good thing since we'll be going into Hell together." I pause. "Have you told my sister what we're doing?"

He shakes his head, coming forward and leaning with elbows on the kitchen island, his hands absently running over a magazine. "It's not for me to tell," he says. "And I'm not sure if it would do any good."

The machine stops hissing. I pick up my coffee and let the warmth flow into my palms. I breathe it in, inhaling the morning. It's the little things that make me happy sometimes and I'm guessing every little thing will start to stand out when you know you're heading to Hell.

I take a sip and sigh. Unfortunately the caffeine can't ward off reality. "I want to tell her. Just in case I don't come back, you know? I also want her to know I've been trying. That…I'm more than she thinks I am. That I'm worth something, too."

"I think she already knows that, Ada," he says, a wistful quality to his voice. "It radiates from you. An energy you can't ignore."

"Regardless," I go on, "she would worry too much. I mean she wouldn't let me go to begin with. Obviously. She would tie me down and lock me in the guest bedroom and

I'd stay there for weeks, forced to watch Dex work on his music videos."

"Not only that," he says gravely, "but she would interfere. She would create portals to try and rescue you and bring you back and we both know things would not end pretty. She can't know, Ada. You can tell her after, but not now. Not while your mother's soul is at stake."

That's exactly the kind of thing that Silas Black would say in an attempt to thwart off my only means of being rescued if everything goes wrong.

But I brush it off. I can't think like that.

"Look, Ada." Jay comes around the island and stops right in front of me. I swear he's going to kiss me, touch me, and my body immediately pulls toward him. But he puts his hands on my shoulders, holding me at a firm distance. "I know you've lost your trust in me. I can't explain what happened last night. All I know is that there is a soul inside me I haven't quite shed, though I'll do everything to bury it. I promise I am here to protect you, to watch over you, to keep you alive. That's my job and duty and nothing can break that bond."

"Silas Black was in league with the Devil," I blurt out. "He was an evil man who did black magic and disappeared without a trace."

He doesn't flinch which confirms that he knew.

"You knew?" I hiss at him.

He exhales, nodding. "I knew. Of course I knew. I had to Google myself the moment I found out my name from Jacob. We're not supposed to, but I had to know."

"And you didn't tell me!"

"You would have treated me differently," he says. "And as I've said before, I am not him."

"But he comes out the more that I spend time with you, let alone sleep with you! Oh my god...what have we done? And you knew. You told me that another side would come out of you, a bad side."

"And you accepted that risk quite well," he reminds me sharply.

The thing is, even if I had known what sleeping with him really meant, I still would have done it.

"Ada," he says, gripping my shoulders tight and peering at me. "I can get this under control. I am still me. Silas is dead."

"But he's not, he *wasn't*, an ordinary human!" I whisper frantically, trying to avoid his eyes. "He's practically a warlock. A disciple of Satan. He's...magic."

"I told you that all Jacobs come from people that have abilities. The person can be good. Or bad. It doesn't matter because it's just a vessel in the end, one we take over and mold to ourselves. But Jacobs aren't good or bad either. We are both. You need the balance to live in the world in-between."

"Sometimes I think there's a bad batch of them," I mutter, remembering Perry's Jacob.

"Look at me," he says. He grips my chin in his fingers, their heat searing into me, and raises my head to meet his eyes. He's sincere. He's pure and powerful and everything Jay.

Some of the fear subsides. "How can I be sure you've got this under control?"

"You just have to trust me." He lowers his voice, leaning in, the world taking on a dreamy quality. His eyelashes are beautifully long, black frames around glacial blue. My mouth parts open, waiting. "And I have to keep my hands off of you."

"What?" I say absently, my eyes drawn to his mouth, dying for another taste of him.

Abruptly he lets go of my shoulders and steps back, bumping against the island. "I can't touch you anymore."

I snap out of my stupor. "What?" I exclaim.

He raises his palms. "Short-term solution, I promise."

"That's ridiculous," I tell him. "I only meant for this time here with Dex and Perry."

"I know," he says. "But until I talk to Jacob about this, I'm not risking anything. The more I'm with you, intimately, the more I feel. The more I open myself to changing, becoming someone else. I don't know how to control those emotions right now but what I do know is that it makes me vulnerable. And right now, I can't be vulnerable. I have to be able to protect you in every single way."

"So then we just don't have sex for a bit," I say and wince at how put-upon I sound. It's been exactly twenty-four hours since he was last inside me and I've been craving him like some junkie on the streets. There may have been a bump or two where the desire was masked by fear, but it's always been there, thrumming like an undercurrent.

"Nothing intimate," he says. "Back to the day I first met you. I mean, outside of your dreams." He pauses. "We can do it. We have to. It shouldn't be this hard."

"Why is it this hard?" I implore him. "What the hell did you do to me?"

He shrugs. "Damned if I know. But I'm sure there's a very good reason why it's forbidden. Being forever bound, forever hungry for the other, must be one of them."

I swallow, feeling my face flush. "You're hungry for me?"

His lips twist in a half-smile. "All the time, princess."

Somehow that makes me feel better, knowing this crazy shit isn't just in my head, that I haven't blossomed into womanhood with a raging vagina. I mean, I know women develop feelings after they sleep with a guy, but this is fucking ridiculous.

"As for Silas," he says, bringing me out of my amped-up thoughts, "maybe going to Hell will be a good way of putting him back where he belongs. If I run into Satan I can just sort of pawn him off on him. You know, I've tried it out and it's not working, here, take him back."

"Are you seriously making a joke about returning a soul to Satan, right before we're headed to literal Hell?" I ask incredulously.

"Too soon?"

"If being around me brings out your sense of humor too, I think a little more distance is needed," I warn him, walking over to the couch with my coffee and giving him the glare to stay put.

It's not long after that Dex and Perry and Fat Rabbit come back from the walk. Miraculously this time, Fat Rabbit doesn't bark or growl at Jay at all, in fact he runs right over to him, licking his hand. That put all sorts of relief back into my heart. Jay was back to Jay for now and

I could only trust he would do what he could to stay that way, even if it was at my desire's expense.

Soon after we get ready to leave, telling Perry and Dex we're heading to the interior to check out the Washington wine areas and will head back home after a couple of more days.

I play it off as casually as I can but I'm not sure either of them believe me. Dex gives me a hug and tells me to watch myself. He then proceeds to tell Jay that if he lays one finger on me, he'll chop it off and feed it to the dog.

Jay has the sense to look worried—even if just for show—and when he promises Dex it won't be a problem, he believes him. Believe me, Dex, we're *way* ahead of you.

When Perry hugs me though, she whispers in my ear. "If you need any help, at any time, you call me." She taps the side of my head. "In here."

"I will," I promise and hope I never have to. I get a sloppy dog kiss from Fat Rabbit and then we're off on our road trip to Hell.

. . .

It turns out Hell is a lot closer than you'd think.

For us, the nearest portal is on an island in the San Juans, hovering between the American and Canadian border. I know that Perry and Dex filmed an EIT episode on a haunted island on the Canadian side, but thankfully we don't have to deal with borders and passports.

We get on one of the Washington State ferries with the Mercedes and head across blinding blue water. The sun is out in full force, the breeze is mineral fresh, carrying the scent of pine and dried moss. It's hard to imagine we're about to leave this world behind. It's the kind of day that makes you believe the Devil doesn't exist.

Once we're on the island, with sleepy towns, tourists, and anchored boats flashing past, I ask Jay how exactly he knows where he's going.

"Instinct," he says, taking off his shades as we turn off one of the main roads and head down a gravel one blanketed by forest. "Doesn't it feel right to you?"

It does. Because the more I'm on this island, the more it looks familiar. The trees, the darkness of the forest. Out by the shore there are cliffs of quartz and tan-colored moss, dried out by the sun, the very cliffs I've stood on in my dreams.

"We're going to a pond, aren't we," I whisper, staring out the window as the dark trees roll past down the bumpy road.

"Yes. I do believe so."

I shudder, feeling as if a black cloud has come over us, shedding sticky tears of tar.

Jay puts his hand on mine before he abruptly takes it away, remembering he shouldn't touch me. "You're going to be okay. You've got me and I'm not going to let a thing happen to you. You hear me?"

I try to make a noise of agreement but it comes out more as a squeak, words compromised by fear.

We keep driving, deeper and deeper into the forest. The sky starts to darken, even though sundown is hours away. It's like the further we drive, the closer we are to night, to a place where light can't enter.

Or perhaps a giant cave that will swallow us whole, take us straight to Hell before we even know what's going on.

"I don't like it here," I tell him, my gut pierced by a corkscrew of unease, thin and sharp and winding its way into the heart of me. "It's wrong. This is all wrong."

"And that's how we know we're going the right away," he says. "Because in no way should this feel comfortable to you. Then I'd really have to worry."

I glance at him. "Does it feel comfortable to *you*?"

He gives his head a grim shake. "No. It doesn't. Every part of me is telling me to turn the car around now."

Every part? Or just most of you?

I don't want to dwell on it, especially as the forest here seems to be more than just trees. It seems...sentient.

When I was younger, a child of six or so, before the subdivisions and developments started popping up in our neighborhood, Perry used to take me to the nearby woods to play. In reality it was probably the size of a block but when I was younger it was a huge, carnivorous beast. I'm not sure why I feared the forest. Perry was thirteen at the time and fearless, a few years away from losing her marbles and shutting herself away from me. But Perry loved that forest and would take me there often.

Normally we just stayed at the area closest to the street, but sometimes Perry would take my hand and lead me through the scaly trees to where the forest skirted the edge of the lake. She liked to try and catch the frogs, often wading up to her knees trying to find them. What can I say, she was a weird girl.

I did as she told me because I liked her attention and I thought she was cool, even if catching frogs grossed me out. She would go into the water and grimace gleefully at how icky the bottom felt on her bare feet, then she'd yell at me to come do the same.

Again, I did it to please her. I took off my shoes and stepped in and squealed because the muck felt like fingers, holding me down.

And then one day, one hot, hot summer day, no different from this one, Perry went all the way in up to her bum, her shorts wet, a net grasped determinedly in her hand as she searched the water.

I stayed on the shore for as long as I could. The lake was shallow and had a very gentle slope in this section where you could walk quite far out without having to swim.

Eventually though, she was too far away and when I called for her, she didn't listen, or maybe even hear me. She just swung her net at the water, lost in her attempts.

I didn't want to stand on shore anymore. A cloud passed over and swallowed up the sun. The temperature dropped dramatically but I was the only who seemed to notice. And the forest, that black, seemingly endless forest was at my back. I could swear that every time I turned away from it, it crept closer. It wasn't just a bunch of trees, it was a hungry, primitive beast that gobbled up girls like me. Of this I was sure.

So I tried to follow Perry. I stepped into the water. It was cold as ice and I was instantly chattering.

The trees started whispering.

Come to us Ada, we'll bring you home.

I whipped around, nearly losing my footing in the gooey bottom.

The forest was still.

But still in the sense that a snake is still when really it's waiting.

Waiting.

I called out for Perry, my voice sounding so small and weak, because I *was* small and weak. I moved a few more steps, the water coming up to my knees now. The mud clung to my legs.

And then I couldn't move. My feet sank into some kind of hole and no matter how I tried, I couldn't bring them out.

Now I was really yelling for her and finally she turned around and saw me. Started moving toward me fast, water splashing.

But I had the most real, succinct feeling that she wouldn't be fast enough.

I looked over my shoulder at the forest.

It was now at the water's edge.

It had *moved*.

And more than that, the shadows inside it were moving too, clicking like insect legs, branches reaching forward like stick fingers.

You're almost home, it hissed.

It was going to swallow me whole.

Then I don't know what happened. Next thing I knew I was back at home and running a fever. Later on, like a decade later, when I brought it up around the family, Perry said I was sinking into the mud and if she hadn't gotten there in time I would have drowned.

She never mentioned the forest moving closer on its own, one giant whispering creature that oozed evil. She never mentioned it and I never brought it up. Chalk it up to childhood memories gone wrong.

But now, now that I was here in this forest, I knew I wasn't wrong. It wasn't in my head back then and this isn't in my head now. This forest isn't just made up of trees, it's made up of something much larger, blacker, unfathomable.

And it's waiting too.

"I think we're here," Jay says as the car bumps over a pothole and comes to a stop. We're at the end of the road, the gravel tire tracks fading into Salal bushes, ever grainy in the descending darkness.

I don't want to leave the car. I grip the pebbled leather seat as if it will tether me to this world.

Jay twists in his seat to face me. "We don't have to do this," he reminds me. "Some things are beyond one's capabilities and there is no shame in that, only sensibility."

"We're getting my mother back," I tell him and I know now I won't turn back.

He nods and we get out of the car. He stands beside me as we crane our necks back to stare at the sky. It's black, void of stars, blending in with the tops of the trees. In the distance a blood red moon glows.

"How is this possible?" I whisper. "This was my dream."

"Many places where portals exist operate on a separate reality. The other worlds can leak through, mess up physics and what we know as truth. Sedona, Stonehenge, Easter Island, there are many more. And here." He grabs my hand and tugs me toward a faint path in the forest. "Come on. Now or never."

We walk through the forest, the path cutting through the trees like a scar. I hold my breath at first, afraid to breathe the air. The branches seem to reach for me and when they brush past my skin, I can feel them try to take hold, like fingers wrapping around my clothing.

Jay holds my hand for the first few minutes, bringing me comfort, until he drops it. I know he's too afraid he'll lose himself, his duty, if he feels me for too long.

So I follow him down the path until it becomes a slope and then we're winding down rocky terrain, moss and vines and branches tripping up my feet.

The crimson moon is glowing now and even though I don't hear the song from my dream, the one my mother was singing, I can feel its rhythm pulsing in my blood.

So hurry now and listen

Run to the pond that does so glisten

They knew. They knew all along that I would come to this exact spot to do this.

Everything has been destined.

The only thing I don't know is what fate has been chosen for me.

Or if I get to choose my fate.

Eventually the forest starts to open up, letting in more of the blood red glow until it's like we're standing in an old-fashioned darkroom, developing film. Giant bats flutter in the distance, not seen but definitely heard. Leathery wings that flap the hot air, stirring up a putrid smell that makes bile slide up my throat.

Then in front of us is the pond.

Skinny alders grow around it, some leaning over as if trying to reach it—or escape—while one large tree slices through the middle. Reeds and lily pads pop up around the edges of the brackish water while the middle is black as sin. It's not large in diameter but it looks infinitely deep. I know that it doesn't have a bottom, that it keeps going and going, to no end.

"I'll have to go in first," Jay says softly.

"What?" I exclaim. A flurry of wingbeats emerge from the trees. The whole forest seems to take in one giant breath.

"Shhh," he shushes me, finger to his lips. "You have to be quiet."

"But we're not in the Veil," I say.

"But we're definitely surrounded by things that have escaped," he says, just as I hear something rustle in the bushes. A raspy, wet breath.

"Ada," he whispers and takes my hand in his. "You need to listen to me very carefully. I have to go into the pond first. I have to be the first out the other side. If you go first, they'll see you. I can make you...invalid."

"Invalid?" I'm not sure I like the sounds of that, even though if you have to be invalid anywhere, Hell is a good start.

"They won't see you if you stay quiet. We'll have to communicate otherwise but they won't see you if you just stay beside me and don't make a sound."

"But what if they *do* see me?"

He grimaces. "Then we better make sure we can find the nearest portal out of there." He lets go of my hand and walks toward the pond. He glances at me over his shoulder. "As soon as my head disappears into the water, you follow. I'll be there, I promise."

I can't believe I have to walk in there. What if I drown? What if I get to the other side and he's not there?

"How can you promise you'll be there waiting?"

"Because I can," he says. His eyes grow tender. "Ada, you can do this. Just think about your mother. Walk into the pond, hold your breath and go under. Think about her the whole time. Imagine her face, her voice, her smell. Hold her to you as close as you can and do not, do not let go, no matter what."

Oh my god. Oh my god. Oh my god.

I can't.

I can't.

"If you want her back," he adds, "you have to."

I have to.

I nod, my mouth gone dusty with horror.

"I'm very fond of you, you know," he says softly.

I'm not sure if this is Jay's equivalent of telling me he loves me but I'll take it.

"Fond enough to wait for me?" I ask.

"Always." He looks behind me, eyes fixed on something in the forest. "Now we have to hurry. Don't dawdle here too long, come in right after me. As soon as my head is gone under, step in and don't stop moving."

"Why, why?" I ask but it's too late, he's striding into the water like a man on a mission, the water quickly rising from his shins to his thighs to his waist as he approaches the middle.

I make the mistake of turning around to see what he was looking at.

There is a woman hovering at the edge of the trees, on all fours, naked and pale as milk, the moon tinting her red.

Long black hair hangs around her face.

No eyes at all, just smooth, taught skin.

A smile full of shark's teeth.

She can't see me but she's watching me all the same. Waiting.

I turn around just in time to see Jay go under, the pond swallowing him whole. There's one ripple and then it stops and it's like he never went in there at all.

A gurgle spins me back around. The woman is crawling toward me, upside down, like the scene from the fucking *Exorcist*, scuttling fast like a crab. Her mouth snaps open and shut with sickle teeth, a piranha.

I have no choice.

I practically jump into the pond, splashing in the ice cold water that takes my breath away, disorients me, freezes me in place. It's like jumping into a frozen lake, hypothermia just minutes away.

I don't have minutes.

I can hear the woman splashing into the water after me. If she's like a crab at all, it won't slow her down. I can imagine her fish mouth closing around my calf, the teeth going all the way through flesh, muscle, bone.

I manage to lift my leg, then the other, numb stumps I can't feel.

I go and go and go, the muck of the bottom pulling at my shoes just like the lake did. It too wants to hold me here so the forest can suck me in, eat my soul and turn me into whatever this woman's been turned into.

A creature that even Hell didn't want.

Now the water is at my chin, my mouth, then my nose. I'm almost under.

And she's right behind, her snapping mouth at my ear. *This is it.* I shut my eyes.

Then the bottom drops beneath me and instead of floating, I freefall.

Straight down underneath.

But it's not so much that I'm sinking, as my ears pop and the darkness envelops me.

I'm being pulled.

A hand around my ankle.

A hand that isn't Jay's.

CHAPTER NINETEEN

I can't breathe.

I can't breathe.

The world around me is black, my ears filling with pops and clicks, like the sounds you hear from the bottom of the sea. Things brush past my limbs, bare branches or skeletal fingers, it's hard to tell.

I go down, down, down until I'm going up.

My head bursts out of the water and I instinctively inhale as big and deep as I can, trying to fill my lungs.

But there's no air to be had.

I make a faint choking sound, my eyes opening in throbbing terror, a brown grey haze staring back, momentarily forgetting where I'm supposed to be.

I'm here, Ada, Jay's voice comes in my head. *Swim to me.*

I can't even look around to find him, I just start moving my arms and kicking my legs in the direction I feel his pull, surprised that they're even working with no air coming in my lungs.

Somehow I crawl onto solid ground. I feel strong, familiar hands wrap around my arms and pull me further up, the icy water letting go of my feet with a nasty *slurp*.

I flip over on my back, gasping for breath, panicking when I can't get it. The grey brown sky presses down from above.

Take it easy, Jay says. *There is no air here. You don't need it.*

I know he's beside me, I can see him out of my peripheral, but I can only stare up at that oppressive sky, alien and alive, and fight along with every natural instinct I have.

Eventually though I realize that I should have died a long time ago. It's been minutes (years?) without air and that breathing will be one of the things I miss about our world.

I sit up slowly, Jay's hand at my back for support, and look around.

Hell isn't fire and brimstone.

It's New York City.

To be more specific, the look of New York City in January but with mid-July weather. A bleak and grey sky above dark and hollow buildings, a jungle of mildewed concrete and decaying plants, dead trees, and shrubs reduced to skeletons. The air is no-air and it's thick, muggy, brimming with humidity that has beads of sweat already rolling down my face. The only smell is one of garbage and something so vile that I can feel it eating away at my core. A smell that makes the lizard-brain of my cortex shrink in fear.

Of course how can you smell without breathing? Hell has many tricks up its sleeves, that I'm sure.

For one, I'm lying at the edge of a pond in Central Park.

Are you okay? Jay asks.

I think so, I tell him, having a hard time conjuring up my "inside" voice. *Considering where we are.*

I twist around and look at him.

I balk.

I don't look so good, do I? he asks with a dour expression.

No. He doesn't. It's not that he looks horrible or gross or even really that different. At a glance he would look the same. But the more I stare at him, the more his face seems to separate from his skin, like he's wearing a mask and it's hinting at something terrible underneath. It's the debilitating sense that he's been taken apart and put back together and the end result isn't human at all.

Do I look the same? I ask him.

He gnaws on his lip for a moment before answering. *You're never not beautiful, Ada. You just look like a doll that someone's made to look like you.*

That's a pretty good summation of what I'm looking at too.

It's good for me to keep using your name, Ada. Names have power. You'll need to be reminded of who you are in here. You'll need to remind me too.

I glance around. Aside from the smell and the awful humidity, there isn't anything too terrifying here. Still, I can't say I feel relieved in the slightest.

Are we actually in Hell? Why is it New York? I ask. *Where is...everybody?*

Careful, Ada, he warns me, slowly getting to his feet. He hauls me up effortlessly before dropping his hands to his side. *Don't question things too much. I have no doubt this place would act upon it. Hell itself isn't just governed by Satan and his disciples, it's governed by the very essence of Evil itself.*

More Evil than Satan? I ask, finding it hard to believe, though a chill sinks deep into my flesh like ice-pick claws. *He's the prince of fucking darkness.*

337

Satan is a fallen angel. He fell here. This place already existed. It was waiting for him to lead. He says this simply, just another fact. *It can feel you, hear you, even now. It will start to mess with your head pretty soon.*

Can...can it keep me here? I wish he'd keep a hold of my hand, my skin is pins and needles in new fear, craving his stability.

No. It is sentient but it cannot become physical. If you remember who you are, where you came from, you'll be okay. He pauses. *Who are you?*

Ada Palomino.

Where did you come from?

Portland, Oregon.

He nods. *Good enough. And to answer your question, I don't know why we're in New York but I have an idea.*

So we're actually in New York, not just a place that looks like it?

Hell is your world, many layers below. Your mother died here and she's your reason for all of this. This is where you'll find her.

I glance around nervously.

And there are people here, he says. *We'll see them soon enough. Souls of the damned. But there are layers to Hell too. It's not just full of murderers and rapists and pedophiles. Hell has a hold on the guilty.*

The guilty?

Self-guilt. Self-loathing. Feeling that you belong here, that you deserve eternal punishment. I'd say most of the souls you see here belong in that category. Not bad people, just...unable to deserve better. They most likely lived their lives the same way, unable to escape from the wrongs of the past, the scars on their souls. If they were never happy in life, they can't be happy in the afterlife.

Shit. I never thought about it that way. My heart aches for them, to think that this is what they deserve.

That's good, Jay says, studying me. *Keep feeling. It's the only thing in the end that will remind you that you don't belong here.*

I have a hard time looking at him. *So where to now?*

Reach inside your head, he says. *Call for her. Feel her.*

I close my eyes and try.

I imagine her, I call to her.

Nothing happens.

Again.

Nothing happens.

Moooooom!

Nothing. Just an inky void in the base of my skull that gets bigger and bigger and bigger...

Jay lays his hand on my shoulder, bringing me out of the darkness. *Focus on her as a person, not a thought. Don't imagine. See.*

I try again.

I try and put her pieces together until suddenly she's in our kitchen making cookies at Christmas time. My mother was never like everyone else's moms. She had a cold way about her, always a bit distant, even from me. But I never saw any malice in it. It was just the way she was. Like someone who never wanted kids or marriage or that whole suburban life but she got it anyway and was just trying to do her best.

But at Christmas time, my mother wouldn't just look the part of the beautiful Scandinavian housewife, she would act it too. She would make ginger snaps, a million times better than the ones you get at IKEA, and light the kitchen with vanilla candles and every time you stepped inside the smells made your mouth water.

And my mother would smile—genuinely this time—and take the cookies out and we'd all stare forlornly at the tray, waiting for them to cool, and when they were ready we'd dip them in eggnog and they would be the best things we'd tasted all year.

My mother watched us the whole time, only having one cookie for herself, and against the candle light her face would glow and I knew she was happy.

The rest of the year was always touch and go, but at those moments I knew it, and I would look forward to that even more than the Christmas presents (which usually sucked anyway, I don't know why my parents would always get me those shitty Pot of Gold chocolates, there was only one good piece in the box and you had to bite your way through so many disgusting ones to find it).

I can see that scene in front of me, my mother, Perry, the cookies, the candles. I'm in it. Living it.

Ada!

My mother's voice is calling me. Her spirit tugs my arm to the left.

The mother in my vision is oblivious, trapped in that time and watching her children happily, but I know I feel her all the same and she can now feel me.

Ada, she cries out again. *Hurry.*

Where are you?

Silence.

Where are you?! I repeat, yelling so loud inside my head my blood vessels nearly pop.

You know where, her voice trails off into a whisper and I at once know that she can't tell me outright.

But it doesn't matter. I know all the same.

I open my eyes at look at Jay, his face taking on a plastic sheen. Doll-like, indeed.

I know where she is, I tell him, ignoring the change in his face. *The subway tunnels. Where she died.*

He nods and waits for me to walk. He doesn't know where she died. He wasn't there.

It's up to me to lead us through Hell.

I take in a deep but eternally empty breath and start walking toward the Empire State building, Jay falling in step behind me.

. . .

The first rule of Hell is: don't talk about Hell.

The more your brain wants to process where you are, the more your brain starts to leak out, like a draining bed pan. Your heart goes next, a gummy mess at the bottom of your shoe. Inconsequential. Then it's your soul, siphoned from the marrow of everything you are.

I don't know this yet, but I can feel it. I can feel Hell as one fathomless hungry beast, watching and waiting for me to just give in. I know this like the blood in my veins.

So I try not to think about where we are, I just keep moving through the streets, ignoring everything I see and hear.

Well, almost everything.

So far Hell has been disquieting. Jay and I do a fast walk down Fifth Avenue (the thick airless air holds us back from a run like an invisible hand), the dead weeds of Central Park to our right, the dark and silent buildings to our left. I get the creeping sensation, spiders up my spine, of being watched through all the windows. Sometimes I see a curtain pulled violently across a window, other times hear the sound of a door slamming but there is no one there. I'm reminded of Shakespeare: "Hell is empty and all the devils are here."

But Hell isn't empty. It's an illusion, one to lull you with a false sense of security, the way a cat might lick you before it bites.

Slowly you start to hear the screams. At first they are in the distance, maybe blocks away. Short yelps of surprise. Then they turn to screams of absolute horror, someone being tortured over and over again. It comes closer.

And then it's behind you.

A sharp inhumane scream that curdles your blood instantly, the type of scream that's also a plea for it all to stop.

I whirl around, Jay grabbing me by the elbow to steady me, and see a little boy standing ten feet away from us. Big big eyes, bowl-cut hair, holding an old-fashioned doll with a cracked open head, the ones that roll open their eyes when you move them.

Why is a child in Hell? I think, my mind trying to wrap around the sight of innocence.

Jay hears me. *That is not a child.*

And the moment he says it, I know it.

The doll in his hands opens its eyes.

The boy smiles.

Wider and wider.

Splits his face in two.

Opens his mouth to let out a scream.

At the back of his throat, a long, thin hand comes out, skinny black fingers that belong to something charred.

I am caught, unable to look away as the child's head splits open, his skull cracking into jagged rivets, just like his doll, and a bony, charred arm comes out, placing long fingers into the child's eyes and gripping them like a bowling ball.

The creature starts to emerge.

We have to get going, Jay says, pulling me toward him.

I'm yanked helplessly, even though Jay is straining to pull me along.

Ada! he yells. *Focus Ada. Think about your mother.*

My mother. My mother.

I want to stay and look at the creature but I must think about my mother.

Jay leads me down the street until the creature is just a dot in the distance, then two dots going two separate ways. He grabs my shoulders and pulls me to him. One hand goes to my cheek.

Soft. His touch is soft.

Everything here is hard but he is soft.

Ada, he says and I'm reminded of the doll in the boy's hands, the way Jay's blue eyes seem made of marble, unseeing. *You can't lose it now. We are close but we're running out of time. I can feel it. Focus. Focus.*

I close my eyes, letting his touch soothe me, sink in beyond the skin, fusing us together as we should be fused.

He feels good.

He always feels good.

Feels.

I feel.

I am alive.

I don't belong here.

My eyes snap open. My gut churns with tiny pinpricks. I feel like I've been seconds away from going over the edge of a cliff and he's pulled me back just in time.

Oh my god, I cry, trying to get my brain back on track.

He can't hear you, is Jay's answer. *Come on. You said the station at fifth and fifty-third, right?*

I nod quickly. We hurry down the street again and I do my best to ignore the sights that this New York has to offer.

I wonder what Hell's Kitchen is like here.

Is that a joke? Jay asks, peering down at me as we walk, sweat streaming down his plastic face.

I'm not sure. I don't know what's funny anymore.

I can't remember what laughter is.

Call for your mother, he tells me, grabbing my hand and pulling us across the street. A bike messenger speeds past in a hurry, no helmet, the back of his skull blasted open and his brains trailing behind him like streamers.

I ignore the bike messenger, ignore the cabbie a few feet away sitting on the top of his cab and tossing bread-crumbs to the empty pavement. I call for my mother. Loud and louder and louder.

Nothing.

But I know she's there. It compels me. There's a golden rope around my soul linking me to hers. I can't see it but I can feel it and it's tightening on the winch as we go.

So we keep going.

We pass the Apple store which looks the same as it does in real life, only this time it's teeming with giant wood lice, thick as trash cans and shining a slick grey. They burrow through the walls with their shearing mandibles, slowly destroying it. Outside on the curb, a couple sits, iPads in their hands. iPads that don't work, given the agony on their faces.

"That's someone's person Hell," I comment.

My voice sounds so foreign and robbed of all essence that it takes me a moment to realize I said it.

Ada! Jay admonishes me.

Shit.

SHIT.

I wasn't supposed to talk out loud.

The couple with the iPads look up at me.

Dead eyes.

Angry eyes.

They see you, he says to me. *We have to try and run.*
What about before? The little boy. With the thing inside.
It only saw me, he says. *If it had known you were there...*

He doesn't have to explain.

The couple is getting to their feet.

More than that, the wood lice have all paused, their antennas flickering in my direction like leathery pipe-cleaners.

Down the wide open street, the bike messenger is turning around and coming back to us.

We start running.

The wall of humidity pushes back against us, just like those dreams when you can't run, but we stagger on and on until my legs turn to jelly, my thighs on fire. Jay picks me up, throwing me over his shoulder and his supernatural strength powers us both through.

We round the corner onto fifty-third and from my angle, my head hanging down Jay's back, I see a parade of people coming toward us. They're running, a stampede, their angry screams and shouts climbing.

We don't belong here, Jay tells me. *They know we can leave and they can't and they'll try and stop us. It doesn't matter. Here we are.*

Suddenly the street starts to rise above me as Jay runs down the stairs into the subway station. It's familiar. Too familiar. I feel like I'm heading into a tomb, that the ceilings will collapse on us and we'll be buried here for all time.

Down, down, down.

Further than the station is in the world above.

Jay leaps over turnstiles made of razor blades like a track and field star and I bounce wildly on his shoulder, his strong arm keeping me from flying off.

Then he runs down a few steps, the slick, oozing tile walls of the stairwell rising up around us like a crypt, and *stops*.

Suddenly, like he hits a wall.

I'm about to ask him what happened but before I can form the question, my mouth goes dry with the acidic tang of pure fear. Terror buzzes in my brain like angry yellow jackets. I'm certain…certain…

I am no longer Ada.

I am just a small mass of tissue, insignificant against purest horror.

Put her down, a voice says.

No, not one voice but a *hundred* voices say, metallic and empty, all at once.

Jay's grip on me intensifies.

You'll have to kill me first, he says.

You know we can't, the voices say, buzzing like a million flies on shit.

Then we have a problem, is Jay's firm response.

I try and twist to turn around to see but can't. I can only stare up the staircase.

The mob has crowded around the top, staring down at us with hateful eyes.

But they don't dare come closer.

Because there is fear in their eyes too.

They watch and wait. I know they want us to be ripped to shreds.

Perhaps we will be, the thought comes into my head.

I find that I don't care.

We have a bargain for you, the voices say. *A fair one. Give us the girl. We'll give you the mother. It's what she wants.*

I'm not sure who they're talking about. She? Me? Mother?

The words make no sense.

Blood leaks out of my eyes, drips onto the stairs. I think my soul might be contained in some of those drops. It too wants to leave me, leave this place.

Stay with me! Jay's voice comes slamming into my head like fist. *Ada!*

My head jerks up and a snuffling noise escapes my lips.

The crowd at the top of the stairs stamp their feet, drool spilling from their gaping, hungry mouths.

No bargain, Jay says. *Her mother, Ingrid, doesn't belong here. Neither does Ada.*

He puts special emphasis on *Ingrid* and *Ada*. All it took was a second for me to forget them again.

She's Ingrid. My mother. I'm Ada.

She's Ingrid. My mother. I'm Ada.

Names have power.

That's right, Jay encourages.

That's right, the voices leer. *Very right. Silas Black.*

Jay stiffens. His heartbeat slows.

Silas Black. The name means something to me.

Images of fire and screaming babies and gaping knife wounds.

Dead horses with their intestines cascading into a field.

Body parts scattered down a dark alley.

Birds with their wings chopped off.

Silas Black is evil.

Silas Black is holding me.

He is walking down the stairs with me.

Silas Black will kill me.

I start to fight against him with every muscle I have but Silas Black is huge, laced with black magic and preternatural strength.

With one swift movement I am tossed through the air. I spin, wet tiles sliding past my face and I land on the ground in excruciating pain. It shoots up through my knees, my hands, splinters my sense of self. I try to move but collapse.

It was over so fast. How long was Silas waiting inside of him to do that? For Jay to just switch, to forget. Jay was obliterated in the blink of an eye. A snap of the fingers at the demons' indulgence. It was almost like they'd forgotten and had done it on a whim.

We'll still hold the bargain, the voices say. They come from under me, rumbling the ground like passing train, they come from above me.

Inside me.

We'll let your mother go if you stay here, they say. *We promise.*

The devil lies, I tell myself, my head pressed against the hard ground. I don't even want to get up, to see.

We are all devils, they say. *Every one of us. Maybe even you. If you let yourself.*

The voices get closer, like they are whispering in my ear. I feel hot, sulfurous breath. *We know all those little things you'd like to do. The things you would never admit to yourself. The pleasure you get from them. The difference between that world and this one is freedom, my girl. Here you are free to act in any way you please. The ways you truly want.*

And yet somewhere, somehow, I hear Jay.

I hear him from a small, dark cage, like a bird under sheet.

Get your mom. Use the walls.

My heart glows in response.

And then it's gone, snuffed out.

Hands dig into my hair and pull me up by the roots until I'm nearly on my feet.

I open my eyes and stare into the face of something I don't have words for.

It yanks me up further and then shoves me back until my back hits a wall, my head cracking on it.

My eyes dart around, taking in the scene.

Jay is gone.

So are the people.

There aren't hundreds of devils here.

There is only one.

CHAPTER TWENTY

I am alone in Hell.

Aside from the demon standing across from me.

Studying me.

Waiting.

I still can't look at it, my retinas balking at its appearance before I can even take it in. It's like looking at the sun if the sun held unimaginable, mind-bending horror in its rays.

So while I can't look at its face, I can look at its clothes.

It's at least ten feet tall, dressed in what looks to be a cloak of purple and black, the structure made from charred animal bones, leathery wings and human hair, with baleful and blinking eyes, and oozing blood, sticky as tar, filling in the gaps.

The demon takes a step toward me, the cloak making a whispering sound. I have no doubt that it's compromised of captured souls.

You're right, the demon says. Its voice causes my brain to cave in. *Lost and forgotten. As you will be too.*

My back flattens against the wall as it steps closer again and I move my head to the side in order to avoid its faceless face. It brings the smell of rotting meat, a cellar full of dead rats and feces and sour milk.

A bony, furry finger reaches out from the end of its sleeve—a hem of eyelashes, wavering like seaweed—and touches my cheek.

Softly at first.

Then it presses in until my skin is being punctured, the finger bones drilling down, down, down into my cheekbones and the gummy flesh beyond.

I scream. It is soundless. Endless.

The demon's fingers are quick. It reaches into my mouth, pinching my tongue like forceps. Spiders, hundreds of tiny red ones, come skittering from out of the demon's sleeve, over its black furred hand and onto my tongue. I can feel each one as it descends down the back of my throat, some slinging webs from one tonsil to the other.

Kill me, kill me, kill me, I think to myself. I am still screaming. I am crying. I am reduced to a shaking mass of fear. A second longer and I'll lose my mind forever.

I welcome it.

Ada...

My mother's whisper settles inside me like snowflakes.

My mother.

Love.

Heartache.

Loss.

It's enough.

It's enough.

I erase the demon from my reality. I create a new one inside my head. A reality born of fury and anger of determination and revenge. A reality built on hope.

Hope is what's missing down here.

Hope resounds in my mother's voice.

She's still here.

I'm still here.

Perry is out there, her face fresher than ever.

Jay is...somewhere.

I will not give up until there is no hope left.

And I know, I know, there is still some.

Despite the spiders filling up my throat, my gut, skittering into my veins, I open my eyes.

I stare at what should not be stared at.

I take nothing of it in, but I give it every ounce of myself. All my scorn and all my power. I aim to freeze it in its place.

And the funny thing is, I think it works.

Its hands drop away from my mouth and in a second the spiders are gone, pouring out of me like vomit.

In that same second I start to run, wiping them from my mouth as I go.

I don't know where I'm going.

I just need space.

Some space.

The subway tunnel looms ahead, no trains.

My mother's echo floats down from one end.

I head there.

The demon is laughing, not even bothering to run after me.

It doesn't know.

But it will now.

In the seconds before I leap off the platform and onto the train tracks—the same train tracks my mother died on—I pull up something from deep inside of me. I imagine my soul a pool of white downy feathers. I bring up something to protect it.

I land on the train tracks, rolling to my feet and when I look up at the platform, I see the devil. The devils. Only one but with many trapped inside.

It stares down at me, radiating amusement along with intense hatred.

The walls go up.

First a steel one at the end.

Then the other side.

The demon swivels its head in surprise from one end of the platform to the other.

Finally one in the middle.

I hear its furious cry, like mangled machinery, in the seconds before all the walls seal shut.

It is trapped on the other side. It can't see me. It can't feel me.

For now, I remind myself, all sense of clarity coming back. I feel like my brain is getting resuscitated by the second, if only seconds mattered down here.

Ada! My mother yells.

I'm here! I call after her, running down the tracks, my legs pumping as fast as they can go.

There is no light at the end of this tunnel. Only darkness. More darkness. But my mother's voice is getting clearer.

Stronger.

We call to each other back and forth, back and forth.

Until finally I see a faint glow up ahead. Maybe another station but in any case, it flickers like fire.

And as I get closer, I see it is fire, burning neatly in the middle of the tracks. It's the only thing I've seen down here that has any symmetry or beauty at all.

So beautiful.

So perfect.

The flames.

I reach out to touch them.

Don't.

A hand grabs my wrist.

It is my mother.

She's got the same appearance that Jay did, like her pieces don't quite fit together, that she's just a shell, a pretty coating. But it's still her. My heart thumps happily like it's springing to life.

I might cry.

I might scream.

I just stare at her, taking her in, feeling her love.

I feel it, everywhere, giving me the future.

Mom, I cry out softly, not daring to open my mouth.

She gives me a sad smile and reaches out to brush my hair from my face. *You look like you but not like you. Still my beautiful baby.*

She pulls me into a hug and I'm hit with a hundred shudders of grief and sorrow and joy, all flowing through me at once, a raging, unstoppable force.

It's okay, she says soothingly, petting my hair like she did when I was a child. I'm now so thankful for her cool, calm demeanor, present even down here. She's keeping me together when I can no longer be.

I don't know how long I cry into her. I know that there is an hourglass with sand tumbling toward an end. But I'm so afraid of what happens after this that I would rather stay like this forever. In her arms, being loved, feeling safe.

Ada, she says, pulling away and drying my tears with her hands. *They'll find us here. They always do. This is their world, not ours.* She pauses and looks at me with remorse. *You shouldn't have come. I shouldn't have asked. I knew you were my one hope, I understood it, felt it, but I shouldn't have asked. No child should make that sacrifice for their parent.*

No parent should make that same sacrifice for their children, I counter. *You took the demon out of my body and held it in yours. You killed yourself for me, for us. I had to repay you. I wouldn't, couldn't, live with myself otherwise. And I know now what happens to those lost to their own guilt…I would have ended up here anyway.*

With no escape.

But there is an escape for us, I tell her. *I just have to find a portal back to our world. If I was Perry I could create one myself…*

It's too dangerous to involve her. She's had it bad enough as it is. But it doesn't matter, she says. *I know where there is one. I've seen them leave through it. But we would never get there.*

We're going to try. Hope is the only thing we've got on our side, mom. The only thing that they can't control or even begin to understand. Love and hope. Those are the bonds that will break them.

Something wet drips on my shoulder.

Blood.

I glance up.

For the first time I'm really seeing the tunnel we're standing in.

Its round walls are comprised of people, stretching off in both directions until the flame's light can't reach and then they're swallowed by darkness.

All types. Fat, skinny. Young, old. Men, women. Some more alien than anything, faces and bodies warped by torture. All naked, some flayed, some nearly skeletal. All strewn together like sinewy fabric, their eyes glued to us.

I have the same sensation I did in the restaurant when all the eyes were looking my way.

My mother is staring at them too. *They would have alerted them by now*. She pauses, closing her eyes briefly. *They are here*.

And I can feel it too, that buzzing, droning sound of insects in the base of my skull, building and building and building.

Suddenly the tunnel of ravaged people start screaming. Loud helpless shrieks that echo and echo, until it sounds like the whole world is screaming.

Oh they are very near indeed.

This way, my mother says, grabbing my hand.

We run off back the way I had come before, the screams following us like angry wasps, except this time instead of reaching the previous station, the tunnel turns to the right. Up ahead I see a tiny pin prick of light, like we're bugs in a can and someone's punched in one hole for us to breathe. I can imagine Satan himself, sitting outside of this all, larger than all the world, the tunnel in his hand. Ready to squish us if he chooses.

The thought nearly reduces me to rubble.

Keep going, I tell myself. *You have her, you can't give up now.*

I keep going. It gets harder. The light seems to be getting further and further away.

It's an illusion, she says. *We're getting closer.*

357

I trust her, I have to, even though every cell in me wants to lie down and roll over.

But I have faith.

And then suddenly we're under the light. It's an open manhole about forty feet up and surprisingly I think I see blue sky. It's hard to tell, my eyes can't seem to focus through the glaze that covers it like a plastic seal.

Is that...? I ask.

Climb, my mother says, taking my hands and placing them on the iron rungs of a ladder that I hadn't noticed until now. *No arguments.*

But I want to argue. I came here for her.

Climb, she says again. *Now!*

A blast of putrid heat plows into us at sonic speed.

Ants crawl under my skin.

I turn to see a single match is lit, illuminating the demon from before, standing in the middle of the tunnel.

It's smiling, I think. I still can't look at its face.

The manhole cover slides on from above like rusty scissors.

We are enveloped in darkness with no escape.

I try to put up the walls, try to think but my brain is slush, dark and wet and melting.

Suddenly candles light up all around us, one by one, a magic trick on slender white wax sticks, held by aged candelabras.

We're in a crypt of bones and altars and cracked stone slabs and rising up the tunnel walls are skulls.

Of men.

Of children.

And of beasts.

Terrible, terrible beasts that watch us with empty sockets.

The demon raises its hands as if to cast some spell on us, its horrible cloak screaming, then it lowers them.

Steps forward.

We would have upheld the bargain, it says. *Truly. But then you pissed us off.*

The sound is hatred personified.

I don't say anything. My mouth has been strangely muted and my brain has stuttered. The pillowy down of my soul has been severed from my reach.

If only I'd known I would get only *one* shot at this.

Don't feel too bad, the demon(s) say. *Your guide didn't do a very good job with you. It's not your fault.*

My guide.

Jay.

My Jay.

Even the thought of him hurts, hurts me like I never thought possible.

Down here there is pain after pain after pain.

Infinite.

Yes, they say. *Yes. We are infinite. You will be too.*

They. Demons. What was its name again?

Suddenly the demon stops, a buzz roaring from its body like hostile flies.

What is your name? I ask, my voice sounding hollow.

My mother holds my hand.

She knows we are running out of time.

It will do you no good to remember, it says.

Jay.

Jay.

I was seeing his face flash through my head. My heart. I could feel him, feel him tugging at me the way my mother was earlier. Golden rope. Effortlessly strong. Alive and ageless and tying us together.

It is over, the demons says.

Sickle blades appear in its hands.

And behind its shoulder I see a shadow.

Large, solid.

It comes closer.

Closer still.

The demon doesn't notice.

Waning candlelight illuminates the sculpted planes of Jay's face.

Beauty in the darkness.

His eyes lock with mine and I don't have to question, I just have to trust.

What had Pippa said to me in that cell? That I couldn't even trust myself.

I had to trust my heart.

My true heart.

My inner compass.

I reach down inside and give it a push.

It spins around, pointing at Jay, glowing truth.

It's him.

And I know the demon's name.

"Legion!" I cry out, my voice sharp and unnaturally loud in this tunnel, bouncing off the miles of bones.

The demon stills, surprised. If I could describe its face I'd say it was hearing its name for the first time and trying to figure out who the hell Legion was.

Then it bares its teeth at me, grey gravestones in a row.

But it doesn't matter.

Jay comes flying at the demon from behind.

Tackles it to the ground.

For a moment Jay is lost in the folds of the demon's cloak, only his hair poking through, here, there, here, there, shimmery red against black as they roll and tumble.

They fight and it's enough for me to yell at my mom to move.

She goes up the ladder first, knows there is no time to argue.

She climbs, she's halfway there, and she's heading to darkness, a roof we can't see. But there has to be a way to open the manhole. There has to be.

Hope. Keep the hope.

I grab the rungs to see Jay's hands on the demon's throat, covered in black tar, before the demon fights back, waving the sickles. They slice into Jay's arms, his shoulders, his beautiful face, blood flying in arcs. If he slices off Jay's head, he might truly be done for. No wonder he never gave me a straight answer on that one. He probably didn't dream he'd be beheaded anytime soon.

Ada, go! Jay yells without looking at me. *I'll see you on the other side.*

I pause, only one foot up, not wanting to leave him. My heart wants to stay with him. My instincts want to leave. My instincts believe in putting survival first. My heart believes that you can't survive without love.

But I do have love. I always have. And one of my loves is above me, making a frantic dash to freedom.

I start climbing, my feet slipping a few times, the ladder growing more and more slippery. Soon the black tar that was on the demon is now coating my hands and it takes everything to lift them up and go to the next rung.

Finally I'm up high enough that Jay and the demon are just two small figures surrounded by bones and I know that only one will survive. I also know that it's unlikely either will die.

"I've got it," my mother cries out from above. "I feel it!"

"Push!" I yell at her.

"I'm trying! There's a film, like a gel. But I can put my hands through it."

The Veil between this world and the next.

"Hurry!" I tell her, feeling like our luck is running out even if Jay is helping. Hell itself will do what it can to ensure we're bugs under the glass.

"There!" my mother cries out. "I think I got it! I think…"

The slide of metal on concrete, so rough and grating I can feel it in my fillings.

Light bathes the both of us, filtered by the portal, and my soul sings. If it had wings, it would fly high into those precious clouds and never ever return. It would live in the stars and eat stardust. To say I'm elated is an understatement.

Then the light is momentarily covered as my mom climbs out of the hole. She disappears. The light comes back. I hear her gulping for air, out of sight.

Her hand appears. Then her face, her blonde hair hanging down.

"Hurry Ada!"

And I do.

Just a few rungs.

Just a few feet.

Then the ladder begins to shake below me.

Something large rushing up it, in hot pursuit.

Oh shit.

My skull buzzes with frantic panic as I shove my hands through the Veil, waving them for my mother on the other side. In these seconds I feel like a hot blade will slice me at the ankles and I'll fall into a gaping mouth, a feast for Legion and all inside.

"Mom!" I yell.

Nothing. Then I gasp in relief as she grabs my hands and pulls me upward. My feet kick at the rungs, trying to get out, then the manhole is digging into my stomach and I'm bring dragged across hot ground.

"Something is coming," I yell, trying to get my feet out of the way. "Get the cover on."

My mother picks it up, about to slide it over when a bloodied hand comes out of the hole, waving at us, trying to grasp the edge.

We both scream.

Then Jay's head pops up, gulping in air.

With ease he pulls himself out of the manhole and quickly takes the cover from my mom, flashing her an apologetic smile before sliding it on.

There is too much to take in, too much to say. I hold my temples and rock on my heels, trying to put reality back together.

"Are you sure that will hold them?" my mother asks. "They've used it before."

"Reinforcements will be here," he says. He glances at me but I only stare back blankly. He looks back to my mother and holds out his hand, bloodied and all. "By the way, I'm Jay."

My mother takes it. "I know," she says with an approving smile, giving it a shake. "I'm Ingrid." She looks around her which in turn makes me finally take in my surroundings. The place on the other side of Hell.

It's downtown Portland. The Pearl district.

Early morning it seems. Not a soul stirring except for us, which is good since the three of us just came out from the sewer.

The smells—the river, the urine, the trees—nothing has never smelled so sweet.

Air has never felt so fucking good.

"I hate to complain," my mother tells him. "But I don't quite belong here either." She gives me a sympathetic look. "Pumpkin, I wish I didn't have to leave you in the end, especially after all this, but this isn't home. I have a home. And I have someone waiting for me."

Pippa.

I nod. I know.

It's tragic all over again.

But I know.

"Come with me," Jay says. He takes her a few feet away from me and waves his hand at the air until it wavers. A sight so familiar to me now. So many veils. So many layers. So many worlds.

"We'll go in together," he tells her. He looks to me. "You stay there. Jacob is on his way."

But I want to go too.

I almost say it but I know my mom wouldn't allow it. It just hurts so much to lose her all over again.

"You saved me, Ada," she says to me. "Don't forget that. I won't."

I can't even speak in response. Everything in me is choking in grief. I know it's best if she leaves right away, that it's the safest thing for her, but part of me hoped that she could spend some time with me here. Maybe even in the Veil. That we could be with each other, as mother and daughter, as friends, for just a little bit longer. Part of me thinks this is over too soon. Just a few more days, a few more hours, a few more minutes.

Please.

But I should be so grateful that I got any time at all. And I am. Most people don't get this chance.

But it still kills me all the same.

She's about to step through with Jay when she comes over, grabs my face and kisses me on the forehead.

"I love you," she tells me. "And I'll be back to make sure you remember."

The tears cloud my vision. She steps into the Veil with Jay—it glows brighter than the sun—and then they are gone and I'm alone.

All alone on an empty Portland street.

With Hell right below me.

And demons at the door.

"Not anymore."

I spin around and see Jacob standing on top of the manhole.

There's no point asking where he came from. He sifted in here like the best of them. Probably could have used his help in Hell though.

You did okay, princess, Jay's disembodied voice comes through my head, like it's lifted up a sheet of the Veil. Then it's gone.

I wave my hand dismissively at Jacob and sit down on the curb. I stare dumbly at the bricks on the street, trying to find some sanity in them.

Jacob sits down beside me. "It will take you time to process what happened. For most people I'd say ignorance is bliss but not you. You'll take what you saw and you will learn from it. And you will be stronger."

"Jay should be back," I say feebly. "He has my mother."

"He took your mother home, where she belongs, where she's happy," he says. "He's her guide for a short while. We'll call this a loaner."

"But he will be back, won't he?" I pause. "As himself?"

He nods. "One would hope so." He gets up and pulls me to my feet. "Dawn and Sage are on their way over to take you home. I have to stay here and really make sure this bloody thing is sealed." He sighs. "Such a thankless job, really." He gestures to the street, the buildings, the one old man walking in the distance. "If people only knew the trouble we go through to keep the world safe..."

"We?" I repeat.

He grins at me. "Ada Palomino—demon slayer."

CHAPTER TWENTY-ONE

Two weeks later

"You have one dark, twisted mind, you know that?"

Jorge is leaning over my shoulder, peering down at the sketch I'm furiously trying to finish before class is over.

I ignore him, my tongue sticking out in concentration as I try and get the shading just right. He doesn't say anything else, just keeps watching me as he always does. I'm starting to think Jorge has taken a non-sexual shine to me. He'd just moved to Portland with his older brother a week ago from San Diego and still has that fish out of water look to him, which dissolves when he's around me, turning into a whip-smart attitude full of withering commentary.

Finally I'm done, holding the paper up so the both of us can see it properly. "I wouldn't say it's dark and twisted," I muse, inspecting every mark my pencil's made.

"Honey, there is no point in denying it," he says. "You're dark. You're twisted. If you didn't have Courtney Love's hair, you'd fit right in with Wednesday Adams."

"Oh please," I say, giving him a look. "You don't even know who Courtney Love is."

"I know the bitch shot her husband and has a horrible bleach job," he says with an exaggerated shrug.

My eyes narrow and for a moment I think he freezes. I think I've done it again, the thing that's only worked on Jay and demons.

But Jorge quickly laughs, swatting at my shoulder. "You know I'm joking, girlfriend. Your hair is preciosa."

Even so, I see a glimmer of fear in his eyes. I feel bad. I need to be a bit more careful. After spending some time in Hell, I'm not quite sure what I'm capable of anymore.

Case in point: my current sketch is a dark purple evening gown made of sequins, shiny black tar and charred animal bones. A sexy version of a demon cloak if I ever saw one. I've been drawing a whole line of designs based on what I saw in Hell. I guess to some it would creepy, not to mention morbid, to fixate on these details I would rather soon forget. But for me it's more of a coping mechanism. Turning the horrible things I saw into something I understand, even something beautiful.

"What are you doing after this?" I ask him. We've only know each other a week really—it's been ten days since school started—but I feel it's time I solidified this into a friendship. Jorge is the only guy in our class and the rest of the girls are nice but all local, so they all have their cliques. I may be local too but I'm still like a boat without an anchor. I've made peace with the fact that Amy and Tom don't talk to me anymore (and Jessie's emails have become distant at best) and the only real tie I have to anyone is Jay, who I haven't even seen since it all happened.

And believe me, it hurts every fucking day.

"I have to work," Jorge says. Then he lights up. "But hey, tomorrow night I'm making dinner for Roberto. Come on by. Roberto will get us wine and beer as well."

So lame. I can go to Hell (not to mention vote) but I can't buy alcohol. In some ways the past month has made me feel old beyond my years and it's like the real world is still struggling to catch up.

"That sounds like a date," I tell him with a wink.

"Easy now," he says with a discerning shake of his head. He runs his hands seductively down his chest and abs. "You may wish you can have all this but until you grow a penis, we'll be staying friends."

I roll my eyes and promise I'll be there. Also promise I won't be growing a penis. Then I wrap up my stuff and head for the bus stop, going home.

Yeah, a lot has happened in the last two weeks since I stepped back from the underworld (and yeah, I know I keep mentioning it but it's a hard thing to just gloss over). Mainly good things. Really only one bad one.

But first the good.

My mother is in heaven. Still. I mean, she's there permanently. Not in the Veil and definitely not in Hell. When Jay took her off into the light, she stayed in that light.

I know so because I've seen her ghost.

Just once.

But it was enough.

It was a few days after and I was lying in bed, doing my usual scroll through Instagram and rolling my eyes at the drama on my feed when she appeared in Pinkie. I felt her before I even saw her, a sugary hit of her lilac perfume, a warm glow to the room.

I turned my head and saw her sitting there in the chair like she used to. She was wearing a long white dress, like a nightgown someone out of the Victorian era would have worn.

She didn't say anything to me.

She just smiled.

In her eyes she told me everything I needed to know.

She was safe.

She was thankful.

And she loved me.

Naturally I burst into tears, completely overwhelmed by the emotions that had been waiting inside. By the time my eyes stopped being a veil of tears, she was gone.

All that was left was the scent of her perfume and this intense feeling of calm, like the room had been blanketed with morphine.

A half-hour later I got a call from Perry.

She had seen her in her kitchen, drinking a cup of coffee.

Dex saw her too. So did the dog.

She didn't say anything to Perry either but Perry knew it was the first time she'd really reached out to her, to tell her she was sorry.

It ruined Perry as well, making her collapse into Dex's arms. More tears.

The next morning my dad had brought it up over breakfast.

He had seen her hovering by his window in the middle of the night.

And then my father broke down in tears.

Three for three.

He'd said that this was the first time he was ever really certain that she was in heaven. I couldn't believe my father, the theology professor, had carried this unsaid fear inside him all this time. No wonder the grief over her death seemed to destroy him in more ways than one.

So there was that. And in my heart I knew she was safe.

The dreams stopped too, at least the nightmares did.

I didn't see any more demons.

More importantly, I didn't feel them.

And school has become a wonderful distraction. It feels good—it feels right—to head there nearly every day and work on something I love. It's hard, my teachers can be frustrating at times and I know it's only going to get more intense as the semester goes on, but I'm up for the challenge. After everything I've been through, this is a walk in the park.

But I still can't say I'm happy.

Because there's still a huge chunk of my heart missing, and the man who has it hasn't been around lately.

I know Jay is still next door, at least I sense him. But ever since we got back, he's been gun shy. Avoiding me. Sometimes I think I'll catch a glimpse of him getting out of the Mercedes, other times I think I spot him through the Knightlys' windows. I'm too afraid to go after him though.

Besides, Jacob warned me.

He showed up at the door a week ago and asked if I would go for a walk with him. It wasn't exactly an exciting concept. For as charming as Jacob is, there's still something about him that keeps me on my toes. He's not malicious but he's definitely not to be trusted. I'm pretty sure you can't be in his position—whatever that position is, King of the Jacobs?—and not be adept at manipulation.

We walked down toward the lake, the September air feeling fresh, even though the heat of summer had yet to wane.

"I want to tell you I'm proud of you," he'd said, flashing me that crooked smile. Even in the hot sun he was wearing a tacky 70's suit. "I've been to Hell myself and it's not a pretty place." He paused. "We've been monitoring you from afar, to make sure there's been no...after-affects."

"What?" I asked. "Monitoring me?"

"Me. Jay. Casually dropping in on your dreams, getting a read."

"Gee, that's not totally invasive or anything," I'd said, though my mind was transfixed on Jay. All this time he'd been watching me. He really was here.

"You should be used to it," he said. "It's part of who you are now. We had to make sure you came back alone, that your mind and soul hadn't been compromised. You're clean, Ada. And you're ready."

"Ready for what?"

"The next step."

"And what is the next step?"

"You'll know when you're ready," was his cryptic answer.

"Will Jay be there? When I'm ready?"

I feared the truth.

Jacob sighed, his chest rattling like it was something he'd been keeping inside for a long time. "I don't know," he said reluctantly. "To be honest with you Ada, I'm disappointed in the boy. There was a lot riding on this, on you, and he could have easily made a bloody mess of it all."

"Then you know about Silas. About us."

"Yes. I know. And I'd warned him about it, repeatedly. Some good that did. I guess there's just enough human still in him to succumb to temptation. That's the thing about Jacobs. We aren't perfect. But we sure as hell should be."

"But is he still...mine?"

Jacob gave me an odd look. "He'll always be yours so as long as you need him. I'm not transferring him, if that's what you're wondering about."

"You can do that?"

He flashed me a grin. "I can do a lot of things, love."

"Then why is he staying away from me?" I asked.

"Because he needs to for the time being, to go back to the way he was, to forget you in...that kind of way. You don't need him right now anyway, you've got the rest of your life to attend to. You can't just sit around and wait for demons to pop on through, you have to go on with your future, day by day."

To forget you in that kind of way.

His words slammed into me like a sledgehammer.

And today, on the bus ride home, it's all I can think about.

Jacob had said I couldn't sit around and wait for demons to pop up.

But I was waiting for Jay.

Waiting for him to come back to me.

Waiting for him to act like I'm nothing more to him than some pupil he has to watch over and train. A glorified babysitter.

I'm both dying to see him again, to be near him, and absolutely terrified that I won't survive it. That it will hurt too much to mean nothing at all.

I get home to an empty house—my dad's gone to visit his brother on the coast for the weekend—and sneak a bit of his wine before heading up to my room.

I step inside.

Nearly drop the glass.

Jay is standing in the corner, idly flipping through some of the books on my shelf.

The very sight of him knocks the breath from my lungs, like I've been winded by a blow.

He raises his head to look at me. His eyes reach mine, burning with a familiarity I thought I'd never see again. I'm immediately engulfed in his gaze, fevered with heat, my heart lurching heavily against my rib cage, as if trying to go straight to him, where it belongs.

Every part of me aches, not just with a hunger of the body, but a yearning of the soul. I feel pulled toward him, compelled, and it takes all my strength to stay planted where I am. If he has to stay strong, then I have to too. The last thing I want to be is some lovesick, sex-starved psychopath throwing myself at him, no matter how right it feels.

"Hey," he says, voice so low and gravely that I feel it inside me. He nods at the wine. "Am I interrupting something?"

"Only my happy hour," I manage to say, amazed how calm my voice is.

He smiles sourly. "Sorry to make it unhappy then. I didn't mean to just show up..."

"No," I quickly say, crossing an arm across my chest, not daring to come closer, not trusting myself. "It's okay. I'm...I'm really glad to see you."

He nods impassively. I can't tell if I'm having an impact on him or not. If this is hard on him at all, he's not showing it. He's back to looking stern and borderline surly, like a sculpture of marble or ice, his jawbones and brow chiseled, his eyes cold and empty.

But they aren't, are they? The more I stare at him, the more he starts to fidget, his composure slowly unraveling until he has to look away.

He clears his throat, running is fingers along the tops of my hardcovers. "I heard you talked to Jacob. He told you why I've been away."

"He did. Can't say I was happy about it."

He licks his lips, tapping his fingers against one book. It has his rapt attention. "I failed you when I shouldn't have. The one place I should have never brought you to to begin with. I let what I felt for you, what I shared with you, complicate everything. And that's on me. If something had happened to you, I wouldn't have been able to live with myself."

"You would have gotten your memory erased, I'm sure."

"No. I would have lived with it, as punishment."

The gravity to his voice tells me he's not kidding around. I sigh. "Look, stop beating yourself up over it. You saved us in the end. Without you, I'd be dead and damned, as would my mother."

I'm not sure if he's taking it in or not. His eyes are still focused on the book, blazing with contempt for himself.

"Jay," I say softly and, against my better judgement, I place the wine down on the desk, taking a step toward him. The closer I get the more his posture stiffens.

I stop where I am. It takes all of my strength. I know I should just let things be as they are, as the way they need to be.

But that's the problem.

Because the way things need to be involve the two of us together in ways I can't even begin to explain. It's not even that I gave Jay my heart—I'm not sure if I did—but I gave him every inch of my body and soul. He's the only one who truly understands me and even though there is so much more to discover about him, so much more for him to discover about himself, we're fused together for better or for worse.

I don't want to fight against something that's meant to be, something that every single instinct in my body is saying is right. For once, I feel *right*.

"I miss you," I whisper.

He closes his eyes, a strand of hair falling across his forehead. He takes in a steadying breath.

"I know how it is," I go on quietly. "I know what Jacob said. I know what you have to do. But I just had to tell you. I wish this could be any other way but I don't know what I can do."

"You can't do anything," he finally says after a long pause. His eyes flit to mine, holding me still. Everything inside me slows to a crawl, a warm, sweet stillness.

Then at least tell me what you feel for me, I beg inside. *Tell me so I know, so I can take it with me and hold onto it before we're forever changed.*

KARINA HALLE

A softness comes over his eyes and I can only hope he knows.

"It's all up to me," he says, straightening up, determination in his jaw. "I've been assigned to you, to teach you and protect you. You're mine in that respect and will be for as long as it's allowed."

A sorrowful sigh catches in my throat and I look away. I know all of this. To hear it again is another nail in the coffin.

I try to put on a brave face, to tell myself it doesn't really matter, that I never really knew him anyway, that this has been a mad crush, a hormone-fueled infatuation, that all it came down to was the fact that I had amazing sex for days with an immortal being and now I'm caught in the lovelorn, addicted tailspin of it all.

And that might all be true.

I'm sure it is true.

But it doesn't mean that it's the only truth.

That he is just as much mine as I am his.

That our souls crawled out from their hiding places and met in the bedroom, that they fused and grew and became something neither of us could have predicted. We've been to Hell together. If that's not a bonding exercise, I don't know what is.

"We're not supposed to be together," he says roughly. He takes a step forward and my brave face falters, wondering how the hell I'm going to get through the rest of our time together when I have to constantly fight against my own body's needs.

"It's not allowed, plain and simple," he goes on, taking another step, his gaze growing more intense by the second. "Jacob threatened me in more ways than one. That he'll transfer me to someone else, that he'll become your guardian if he has to, that my duty to you absolutely can't be compromised."

"I know, I know," I cry out, my cheeks flaming in frustration. "I know all this."

"He says you'll deal with it in time. He says I'll deal with it in time. That time will erase whatever thing it is we have," he says. "But I know that's not true. We're just at the beginning. This is just the start of what we are together, who we are to each other deep inside. I know you, Ada, and even though logic says you can't, you know me too."

"What are you saying?"

He's just a foot away now, that musky, spicy scent of his flooding my nose, coating my nerves with honey. My body tingles from head to toe, the air between us starting to crackle as if it's fighting to pull us together. One faint but glowing rope of livewire around my waist, connected straight to his.

"I'm saying," he says, reaching out for my hand. A spark jumps from our contact, his palm warm as his strong fingers wrap around mine, grounding me instantly, "we can't be together. But that doesn't mean we won't be."

I blink dumbly at him, afraid to take in what he's saying.

"You're mine, princess," he whispers, cupping my face in his hand. "And you're mine in more ways than one. You're mine in the way that really counts. I may not be mortal but it doesn't mean you should be denied to me, just as I shouldn't be denied to you."

I nearly cry. His touch, his words, are a balm to my wounds.

But I can't, not yet.

"Silas," I whisper. Scared of his answer. That he won't have an answer.

But he does.

"Silas Black was left behind in Hell," he says. "I saw to that. Names have power and the demons brought him out, albeit at the worst time. And you know I can never stop apologizing for being so weak, for not seeing it coming. It's something that will never happen again but it happened. But when I fought back, when I felt you, and you alone helped me through it, I banished him from every corner. I said his name myself. And in Hell now he will stay."

I stare at him with uncertainty, even though I want to believe him so badly.

"Are you sure?" I whisper.

He gives me a faint smile. "When you shed evil from your soul, you know it. It's no longer a shadow always following you, a black crown on your head. He's not here." He gestures to his chest. "It's just me. J.J. Abrams."

I can't help but grin, then quickly bite my lip, trying to keep it together. "What about Jacob?"

"I have free will, remember?" he says, running his thumb over my bottom lip. "And what he doesn't know, can't hurt him."

"But," I try to say but he just pushes his thumb gently into my mouth. Hmmm. This is new and not entirely unwelcome.

"Can you put up the walls?" he whispers, eyes glued to my mouth as he removes his hand.

I swallow anxiously. Nod. I reach back into my head, my soul, the same way I'd done before, and instead of a steel door that can withstand the hot and cold of Hell, I imagine black velvet curtains rising from the floor, curtains made to conceal us inside and out.

Pop, pop, pop.

One by one they emerge around the room, billowing out and circling us in until it's just Jay and I standing in world of soft black.

We grin at each other in amazement. I'm just as surprised as he is.

"Problem solved," he says proudly. "What else can you do?"

I lick my lips and squeeze his hand tight, leading him toward the bed. "Let me show you."

We stand at the foot of the bed, my hand pressed against his hard, heaving chest, ready to push him down. Before I can, his mouth crashes against mine, waves at sunset, kissing the shoreline. It's like being swept into a whirlpool, warm and electric, spinning and pulling until I'm drowning, wild and free.

Are you sure? I ask inside my head.

And his kiss tells me, *Always.*

We fall into bed, wrapped in each other's arms, cocooned by the dark.

We make our own light.

THE END...or keep reading.

A SPECIAL NOTE FROM THE AUTHOR

Thank you for reading Veiled until the end.

Wait a minute? That was the end? THAT'S IT?

Well…probably not.

Hear me out.

When I first plotted this book I plotted it as part of a three-part series—a trilogy. However, I waited a very long time to be in the "mood" to write Veiled and revisit this world (more on that later). And when I finally felt like, yes, Ada, let's do this, I could only commit to one book, not three.

Trust me, there is nothing worse than a book you HAVE TO WRITE. The pressure is insane. For me, I can't write unless I feel it, so I was scared that though I was in the mood to finally tackle Veiled, I didn't know if I would be in the mood to commit to two more books and write them in a timely fashion.

So I wrote Veiled as a standalone. I wrapped up as much as I can—knowing I have so much more to explore with Ada and Jay (Oh, Jay, you have NO IDEA WHAT I HAVE PLANNED FOR HIM. And Silas. Plus what about Ada's training? Dex's secret documentary? Will Sage Knightly ever put out another album?)—in the event that I could only get this one book out there.

In fact, when I first talked to my agent about approaching a publisher with this series (in the end we never did), she said that the first book would have to be written as a standalone, even if you have the other books written. It's just the way it is since a publisher may just buy one book and not the whole series.

Also there's the fact that Veiled might bomb. There might not be an audience for another book, even if I felt like it. No point releasing a book if no one cares about it (doesn't mean I wouldn't write it, but releasing it is another story).

So, time will tell. And what I need is to hear from YOU! Write me emails, message me, share the book, share the love. Let me know you want more! But I will tell you this, and I'm VERY optimistic, if it goes forward as a trilogy, I will know *very* soon. And I will let you know the moment I do.

How?

- You can follow me on Amazon
- You can join my super special Facebook group
- You can join my amazing newsletter (you'll never miss ANY news this way. Everything new and cool goes straight into your email inbox. Sometimes there are cool giveaways too AND I give away free books once a month!)
- You can follow me on my Instagram (I live on IG and always have great shoes, travel pics, puppy and cute husband posts)
- And my Facebook author page

Meanwhile, thank you for reading Veiled. This book, as I mentioned before, was a long time in the making. After I finished The Experiment in Terror series (Perry and Dex, which you can find on KU, starting with Darkhouse), I didn't want to touch a paranormal/horror/UF genre again.

I had to repeat myself a lot on why.

Because writing a book is hard.

Can you imagine writing a book? It's not easy. It takes time and heart.

I wrote 13 books in those genres. THIRTEEN.

That's a lot, is what I'm trying to say. I was burned out.

I have a rule, a personal code and motto that I follow: *I don't write what I don't feel.*

I didn't FEEL like writing anything like EIT again. And no matter how many people begged, or how many took shots at my other series ("Go back to writing horror, I hate your new stuff"), it didn't change a thing.

I don't write what I don't feel.

I even tried to write Veiled last year. Wrote half a chapter and lost interest. I was more interested in what Lachlan and Kayla were up to in The Play. THAT was my passion and you can't force passion.

Sorry.

You can't.

Just like you can't be forced to love someone.

So I shelved Veiled. And guess what? I've shelved or delayed other books before. Some of them are contemporary novels that might be "big hits." I don't talk about it. But I have. I stop writing them because I don't care, I don't live and breathe it and I have to live and breathe it to write.

I know many of my original fans probably won't believe this and that's fine. But the truth is, I feel and love and breathe every single book I release. Smut...that was a romantic comedy. Crude and light. But I wrote it because I lived it, I felt it. The Lie. That was angsty as hell and even painful. But I LOVED writing it. Where Sea Meets Sky, Racing the Sun...some of my favorite books. None of them are gritty or dark but I adored writing them. They made me happy. They gave me LIFE.

Isn't life about that? Being happy and really living it?

That's what I need to write.

Contemporary romance still makes me very happy. I'm still going to write it until maybe one day I get burned out on it. Then I'll mix it up. Who knows. But it makes me happy, it fills my days with joy and it makes me look forward to my job. So say what you will about the genre (I get disgruntled emails from time to time, though thankfully I know most people love the books), but it's mine and it's honest and it comes from a beautiful place.

But Veiled...finally Veiled was coming from that place too. I shoved aside a contemporary romance in order to write this. I am mercy to my moods. And I felt it. I loved being back in this world. I loved seeing Dex and Perry and Dawn and Sage again. While those characters' stories are over (let me repeat that: those stories are over. I am a romantic at heart. I wrote Dex and Perry and Dawn and Sage perfectly. All their books dealt with the rise and fall of their relationships. As an author, personally, this is the only thing that interests me. I have no desire to keep writing about couples who have a happy ending, let alone are married, because that's boring to me and I just won't do it. UNLESS I ruin their HEA. Which is fun! But do you REALLY want me to break these couples up? I don't think so!), I loved being in Ada's world and seeing how her relationship with Jay will develop.

For those who read EIT, you'll sadly lament that it wasn't like EIT. That's on purpose. EIT is it's own thing and own genre. This is different. This is about Ada. And Jay (Jayda?). Their journey is unique. EIT had nine books of Perry and

Dex's on and off quest to find love and happiness. Ada and Jay get one book to come together and three in total to test them (let's hope). (Also, the fact that EIT had nine books explains why Dex is so many people's favorite book boyfriend. Of course he is, he's had NINE books. Most romances are standalones and you get ONE book to love a guy).

I'm blabbing on. I know this. But I've had a lot to say for a long time (seriously, I just wrote 1,000 words here when I should have written 1,000 in Veiled, oops).

But know this: I am very happy that the passion to write Ada came back to me.

I'm happy that you've stuck around. And if this is a new genre for you, I'm happy you took a chance on it.

Thank you.

From the bottom of my heart.

And I will continue to bring you novels that will make you fall in love. I'll keep staying true to myself and keep writing what I feel from the deepest parts of me.

PS if you want an example of what I'm loving, you can preorder my next book, The Debt. It's coming out August 29th and my heart and soul is being bled onto every living page. I hope you love it!

PPS If you want to read more about Dawn and Sage (the epic story of their lives, plus Jacob and lots of sex, drugs and rock and roll), read The Devil's Metal and The Devil's Reprise – click here for the Duology. You can always purchase the books separately as well!)

Much love,

Karina <3

ACKNOWLEDGMENTS

I spent a thousand words on my special note so I'm just going to make this part quick.

Major thanks to:

- My beta readers, Paula, Pavlina, Arabella, Nina, Rebecca, Kim and Sandra (kind of), plus Jodi Casalles, Amy Harmon and Jay Crownover for wanting to take a read! Also Stephanie, because I have to thank her or she beats me.

- Maryse for all your help — without you taking a chance on Dex and Perry, I wouldn't be where I am today. It's all on you, lady. Love you!

- The Hallewood crew and my Anti-Heroes for being so so so supporting and excited and wanting to take a chance on something that's a bit abnormal in terms of romance. Hope it's been a wild ride! PS leave a review and I will bless your house with rainbows and Fat Rabbits.

- Laura Helseth for your commitment, spontaneity and encouragement (but NOT for that teddy bear picture, I swear to God, if you show that to me again...)

- Hang Le, I bow to you. Your cover for this is just <3 <3 <3

- Scott Mackenzie for being thoroughly creeped out while I explained certain scenes in detail and for being all "this sounds like a fucking awesome book!" Let's hope you were right! Also, I still think it's weird that you like pie as much as Dex does (not sexual innuendo, don't worry!)
- Special thanks to all the EIT fans AND all my contemporary fans who read this book with an open heart and open mind. I hope you had a lot of fun. I know I did.
- Finally, Bruce. For *not* being one of those dogs that bark at the wall and make me think there's a ghost there. Not sure I would have survived this book if you were.

CPSIA information can be obtained
at www.ICGtesting.com
Printed in the USA
LVOW12s0321251016
510074LV00001B/178/P